SECRETS OF THE GOLD

BAER CHARLTON

MORDANT MEDIA

Rogena Mitchell-Jones, Literary Editor
RMJ Manuscript Service, www.rogenamitchell.com

Published by Mordant Media, Portland, Oregon

ISBN: 978-1-949316-20-9 [paperback]
ISBN: 978-1-949316-21-6 [ebook]

10 9 8 7 6 5 4 3 2 1

EIGHT YEARS BEFORE

Someone unexpected at the front door is exciting—for a nine-year-old girl. But time and experience change people.

"I'll get it," she squealed.

The sound of cheap sneakers slapped on the cheap flooring. Military housing, even off-base, has never changed. Expensive big toys were always more exciting for congressional representatives than looking after the troops and their families.

"Check the peephole before you open the door."

The polished brass belt buckles dully reflected the peeling white of the door. The dark blue of the uniforms wasn't what she was used to seeing around the base, but she had seen them occasionally.

Pulling on the door, she yelled over her shoulder. "It's a couple of marines like Daddy."

The enormous crash at the back of the small apartment ricocheted off the rigid walls and out the open door. It hit the two lieutenants hard.

One with their mouth half open.

The man looked at his female companion as she hurried into the apartment. The man reached for the girl's arm.

"Mom?"

———

THE CALIFORNIA SUN did nothing to brighten the day. The two lieutenants in dress blues stood a short distance away. The casket sat draped with flowers, but only two adults and a young girl filled the fourteen chairs.

The girl's hazel eyes appeared washed out—more watery-blue than green. The swell of her lower lip slowly sucked in and then released over and over. The blink had nothing to do with what the chaplain was saying. It had nothing to do with her world. The black dress didn't fit her, but at least it covered the scrapes and scars on her knees. The long sleeves performed the same service for her arms. The rusty blonde hair, chopped at the center of her neck, was the only acknowledgment of her being less than delicate.

The deep low rumble of the officer's voice left his Minnesota lips motionless. The sound carried only to his partner. "What now?"

The woman shrugged slightly.

"Any relatives at all?"

The woman turned her head slightly. "There's an older uncle. He'll be available, possibly in ten to fifteen—if he behaves this time."

The man frowned and looked out from the side of his eye. They had worked together long enough for the silent shorthand.

"Aggravated homicide with extenuating circumstances."

His eyes didn't move. He was waiting for the boot to drop.

"Beat his wife and then cut off her breasts and legs to let her bleed out." Her eyes moved to lock on his. "He caught her in bed with his best friend."

The man's frown furrowed deep. "And his friend? What did he do to him?"

The woman's eyes snapped to a distant tableau—seven marines with seven rifles for a different burial. "You mean *her*. His best friend since high school. He beat her to death with the waffle iron."

They both came to attention and saluted the three-shot salute of the honor guard from across the cemetery. The other funeral was well attended, even though it was unusual for military internment with honors to be held in a civilian cemetery. The passing thought was that the funeral was for a much-loved senior member of a large family.

"Did they cross-check the weapon of choice for a match...?"

If the dead were not theirs or family, they were fair game for lighthearted banter.

"The prints matched. The iron was still hot when he struck."

The last rifle volley faded away as three riflemen gave their squad leader a cartridge. The two officers watched as the squad leader marched over to the casket and began folding the flag with the rest of the honor guards. The three shells folded into the flag forever. Some thought the seven riflemen firing three volleys was a twenty-one gun salute. But the tradition didn't come from salutes of Man-O-War dreadnaughts but to let an opposing army know they had cleared the field of battle of *their* dead. The three spent shells also had a simpler meaning than many thought—the flag was from a military funeral. Nothing more. They presented the folded flag to the soldier's spouse or parent.

The two officers couldn't tell the woman's age through the black veil. The man nodded his chin toward the small girl, who looked frightened by the whole proceeding. After that, they resumed standing at ease.

The female lieutenant spoke softly. "Child Services is picking her up this afternoon."

"None of the family friends could take her? Keep her in the same school or with people she knows?"

The woman rolled her eyes shut and opened them again as she faced the man. "You grew up a navy brat. How many new schools did you go to before you got out of high school?"

"Fifteen or sixteen." He looked back at the woman. "Dad was on the fast track. We lived on sixteen bases in seven different countries. He wanted dragons on both arms."

She nodded. "Yeah. A double shellback. I've seen a few. The tattoos become muddy, ugly, and smeared by the time you're eighty. But by then, who cares?"

URANIUM MINE, SOUTHWEST COLORADO

Not for the first time, Duff fanned out his driver's licenses, certificates of operation, and credentials. They issued the primary license from the fourth state he had lived or worked in the last two years. Duff wasn't sure if the licenses, certificates, and credentials were real, but he trusted he could do everything they said he could.

He closed his hand around the small stack and shoved them back into his large wallet attached to his belt loop with a chain. He rarely thought about it, but he knew the wallet and chain gave him their own credentials in certain bars and greasy spoon diners.

The size of the wallet was half wasted, carrying only money and IDs. The pack on the back of his Indian motorcycle was only sparsely filled, as well. He had learned it was easier to pack a six-pack of inexpensive undershirts and a couple of work shirts with his three pairs of jeans and six socks. Then, when the entire pack was dirty, he could buy new or spend a couple of hours washing his clothes in shifts at a laundromat. The half-hour of buying fresh and then washing the old, allowing him to help someone down on their luck, was his preferred. He didn't know why, but he liked the feel of fresh new clothes.

He squinted out at the man with the white helmet twenty feet below and half a football field away. The man sat at a desk. The desk was on top of a slight rise six feet above road level. You could imagine the man was in an office from the laptop computer and radio instead of under a sun canopy.

Duff's right hand fiddled with the gear shifter back and forth in neutral. Waiting made him nervous.

There had been a minor collapse of the road going down into the mine. For the last three days, the man and his twin at the bottom of the mine had controlled the giant dump trucks crawling up and down the side of the two-mile square pit. For now, six dump trucks waited at the top for the six corkscrewing their way up from the bottom. The first would almost crest out about the same time as the last finally finished loading.

Duff took a long pull on the gallon jug of water. The Colorado desert mountains were a long way from the greasy water he had woken up lying in two years before.

The hollowed-out shell of a building looked like it had been rotting and crumbling since the last world war. Many abandoned war-effort factories fell into disuse when Korea hadn't been the cure to keep them going.

Duff looked out the open truck window to the east. The lone wire strung from pole to pole was the last trace of a telephone system becoming as useless as flags and semaphore. The cell phones in every pocket replaced first payphones and then desk phones.

When Duff regained consciousness in the falling down building, he didn't have a phone. There were no business cards in his wallet, not even a small black book. The gash on his head was more swelling than cut. But it didn't give him a clue as to who he was.

It wasn't until he took time to hole-up in a cheap motel that he started figuring out what had happened. But still not who he was. The three bullet holes in the back of his overly heavy leather jacket were only a mystery until he took out the inner liner to patch the holes. The bullets lay buried in some heavy plates of gold.

The man under the canopy rose from the chair. He watched as the last truck gathered itself out of the pit and lumbered past Duff and the other trucks. The man swept his arm and hand in a dramatic gesture, inviting Duff to lead the next group. Without looking, Duff slipped the three-story-tall truck into gear. The truck was in fourth gear before the front tires left the desert level and began the two-mile-long descent down to the bottom of the pit where the deadly-looking praying mantis of a dragline excavator towered over everything.

The bucket of the giant crane named Big Mac could hold enough earth to fill four standard-sized dump trucks. The Big Mac was taking the soil, hiding the carnotite ore being mined. The ore produced uranium. Duff's job was to move the dirt to the giant hill they were building—a mile from the edge of the pit. Years after the ore played out, the company would reverse the process and return the dirt to the pit.

Duff knew it was a promise rarely kept. First, the mine would sell cheap to a small paper company. Then, after a time, the company would file for bankruptcy, and the hole in the earth would remain an unfilled promise, an eyesore, and a source of pollution with wind or rain.

———

"BUT YOU'RE one of my most dependable drivers. And in the three months you've been here, you haven't broken my rigs, you've never been late, and you've never been drunk on the job."

Duff shrugged and held out his hand. "You need to hire better people. Maybe if you paid more…"

The man scoffed. "In this shit hole? Not hardly. We're the highest paying job within a hundred miles. We have sheriff deputies who would rather drive than be a cop."

Duff cocked his weight onto his left leg and nudged his hand again. "Then hire them."

The man leaned back and barked a laugh hard enough to make his bad toupee move. "Hah. Not hardly. They're so crooked that the corkscrew highway across the desert used to be a straight shot until they had to run it across every cop's land and pay a land lease. No thanks." He rolled his slender frame onto the desk. "Besides, they have a dozen cars just so the mechanics can keep at least three still running."

The man squinted at the pale stamped numbers on the time-card. "What do I owe you?"

Duff sighed at the stalling. Everyone else made more but got a paycheck. The company only gave the check to the wives or live-in girlfriends. There were three bars between the uranium mine and the bank. All three would cash the checks—for a fee. Duff's arrangement was for cash only. Due on Friday, after the workday, or with an hour's notice, if he needed to leave town suddenly.

The only place Duff had stayed longer was just north of Las Vegas. He had dealt blackjack at a small family-friendly restaurant and casino. A pit boss from the Sands had hired him away with the promise of twice the wage and better tips. The wages of dealers were on a par with servers—nothing a human could live on, even for someone like Duff, living in a cheap week-by-week motel. Tips were the only thing keeping a roof over a dealer's head.

He had liked the small town and the people. His motorcycle went unmolested. He even forgot and left the key in the bike for a few days while working doubles at the Sands. The bike sat washed and polished by the owner's twelve-year-old son when he returned. The owner gave him the key back, saying the kid had thought about taking it for a ride until he figured out the weight would flatten him like a pancake. Duff slipped the kid a fifty for the work.

Naturita seemed like a similar town. Small with friendly people and a couple of decent diners. The important people were uncomplicated and easy to get to know. The motel didn't break the bank, and there was a small carport for the bike. But after three months, the air seemed to thin. The buildings felt crowded. And the people... were asking questions Duff couldn't answer.

The man behind the desk licked his thumb and started counting the small stack of twenties. "Where you planning to go?"

"I thought I'd head north to the shale. Drivers are supposedly raking in four to five hundred a day."

The man's fingers stopped. "That's kinda high..." He finished counting.

Duff took the offered money. "Yeah, well, it's twelve-hour days, and they say a camper with power starts at six hundred a week. There aren't any more motel rooms."

The man rocked back in his chair as he sipped on his coffee

mug. The smell of bourbon hung cloyingly in the air. "Yeah. I've heard that too. What were you paying here?"

"One forty with laundry."

The man's eyes shot open. "A day?" The man's pay couldn't cover four nights.

"Week." Duff folded the money into his left front pocket. "I figured it was a steal as long as I didn't have to go sit in a laundromat."

The man winked and nodded as he looked at his coffee mug. "Wife does mine. She's a damn good cook, too. Better than my mother was."

Duff looked at the man. The clothes were little more than a parched bag of bones. He thought the review was more defensive than supportive. He wiggled his eyebrow and patted his front pocket, turned, and left. Another job. Another town.

2

SAVE ME

The crispness of the morning light belied the later heat of the day. Even at this altitude, the intense sunshine of southwestern Colorado could make rocks sweat. But Duff would take the sweat over the mind-numbing cold and ice of working in Alaska. A company offered him a king's ransom to drive support trucks for drilling rigs at the end of a pipeline. A company mechanic told him they changed the oil with the engines running. If they turned them off, the oil congealed solid before they could drain the engines. Duff dragged up his pay the next day and headed for California and the heat.

Duff turned, leaving the door open to the air and morning. He shoved two shirts and one pair of jeans in the pack. Weighing in on the three pairs of socks lying on the bed, he grabbed them, pushed them into the bag, and topped them with his toiletry kit as he heard the step on the doorsill.

"So y'all are seriously leaving."

Duff turned and smiled. The man was the kind you could see and never remember. He was a tableau of beige from his dusty-brown hair, his tan shirt and pants to his yellowish dirt-colored work boots. But he played checkers like a high-paid professional. The evenings had been a great distraction for both. His small bookcase was a wild collection of information, from archaeology to geology to aerospace design. The man had one picture on his walls other than family. The picture was a four-foot-tall rocket launching. He and a friend had built it as seniors in high school. They had watched it with binoculars as it disappeared into the sky—still going straight up. The plans had called for twenty thousand feet. They built their rocket four times larger. They never made another.

Duff looked around the spartan room. Even the bed stood squared away, military tight. He had little to leave behind. He pointed at the two khaki work shirts still on the bed. "They might be a little loose on you, but I left you a couple of work shirts. Where I'm going, they'll be too hot."

"Heading out to California to soak up the surf and sun? That's T-shirt land."

Duff shook his head. "Nevada. Driving tankers is paying a lot better than the dump truck." He picked up his leather jacket and slid it on. The floorboard under his left boot groaned with the extra weight. He looked down at the old pine flooring. "I think you have raccoons or rats under there, Taylor."

The man shrugged into his cocked head and rolled his eyes. "I'm sure the next guest will be too drunk to care." He rubbed at the back of his neck. "You sure I can't talk you out of leaving. Ain't nobody in town plays checkers as good as you do. Hell, I won't even get into the sort of conversations…" He looked shyly at Duff.

"Taylor, if I were a settling down kind of guy, I'd want you to be my neighbor. But I'm not that kind of guy, so I don't get you for that neighbor. When the feet itch, the wheels gotta turn."

He slid out around the man, noting the thumbs jammed into the front pockets and pushing down on the fabric. It wasn't the first time Duff had seen the stance. He knew it wouldn't be the last.

Duff grabbed the bungee cords, pulled them over the pack, and hooked it all to the rack on the back trunk. Not for the first time, he sensed he should also strap a bedroll or something over the headlight for balance. But there was nowhere to clip the ends of the cords. The fairing had nowhere to put on a bedroll. It wasn't a chopper or even close. And motels were more comfortable.

He turned. "I'd say something stupid like I'll drop you a postcard…"

Taylor nodded, his eyes closed, agreeing. "We both know it would be a lie. You never got a single piece of mail the whole time you were here. And I never mailed out even a card for you. You're not that kind of guy."

Duff paused and then stepped over with a handshake. "I'm serious. I never enjoyed living anywhere as much as I did here. Just keep the kid out of trouble. It won't be long before he wants a motorcycle of his own."

The man pulled his grimace tight. "I've known that for about a year. We're sticking a bit away here and there. He isn't college material, but we're hoping he doesn't just end up in the bottom of that pit out there."

Duff threw his leg over the big red motorcycle with the Indian on the tank. He fired up the engines and let it warm as he pulled on his gloves.

Taylor waved as he watched him turn left onto the highway.

A few minutes and a mile later, Duff eased the big Indian into the diner's parking lot. Parking in front of the large window in his usual spot, he watched himself and everything behind him as he slid off his helmet. He dismounted as he watched Doreen, the waitress, pour a cup of coffee at the counter. The bubble of her bleached hair was larger than his full-head helmet in the trunk. She felt the big-hair eighties never went out of style. Duff smiled as she waved with her hand near her chest. Only the ends of her fingers wiggled—something a shy girl in high school would do.

He set the half helmet on the motorcycle seat, unzipped his jacket, and walked to the door. His eyes scanned the reflections in the large windows. Everything, moving or stationary, was noted. He wasn't sure why. It was just something he always did. He had pulled open the same door ninety-four times. By the time his hand touched the aluminum pull, he knew who or what might be a threat and where his three exits of escape were. He chuckled about watching too many spy movies, but inwardly, he wondered what drove his obsession for safety.

The bell on the top of the door hit the clacker and tinkled a greeting of cheer. The five notes never changed.

"Morning, Doreen." He stopped at the cash register and picked up the morning paper. The headlines rarely changed. Some jihadists in some Muslim country blew up a building or car and many other people. If a cat were rescued from a tree by a fire department—it would wait for the seventh page, right before the obituaries and the weekly specials at the grocery store.

Duff laid the paper on the counter to read the bottom of the front page while he sloughed off his jacket. He wrapped it over the back of the stool and bent forward with his hands on the jacket. The article was about a mine an hour north. A rockslide caught three miners when a blast had gone wrong. One was still in critical care, but the hospital said they released two the previous night.

Duff flinched at the sound of the front door. The young girl had pulled it open with such urgency that the bell rang seven times. She stood looking along the counter, and her gaze landed on the faded battered leather jacket. Her stride was purposeful. Her eyes searched Duff from head to toe as she approached.

She swung behind him and took the next seat, then removed her hoodie and jacket and threw them down at her feet. She raked her long mottled blonde hair with her fingers and fluffed her head.

Duff studied her brazen actions as he cautiously slid into his seat and continued to watch her.

She glanced out the window and took a breath. Then, letting it out, she leaned into Duff's shoulder. "You're my uncle or something. I'm with you, and we're just passing through or anything you want. Just don't let them take me."

The look in her eyes was pure fear. There was no room for anything else. Duff ignored the door and nodded. "Sure, Bunny Bean, we'll get breakfast and then go sort this out with your mother."

"Hey!" The voice was demanding with a cruel edge. Duff ignored it as Doreen set his coffee down and another in front of the girl.

"Hey, I'm talking to you." Doreen and Duff turned their heads to take in the two deputies. The forward one had his hand resting on his sidearm. By the spread of the man's hand and the weight on the belt, Duff knew it was an old Browning high-power 9mm with thirteen bullets in the grip and one in the chamber. The weapon was long out of favor because they were finicky and jammed when your life depended on it. But in the backwaters of Colorado, he was sure the job didn't come with an issued sidearm or uniform allowance. Both deputies wore faded jeans and scuffed work boots.

Duff cleared his throat. "Something I can help you with, officers?"

The man was sensitive to being called a police officer instead of a sheriff's deputy. "Sheriff, and our business is with the girl."

Duff eased his right knee out from under the counter. "She's my sister's kid. What do you need with her?"

"She's a runaway."

Duff reached for his mug, raised it to his mouth, and shook his head as he took a leisurely sip. "Nope. She's just been with me. No runaway. Her momma kind of went on a bender, and we're just letting her wear it off."

The man rocked subtly from foot to foot. His authority was in doubt, and he wasn't sure where to take it. "We saw her run in here."

Duff pushed up his lips and glanced back at the girl with the long blonde hair. He turned around, shaking his head. "Someone rushed in here right before you..." He nodded toward the door leading to the bathrooms and back door. "But they went into the bathrooms or out the back." He smirked. "Butter Bean here regularly gets detention because she won't run in her PE class."

Doreen set down two breakfasts and turned on the deputies. "Reggie, you boys either get to your booth and drink your coffee you never pay for or leave. But stop bothering my paying customers."

The deputy glanced back at the other. "Let's go check out the back. Maybe she's running up the back hill."

Duff turned back to the counter and opened the newspaper.

Then, turning it inside out, he started reading as he picked up his fork. He didn't look at the girl. She was bent sullenly over her food. "Eat, or I'll call them back."

Doreen turned her right hand backward and jammed it onto the edge of the counter. She leaned into it as she looked down at the girl. Her voice was low. "Everything okay, honey?"

The girl's head snapped up—scared. She searched the waitress's face. "Syrup?"

The woman paused, waiting for more of an explanation. Her elbow bent with a snap. "Oh, shoot, honey, of course. Coming right up." She stepped over three feet to grab one of the dozen bottles of syrup along the counter. Her right eye was slightly more open than the left. She put the syrup down in front of the girl, pausing before she looked at Duff, carefully acting like he was reading the paper without a care in the world. "Everything okay with your skunk burger, Duff?"

His eyes never left the paper as he shoveled in another bite of the strawberry-smothered waffle with two eggs on top. "Give the chef my best. He really outdid himself this morning."

The two deputies walked out from the back. As they passed behind the girl and Duff, they gave her a stern look. She chewed leisurely. "She must have gone out the window. The back door's locked somehow."

Duff looked up. "Isn't that illegal or something?" He looked over at Doreen. She smiled and shook her head with a slight jerk as she turned back to the coffee machine.

He watched the deputy wave it off with a flounce of his hand. His radio squawked as he turned out the door.

Doreen patted the full coffee carafe and started pouring as Duff nodded. The girl held her mug out.

"Nothing wrong with the door. If you're not too lazy to turn the knob before you hit the breaker bar."

Duff folded over the back section of the paper. "Thanks. I'll take the check when you're ready."

Doreen set the carafe down on the counter. "This is really it?" She nodded her head at the window. The packed motorcycle sat red and warm in the parking slot. "I see you've already packed."

Duff leaned back and nodded. "Dragged up the last paycheck yesterday at the mine. I paid off Chet this morning while I packed. I'm going to miss his checkers." He looked out the front corner glass door as he sighed. "It sounds strange, but he's the only one I ever knew who played an honest game of checkers."

She chuffed softly. "How many checker players do you know?"

"Chet."

Her laugh was a bark. "Trust my father and me. He cheats."

Duff smiled. "I'm still going to miss playing with him."

Doreen closed one eye and tossed her head at the girl. "What about her?"

Duff looked at the girl with the fork, slowly pushing the wad of waffle halfway into her mouth. Her eyes were wide as she froze, listening to the conversation that suddenly had turned in her direction.

"Whuff?" A tiny piece of the waffle popped out and landed on the counter.

Duff snorted through his nose. "See, I can't take her anywhere."

Doreen leaned in with a frown. "That's not what I meant. What are you going to do with her? You turn her back on the street, and it will take about twenty minutes for Reggie and

Franklin to round her up. This town is a one-horse town, and that horse is red and out front, packed to hit the road."

Duff looked down at the flake pattern of the soft green Formica counter. Someone probably installed the aged nickel trim after the last world war. He looked over at the girl chewing like it was the first meal she had enjoyed in a long time.

He looked up at Doreen. "No hurry on the check. This might take a while."

Her smile was sober as she glanced at the girl. "No rush, sweetheart. I'm here until three." The order book slipped back into her white apron as the pencil disappeared back into the fluff of bleach-blonde hair.

Duff watched the pink dress move back down the counter to the only other customer.

As he turned back to the girl, he could sense the tension in her shoulders. Her face was the look of a dog afraid of being beaten. He glanced beyond her to the empty booth at the back of the diner. It would give her sanctuary and privacy to cough up the information Duff needed.

3
___

WHY?

The booth wasn't the perfect spot, but it was enough. Duff sensed Doreen clearing the counter but never saying a word. She'd been through enough of life's battlegrounds to understand. The same way she had doubled the breakfast order —silently covering for the scared girl.

Duff studied the young girl's face. A few pale freckles showed dully. None showed like on redheads. Genuine red hair, pale, easy-to-burn skin, and a face of freckles are as rare as Vikings with horns. Horns on helmets were plentiful only in Hollywood. Not with Erik the Red on the open sea. But her long hair had streaks of more brownish mahogany than red. He guessed the tan came easily without burning.

The daylight shimmered across her hazel eyes as she watched the street and the few passing cars. Duff could tell by the fix of her eyes that her focus was elsewhere. He waited.

Her soft-toned voice seemed as disconnected as the plastic bag slowly blowing down the sidewalk across the street. The only thing moving was her throat when she swallowed.

"Four days after my ninth birthday, two marines came to the

door of our apartment. A month later, the military police came to my school to get me. My mother… was gone too." Her head ground around. Duff could see the wet eyes but no tears. She had dried out years before.

"So they placed you in foster care?"

She blinked and gazed down at her mug. There was no answer there. It was just a safe place to stare.

Duff put his mug gently on the table. "And this morning?"

Her eyes rose to look at his shoulder or somewhere behind him. She toyed with her mug. The handle distractedly swung back and forth.

Then, lifting the cup, she glanced inside. "It wouldn't have worked out."

Duff waited. He could feel Doreen float up behind him. She had a sixth sense about an empty mug. She poured and left as silently as she had shown up. The air changed. Lighter somehow.

He stirred the cream into his coffee. "Worked out how?" He kept his face passive.

She looked up from her mug. Her eyes held a sad challenge. "How much do you understand about foster care?"

He shrugged with his eyes and face. "I think… nothing."

She pushed back from her mug as her face rolled toward the window. The silent moments stretched longer. Her eyes stared past the street—avenues taken in the past or not. It was as if she were talking to the window or somewhere beyond. "Us foster kids hear stories about homes where you can feel safe, where the foster parents care. Some even where the arrangement becomes permanent. But, for most of us, it's just fantasy." She glanced back at Duff. "Some might luck out with a roof, food, and a bed to ourselves. Some of us…" Her face drifted back to the street.

"Food… or bed to yourself?"

Her voice was soft. "Mostly both."

"And you know this in the first week?"

She looked at him. Her face was hard. "In the first minutes. The locks on the cupboards and refrigerator, and no knob on the bedroom door. I've been in homes where there are no doors, even for the bathroom."

"What about…?"

She snorted softly. "Privacy? That's the point. There is none. They watch. The last place they did more than watch."

"The man molested you? Aren't there controls for…?"

"Not just the man. And no, there are no controls." She made quotation marks in the air. "Most of the time, the state inspector is in cahoots with the people. That's why they're in the business. And if you thought they were fosters because they have a big heart… forget it. It's money. Big money. I'm worth over twenty thousand a year. And at the last home, I was one of four kids."

Duff blinked a few times. She didn't. The enormity of her life was sinking in.

Duff watched a dusty green truck crawl down the main street headed north. All the tin on the vehicle had small dents from years of use. A large crack crossed most of the small back oval window.

He looked at the girl, who was also watching the truck. "Why me?"

"What do you mean?"

He blinked, and his right eyebrow and eyelid shot up. His

head tilted as he studied the mug in his hands. "Maybe I should ask instead is what do you want from me?"

"Take me with you."

He frowned as he sipped his cooled coffee. "Just like that? You choose a random guy and ask him to take you with him? How is that better than the home?"

"The home I've seen before. I'm seventeen. In eleven months, I'll be eighteen. Then I can go wherever I want on my own. But, for now, I think a guy with a well-maintained motorcycle beats the hell out of getting beaten or molested or even raped by a system with two blind eyes."

Duff's eye on the streetside pinched into a squint from the sun reflecting off a car's window. "But you don't know if I'm a killer or pedophile or just a child molester—just that I'm a guy with a big red motorcycle heading out of this town."

The girl pointed at the waitress approaching. "And she likes you."

Duff flinched to turn as Doreen leaned against his shoulder and poured more coffee.

The girl looked up at Doreen. "Can I ask you a serious question?"

Doreen smiled. "I was home all last night watching old western movies with my cat. And I'm not gonna tell ya what we were eating. But other than that, honey, shoot."

The girl smiled with a soft snort and then sobered. "If you needed someone to rescue you"—the girl pointed at Duff—"would he work?"

Doreen studied the girl's face. Her hip leaned slightly harder against Duff's shoulder. Her voice was more serious than Duff had ever heard her. She understood the girl. "Yeah... honey, in a heartbeat." She lightly rested her hand on his shoulder. "There are several available guys in this town. And, as I said, I was watching old westerns with the cat last night."

"How do you know he's not a child molester or a wife-beater?"

Duff could feel Doreen take a long, soft breath. "Those two deputies earlier... I grew up with them. I wouldn't climb into the back of their sheriff's car if you paid me. But climb on the back of his big red motorcycle and blow out of here with no idea where we're going? Let me grab my purse."

She lowered down and pushed Duff with her hip so she could sit in the booth next to him.

"Look, honey, I know what you're asking. And it's a tricky question. I'm twice your age and have been asking that question four times longer than you. But it always comes down to your heart and your gut. Sometimes they're wrong, but more times, they're right. Or at least right enough. But just as serious a question is the same for Duff. You blew in here, running from the law only an hour ago. So how does he know you're not a serial killer who gets her jollies by stabbing guys in the back when you're on their motorcycle? Or worse, start yelling he kidnapped and raped you? So you see, trust has to run both ways."

Duff cleared his throat as he looked at Doreen in a different light. He looked at the young girl. "But then, how can you be sure Doreen's telling you this because she has your best interest at heart?"

"I don't. But I see her point."

Doreen stood, poured some coffee, and left but turned back. "It's not always a straightforward answer. And it doesn't get any easier as you get older—in fact, it gets tougher." She turned and pensively walked back behind the counter.

Duff looked at the girl chewing on the inside of her cheek. Her eyes focused on the middle of his shirt—if they were anywhere in this universe. The brownish blonde hair hung loose on her head until it gathered at the back of her neck. The rest lay on her left shoulder like a lazy dog in the sunshine. He studied the worn collar on the light blue T-shirt under the red flannel checkered shirt. The left front pocket showed a semi-circle wear mark from many cans of chew. There was no can of chew now, but the past had frayed the impression and wear into the cloth. Duff didn't think the girl chewed or smoked, but it reflected the territory of hand-me-down clothing two sizes too large for her gaunt frame.

"So why should I strap you to the back of my bike and risk getting caught transporting an underage girl across state lines?"

She looked up. "Who said I was underage? By law, I can ask a judge for emanc... to be an adult."

Duff sipped his hot coffee. "It's called emancipation. Same as the enslaved people after the Civil War."

"Yeah."

He placed the mug softly on the table. "Except by the time you get to see a judge, I would already be under arrest. So again... why?"

She thought about her words as she toyed with her mug. She looked up. "If you saw a guy or two raping a girl in an alley, would you stop them?"

He saw where she was going. "Sure."

"What if you could stop it a few days before it happens?"

He nodded slowly.

She pushed her mug forward. Finished. This was it. She was all in. "When I woke up this morning, Virgil—the husband of the new family they placed me with—was taking the door off the bathroom. I must have been out of it because the door to my bedroom was already off. Hinges and all." Her eyes were pure stone.

Duff sat watching the hazel eyes. There was no more information needed. But then, he had been managing with scant details for two years.

Doreen rushed up with two brown sacks and a thermos. She placed them on the table as she scanned the street. "Get out." She looked down at Duff. "I'd love for ya to stay forever, but you have to leave. Now. The deputies cruised by a few minutes ago. They were eyeballing your motorcycle hard. They're just working up the balls to come back and go head-to-head with you."

Duff leaned up on his left hip and reached for his wallet. "Which way were they headed?"

Doreen pulled at his arm. "South. Which part of *now* was confusing you? Today is on me. Stop by again sometime and take me for a drink. But now you need to go. North will get you across the county line the fastest. But west will get you across the state line. I don't think even Reggie is stupid enough to chase you into Utah."

Duff dragged his jacket from the booth as he rolled out. The girl stood with her hoodie on and a large woven bag of a purse sitting on the table. She slid the thermos and two bags into the seemingly cavernous maw of the bag. She fed her arm through the braided rope strap and turned.

"Let's go."

Duff pointed at the back door. "Bathroom?"

She shook her head. "There are safer trees down the road." She dodged around Doreen and headed for the front door at a quick walk. "You coming? Or are the keys in it?"

Duff looked at Doreen. His mouth was just opening as her finger pushed on it. "Shh. Go. Now." As she watched him rush for the swinging front door, she called. "But you're breaking my heart, Duff Akens."

He waved an arm back as he shot through the door. He had just remembered where he had left the key.

4

RUN

Duff opened the back trunk and pulled out the battered spare helmet. Handing it out, he exchanged it for her oversized purse. As he laid it into the bin, he thought he remembered seeing a girl with a headband and tie-dyed T-shirt, torn jeans, and bare feet with a similar bag hanging from her shoulder. In his mind, the long hair was blonder. He closed the lid and looked at the long browner blonde hair hanging from under the white helmet.

"Let me get on first."

She found the passenger footpegs and folded them down. She rested her hands on his shoulder as he pushed the button to start the enormous engine. He revved the engine to warm it. He knew the noise always attracted attention.

"Hang on tight. It's going to be a bumpy ride, and no screaming allowed."

The transmission clunked into first gear as he let out the clutch. The rear tire spun on the asphalt as he held the front brake tight. The large motorcycle slewed around until it pointed up the street. He let go of the brake, and they shot out of the narrow parking strip and up the road, heading north. They were over the speed limit before the end of the block. Subconsciously, Duff counted at least six people on the sidewalks turn to watch the motorcycle with two riders racing north out of town. He hoped at least one would point which way they had gone when the sheriff's deputies returned.

The motorcycle and riders were a blur as they passed the population sign at the end of town. Duff slowed enough to make the tight right turn onto a narrow old road a quarter-mile later. They quietly motored up the hill.

"I thought we were headed north?"

Duff's helmet shook as he eased over to the cutout where the road turned. The inner cutout was considerably lower than the berm along the pullout side. Then, turning off the bike, he pulled off his helmet. She stumbled out from behind him and stood, removing her helmet.

Duff pointed at the other side of the road and berm. Sitting low behind the ridge, they could see the highway in the distance —the sound of cars carried across the barren dirt in an eerie distortion. The diesel truck pulling an extended trailer they heard before seeing it and the Volkswagen going around the bend that turned west before they heard it.

"What are we waiting for?"

Duff smiled. "It's forty miles to the county line."

"So...?"

"When the deputies go past, we'll have an hour to get south, less because I need gas. But enough of a head start."

"We're going south?"

He nodded. "Sort of. Eventually, we're going west. But we need to get out of their jurisdiction, and New Mexico is the last place they would look." He continued to watch the highway.

"Can I ask you something?"

He didn't turn. "Sure."

"The patched holes in the back of your jacket...?"

He glanced back and then continued to watch the highway. "Bullet holes."

Her eye narrowed. "Who shot you?"

"I don't know."

She watched the back of his head. It didn't move.

"And when I was holding on tight to you, I wasn't holding on to a body. It was like grabbing a garbage can..."

"Bulletproof. Metal plates."

"Doesn't that weigh a lot?"

He looked back. He lowered his wrap-around dark glasses. "I'll make you a deal. You tell me your name, and I'll tell you about the jacket."

She looked out across the barren land. There was more rock than scrub brush. Nothing hidden—everything exposed. "What did you call me back when the cop wanted to know who I was?"

Duff shrugged. "I don't know. Lima bean or something."

Her head rocked as she thought. "Let's leave it at Bean for now."

Duff smiled. She was quick. He listened and then held up his finger. The sheriff's cruiser was speeding and cut across the dirt inside the sweeping curve. As the car raced north, a cloud of dust hung in the dead air.

Duff stood. "Time to go."

As they climbed on the bike, she wouldn't let it go. "The jacket."

"Forty-eight pounds."

She leaned forward as they turned on the highway and headed back into town. "What about forty-eight pounds?"

"That's what it weighs."

When they stopped at the last gas station in town, she was still thinking. "Why bulletproof?"

He looked at her as he counted out the bills to the kid with a face full of zits. Then, he got on and nosed the bike out onto the highway. "Did you want the deputies to take you back to that house?"

"No."

"Well, that's why my jacket is bulletproof. Someone tried to kill me. And that brings up another thing. Do you have anything back at the house you need?"

"No. Everything is in my bag."

They turned left onto the state highway. Not much larger, but better paved. "Everything?"

"Three shirts, two pants, socks, and underwear. When you're a young foster, you don't think about all your stuff fitting into a garbage bag. But when your suitcase being a garbage bag becomes embarrassing, you get creative."

He peeked back at the girl, now leaning against the padding on the trunk. He'd never had a rider, but it didn't seem to make a difference. "Hence the hippie purse."

He heard her mumble confirmation about the purse.

———

HOURS LATER, they pulled into a truck stop outside Farmington. Out of Colorado, but barely. They wandered with purpose in the small market that supplied truckers who lived on the highways.

Duff found what he was looking for. The leather jacket

wasn't of outstanding quality, but it had a nod to female flare with white leather fringe on the black leather jacket.

Duff pulled it off the hanger and held it out as far as the security cable would allow. "Here, try this on."

Her eyes squinted at his intentions. "Why?"

He stood solid with his arms holding the jacket. "Because it's going to get cold tonight across the desert."

"Desert?"

He nodded. "And cold. No heater on a motorcycle."

She pulled the jacket on and zipped it up. He grabbed at the sides and shifted it around on her.

He swung his arms and shoulders in a rowing motion. "How do the shoulders fit?"

She moved her arms until the cable stopped her right. But her left swung okay. "It fits okay." The price tag swung into her view. Her eyes grew. "Are you sure about this?"

"You want to freeze?" She held up the price tag. He looked and shrugged. "It's probably made in China or South Korea. That's why it's so cheap."

"This is cheap?"

He leaned into her face. "Just be glad it doesn't weigh forty-eight pounds." He backed out. "You need a pair of shades and gloves too."

The gloves were bulky, more like ski gloves than work gloves, but as they raced along the high-altitude desert, she was thankful for the warmth. The wool scarf she buried her chin into. The trees and brush had all but disappeared. She wondered about the first person who rode across this land on a horse and thought there should be a trail or road. She found her eyes drawn back to the three patched holes. She took her right glove off and placed her fingertip on the hole. She tried her thumb, and it fit better—a big bullet.

As the gloom turned to dark, they rode slowly through a small town.

Finally, they pulled into a gas station just before the freeway overpass. The bathrooms were calling as strong as the low fuel. Paying, Duff pulled a couple of sticks of local jerky out of a plastic jar with no lid. The jar of a national brand jerky looked shopworn but still full of meat.

As they chewed on the spicy meat and walked back to the bike, Bean looked at the piece in her hand. "Why this jerky and not the other one?"

Duff moved the wad of meat to his cheek. "This is better. It's local meat not made by machines in Chicago."

"What makes it better?"

They stood next to the bike. "For one, they hang the meat outside where the flies can land on it and add their flavor. Then the blind woman throws ground peppers and salt on it."

She looked at the meat and then up at his face to see if he was laughing at her. "And that's why you buy it?"

Duff pulled on his helmet. "Nah, I buy it because I like coyotes better than I like cows."

Her hands froze with the strap unsnapped.

He fed his leg over the bike and started it. He noticed her still staring at the meat. "I was just teasing about the blind woman. I don't know if she's blind or not."

She stuck the rest of the stick in her pocket. Possibly later. She would have to think about it. She climbed on, and they thundered up the on-ramp headed west.

The night air was crisp. The lack of city lights let the stars fill the sky. Duff could feel the extra pressure of her thighs pushing against his butt. He smiled. "Ever seen the real night sky before?"

"Not this many stars. Where did they come from?"

As they peaked on a slight rise, he pulled over to the side of the road. "They're always there. But if you're always in a city, the lights cause an illumination fog, and you can't see through it. Get away from civilization and the light pollution, and bingo." He spread his arms in an arc. "You get the entire show of the Milky Way." He turned the headlight back on and pointed at the sign. "Do you know what that means?"

"The divide of the continent is at this point?"

He smiles at her parroting the Continental Divide sign. "Yes, but do you know the significance of this divide?"

"Does this mean I have to go back to school?"

Duff laughed. "You don't get it. You'll be in school all your life. The day you stop learning is the day you start dying."

"So what's so important about this piece of desert?"

He pointed back the way they came. "Every river, stream, or lake over there runs downhill to the Gulf of Mexico." He swung his arm forward. "Every water over there runs into the Pacific Ocean. This is where it divides."

"What about water right here under the sign?"

He snorted. Her smartass mouth had some real brainpower behind it. "It soaks into the sand, silly."

His stomach growled, and he remembered the last food was breakfast. And cold sandwiches didn't sound as appealing as warm soup. "Maybe one of these days, we'll get some sleeping bags and spend a night out in the desert under the stars."

She pushed at his shoulder. "Don't make promises you can't keep."

"Well, let me start with the best soup on this stretch of the interstate."

"Not the sandwiches?"

"Those are for tomorrow."

She frowned. "Why tomorrow?"

He thumbed the white start button, and the engine rumbled into life. "Because tonight, you get to meet Shaky the Sikh. And if we're lucky, his wife is also working."

He nosed the big bike back onto the asphalt.

"What's he seeking?"

Duff laughed. "For us to have happy tummies before he takes our money and shows us to our beds."

She settled back against the backrest. She pulled the piece of jerky from her pocket. She thought about it and put it between her teeth. The pepper and spices made her mouth water, and she softened the meat as she thought. Her head fell back in the wind as she watched the tumbling waterfall of stars spread across the night sky. It had always been there. She just never knew to look up.

5
___

STAY

The gigantic field of asphalt still radiated the day's desert heat. The parking lot was only a quarter full, but Duff knew it wouldn't fill until just after dawn. The truckers would rather spend the fuel to run the air-conditioner in their cabs and sleep off the heat than stare into the mind-searing desert heat and glare. The interstates were full of long-haul trucks during the desert nights.

Three truckers with stark white turbans had just left what passed as the restaurant. As they walked past, they talked in a rattling tattoo of what Duff recognized as Punjabi. Duff laughed as they walked toward the door. Bean's mouth had dropped open at the sight of the three bearded men. As they walked past, she spun to walk backward and watch them. Her finger poised in the air—floating at a random point. Her mouth was open, but nothing came out.

Duff reached over and pushed up on her chin and down on her hand. "You catch desert mosquitos that way. Big enough to lose your appetite. Besides, it's not polite to point."

"But... but...?"

"Who? The truckers?"

She looked over at Duff. Hard.

"They're Sikhs. Same as Shaky. They are from Pakistan, or their parents were probably."

"But they were wearing…?"

Duff pulled open the heavy sandblasted glass door. "Turbans? What did you expect them to wear, cowboy hats?" He smiled his best goofy look. "They don't cut their hair, so the turban keeps it clean."

They walked down a short hall to a pass-through window in the wall. On the wall was the menu. A few feet away, a couple of truckers in cowboy and baseball hats leaned against the wall—waiting. Duffy leaned in to see who was working. He grinned. "Can I get some roadkill shawarma with tiki sauce?"

The woman turned around as the man looked up. They harmonized. "Duffy. Where you been?"

"I had some family stuff to do. Darla, Shaky, I'd like you to meet my sister's kid, Bean."

They came over to cluster at the ordering window. Darla smiled. "Oh, your sister kept all the good looks in the family." She nodded. "Nice to meet you…"

"Bean. Just like the bean you eat." She held her hand out through the window until she realized nobody was going to shake it.

Duff rested his hand on her shoulder. "It's a cleanliness thing. If they shake your hand, they will have to wash their hands after, which would appear rude. So the only Shaky here is Shaky."

The man nodded and smiled. "Nice to know Duff has someone to look out for him. We worry sometimes. He goes away, and it feels like years. We have nobody else to sell the roadkill to." He nodded and went back to the stove.

Duff looked at Bean to see how she was dealing with the strangeness. She rolled her eyes. "It smells so good."

Duff chuckled and turned to Darla. "What are we having for dinner, Darla?"

She wiped her hands on her apron. "What do you feel like? You already know it's all good."

"The last few miles, I've been thinking about biryani…"

She bobbed her head and smiled. "Lamb?"

Duff looked at Bean. "Have you ever had lamb before?"

She rocked her head back and forth. "Oh, sure. All the time."

The woman laughed. "We also have goat tonight…?"

Duff snorted. "Let's start her with lamb. I'll take the goat. Also, some flatbread and a couple of orange sodas, please." He pulled a couple of twenty-dollar bills out of his wallet and then thought. "We'll need a couple of rooms if you have them."

"Sure. You be out by eight in the morning?"

He stuck the twenties back and pulled out a hundred. Laying it on the counter, he looked up. "By eight. I want to be down at Mickie's for breakfast."

She didn't touch the bill but used a stick to move it to a box. "I'll bring it all out to you."

"Thanks, Darla." He waved through the window. "Good to see you, Shaky."

The man glanced back and waved.

Duff guided Bean past the truckers as they headed into what passed for the dining room. Most of the tables were long communal tables in the middle. Booths were along the far wall. The white walls, gray tile floor, and sparse furnishings spoke loudly about the utilitarian nature of the truck stop.

They took the booth away from the few truckers. Then, sliding their jackets off, they tossed them into the booth bench seats. Bean's jacket puddled into a heap. Duff's landed in a stiff teepee. Duff watched Bean stare at it as he lowered into the booth. "Sit before someone else wants to know."

She shook and slid into the booth. Looking around. "I don't know what I thought a truck stop would look like, but this isn't it."

Duff glanced around. "Yeah, the down-home hillbilly nature doesn't shine through here. This is different from every other stop we'll go to. Some have a ceiling filled with trucker hats from all over. Others have truck parts on the walls like bumpers and headlights. There's one in Oklahoma where the ceiling is covered with one-dollar bills held up with forks." He explained the strange tradition. "The first time you go there, it's tradition to take a dollar, write your name and where you're from on it, stick the tines of your fork through it, and throw it up to stick in the ceiling panels."

Her eyes narrowed. "Isn't it dangerous?"

Duff shrugged with his face as he leaned back. "Maybe. But just spending a hundred fifty thousand miles a year on the road seems more dangerous."

"Is that what you do?"

"Drive?" He rolled his lips as he shrugged his face and shoulders. "I guess."

"You guess?"

They paused as Darla set down the tray with cast-iron pots, a basket of flatbread, plates, silverware, and drinks. She reached in her apron and pulled out two keys with round brass fobs. "I gave you two next to each other, but back where it's quiet. I'll let you show her about the showers. You know how to set the alarms and all, so I'll leave you to your dinner. Good to see you again. Say hi again before you turn in. Shaky really has missed you."

"I've missed you two, as well. And not just the food. We'll stop by on the way out."

They watched her walk back toward the kitchen. She picked up plates and silverware as she walked. If she moved, she was working. Any movement was a reason to clean, straighten, and clear tables.

Duff quietly served the two plates from the cast-iron pots. He knew there were few of the pots. Only the revered customers were blessed with the old country's way of cooking the traditional meal. The yogurt-marinated lamb or goat and vegetables were on the bottom. Next came a layer of rice with saffron drizzled on top. The lid covers the pot, and the whole cooks while blending the flavors.

The tantalizing aroma boiled out with the steam as he served from all the layers. He chuckled at the large hazel eyes growing even larger. "Smells good, huh?"

"I'll never look at sheep the same way." She reverently took the plate. Then, taking up her fork, she tried a small bite of the mixture. Her eyes rolled as she leaned back against the booth.

Duff nodded. He remembered his first experience a couple of years before. One bite, and he hadn't cared if the pass was closed. They ate in silence until the pots were empty and the soda bottles almost so.

Bean held up the last sip in her bottle. "The orange is a perfect choice with the curry. A coke would be too sweet."

Duff snorted. "Now she's a connoisseur of drink and food."

She placed the empty bottle on the table. "I'm just saying..."

"Nope. You're right. I'm not even sure Shaky sells any other soda pop. They have coffee and tea, but those are fuel for drivers. And I'm sure he has milk and maybe even kefir, which is a milky yogurt drink. It goes great if you're eating exceptionally spicy food."

She pointed at the pot. "This wasn't spicy."

Duff cocked his eyes. "For some meat and potato drivers, it might be too spicy."

She crossed her arms. "Then they don't have to stop here."

Duff rocked his head. "They don't. Mickie's is twenty down the road. They can get a greasy bland chicken fried steak with whipped potatoes out of a box, drowning in brown gravy from a bucket."

Her eyes narrowed. "But we're eating breakfast there." The question was more of an accusation.

"Because the waffles are fresh and light—perfect for warm strawberry compote from a can, topped with two eggs, and with bacon on the side. And they understand coffee."

"What if I only like pancakes?"

"Same batter. Big, thick, and fluffy. You'll love it."

She turned and leaned back into her jacket and the wall. Her legs spread out along the bench. "So how long did you drive trucks through here?"

"The first time? Only about a month or so. I was running a reefer box from Phoenix to Flagstaff. And because I delivered their food, I also got to know a lot about the restaurants and what they served."

"A what?"

His eyes scrunched and then opened. "A reefer box is a refrigerated trailer. The one I was hauling was only thirty-six feet long but held a lot of food. Being cold, I hauled produce as well as canned goods. Anything frozen would come in a freezer truck, and they only carry frozen foods."

"And the next time you drove this way?"

Duff stacked the dishes at the outside edge of the table and moved toward the wall and his jacket. His forearms rested easily against the edge as his fingers interwove loosely. "The next time, I was hauling explosives to some of the mines around here. That lasted almost a month."

"You got fired?" She was laughing at her joke.

"Nope. Someone blew up the company. So I left town."

"Then what?"

He squinted. "Hauled lumber."

"All you do is drive."

He thought about his jobs for the last two years. He rolled up on his left hip and pulled out his wallet. Laying it on the table, he leaned in. He opened the large flap. Money stuffed the back half while the front pockets contained his licenses and certifications. "This is the easiest way to explain." He spread out all the documents.

"Two years ago, I woke up or came to in an old, abandoned warehouse in Pennsylvania. Pittsburgh, to be exact. I was lying face down in grease and water. I had an enormous crack on my head and those bullets stuck in the plates on my back. My head hurt like hell, and I had no clue where I was, why I was there, or even who I was. Still don't. There was a bunch of money in the inside pockets of my jacket, and my wallet had these documents. So now you know everything about me that I know." He looked down at the driver's licenses on the table and then looked back up. "Yeah. I drive. As far as I know, I can drive anything."

She pulled the small stack of licenses to her. Looking through the pile, she sorted out the primary driver's license. She held it up. "Garden Grove, California." She looked over the license. "Did you ever go back?"

He shuddered his head.

"Why not? There might be your answers."

"Or worse. Remember, I have good reason to believe someone wants to kill me. If it weren't for the... plates in my jacket, I'd be dead. The address is the same as when I got shot."

She cocked her head, and her hair swung over her shoulder. "But you don't know that. Pittsburgh is, what? A couple thousand miles away from California? Maybe there's no connection."

"And then maybe there is. Maybe I get shot again just walking up to the door."

She studied his face. "And then, maybe the address is just an empty lot. You'll never know because you're afraid to go look."

The silence spread as they sat watching each other while the busboy cleared the dishes. For two years, Duff had danced around what Bean had deduced in mere minutes.

6

STAY AHEAD OF THE SUN

Desert heat starts with a hammer blow. The frigid chill of the night can reach the marrow of a person's bones. Swiftly, it can stupefy any thought. The muscles tighten and harden to a firmness rivaling stones on the side of a trail. The body seeks salvation in the black before the gold knife-edge slices the heavy dark below from the fragile dark above. Both are deeper than a man's soul is capable of—but hold the redemption of salvation a soul searches for in such an hour of need.

The heavy glass door swung in. Duff waved the smiling Bean out. The tremendous blazing hammer in the sky had seared back the night's cold and was already beating heat into the large parking lot and the gathering trucks. The cabs pointed at the rising sun in the east as a defense against the hotter pounding of the afternoon. Every truck would idle. Burning eighty dollars of precious fuel while the drivers slept—burning the clock of the hours they had to spend not driving.

Bean was still laughing. "How many trucker hats do you think they nailed to the walls and ceiling in there? I don't mean the cowboy hats and sombreros."

Duff laughed at her. "You missed the two turbans and the firefighter's helmet. But, yeah, a thousand or more. I think Mickie had collected at least several hundred before she thought about opening the place. Someone told me she put out a cargo crate and said if truckers could fill it with hats, she'd buy the restaurant and hang them on the ceiling. It was overflowing before the end of the week. Truckers love a good-time challenge. I don't think those wooden beams are real—just a great way to hang more hats."

"I was looking at all the trucker hats for sale in the store. There was one that made no sense at all."

"Which one?" Duff shoved the four water bottles into the side bags on the bike.

"It said Hawaii long haul. Isn't long haul like from here to New York or something?"

"I've met a few Hawaiians who drive long haul. They just do it here on the mainland. Most live in Washington and Oregon. One told me more Hawaiians were living in the Pacific Northwest than in the entire state of Hawaii. Most of the truckers wear hats about where they're from." He looked at the two walking toward them. The one was wearing a Green Bay Packers hat. Green with the G logo. Duff held up his finger, pointing at the man's hat. "Are you from Green Bay?"

The man smiled and shook his head. "Nah. Born and raised next to the Schlitz brewery in Milwaukee. But I hate beer, and the boy plays for the Green."

Duff looked at Bean. "See. Same state and a peaceful drive to watch your kid play."

The man snorted a laugh. "Easier to take the bus down to watch them beat on the Bears." He slugged his partner in the arm, laughing.

The man with the Springfield Feed hat gave him a hard look. Obviously, the rivalry was in good nature and long-standing. Duff noticed the middle finger rubbing the side of the one man's nose.

The two men laughed loudly as they pushed through the glass door.

"Do they all wear trucker hats?"

Duff paused before getting on the bike. "This is the busy time of day." He tipped his head over toward Bean and winked. "They love Mickie's breakfast. Let's look at the next twenty drivers. You have ten fingers and thumbs, and so do I. If they're wearing a hat—any kind of hat, you turn a finger down." He sat leaning into the large seat on the bike, with his hand folded in his crotch. "Here's three."

She pulled in a thumb and forefinger. "And two."

Duff nodded his chin at the two men and a boy climbing down from a dark blue Peterbilt pulling a moving van. Bean looked over and smiled. The two men wore turbans, but the boy wore nothing.

"I think only the drivers should count. Two more."

Bean had all her fingers curled at twenty, and Duff had two. "There you go. Twelve out of twenty. What's the percentage?"

Bean scrunched her nose and face.

Duff snorted softly through his nose. "It's easy math. Cut it in half."

"Cut what in half?"

"What's half of twenty?"

"Ten."

"And half of twelve?"

"Six..."

"Now add a zero behind both."

"One hundred and sixty?"

Duff didn't move. He just watched her.

Suddenly, her eyes grew larger, and she smiled. "Sixty percent."

He wiggled his eyebrows as he pulled on his wraparound dark glasses. "Time to make tracks."

A trucker bumped his horn and waved at them as they nosed out on the highway access road. Duff looked at the logo on the side of the truck and the trailer. He didn't recognize either.

"A friend?"

His shoulder rose. The bike eased left and down the on-ramp. The air seemed cooler, but only because of the speed. The day was before them.

Shortly after they passed into Arizona, they stopped for gas. Duff watched Bean's face. The dark glasses hid her eyes, but he could tell from her head that everything was being watched and remembered. He had been there. Now, it was more of sensing where everything was.

When he walked into a room, he knew in a moment where the exits were and how many people were in the room. He had a sense about whom could be a threat or not. He didn't know why he did it, but he felt it was an old habit. And his being alive was a good enough reason to keep the tradition up.

As they pulled back onto the freeway and away from anyone else listening, he felt her shift and lean forward.

"Do you ever wonder why you have the metal plates in here?" She poked him in the back—on the jacket. "I mean, there are other ways of wearing bulletproof vests and all."

"I wondered why I even had a bulletproof jacket. But then, it having saved my life put that question to rest. It wasn't so much an *IF* as it was..." He pointed to his left. "See... You needed it."

He shrugged. "After a few months, I got to thinking about lighter ways to do the same thing."

"And?"

"Give me a few days." He glanced back. "We'll go do that camping thing, and I'll show you. But I need to talk to a man in Phoenix first. He might have a job for me."

"What kind of job?"

He glanced back with a laugh.

A moment later, she got the joke. "Driving. Of course." She leaned back and watched the desert.

After a while, she caught herself curling in a finger, then two. Soon, her hands lay curled into fists. She laughed softly.

"What?"

She leaned forward halfway. "For a desert, there weren't as many cacti as I thought there would be."

He thought about why she would laugh, and then he chuckled. "Were any of them wearing a trucker hat?"

"No, but one looked like it had a turban."

Duff nodded largely. "That one they call the Naughty Man cactus."

The silence told Duff she was thinking about the name and why. For some, it wasn't obvious. But he knew some truck stop stores sold postcards of the cactus.

They eased off the narrow but decently maintained freeway and turned south. The cacti became fewer and fewer. The strange yucca plant took the cacti's place and then faded away as well. Sand became rocks, and the temperature cooled some. Finally, the highway led through nothing and headed to nowhere.

Bean eased forward. "Where are we going?"

Duff could hear the worried edge in her voice. The thought

of being taken out in the desert and buried was something even he had once thought about. Now he embraced the desert as a place of opportunities and wonder.

He glanced back. "What if I told you I was going to show you a snowflake in the desert?"

"In this heat?"

He nodded. "Give me about twenty minutes. Meanwhile, enjoy the scenery."

She looked to her right and then left. "Where?"

He laughed. "In a week or two, I'm going to remind you that you said that. You'll either laugh or growl, but you will never look at the desert as a place of nothing again."

She kept watching to find the scenery he was talking about, but all she saw were hills, sand, stunted brush, and powder gray highway. Not even a flatbed truck passed, none driven by a girl nor anyone else.

Only the staccato of the deep-throated motorcycle drumming on the highway kept her focused. The dull vibration had become the usual. The wind around her face caressed with the heat on the east side and cooler on the west. The three small patches on the jacket distracted her. She pointed at each—imagining where the slug would have traveled through Duff's body. Her guess was heart and lungs.

"Are you alive back there, or just quiet?"

"Thinking."

"What about?"

"I think the bullets would have gone through your heart and your left lung."

The motorcycle's throat softened as he eased off the gas. He downshifted as they came over a small rise, and a town appeared. He stopped at the sign: Snowflake, Arizona. Population 5,580. 1,700-feet.

"Why a snowflake?"

"Two Mormons found it. One named Snow and the other named Flake."

"Someone lost it?"

Duff looked back at her with a questioning eye. And then he realized she couldn't see his eyes as much as he couldn't see hers.

"Smartass." They both laughed.

Duff put the bike in gear and resumed. It felt good to have someone to laugh with. Her remarks aligned with the commentary he usually played in his head. Most of his days were routine, serious work. But to take a few minutes and just count who wore a hat... It reminded him that life wasn't only about work.

Phoenix isn't large with high-rises in a concentrated downtown or a financial district. Instead, Phoenix is a gigantic city made up of more strip malls, outdoor malls, and fashion centers than all the rest of the southwest combined. When the greater Los Angeles area gave up strip malls and open-air malls for five-story behemoths with even larger parking structures, they didn't die. They just packed up and moved to Phoenix—taking the retirees with them. The Angelenos were used to driving seventy miles for dinner, ten more for a special event, and then the combined hour and a half back home. What had started as a manageable city in the desert had ballooned to over four thousand square miles of semi wall-to-wall people.

As they rode the one freeway to another freeway and yet another freeway, Bean leaned forward. "Are you lost?"

"Nope. Why?"

She pointed at a giant cactus holding a sign for a shopping mall. "Because I swear, I've seen that same cactus at least four times." Next, she pointed excitedly at a white luxury sedan. "And I know I've seen that same car at least twenty times."

Duff laughed. "That's an electric car. I think they've sold half a million of them in Phoenix alone. And they're all white." He waved his arm and hand. "Look at all the cars. Most of them are white. It's the desert."

He eased the bike right and down an off-ramp. At the bottom was a stoplight. The street to their right only ran for half a block and dead-ended at a fence. They sat with their blinker flashing left. They were the only people at the light.

Bean was aghast. "Why even have a light?"

Duff snorted and nodded his head. "When they put this off-ramp in twenty-five years ago, the next year they were going to build a convention complex over there. The big hotels ended in a bidding war, and this light was going to control the gateway to a seven-billion-dollar complex."

"What happened?"

"On Monday, they wanted twenty million for the land. Then, word leaked out on Wednesday, and a large landholder across town said he'd sell them the same amount of land for only ten million. By Friday, five other landowners had jumped in, and the prices had dropped to a million."

The light turned, and Duff eased the bike left. Four quiet blocks later, Bean ran out of patience and poked him. "What happened?"

"Economics." He glanced back at her. "After two weeks of the ball bouncing all over the city like a Pachinko ball, a smart guy in Las Vegas called. He said he had an old casino sitting on a parcel only a quarter the size. They would have to redraw everything to go vertical, blow up the old casino, and clear the land before building. And for the land, he was willing, for that day only, to sell it to them for eighty million. But he would get one percent of the convention center, casino, and hotel complex for the rest of his life."

"But that's crazy. Why would they pay so much more for so much less land?"

"Because Phoenix had already proved the land wasn't worth anything. Location was worth everything."

"So they moved to Las Vegas instead."

Duff turned left up a long driveway. Only when he turned right into the small parking lot with a valet did Bean genuinely see the low-lying buildings discreetly tucked into the desert foliage and landscape. The valet pointed with both open hands at the space where he could watch the motorcycle.

Bean leaned forward and asked quietly, "Do they know you?"

Duff turned off the bike and set the kickstand. The valet walked up with what appeared to be a thin, flat rock. He bent down and held it next to the end of the kickstand. Duff eased the bike upright, and the valet placed the stone underneath. He looked up. "It's probably not that hot today, but just in case, we don't want your bike to melt its way into the asphalt and tip over." He stood. "Checking in?"

Duff pulled a bill out of his front pocket and slipped it into the young man's hand. "No, not today. I have a meeting that I only wish was down in the spa's steam room."

"Very good, sir. We'll watch your bike. Enjoy your stay."

7

SANCTUARY

Duff wound his way past the reception office and into the restaurant's bar. He looked around. There were only a few people apart from the staff. The two bartenders were polishing glasses as bartenders always do.

Duff leaned on the end of the bar. "Excuse me?"

The brunette with a ponytail looked up and smiled. She put down the glass and closed the gap, pointing out the panoramic glass wall with a glass door at each end. "If you take this door and then down the stairs over here, they will take you down to the pool. Your daughter looked bored and hungry, so I set her up with some food and refreshments. You raised a delightful daughter."

Duff rolled his eyes under his closed lids. "Niece, and I hope she didn't order a vodka holy terror… again."

The bartender smiled warmly. "Well, someone raised her right. And she settled for a Plain Jane Harvey Wallbanger without the alcohol, fruit juice, and umbrella. But I'd love to hear about the holy terror."

Duff smiled. "Another time, perhaps."

As he started toward the door, she asked if he'd like any food, as well.

Duff's stomach growled, and he stopped with his hand on the door. He looked back, and the woman was holding a menu. He smiled and pushed on the door. "Surprise me."

———

THE PONYTAIL FELL over the back of the chair she was slumped in. The leather jacket and hoodie were draped over another chair at the umbrella-topped table. Duff looked for a seat that would hold his weight. Finally, he shucked off his jacket and stood it up just under the table. He pulled out the pool chair and sat. The infinity pool stretched out away from them, and the two palm trees on the other end reflected in the calm water. The distant mountains made a cresting at the other end of the pool.

Bean reached up with her finger and pulled her dark glasses down on her nose. She slowly rolled her head along her shoulder and looked at him as if she were in a movie. "Have a nice meeting?"

Duff sat back in the chair. "We have a place to live that comes with a housekeeper, grocery delivery, secure parking for the bike, and a job that will have me home most nights."

She rolled over and sat up in the chair. Her voice lowered. "Who do you have to kill?"

Duff snorted. "Nothing I haven't done before. Medium haul. So I'll be killing bugs on the interstate." He looked at the empty plate with a sprig of parsley nibbled around the edge.

She followed his questioning gaze. "I highly recommend it. It was a chicken sandwich on bread I'd eat by itself. We're not talking a boring old sourdough."

He pointed at the small bowl.

"It was a peeled cucumber something with a sweet and spicy sauce. The lady said it was no pals or something."

Duff smiled largely. "Bean, meet Nopales cactus. Nopales, meet Bean."

She sat up straighter. "I ate a cactus?"

"Yes, you did." The bartender took another bowl off her tray. "I figured you might like some more. Also, your uncle." She placed a plate down also with a large sandwich and a larger bowl of the cactus salad. The tall water with cucumber and lemon slices mirrored Bean's.

"Anything else you'd like, just wave. You're on closed-circuit TV, and I'll come right down. And don't worry, Mr. Akens, it's all on the house as you are guests of Mr. Kaminski. So don't forget the dessert." She placed a dessert menu next to his plate.

"Thank you. And thank Mr. Kaminski, as well."

The bartender nodded and silently disappeared back up the stairs.

Duff eyed the sandwich. He remembered the artisanal bread from the first time he was here. The memories weren't wrong as he bit into the sandwich. His eyes fluttered shut as he chewed. His head gently bobbed as memory met the crossroads of juicy chicken, a salad of fresh greens, and a sauce he would be willing to learn how to make.

Bean turned back in her chair and put her feet back up on the small ottoman. "I told you so."

Duff's eyes slowly opened, and he chuffed at the sight of her second empty bowl of cactus. As he ate, he watched a distant bird soaring over the desert—only the occasional flapping of wings ensured the reality.

As he was wiping his hands and mouth on the cloth napkin, a young man in a white shirt and black jeans of the staff bent over, placing a room key on the table. "With Mr. Kaminski's complements. Bungalow 104 is just down these stairs. Turn left, and it's the second bungalow on your right. You and the miss have spa appointments at three."

Bean turned at the word miss. She lowered her dark glasses at the word spa. "What appointments?"

Duff cleared his throat. "It is 'What appointments, *please?*'"

She sat up straighter. "What are the appointments"—she glared at Duff—"*please?*"

The young man smiled. "Just in case this is your introduction to a spa day and massages, I believe you will start with a facial followed by an enjoyable Swedish massage and finish with a manicure and pedicure. If you feel the need to have your ends trimmed of windblown damage, the stylist is in-house until six."

She smiled cutely and pointed at Duff. "What about him."

The young man rolled his eyes. "Well... I believe he's scheduled for his usual wrestle a gator, kicked by a mule, and get thrown to the wolves. But I think the wolves will take care of his split-ends."

Duff looked back around as he chuckled. "Well, good to see they didn't turn Igor loose yet."

The young man smiled at his flirting and fun being taken in the nature given. "Enjoy your Rolfing, sir. And your dinner reservation with Mr. Kaminski is at seven."

Bean's frown had a concerned look as she watched the young man make his way back up the stairs. "What's Rolfing?"

He looked at her and assumed a sober face. "You know those patched holes you've been worried about?"

"Yeah?"

"About like that. But it also feels like what he described. It's a form of deep tissue massage. But not what I'll be getting. I'm more of a Shiatzu kind of guy. Kind of like what you'll be getting, but with more sticks and rocks."

Her eyes opened. "Sticks and stones? As in, break your bones?"

"They throw a little Thai into the mix if it's the same masseuse I had a year ago."

He looked at the key and beaten copper room fob. Then, glancing at his wristwatch, he chewed once on his upper lip. "Let's go see what we have for a room."

She stood and grabbed her jacket and hoodie. "What's a bungalow?"

Duff rocked his head. "Bigger than a room and smaller than a house."

As they walked from the foyer into the living room, he knew he had undersold the size. The slate floors extended both ways into two master suites. The closets were open and in one hung a pair of black jeans and a white top favored by the Mexicans and Navaho. Bean frowned. "Hey, Duff? I think someone left some of their clothes."

Duff walked into the room and looked at the pants and top. "Try them on before we go up to the spa. Just in case you need different size jeans."

"Try them on?"

Duff smirked and twitched his head as he danced his way out of the room. "They're for dinner. It's a nice place and Mr. Kaminski, it seems, thinks you should look nice but relaxed. It's not like he left you an evening gown and glass slippers or anything."

"What are you wearing?"

He called back from the other side of the living room. "The gown and glass slippers, of course."

8

———————

CAMPING ANYONE

Breakfast by the pool was a pleasant relief from the heat. Dawn broke with low gray clouds. The overcast dropped the temperature while they ate, looking across the desert.

The cubes of sweet-pickled cactus hearts were tossed with blackberries and raspberries—a refreshing and perfect southwest desert-load of vitamins. It was the ideal complement to the machaca and avocado omelet drizzled with salsa compote.

Back in his standard desert attire of a white T-shirt under the leather jacket, jeans, and boots, Duff had comfortably closed the closet on the lent black jeans and dress shirt. He knew they wouldn't go begging. At six-foot and two hundred pounds, Duff was a close match for many other men who could put the clothes to good use. He had what he needed.

He slung the light bag over his shoulder and waited by the door. The new phone in his pocket vibrated. The text was from a two-digit number. *Enjoy the week.*

He texted Mr. Kaminski back. *Thanks. And thank you for the great stay.*

Anytime.

Duff slipped the phone into his pocket as Bean came out of the other bedroom. "I could get used to living like this. But I know it's not real." Duff felt the soft sadness in her voice.

As they walked up around to the valet station, he watched her face. For once in her life, someone had catered to her, with nothing asked in return.

He cleared his throat. "It's real, but it's just another way of living. There are many memorable experiences in this world. Some cost a lot, and others cost little at all. Like camping out in the desert and looking at the Milky Way."

As they walked to the valet station, Duff noticed his bike. The red paint and chrome hadn't shined with polish for a few months. He had washed it but didn't have wax and chrome polish. He knew he was looking at a few hours of sweaty labor. He walked around the bike with an appreciative eye and looked up at the three valets. "It's pretty. But where's my old beater?"

The three chuckled. "We think Pedro got bored last night."

Duff looked across the flat chrome on the gas tank. There wasn't a single dot left from morning dew as he had seen on the breakfast table. This wasn't a night job as much as it was a morning job split two or three ways. He quietly slipped a hundred out of his wallet and folded it with his fingers. He passed it to the older of the three. "See that Pedro gets thanked for a superb job."

The three tight-lipped smiled in unison.

Duff frowned and then figured they might know. "We want to go camp out under the stars tonight, but we need some gear…"

The two younger guys smiled. "Bunkers." The blond ran back over to the valet station. "I'll draw you a map."

The brunette pointed back the way Duff and Bean had come.

"Just before the freeway, there's a big street and light. Turn right. It's down about a mile on the left. There's a gas station with an old truck on the roof. The place called Bunkers is behind there."

The blond ran back up. "Here's the address and phone number. My older brother works there. They have new gear, but Mike runs the rental or used shack if you go in the back. If you aren't going to use it much, that's the way to go. I'll call him and let him know you're coming and to take care of you. If you're just going out to hang out for the night, just a bedroll and tarp are pretty much all you'll need this time of year."

The older valet cocked his head. "Where were you thinking of camping?"

Duff pointed at Bean. "We stopped at the Continental Divide the other night. It was the first time she had ever seen the Milky Way. So just someplace between here and Vegas where city lights won't interfere is fine."

The valet smiled. "Try it in the middle of the Pacific. I remember standing my first watch on the conning tower. The chief asked me if I'd ever seen the Milky Way. And then he shut the hatch. There wasn't light anywhere *but* the Milky Way."

"Where were you?"

"About six hundred east of the Philippines. Fast attack sub, sir."

Duff almost felt a salute in there somewhere. "Is the Southern Cross as spectacular as they say?"

The valet nodded. "Memorable. I'll always want to go back. But not in a boat that sinks."

"Sedona is a nice place to camp. But many tourists looking for an"—he hooked his fingers in the air as he rolled his eyes—"*experience.*"

The blond finished the thought. "But if you're going up through Flagstaff, head up eight-nine. About a half-hour north on the right is the Trading Post. You can get gas there as cheap as in Flagstaff, but they can point to the dirt road going west to the craters. They're old cinder cones, but the big one is where people think a meteor hit."

The brunette jerked his head up. "It's just an old cinder cone worn down. But it's huge. When the sun sets, you have about five minutes until lights out. And I do mean lights out. So we haul the telescope out there. At the bottom of the big cone, we've seen Pluto and some of the distant nebulas. But we have a ten-inch parabolic mirror on an eight-foot tube."

Duff smiled. "I think we'll just take some MREs and our eyeballs this time."

The older valet nodded. "I think Bunkers can outfit you with something better than sea rations. Even I wouldn't make my little brother eat c-rats. But then, he's flying air force."

———

DUFF FOUND BUNKERS, Bean found some boots she liked, and then they found their way to the amazing crater. It was as large, if not larger than what the valets had said. The woman at the trading post had told them how to take the road north to the massive lava bed where the volcanos had emptied their guts. So they stopped and walked across the moonscape for a couple of hours. Not because there was so much to see, but because it was so much to get their minds around. The landscape in the first minute was the same as the sixtieth and the hundredth. But looking across the desert of dark black lava cinders was to clear one's mind of anything else.

"It looks and feels like just before I go to sleep."

Duff looked at Bean. "How do you mean?"

The young woman stopped and looked north. As far as the eye could see, it was the same black—the same sky. Nothing moved. "Nothing reflects back. It's just black. But not deep dark blue-black, and not really a gray either. A charcoal gray would have some gray, but this is black. And not like the so black of an Asian girl's hair, but just black." She looked down and shook her head back and forth. "I don't know. It's hard to explain. But it's what my mind sees as I'm going to sleep... and then I'm waking up."

Duff kicked his boot at the scree of the lava and gave the idea a try. "Try matte black. The type of black on a black dog. It doesn't shine. It just absorbs the light."

She pointed at him. "Yeah. Like that. A black dog. Or a bear. Or a gorilla." She looked over. "I read an article once. It was an interview with a wildlife photographer. He talked about how every animal had difficulties getting an excellent photograph of them. He said the mountain gorillas like in the movie Gorillas in the Mist were so black that the light got trapped, and all you got most times was just a black blob in the photograph."

They looked out across the lava flow. Duff snorted softly. "A gorilla of a lava flow."

Bean started laughing and then looked at Duff and laughed even harder. Grabbing her stomach, she bent over and finally fell to the ground. The more Duff stood waiting, the more she laughed. Duff looked around for a rock to sit on. He walked the thirty feet and sat down. She laughed even harder and rolled over so she couldn't see him. He finally turned around on the lava boulder. He mused to himself that at least it wasn't pumice

—the foamed glass would have cut the backside out of his pants.

She finally stopped laughing. But she didn't move.

"Have you ever seen videos of monkeys throwing shit at the people who go to the zoo to see them?"

He squinted behind his glasses. Trying to figure out if he had ever seen a video of anything in wildlife. "Yeah...?"

"Well, that is a monkey-sized shitstorm. This must have been a King Kong gorilla shitstorm."

Duff looked out across the field at what had been hot molten lava thrown over dozens of miles. Maybe not his humor, but it made sense. And the more it made sense to him, the funnier it became.

He looked back at her lying on the lava. Her hands clasped behind her head were comfortable, her one leg bent with the other boot resting on the knee. She was calm. Even by the pool, she had draped her jacket and hoodie, ready to run. And now, she lay relaxed and defenseless.

Duff turned back around. Even from thirty feet away, their nearness in the vast expanse of lava seemed close or even intimate. "Still want to run away?"

Her head rolled toward him. He waited.

Her head rolled back. Looking at the sky. "No." Noticing his silence, she asked, "Why?"

He shrugged. "I was just wondering what changed. This is the first time you don't look like you have one foot out the door. You asked to go with me, but you were still ready to run."

She sat up, clutched her knees, and gently lowered her head, resting her chin on her knees. "I don't know. But being out here, and yesterday... I always knew what I was running from but didn't know what I wanted to run to. These days... I don't think

I could even have imagined them." She spread her arms with her hands palm up. "Look at this. There's nothing. Nothing. And yet, it is perfect. This is what I ran to, and this day—I don't ever want to run from it." She lifted her glasses and looked over at the silent man. "Does that make sense?"

He cleared the frog in his throat. Then he cleared it again. His voice still croaked. "Yes. Yes, it does." He looked around. "Before today, before these three days, I would have never thought to just wander out into the desert with a bedroll. The desert was just an enormous area to drive through."

They sat silently in the magnitude of their personal revelations. The sun hung late in the day.

"Ready to find out what's in those bags for food?

———

WHEN THE FOIL-PACKAGED space food had turned to wrappers, the stars were revealing themselves through the last of the sunset. The first was the dog star, but Duff couldn't remember why. By the time Polaris showed up, they were lying side by side, and Duff was naming off constellations and pointing them out. And soon, the individual parts of light were clusters, and then vast washes of lights across the sky.

"Why does it go from there to there if we are inside of it?" Bean's hand dropped onto her belly. She looked over toward the silence. Duff's eyes were closed, and she could tell he had drifted off.

Quietly, she unzipped the flat sleeping bag and pulled it over them both. Then, she curled with her back to his side for heat, and using her leather jacket for a pillow, followed him into sleep. It had been quite a day.

9

MORNING ILLUMINATION

Bean remembered Duff telling her how bone-chilling the predawn morning would be. She didn't have a choice. Nobody was going to wander off behind a bush and pee for her. As she walked in the gloom, partially lit by the stars and partially by the dark gray moving in from the east, she tried to remember if there was a bush or just gravelly desert sand. Her bladder decided it was far enough for her to look back toward the dark mound under the tarp. And then, squatting with relief, she remembered what they had forgotten to bring. She wondered if it would dry before it froze—but then decided she didn't want to find out.

The crinkling of a water bottle was as loud as a gunshot. She didn't have to lift the black plastic tarp to know Duff was drinking water. Instead, she pictured him already dressed in his leather jacket against the cold air.

"How's the coffee?"

Duff took another pull on the water bottle. They had packed a six-pack of two-liter bottles. They had split one over dinner.

"Hot, steamy, tasty, and about ten minutes that way. Were you planning to sleep all day?"

She raised the edge of the tarp. Then, throwing it aside, she sat up. Blinking, she looked around. Duff sat cross-legged in his jeans, boots, and a T-shirt. It was already getting warm. "What time is it, anyway?"

Duff glanced at his wrist. "Quarter after nine."

Bean vigorously rubbed her face with the palms of her hands. She smacked her lips and stuck out her tongue. "Yuck." She reached out with her hand, and he handed her the half-full bottle.

She took a long pull. Her face screwed up. "Whoa. That's cold."

Duff looked over and shrugged his face. "Well, at least the ice has melted."

"Ice?"

"Well, kind of like a slushy, but with some hard slivers. It's an acquired taste." He sneered.

She bent and rolled up the one sleeping bag and tarp and then looked around, confused.

Duff pointed at the bike. The trunk was open, and he had leaned the side bag lid against the cycle. "Packed. But first, I want to talk to you about this." He patted the jacket standing up like a dark brown leather teepee.

She put down the rolls and sat on the smaller chunk of lava. "What about?"

He pointed at the jacket. "Go ahead. Open it up."

She braced for the weight and dragged it up onto her lap. The interior lining was a mass of small flaps large enough for a credit card or six. She ran her hand over the smooth satin. "Why...?"

"Pick one. Any of them. Open it. They're all the same."

She moved a flap up. She could feel the thin padding diffusing the outline of the metal plate underneath. She looked at the edge of the metal showing. She drew the plate out. The yellow shone dully in the sunshine.

Turning it over several times, she finally looked up, frowning. "Brass or gold?"

She looked back at the lining and started counting. Duff laughed. "You'll need to take the lining out to count them all. Eighty-eight, all total, stacked with a slight overlap. They make a flexible wall of protective gold. They're fourteen troy ounces or sixteen regular ounces each."

She looked at him blankly.

Duff frowned. The smartass mouth wasn't snapping. "What?"

She waved her hand at him with a shush. She kept looking at him, but he noticed her mouth was moving ever so slightly.

"It doesn't work out."

He frowned. "What doesn't?"

"Eighty-eight."

"Why?"

"Because, if they're a pound each, which is sixteen ounces, just the metal weighs eighty-eight pounds. But the ingots each weigh a pound, which makes it eighty-eight pounds of metal, plus the leather. Not the forty-eight you told me."

Duff smiled at her quick math and then laughed. "If I told you, it weighed a hundred pounds with my gloves in the pockets, would you have even tried to pick it up?"

Her left eye narrowed. "Why do the gloves matter?"

He pointed. "Pull one out."

She drew one out and frowned as she tried it on. She flexed the large gloves as she felt along the fingers. "What's in here?"

Duff snorted. "I figure it's lead powder. But with the jacket, it might be gold dust. The gloves are two-point-six-pounds each."

Bean stuffed the glove back into the pocket. "Why?"

"Well, it came with the jacket." He shrugged and laughed. "If I were a gangster or something, they're like a pair of brass knuckles. It protects your fingers but adds weight if you hit someone."

She slowly folded the jacket as best as it would allow. Finally, letting it slide off her lap to stand by her foot. "Should I be afraid?"

He shrugged his one shoulder. "It's up to you. I used to be afraid of the person I might be, but then I found it exhausting. So now I drive and look at the world around me, and don't worry."

He stood and effortlessly picked up the jacket and slipped it on. Then, bending, he grabbed the sleeping bag and tarp.

She followed. "There were large pockets too...?"

He nodded. "Great for maps and paperwork."

"Someone went to a lot of work to make pockets for the gold ingots. But then just general random-assed pockets for maps and paper?"

Duff lifted the clothes and gear out of the large back trunk. When it was empty, he pointed at two small pieces of fabric, unlike the carpet-like lining. He carefully grabbed the small fabric loops and lifted the floor liner out.

Bean's eyes grew, and her mouth dropped open. "Holy... catfish."

Duff returned the lining, covering the stacks of money, and

repacked the gear. "The reason I'm showing all of this to you"—he stopped and turned toward her—"is in case something happens. I want you to know why you don't leave my jacket or the bike in anybody else's hands."

He closed the lids and locked them. "There's more in the bottoms of the side bags. All total, there's a little over a quarter-million dollars. There's a bunch of euros mixed in." He peeked at her. "And Canadian and Mexican, too… in case we need to take a vacation or something."

His stomach growled. "But right now…"

Bean shooed him with the back of her hands. "Hurry up. I need to pee."

The morning desert swallowed up the deep throat of the motorcycle. The dirt road wasn't difficult, but it also wasn't smooth.

"How do you know Mr. Kaminski?"

"About a year and a half ago, he reached out. He said I came highly recommended."

"By whom?"

"He never told me."

"Did you ask?"

Duff glanced back and then did a second fast glance. She got the point.

They parked in front of the Trading Post. Duff noticed the beautiful polish job now had a fine layer of gray dust. He knew the type of dust. It wouldn't blow off at sixty or even a hundred. He would have to wipe the bike down or wash it.

The omelets were standard. Three mixed eggs with bacon chips, onions, Ortega chilies, and cheese smothered in a salsa out of a large can. The bread came from a bakery at least a few days away. Duff eyed Bean as she pushed the food around with lackluster interest.

She looked up. "What?"

He looked at her food. She fell back against the bench, placing her hands in her lap. "Wow, you have one great breakfast, and everything else just seems like dog food?" The chuckle came from somewhere deep in his gut. "Just making sure I hadn't spoiled you into becoming a delicate hothouse flower."

She stuck her tongue out at him as she forked a piece of omelet into her mouth. Her chewing slowed as her elbow stood on the table. The fork bobbed gently in her loose hand.

Duff raised one eyebrow. "What?"

"Hothouse flower."

"What about it?"

Her face pulled to one side as her other eye closed. "What is it?"

"Do you know what an orchid is?"

"Heard of it."

"It's delicate. They originally came from some hot, steamy, tropical jungle or something. But now, they raise them in hothouses that are hot and steamy."

"So I would be a delicate hothouse flower because I liked the steam room at the spa?"

Duff gave her a goofy look. "They had a steam room? We should have stayed another night or two."

Bean chuffed a snort. "You would have gotten fat or ran off with that bartender."

Duff wiggled his eyebrows. "You're younger."

They went back to quietly eating. Finally, the waitress came, poured coffee, and left.

Duff pushed his empty plate forward and leaned back with his mug. He studied Bean.

She felt his scrutiny and looked up. Her voice was quiet. "What?"

"Just thinking. Nothing specific or important."

"Like what?"

He gently put his mug down. "Let me ask you. You don't have to answer now or even think your answer is final."

"Okay...?"

"What do you want?"

"When?"

He pushed his lower lip out as he shrugged his face. "Now. Next week. A year from now. Even twenty years from now when you're old and gray. Just... what do you want? Something in general or something specific. Small or big, it doesn't matter."

She studied his face and then looked down at her mug. Then, turning, she leaned her back toward the windowsill and studied the coffee in her cup.

Her voice was soft and distant. "I never thought about anything like that. Everything was just responding to whatever was going on at the moment. Every night I'd go to sleep. I didn't think about the next day, of going to school, or anything but getting through the night."

Duff's jaw and lips locked. His eyes wandered over the youthful face. The sentiment didn't fit the age of the person. And then he thought about his own dealings for the last two years. They were just alike but from two different circumstances. Hers forced on her, and his by his choosing not to examine or correct his lack of knowledge or memory.

"I guess now you get to think about more than even just tomorrow."

Her face shrugged as she looked at the mug distractedly. "I guess one thing would be to graduate from high school." She looked up at him. Her face wasn't asking, begging, or making a statement. It was just a passive look as she waited for a response.

Duff sipped on the cool coffee as he thought. "It's kind of a basic requirement these days."

Bean turned to face him. "When you apply for a driving job, do they ask if you graduated high school? I mean, do you have to show them your high school diploma?"

Duff chuffed softly. "Heck, I've never even filled out an application. People already knew I drove, and with all the licenses and certificates I have, I guess they just assumed I had. Driver-wise, I'm probably a master's or Ph.D. level."

"But you don't know. I mean, for sure. You haven't made sure by finding out what high school you went to or anything?"

His eyebrows raised as he looked at his coffee. "I wouldn't even know how to start looking." He looked up with a crooked smile. "Got any suggestions?"

She snorted as she leaned back. "Oh, we're a fine pair."

His head rocked in a short bobbing. "But at least we're a pair. And that's better than last week."

She watched the far wall. Collected desert findings of past human off-casting covered the upper section of the board-paneled wall. Her right hand in a fist, she extended it toward him. He softly bumped it in acknowledgment.

As Duff paid for breakfast, more waters, and their gas, he looked at an old photo on the wall. "Where was that taken?"

The woman didn't even turn to look. Obviously, it wasn't the first time she explained the photo. "Curtis took that photo from the deck of the El Tovar Hotel when it opened back in 1915."

"Where's that?"

"Over on the south rim at Grand Canyon Village. Right up here, turn left on sixty-four. It's a minor road, but a pleasant drive. It'll be great on your motorcycle."

He pushed the change back to her. "Sixty-four. Thanks. Is it far to the hotel?"

She pursed her lips. "It's a pretty ride along the rim. And an easy hour's drive."

He turned to look at Bean. She shrugged. "Sounds good to me."

10

NEW ASSIGNMENT

The valet looked up from the shack as the large red motorcycle made the last turn into the parking entrance. Grabbing the wide, flat rock, he walked out to meet Duff and Bean. The engine chuffed one last mutter and went silent. Duff eased out the kickstand with his foot. The valet squatted and set the stone under the end of the stand. Duff eased the bike over into position.

"What if we brought home a few other bikers?"

The kid stood, smiling. "I have six rocks in the shack right now, and we have more down in supply. There's an event every year. This parking lot is full of a hundred or more motorcycles. We look forward to it. There are some spectacular antique bikes. And a few of the guys ride unmarked bikes that aren't in production yet. We get to see it all for five days."

Duff looked at Bean, both smiling.

"That would be amazeballs to see." She smiled, and being silly, nodded her head in tiny twitches.

Duff rolled his eyes as he slid off the bike. "Let's see if we can still get a room at the inn first."

The valet snorted. "You're still in bungalow 104."

Duff frowned, and the kids grimaced comically as his eyes rolled to one side. "They arrange these things way above my pay grade." He looked at the dust on the bike. "And we'll get this volcanic dust washed off before it scratches the paint."

Duff slipped him a hundred. "I noticed some specks of rust or something on the chrome..."

The kid recoiled in mock horror. "No. Say it's not so." He returned to his usual smile. "We'll get it done. And if you want to pull your bags, we can get them down to the bungalow for you." He glanced at his watch. "I believe you're just in time for your dinner reservation by the pool."

Duff rolled his eyes and turned his head to face a smiling Bean.

Bean made a production of looking at her empty wrist. "Well, after all, we have eaten nothing in, what... the last four hours?"

Duff looked at the valet as he unlocked the trunk. "Growing child."

The valet nodded. "I know. I've got one of my own."

Duff froze and looked hard at the kid. His look lingered as he studied the face, still unfamiliar with a razor.

"A seven-month-old Great Dane. We call him the flow-through digestive system."

Duff handed him the two small bags. "Good luck with that, Daddy."

The graying gentleman stood as they walked down the stairs. Duff noted the still properly snugged tie but with rolled back cuffs. The double fold back appeared flat enough to be ironed in place. And why not?

Duff stuck his hand out as they walked up. "And we just

happened to have dinner reservations where our attire is suitable?" He looked at the empty tables around the pool. Only one stood draped and set for dining.

The man smiled and shrugged. "I thought it would be more comfortable on such a pleasant evening." He turned, facing Bean. "And how did you like one of our oldest accommodations, my dear?"

"El Tovar is amazing, Mr. Kaminski. I thought the heavy beams and wood paneling echoed the magnitude of the large hole in the backyard."

The man laughed. "Please. We're almost like family. Call me Itzhak, or Ziggy. And the oldest accommodation was where you spent the night. Camped by the crater. *The* oldest craters of North America, if I'm not mistaken."

Duff narrowed one eye. "Itzhak?"

The man smiled and looked up at him. "That would be Mister to you, *Mr.* Itzhak. You still work for me. But I'm going to adopt Bean here as my new grandniece." He put his hand out toward the table as he saw the server coming. "Please, sit. You two must be hungry."

As they sat, Kaminski leaned toward Bean. "I understand you took a liking for our Nopales. This is Nopal soup. They cook it and then chill it for desert dinners."

With her first spoonful, Bean was all smiles. "I think I could live on cactus."

The older man rocked in his chair, smiling. "But there are so many other delightful edibles on the desert floor."

Duff snorted softly. "Wait until you try barbecued Armadillo."

Kaminski's eyes lit up in delight. "Ah yes, sand lobster on the half shell." He leaned conspiratorially over to Bean. "Definitely an acquired taste. I'd settle for the wet coyote machaca burrito instead."

As the entrée arrived, Bean grew pensive. She eyed the whitish meat perched on a bed of greens over a small puddle of a light green sauce.

Kaminski pointed at the meat. "This is not from the desert. This is Chilean sea bass caught and flown in fresh. It is the best the west coast offers. The chef marinates the steaks in fresh apple juice, which draws out the oil but leaves a delicate apple flavor. They harvested the greens only a mile from here, and the sauce is more of your old friend, the cactus. And as they say in the old country, Bon appétit."

Bean smiled. "So it's fish. Got it." She cut off a small bite and smiled as she chewed. "I just didn't recognize it without the breading and in the shape of a stick. This is better."

She cut a bigger bite, but she stopped with it on her fork. "You said the crater was the oldest accommodation. Why? It's just a volcano."

Kaminski put down his fork and dabbed at his lips. Then, straightening his napkin back on his lap, he leaned his forearms against the edge of the table as he pulled apart a small piece of the bread. "Did you walk out across the cinder field?"

"Sure."

"Well, some pieces of cinder aren't hard, dense lava, but are not soft puffy pumice either. They are lighter, only semi-puffy lava. They are the magma that should have stayed inside the earth. It becomes pumice when it's still liquid and thrown into the air. But if it flowed out, it would be lava. The light rock with no air only got exposed to the surface after it had cooled but got thrown out by fresh liquid magma becoming pumice. The early indigenous people sought those rocks and shaped them into bowls called mortars and a club kind of thing called a pestle. They put nuts and dried grains in the mortar and pound and grind them into a coarse flour."

"Grains. Like corn?"

He smiled and chewed on a small bite of the bread. He glanced at Duff and then back to Bean. "Well, corn is a controversial subject. There's a new belief about corn or its original form: maize. It didn't arrive on our shores until about a thousand or more years ago. But when it got here, they were ready."

"How do you know they came there to make these... whatevers?"

"People who study those people have found mortar holes out there in larger stones. At first, they thought the migrant people came there to grind their grain and such. And maybe they did. But it made more sense for them also to work or shape the stones to take with them."

"That would mean they could grind flour wherever they found the nuts and stuff."

Kaminski turned to Duff. "She's good. How are you going to keep up?"

Duff deadpanned. "I have a fast bike."

Bean mopped up the last of the cactus sauce with a small piece of bread. As she swallowed, she raised one eyebrow. "I figured someone told you we were at El Tovar, but how did you know we camped at the crater?"

Kaminski deadpanned the girl and turned toward Duff. "Can I borrow your fast motorcycle?"

Duff licked his lips. As his head tilted back, his eyes narrowed. "I was wondering about that too."

Kaminski sat quietly, studying the larger man he had known through business. There are certain boundaries of propriety, and crossing them requires explanations. He leaned to one side as he fished his phone out of his pocket. He turned it on and placed it on the table so Duff could also see. As the phone booted up, the lock screen was a plain wall of black with white letters. The man pressed his thumb into the receiver. The desktop showed a few apps. Kaminski tapped an app icon. A roll call of a few names appeared. Duff Akens was one of them. He tapped the name. The screen cleared and was replaced by a map. A small red dot pulsed in the center. He pinched his fingers and then spread them across the screen. The map zoomed in, showing the property. The red dot still pulsed, but not at the valet station.

"Did you leave your key in the motorcycle?"

Duff pulled it out of his pocket and held it, dangling. "No."

Kaminski smiled. "I hope you tipped them well. They pushed it down to the wash station over here." He pointed behind them. "That's got to be a heavy bike to push back up the hill."

Duff dropped the key on the table. "Can they take these down to them? I'd never push it that far. Much less up hill."

Kaminski raised his left hand and circled his finger. The server showed up seconds later. "Can you run these down to the wash station? We don't want the boys pushing the motorcycle back up the hill. And warn them against taking it for a joyride." He tapped next to the phone on the table. "Or I'll know."

The server snickered. "Yes, sir."

Bean followed all the interactions. "But you don't own the place."

Kaminski turned at the statement. "No. No, I don't. But I'm here more than I am not."

"But it's expensive..."

He nodded. "So is an expensive house with daily housekeeping service, a world-class chef, a Michelin-rated restaurant, and staff who feels like your family. I have a clean bungalow, impeccably laundered clothes, a world-class office, car service to the airport when I need it, and none of the headaches of payroll or running the place."

She smirked. "Not to mention the spa."

"Ah." He raised his index finger and turned on her. "I meant to ask you how you found your first experience at a spa?"

She tilted her head. "I'll tell you... after you explain to Duff why you have his bike nanny bugged."

His eyebrows raised. "Tracked. The term is tracked. The same as with all my vehicles. Cars, trucks, and airplanes. Everything has a tracker for security. So, for example, if we send a truck on a sensitive errand, we need to know exactly where it is and what's going on."

"Why?"

Kaminski glanced over at Duff. The man was passively listening. He held out his hand toward Bean.

"There are restrictions on our shipments. Some of our shipments are worth millions of dollars. The monetary value is not the most important at some points—it's the package. There is a reason armored trucks may not stop at the local doughnut shop for a coffee break."

"Explain value beyond millions of dollars."

He thought a moment as he looked at Duff for help.

Duff closed one eye and thought of something safe. "Eyes only information."

"Right." Kaminski turned back. "Let's say I have some information. It's only about ten pages of paper. I put it in an envelope rigged to burn up if it's opened wrong. This I give to Duff and tell him to drive it to a person in Los Angeles. Don't get stopped. Only stop for gas, and make sure it's the right person. Let's say they have a password, and he has a photo of them."

She nodded.

He continued, "The paper and envelope are only worth a few dollars. But the information contained in those pages could make or break my business." He leaned back in his chair. "Would I want to worry for the next twenty hours about if Duff got through safely?" He tapped on his phone. "Or would I want to track his movements?"

She furled her lower lip. "Nanny tracker." She looked at Duff. "Are you okay with this?"

He shrugged. "I always knew the trucks have trackers. One guy stopped to see his girlfriend… the truck was empty, but that wasn't the point. They never teamed me with him, but I wouldn't want a distracted person in my truck. And I made that trip with an envelope. I just never thought someone would put a tracker on the bike without asking."

Kaminski grimaced. "It's under your seat and slaved to the battery and your phone for a signal. I'd appreciate it if you didn't remove it. Which brings me to work—I need you to make another of those drives for me."

"When?"

"Tomorrow."

Duff pointed at Bean.

Kaminski weaved his head around. "I've been thinking about that. She can stay here, or you can take her with you. Together, you look like you're touring around. Taking a vacation. Alone, you look like you're headed somewhere."

"How far."

"Just north of San Francisco. Near Santa Rosa."

From Duff's questions, Bean knew he was in his work mode. He sounded almost like a machine.

"How fast?"

"Run me the numbers and routes."

Duff sipped on his water, his eyes focused on Bean, but she knew he wasn't seeing her. His face was calm, but there was a tick around his eyes.

Kaminski reached his hand out to her and rested it on the table. "You are watching a talent no one else in my company has. This is the one best reason I hire him."

Duff's eyes changed to Kaminski. "Las Vegas, to Los Angeles, and up the center is just under nine hundred. Two long, grueling days, but I don't think Bean's up to it. So more like three days."

Kaminski agreed. "And if you go north out of Vegas and cross over at Reno?"

"It only adds about a hundred, but the speeds are lower, so it would take four days."

Kaminski rolled his lips in thought as his eyes hopscotched about the table, looking for answers. "Go up the Nevada route. I'll have something else you can drop off at the office there, and you can check out your new digs. I changed where you'll be. There was a school across from the other place, but I think a tutor and homeschooling might be more to her liking." He looked at Bean. "I have a feeling you get bored in regular schools."

She nodded with a silent laugh.

Kaminski looked back at Duff. "Show her around a bit. Then, maybe go up to Lake Tahoe and do a little sightseeing. Have you even been to Lake Tahoe?"

Bean and Duff harmonized. "No."

Kaminski broadly smiled as he held out his arms and hands. "See. Kismet."

Duff squinted his left eye. "Circling the Lake would add another hundred miles or more."

"Then you can go over the Kit Carson Pass and wander down through the gold rush country. Cross over and go up through San Jose. Take her across the Golden Gate bridge and hit Santa Rosa in, say, seven or eight days?"

Duff agreed with a nod. "Still hard riding, but she's tough."

"Taylor will have something for you to bring back to Vegas. But it's not critical. So why not swing out to the coast and spend a couple of days relaxing. I don't have a spa out there, but I'm sure you can find one for the road-weary bodies."

Duff looked at Bean. "Been to California before?"

"I would think so. We lived in Pendleton. The first foster home was in a tiny town called Mentone. I think it was near a city named Riverside."

Kaminski nodded. "San Bernardino County. Southern California. Pendleton. Was your father a Marine?"

Her head bobbed once. Both men could tell it was the end of that conversation.

11

LAKE TAHOE

The sandwiches were standard for *made sometime in the last five hours* and *sitting in the cooler until warmed up in a microwave or steam box*. But they didn't come for the food. The counter and benches looked out over the lake thousands of feet below, attached to the deck's railing. They could imagine how crowded the ski lodge at the top of Heavenly Valley could get on a clear sunny day during the ski season. But it seemed people didn't think about taking the gondola to the top of a mountain they couldn't ski down. There was one other couple at the other end of the deck. Bean and Duff were happy with the separation. The couple was in the gondola behind them, and they could see them arguing the entire way up the mountain.

"Where did we take the boat ride from?"

Duff pointed at the other end of the lake, twenty-two miles away. "See that dark area at the edge of the lake?" He sensed her nodding. "I think that's Tahoe Vista and King's Beach. I don't think we can see Emerald Bay, but it would be over there on the left."

She chewed her sandwich quietly.

Duff sipped on his coffee. It was little more than scorched water with some darkish color. "Why?"

Her voice had a wispy quality to it. "I don't know. But maybe it would be fun to do it again... but longer sometime. Being on the water was refreshing. But a sailboat would be quieter." She turned her head. "Have you ever been sailing?"

He shook his head. "Not that I know of."

Her lower lip furled. She thought and then looked back down at the lake. She took another bite and put down her sandwich. She chewed quietly. "It must be a bitch not knowing what you have or haven't done or who you are or aren't. What kind of life you lived for...?" She looked at him.

"Thirty-six years. I think."

She turned back to the lake. "Twice my lifetime. Enough time to live two lifetimes. And then nothing." She turned to sit straddling the bench. She rested her left elbow on the table and leaned her head into her palm. "But it doesn't bother you. How is that?"

He thought about how she had trapped Kaminski about the tracker. "I'll tell you, but first, let's talk about your father and mother. You admitted to Kaminski that your father was a Marine. So let's start there."

Between the two pairs of blackout wraparound dark glasses, he couldn't read her eyes. Her face was blank. He wasn't sure if she would talk or just run away. In Phoenix, it was apparent it was not a subject she ever talked about. But then, neither was his lack of memories.

"My father died in Afghanistan when I was nine. He was my best friend. He had gone overseas before, but two Marines came to the door this time. After that, I only remember my mother crying all the time. Another base mom came over to stay with us. I don't remember if she cooked or what. I was old enough to get my cereal or microwave something from the refrigerator or freezer." She looked out across the sky. "One night, Mom went to town. I overheard some older kids saying she had driven down to the cliffs and didn't stop. There was only one funeral—hers. She never arranged one for my father. I don't know if they even brought his body home. They kept me at the hospital until the funeral, and then Child Services took me after the funeral. I don't even know what happened to all our stuff."

She looked over at Duff. He shrugged. He couldn't imagine being that nine-year-old or what happens to a house full of memories. His pack was up to three shirts, three T-shirts, three pairs of socks, and two pairs of jeans. All of which needed him to stop at a laundry or buy new. He imagined Bean was in similar shape, but to lose a whole family, you can still remember...

He stood. "We need to get over the mountain." His voice was thick.

———

THE CAMPGROUND WAS Bean's idea. Their site nestled in among what they could tell was the last of the tall trees. It was the farthest from the communal bathrooms with showers, but also there was nobody in the next campsite. It seemed people liked being in nature but not walking. They tried out the little gas cookstove they bought at the surplus store. They also found replacement clothes, and Bean was walking funny because she had never worn new jeans before. Everything in foster care was hand-me-down or used from a thrift store.

"Are they always this stiff and rough?"

Duff pushed his lower lip out. "Yeah. Pretty much. They're more comfortable once we run them through a washing machine."

She plopped down on the picnic bench and watched the transparent flame lick at the bottom of the small pot. "Is that going to be enough?"

"We bought a second can… And that meatball sandwich we stopped for as an after-lunch lunch would feed a family of four in some countries." Duff leaned out and looked at her butt. "Where are you hiding all that food?"

She gave him a stern look. "Are you checking out my scrawny butt, Mr. Akens?" They both laughed at the intimacy. Duff smiled, glad she was comfortable enough to joke about the casual relationship. Not a father and daughter, but not the usual uncle and niece. Just somewhere in between.

Bean scoffed as her gaze turned back to the flame. "Besides, you're the one who decided to stop."

He recoiled with wide eyes. "I only stopped for the pie. You're the one who spotted the meatball sandwich on that guy's plate."

"Yeah, and who added the chili fries?"

"Are you saying you only forced yourself to eat them?"

She ignored him. The flame danced in her eyes. She rolled her head and looked at him with a closed smile. "They were good."

He laughed with a bad James Cagney imitation. "Stick with me, kid, and we'll both be over three hundred pounds before Christmas."

Bean folded her arms on the table and rested her chin on them. Her eyes became more flame than hazel as the gloom replaced the sunset. "I think I've eaten more food in the last week than I've had in the last year. At least better food."

He joined her position, watching the flame. "Food was scarce, or just decent food?"

She rolled her head onto the side. She looked at him. "That's not how this is going to work."

His eyes ticked over to hers. "What?"

"You've put it off all afternoon. As slow as the mountain road was, you could have talked on the bike. You had your chance at that strawberry place. But now… it's your turn to give."

He smirked. He had been mulling over how to say what would make sense. Everything he had thought of sounded wrong in his head. And she deserved better.

His eyes returned to the flame. "When your dad died, you felt like your best friend had abandoned you."

His eyes shifted to her. He waited. Finally, her eyes slowly closed.

"When your mom died—"

Bean interjected the truth. "Decided to kill herself."

He nodded slightly. "Made her choice. It was another betrayal and abandonment. And then the military gave you to Child Services. It was the last unfaithfulness or desertion."

She nodded and straightened her head. Duff could see the flame in her eyes was wet.

"The difference between what you went through, and mine, was you went through every second, minute, and hour of it. On the other hand, I woke up, and it was all done. Anything or everything that was or could have been me was gone." At the sound of bubbling, he reached in with the spoon and stirred.

"I woke up with a splitting headache. I was lying face down

in filthy, greasy water. It was cold, wet, and my head and back hurt. At first, I pulled out my keys. The fob matched the Indian parked in the shadows. I think I would have walked out of there and kept walking if I hadn't scared some birds. They flew out of the shadows, and I saw the bike. I stumbled onto the bike and the key fit. I rode out and left town. Out in the country, I found a small motel. I checked in and then counted the money in my wallet. I had nineteen hundred dollars' worth of bills left in my wallet." He looked at Bean with wide eyes. "What kind of person walks around with two thousand dollars in their pants. That's when I realized I didn't know who I was."

"Or how much was in your bike."

He chuffed. "I found more before I went through the bike. The big pockets"—he flipped open his jacket—"were stuffed with over a hundred thousand in different currencies. Talk about wild thoughts of being some international spy or something."

"But the memories? Or lack of memories, I should say…?"

He rolled his eyes as he dished half the soup into another bowl. He handed it and a spoon to Bean. "Well, I sat next to the stack of cash on the bed. And then the next thing I knew, I woke up when the maid knocked on the door. I went to the door and told her I wouldn't need anything and was going to stay the week. She frowned, and I realized I'd just kicked a chunk of her income out from under her. I went to the bed and grabbed a couple of hundred and gave it to her."

"What then?"

"I think I slept for another day or two."

"But still no memories? Nothing?"

Duff tried the soup. He shrugged his face. "It's not as bad as the sandwich at the top of the ski resort." They laughed. And then they ate in silence.

As Bean finished, she put her bowl down and looked at him. "Do you cook?"

His stare was blank.

"Well?"

"I don't know. I always just ate in restaurants or lunch trucks."

"Haven't you ever lived anywhere long enough to wonder or try? Or do you always just stay in motels?"

Duff thought about his various jobs. He hadn't even stayed in a motel with any kind of kitchen. He ate when he was hungry or didn't when he wasn't. He couldn't even remember stepping inside a grocery store. The closest thing was a minimart at a gas station. He hadn't needed to—a restaurant was just a block or three away.

Bean coughed. "You know? One of these days, you're going to stop to think like that, and someone is going to slap you on the back of the head, and you'll freeze up with that same face."

He frowned at her. "Freeze...?"

"You stop to think. Then you try so hard... maybe to remember or something. But you just freeze. I'm not even sure you breathe. You've done it a few times."

"But I was..."

"No. Stop it. It's scary as all heck. Ease up. If you finally remember your past, I'll bet you're flat on your back and breathing normal-like. Not all bunched up and frozen—afraid to twitch or move because it might come back any second." She gently punched him in the arm. "Breathe. Chill. What would happen if you tried to remember something and we're barreling down the highway at a hundred miles an hour, and a curve came up with an enormous cliff and a lake at the bottom? I'll tell you what will happen. We'd go swimming. But not in a fun way. So stop it."

He blinked. "Yes, ma'am."

She scoffed in dismissal. "I'm not some married old lady."

"Yes, miss."

She rolled her eyes as she hissed between her teeth. "How about just, okay?"

"Okay."

Bean looked at the dishes. "Now, who does the dishes?"

He blinked a few times and then looked at her with a crushed look on his face. "The dishwasher?"

She snorted. "First, the waitress has to take them away."

He looked at the cold-water faucet standing out of the ground. "Umm..."

She rolled her eyes and stood. "I need to go pee. So I'll wash them in the bathroom."

"You think that's okay?"

She narrowed her eyes in condemnation. "If they throw us out, you're driving."

"You've got a deal."

12

DELIVERY

Bean's voice lowered at the deep green carpet supporting the dark wood walls and furniture. "Is this usual?"

Duff looked at her. "The fancy office?"

He could tell she wanted to slug his shoulder. Her fist bunched, but she preserved the decorum.

Her eyes widened with her hiss. "No, goofball, the waiting."

He rolled his head back, looking forward. There wasn't even a secretary to watch or listen to. It was just the endless hum of an office building. He had forgotten what they sounded like. The soft undertone of voices you can't make out and keyboards or phones—but you can't tell if it's in this office or one somewhere down the hall. Just noise, making little or no sense. He'd rather take the sound of his motorcycle, or a giant sixteen piston engine in an earthmover, or a simple Cummins engine in a long hauling truck.

He eased his head forward and yawned as he pressed his palms together between his legs—stretching. He glanced at her. She was still waiting. He fluttered his eyes wide and looked at the carpet. "My usual is fourteen gears and driving from dock to dock. Sometimes it's just a container drop. Others I'm asked to wait while they load the trailer or unload. With Kaminski, if I'm driving a truck, I'm driving alone, or in a team of five."

Bean squinted one eye as she smiled at him. "Isn't that a little crowded in a truck?"

"They build the trucks special for the teams. If they stop for any reason, three are always in the cab. You can't even roll down the windows because they are that thick." He held his finger and thumb a couple of inches apart."

"So they're armored?"

"And then some. Someone can even shoot holes through the tires, and they won't go flat. There's nonstop communication with a base dispatcher in case of trouble. Everything is about protecting the shipment, no matter what it is."

"What the heck are you carrying?"

Duff shrugged. "We never know. Those are the times we drop the trailer, hook up another one, and leave. If I do any of those, those are the times I won't be home that night. They are usually a two-day flip, but I've been to the east coast and back. It takes about five or six days." He reached out his hand and touched her knee. "If I ever have to, someone will let you know or come to be with you."

She scoffed. "Like I'm a little kid. Hell, I want in on the driving."

Duff leaned back and rested his head against the wall. "Do you have a driver's license now?"

Her shoulders and chest visibly deflated. "No."

Duff pursed his lips and wove his head through a few figure eights. "Then I guess we have a few things to work on when we settle down in Vegas."

"Like what?" She side-eyed him.

"I've been thinking about that. First, you need to either get a GED or finish high school. Do you know what you had left to finish?"

She snorted a soft breath. "They never transfer your records. Most foster kids bounce around so much that they just drop out and run away. When you're twelve, you know that you're never finding a family because they aren't looking for older kids. You aren't cute and cuddly, and you usually have problems, anyway."

"And you…?"

"That's why they sent me to Colorado. The guy was some sort of retired teacher or something. He was supposed to whip me into shape so I would finish school before I aged out."

"And…?"

"I never saw it, but I had the feeling the whip was the only genuine part. I was headed to find a bus station or start hitch-hiking when I saw your motorcycle. But I had also heard the jerk call the sheriff. He just wasn't sure what I was wearing."

Duff studied her and thought. "How did you know you could trust me?"

She shrugged her shoulders. "I don't know. If it hadn't been for your jacket hanging on the back of your chair, I wouldn't have even known the bike was yours. But from what I could see, you didn't have any tattoos, and the waitress didn't seem afraid of you… so I took a chance. If you were a jerk, I could run away later. But I needed out of there right then, and you were the best shot at it."

"But I might not have been leaving town."

"I thought it was a good bet. The bike has Nevada plates."

They both looked over at the soft whoosh of the heavy door to the inner office. A man in rolled-up sleeves on his white shirt and dress slacks stood looking at a handful of papers. He frowned behind his wire-rimmed glasses. His mouth opened to say something, but then he stopped and held up one finger. The door stayed open as he disappeared into the other office. He came back with different papers. Leafing through, he stopped at a few pages and then looked up. "When are you going back?"

Duff stood. "We were planning to be on the coast for a few days. But if...?"

The man let the pages gather as his hand swung to his side. His eyes looked to the space above Duff's head as he searched for an answer. "No..." He held up the pages and looked at their body instead of the words. "No, that would be fine. Wednesday morning would be fine. If anything comes up, we have your phone number and will call you. Where on the coast?"

"We looked on the map and were thinking Mendocino. See if we can find a room or two. We heard there was some good seafood and pretty country to see."

"What are you driving?"

Bean stood. "Motorcycle."

The man looked at their leather jackets. "Two motorcycles...?"

Duff's head twitched. "One. Two-up."

The man mouthed the word *ah* as his head lifted in acknowledgment. "Pretty ride." He glanced at his watch. "A little late. Have the desk find you something for the night in Guerneville. But tomorrow, hit the coast and go north to Gualala. North of town, when you see a Russian onion head on the right and ocean on the left, that's the place. Make sure you're hungry for dinner. I'll call ahead..." His face formed a question as his finger moved back and forth between Duff and Bean.

Duff shook his head. "She's my niece. She'll need her own room."

"Bathroom down the hall okay with you two?"

Bean coughed. "Does it have a door on it?"

The man frowned, and Duff elbowed her.

The man's one eyebrow peeked over his glasses. "I'll see what I can arrange. They also have cabins hidden up in the forest with a personal Jacuzzi. If you don't like where they stick you, ask to see what else they have. We have a standing account with them, so don't worry about anything."

Duff nodded. "You can tell them my last name—"

"They won't need it. They don't get many motorcycles. What color is it?"

Bean laughed. "It's an Indian but looks like a fire truck."

The man chuckled. "Red. Easy deal." He looked back at Duff. "How many days to get back to Phoenix?"

"We can make it in two if we need to."

The man blinked. Duff and Bean could both tell the distance, motorcycle, and time didn't digest easily for the man.

Duff thumbed toward Bean. "She's ready to find out what fourteen-hour days are like."

Blinking, the man fanned through the paperwork. "Okay. That'll work. I'll see you at eight on Wednesday." He caught himself. "Oh, if you're coming from Gualala, maybe make it more like ten. Down the coast is slow going, but they don't expect people to come down to breakfast real early. You'll see."

At the front desk, the woman showed him on a map where the man had talked about. She also pointed out and then made a reservation for a small B&B in Bodega Bay she liked.

———

THE RIDE WAS EASY ENOUGH. The rooms were perfect, and the deck out the back looked west over the bay. The owner had delivered a small bucket of fresh local oysters from just down the coast.

Bean talked around her seventh oyster. "Do you remember ever eating oysters before?"

Duff mumbled and then swallowed with a chuckle. Wiping his face, he nodded. "I drove a service rig down near New Orleans. A guy I worked with lived down in the boot's tip. His family was shrimpers and oystermen. Every weekend we were down at the End of the World eating everything from the water." He jabbed his finger at the plate of oysters. "But these don't taste like ocean oysters. These are sweet."

"*Exacta mundo*, my friend. These are Hog Island oysters. Twice a day, they bathe in freshwater while the tide is out. But then, when they're harvested, they spend a whole day in pure sweet water. Here. Try these MacArthur's." The owner, Niles, put down a tray of a dozen broiled oysters.

Duff looked at the oysters with a green and cheese topping. "Don't you mean Rockefeller's?"

"Nope. Randy Macarthur won the state fair with this recipe. That oil fella from back east doesn't play out here. Shoot a little lemon on them."

Duff did as he was instructed and slurped one into his mouth. As he chewed, he made a horrible face and shook his head at Bean. But he continued to chew.

Bean reached over. "I call cow droppings." She took one, drained the lemon wedge over it, and sucked it past her teeth. Two seconds later, she didn't hold back.

Duff rubbed his shoulder, laughing. The strength of her

punch surprised him—until he thought of her growing up having to defend herself.

Niles laughed. "I see I'd better go whip up another dozen."

The door swung out, and Niles's husband stepped out with another tray. "Way ahead of ya, honey." The thin black man gently set down the new platter. He reached over and grabbed one of the original oysters, slurping it into his mouth. He almost immediately swallowed. "Yup, thought so. He's always forgetting the paprika. Paprika is the secret ingredient that wins medals." He pointed at the fresh platter. "You can't taste it, but you can taste when it's not there."

Bean tried a new oyster. She nodded as she chewed.

Randy beamed. He side-hugged his husband and kissed the side of his head. "Pumpkin, you're sweet, and I love you to the moon and back, but you need to follow the recipes. I don't want you ruining our fine reputation by serving stuff they serve in town." He kissed him again and spun around to the door. "Lasagna in ten minutes."

BEAN AND DUFF sat stupefied at the end of the deck as the sun sunk below the knife's edge of fiery gold separating the ocean from the sky. Neither was certain if they could move. The light dinner had finished with homemade orange rum sherbet.

The faded blue sky washed into a hazy taint of gold. It wasn't one of those spectacular sunsets with clouds and rays and a symphony playing softly in the back of your head. The sky just turned from the pale end of the day blue to a washed-out gold.

Duff opened his mouth to apologize for such an anticlimactic sunset, but turning his head, noticed a single tear slide gently down Bean's cheek. The girl didn't move.

His left hand twitched. He didn't know if he should reach out or mind his own business. Obviously, it was a very personal moment.

He rolled his head back and watched the sky deepen into the still of gloom.

13
____

UP THE COAST

French toast from thick homemade egg bread was the secret that got Niles to marry Randy. Randy was the head chef at a fancy restaurant in Los Angeles, but Niles was the baker they bought their baked goods from.

One morning, Niles was pulling his fresh breads out of the ovens when Randy walked in the back door. He picked up the restaurant's order, but he was an hour early. Niles made him sit down, have a cup of coffee, and then sample a plate of fresh French toast slathered with strawberry freezer jam. It all sounded pedestrian until he tasted it.

The bread was Niles's grandmother's recipe. The freezer jam his sister made in Oregon. She sent him dozens of small plastic jars packed in dry ice. The special strawberries in Oregon were sweeter, juicier, and packed more flavor than any other berry.

Niles was slow, but Randy was persistent. It took him five Sunday mornings before Niles figured out Randy was doing the pickups because of the baker instead of the baked goods.

After they found their true love for the northern California coast was as strong as for each other, they worked on buying the lodge overlooking the bay.

Bean leaned into Duff's back. "I could stay there for a week or more."

Duff's helmet juggled up and down. "How many pounds do you think you would gain?"

"Less than you. You have no shame. I felt like a pig having a second serving. But you… eggs on top of it to boot."

He laughed, and she chuckled. He downshifted the big bike for the turn. They hadn't been joking about the road up the coast not being fast. When he shifted the bike into fourth gear, he was braking and downshifting again. Bean was becoming one with the bike. Unlike the first few hundred miles where she resisted the tilt of the motorcycle in turns, she now rode glued to Duff's back. Even if she was leaning back against the trunk, she moved in unison with him.

"Do you have a driver's license?"

She didn't respond, and Duff looked in the mirror. She was staring out over the seaside pasture to the distant ocean.

"Bean?"

She didn't move. "No."

He let it go and watched for the gas station. Niles had warned him he would pass it. He hissed as he slowed to the side of the road, turning around.

Bean chuckled reflexively. "Niles warned you."

Duff growled in mock combat. "You didn't see it either."

Bean hooted, "Some driver you are."

THE GAS RAN slow into the tank. Duff wasn't in a hurry. Bean stood at the highway's edge, looking across the expanse of seagrass and, eventually, some low dunes. Her hands were fists just nudging at the empty back pockets of her pants. Something had her wound tight, but she wouldn't talk. So Duff tried another tack.

"Do you want a driver's license?"

She turned her head only a quarter turn. "Do I get a bike to go with it?"

Quid pro quo. Duff's one eyebrow arched. "What kind?"

"Blue. Like the sky."

"Is that the only criterion? It needs to be sky blue?" He screwed the cap back on the tank and hung up the nozzle. He turned and paid the older man listening to their conversation with quiet amusement. He headed for the office to make some change.

Her head hung as she turned her upper body to glance back at him. "Well, it has to run."

"With an engine?"

Bean didn't respond. The light breeze played with the tips of her braid. She had figured out a braid meant she would lose less hair to split ends. Duff watched her try to weave it tight, but it only hung wonky—so he braided it for her.

The older man returned with the change. "You have your work cut out for you with that one."

Duff lowered his voice to a mutter. "I'm finding that out."

MOST OF THE land around the winding highway was flat with rough grass thriving on the sea air. A hundred yards toward the distant hills, a broken forest gnarled in a confusion of twisted scrub oaks and straight pines. The up and down of the brush mottled the look with dark browns to light greens. An occasional house peeked through from their position of protected privacy. The long stretch of territory lay testament to privilege with time to escape into solitude. But these were no campsites. They were more rustic manors built to appear as lodges.

The road dipped and rose around what may have once been headlands. Bean pointed at the brush ahead to the right as they rose out of a curved dip. "Deer."

As Duff turned his head to follow her finger, the brown flash became a large blot to his left. His foot and hand slammed on the brakes as he twisted his weight to throw the rear tire around. He pushed the bike to force it down and hopefully slip under the large buck in the air.

The timing was wrong.

Duff's head and shoulder hit the trailing rear legs and rock-hard hooves. The pressure at his lower hips gave way to air as Bean was pulled off the falling bike. Everything turned into slow motion as the large deer spun around in the air. The silence of the moment turned into the screaming chrome sidebars grinding on the asphalt and the dull bang of the fiberglass side-bag. Their traveling speed prevented a prolonged skid. The blow to the back of Duff's helmet knocked his face into the edge of the windshield. The spin of his body rolled him along the edge instead of a direct hit. He tumbled over the top of the bike, sliding and tumbling along the asphalt.

He lay dazed on his side. The sound of the deer disappearing up the bank to the brush above broke the silence. A bird twittered in the distance.

Duff blinked. The world was wrong. He blinked again and moved an arm. And then a leg. "Bean?" He rolled over. One lens of his glasses had popped out when the deer's hoof hit him in the face.

"Bean?"

The black leather heaped where the roadside turned up to the small bank. The white helmet rolled. The dirty white fringe rolled back, falling down her shoulders.

"Bean?" Duff moved his other arm and leg. He sat up, wiping at his face. His hand came away, smeared with blood.

"Bean?" He moved to his hands and knees. Raising.

"Bean!"

The muffled voice sounded full of dirt. "Yeah…"

Duff stumbled around her and kneeled to face her. Her face had a couple of scrapes. She looked up at him. Her lip next to her front teeth was white as the teeth biting on them.

He looked at her body. "Where…?"

Raising her left arm slightly, she let it fall back at the sound of a car. They both turned to see the older couple open their doors. The man stepped out. He leaned back into the car and said something to the woman.

The man approached as the woman went to the trunk of the car. "Agnus is fetching the first aid kit. I see your face…"

Duff pointed at Bean. "Her arm."

The woman, in tennis shorts and a white sleeveless shirt the color of her hair, approached with a large case. The box was larger than most people pack for a week's vacation.

The man smiled at Duff's look. "My name is Bob, and this is Agnus. I was a stockbroker, but Agnus was a trauma nurse. The EMT box we just got used to having in the trunk."

"Duff and Bean. We hit a deer."

Agnus turned his face with her finger. "You'll be fine. I'll get you in a minute. Let me look at your daughter first."

Bob touched Duff on the shoulder as he jerked his head. "Let's let the womenfolk do their thing while we see if we can get your bike back up on its feet." He smiled at Duff. "So to speak."

"Nice bike. Eighty-inch?"

Duff shook his head. "One-eleven but milled to one-sixteen. Do you ride?" He grabbed the handlebars, then thought a moment, and stepped back.

Bob frowned. "What's wrong?"

"Nothing." Duff slipped his jacket off. It hit the asphalt and stood in place. The man looked at the strange behavior. Duff smirked and stepped back to the bike. "It's well trained."

They leveraged the bike to upright, and Duff slipped his leg over. He turned the key to off and then back on. He pushed the starter. The bike churned. He turned it off and pushed out the kickstand.

Bob nodded. "Flooded. Give it a minute. Every four-stroke I had in the dirt had that problem. You go down in a race, then you're done. Two-stroke was usually still running."

Duff looked at him. "So small bikes."

"When I was a kid. One-twenty-fives, some two-fifties, and then, I got a Matchless 500 and never looked back as I got older. I put my way through college road racing for twenties."

Duff took off his dark glasses and stuck his gloved finger through the one hole. He looked around on the road.

The old man laughed. "Those cheapies never break. They just pop out and pop right back in. Where did you lay it down?"

Duff got off the bike, and they started walking back toward the curve. "So what was your biggest bike?"

"Biggest, or fastest?"

Duff snorted. "Both."

"Biggest was a fifty-two pan-head Harley. A friend called me one day. They were surveying an old manufacturing plant a guy was trying to sell. He had found something I might want in a storeroom. It was a bike under a tarpaulin with decades of bird poop and dust covering it. It would be part of the salvage, and he would ship it out if I wanted it. I didn't even ask what it was. When I got it, it was brown."

"Rust."

Bob squinted one eye and pointed at Duff. "Bingo. I knew it was a Harley, but nothing else. I thought about it in our garage for five months. I didn't know what I wanted to do. Then one long weekend, I started taking it apart. I stripped it down to three heaps. Paint. Chrome. Or make it go. I found a Harley dealer who knew about old bikes. I dropped off the mill with him and told him to call me if it's worth my time."

Duff scanned his side of the road for the lens. "I'm guessing it was?"

"Nah. But I did it anyway. All my life, I had just beat-up bikes and then sold them. For once, I was wondering if I could get it back to original." He stepped over to the side of the road and leaned down. Standing, he rubbed the lens in his shirt. "Here. See if this lens will fit."

Duff chuckled and took the lens. He pushed it into the frame. Slipping the glasses on, he smiled. "Everything looks darker."

Bob jerked his head and smiled. "That's usually how it works. Let's go check with the doc and see if the bike starts."

Bean was standing, but a clear balloon wrapped around her arm. Agnus was just closing her medical case.

Bob groaned, "Uh oh. That is not a good sign. Which way are you two headed?"

Duff pointed north. "There's supposed to be a building up here with an onion on top."

"There sure is. We're headed there for an early dinner. But it looks like we're stopping off at the hospital first." He looked at Duff. "You better try getting your bike started first. I'll take care of the girls."

Duff picked up his jacket and pulled it on. He turned the key and hit the starter. The bike coughed, farted, and fired up. Looking over at the three, he turned it off.

As he walked up, a car passed by carefully. The family eyed the car, motorcycle, and people with suspicion.

Bob turned. "The doc is pretty certain it's broken. Either way, it's best to get an x-ray. We can take Bean with us, and you can follow. Then we can have that dinner."

Duff looked at Bean and then at Agnus. Bean's eyes closed, but Duff could see her roll them under the lids.

The woman tilted her head at the arm. "It's probably just a simple fracture, but it needs looking at. We can probably get in and out in an hour." She smiled. "Just enough time to work up a real appetite. Bean told me you two have reservations for staying the night. Great choice. And Bobby can schmooze us the change for dinner reservations while we get Bean patched up."

———

THE DOCTOR POINTED at the large monitor on the wall. "You got lucky this time, young lady. This little bone is the radius. So much blood flows around it, and they heal faster than the ulna. This bigger bone."

He looked at Duff. "Your daughter—"

"Niece." Duff and Bean chorused defensively.

The man stepped back and put his one index finger across the other as if warding away a vampire. "My mistake. Niece.

When you get home, you should see an orthopedic surgeon. She's suffered a few breaks in the last few years that never healed right. He pointed to a couple of places." He turned toward Bean. "Do they ache when it's cold?"

Her voice was more of an embarrassed mumble. "Some."

Duff frowned. "If they're old breaks, what can they do now?"

"Shave the bones back smooth. If the muscles don't move smoothly along the bone, it creates nodes in the muscle or tendon. When that happens inside the elbow, the painful result we call tennis elbow." He turned to Bean. "But for right now, let's get you back in the casting room and fix you up for dinner. What color would you like?"

"Color? I thought casts were white?"

He smiled. "They are. But the lollipops are fruit-colored. Before you finish your lollipop, I'll be finished with your cast. Deal?"

She nodded as she looked at Agnus.

The woman waved her through the door. "Go ahead, dear. We're going to be right here."

As the door closed, Duff looked over at the concerned look on Agnus's face as she studied the x-ray. He stepped close. "What do you see?"

She looked at him—studying. "Many questions with no comforting answers."

"Such as...?"

"What's your actual relationship with her." Her face was not accusing but concerned.

Duff thought about all the wrong answers as he felt Bob's presence behind him. Two hours before, they were just strangers on a highway. Now, their concern was that of family.

"I rescued her in Colorado a couple of weeks ago. She's been in the foster system for half her life. She wanted out." He shifted his weight on his hip. "You might say we took a chance on each other. She told me that if I turned out to be a bad guy, she would just run away." His lower lip furled. "She hasn't run away yet."

Bob cleared his throat. "And you're sleeping...?"

Duff turned. "Fair question. Separate. No hanky-panky. I don't intend to either. I kind of enjoy having a niece." He pointed back at the x-ray. "But what...?"

Agnus blinked, thinking. "In the city, we saw a lot of this. Those are defensive breaks—those never seen by a doctor." She looked hard at Duff.

Duff glanced at the display. "Everything I know about Bean, I can hold in one hand. But I also know she's upfront. So over dinner, you can ask her about her time in the system. Ask her about her kidnapping me and forcing me to get her out of town. If she trusts you, you'll get your answers. Ones I'd like to hear as well. But now I know I need to find her help in more than just school and a driver's license."

"But you're not related..."

Duff smirked. "I don't have insurance either. But I can afford anything she needs. Even if that means surgery."

Agnus looked at Bob in the silent communication that comes with many years of close marriage.

Duff shifted. "What?"

Bob shook his head softly. "We both noticed it. Not a tear. That's a painful break. So many nerves run right there." He rubbed his finger along his other arm.

Agnus reached out to Duff's arm. "I've seen big macho cops and firefighters bawling like babies. Those injuries hurt so bad. But Bean? Not even a tear. Have you...?"

Duff wagged his head. Something was there, but he felt it was too personal. "No. Never. Like I said, it's only been a couple of weeks. But I do know when camping out in the desert one night… neither one of us liked the night cold."

Bob shuddered. "That kind of cold… straight to the heart of your bones."

Duff snorted. "Coffee is better in a restaurant."

Agnus bobbed her head. "And clean sheets in a pleasant hotel will always win over a sleeping bag."

Duff stuck up his index finger. "Unless… you have never truly seen the Milky Way."

Bean pushed her way through the door with the doctor trailing. She pulled the cherry red lollipop out of her mouth. The cast on her other arm was a matching red. "Enough of this candy stuff. I need oysters."

The doctor pointed at the fiberglass cast. "As I said, if the arm swells, you can soak the whole thing in ice water. Two aspirin every four hours. And no more than four servings of oysters in a twenty-four-hour period." He laughed at her growing wide eyes. "Okay, I was just fooling about the oysters."

14

SAFE HARBOR

"WHAT DID YOU DO?" As Bean sloughed off her jacket, Niles's voice was almost at a squeal. "RANDY. Oh, lordy me. RANDY. NOW."

The thinner but taller man came crashing through the swinging kitchen door. The door hit its stop and slapped him back. To his credit, he never slowed down. "What? I said wh..." He froze. His face fell open. "Oh. My. Granny's little chickens..." He spun and fussed at the overstuffed leather chair and ottoman. "Child, you sit right here. Here..." He grabbed the plush red silk crepe throw pillow from the divan. Laying it on the ottoman. "Put your feet up here."

Bean laughed at the fussing. "It's my arm, not my legs."

"Hush, child." Niles swept by with a touch on her right hand. "Your *funcles* know what is good for you." He glared back at Duff. "Unlike some other hooligan."

Duff reacted in defense. "It was an accident."

Randy closed one eye and eyed him up and down like the disapproving church ladies of his youth. "Um-hm. Sure. *That* is what they all say." He leaned in and hissed. "We trusted you.

You're the man. The adult. And you took her out and threw her around on the highway like an old disgusting ragdoll nobody wants." He stalked off toward the kitchen as he watched his husband take care of the child.

Bean frowned at Duff from her pillowed perch. She mouthed, "What's a funcle?"

Niles pulled two more small pillows off the love seat. "I saw that." He stuffed the pillows down each side of her hips.

"Saw what?" Amused, she held her arms in the air above his fussing. She noted the small bald spot starting on the back of his head, exposing more of the creamy skin and the gray rimming his ears. She realized the two men were older than she originally thought.

The man straightened. "You asked the thug over there what a funcle was. Why in the world would you think such a gangster would know anything about the refined nature of funcles?"

Bean narrowed her eye at the man as she felt the power of her position. "Well? What's a funcle?"

Randy came back out of the kitchen with a steaming mug of tea. "Here, sweetie. This is chamomile and home-roasted dandelion root tea. It will calm you down and promote healing." He glared at Duff. "Something you're going to need a lot of."

She pushed back at the mug. "No."

He straightened—shocked. "You don't like tea?"

Bean laid her head back to look up at the man. "I like tea." Her head rolled to glare at the other man. She saw Niles flinch. "But not until someone explains funcle to me."

Randy collapsed onto the ottoman, barely taking up a couple of inches along the edge. He presented the mug of tea again as he chewed on the inside of his cheek under the girl's scrutiny. Niles hovered and then lighted on the other side of her legs.

Niles started as he held and stroked the three thin fingertips sticking out from the bright red cast. "Sweetie, what do you call the brother of your father?"

"He didn't have one."

Randy rolled his eyes. "If he did."

"He'd be my uncle."

Niles watched each of the fingertips as he smoothed them. "And if he was gay?"

"Still an uncle."

Randy cupped the other hand and mug in his hands. "Yes, but some use a crude offending term for a gay uncle. They call them a guncle."

Her face recoiled. "Ew. That sounds more like oyster poop or something."

Niles nodded. "Yes, well, that is exactly the way we feel. Especially when we are fun and loving."

She digested their heartfelt explanation and then saw the answer. "Fun uncles."

The two men beamed. Randy closed one eye and pointed at her. "*Exacta mundo*, little one. *Funcles*."

Bean glanced over at Duff, leaning against the wall. Only his one glove was off and held in his other, still gloved hand. "What does that make Uncle Duff?"

Randy stood and blew out a short, scornful sound of air. "A hoodlum who takes out a fragile child and allows her to become battered and broken…?"

Bean felt it was time to come to Duff's rescue. "Who showed me the Milky Way? Introduced me to oysters and two funcles I never had before? Saved me from my past life and then introduced me to cactus…" Her voice trailed off.

Niles tossed his head with rolling eyes. "Well... Maybe there could be *some* redeeming qualities..."

Randy glanced at his watch. "I want to hear about the cactus, but first, I need to run down to Hog Island really quick if we're going to have any oysters for dinner." As he walked out the door, he held his two fingers in a *V* and waved them back and forth from his eyes to Duff as if to say he was watching him. And then he smiled with a soft laugh and slapped him gently on the shoulder. "Take off your jacket. Relax. Stay awhile. I'll be back with dinner in a short bit."

Duff held up his gloved hand and looked at the gloves. He realized the two whirlwinds had overtaken him and left him adrift by the doorway.

Niles rose. "Here. Why don't you relax next to your niece? Let me take your coat, and I'll hang it up."

Bean snickered. "That I'd like to see."

Duff shot her a stern look as he stuffed his gloves in the leather pockets. Sloughing off his jacket, he kept it away from Niles's grasp. He didn't want a second broken arm. "It doesn't hang up well."

He stepped around the man. Then, standing next to the couch, he let the jacket fall the last eight inches to the hardwood floor—the muffled boom echoed through the structure of the house. The jacket looked like it was hiding a highway cone.

"Oh, my." Niles looked up, blinking. "Leather has gotten a lot heavier than it was back in my day."

Duff and Bean looked at him for clarification. He blushed. "Well, chaps, boots, hat, and a vest. I never got the motorcycle."

Bean laughed as she pointed. "You were a leather boy? Oh, my gosh. You really are a funcle."

His right knee bent in front of his left as he double-handed gripped at an imaginary rodeo belt buckle. His voice dropped to an attempted deep John Wayne rumble. "Just riding the range, miss. Just riding the range."

———

NILES LEANED INTO RANDY. Randy kept dishing the finely chopped spinach onto the tray of oysters. Niles's voice was soft. "When you get those under the broiler, go try to move Duff's jacket. I tried to scoot it out of the way with my foot." He looked up with surprise, eyes wide. "I think I broke a foot."

Randy frowned as he sprinkled the cheese. "What's wrong with it?"

Niles rolled his eyes as his head arched up and over. He lifted the tray of cooked oysters. "Oh, nothing. It's just an enigma as big as the two of them."

Randy narrowed one eye and looked at his partner. "What's wrong with them?"

The man stopped and thought. "Probably nothing."

"Then what's the problem?"

"Just go try to lift his jacket."

Randy looked toward the front room. "Where's it at?"

"Between the chair and the divan."

Randy shrugged as he lifted the next tray and opened the oven.

———

NILES HUGGED Bean while Randy waited his turn. He studied Duff out of the side of his eyes, his hand shading against the rising sun.

"And you write, you hear?"

Bean laughed. "I've got your card. I'll get an email address and let you know how we're doing. But it's going to take a while. We don't even know where we're going to be living. But soon."

He rubbed his hands on both of her leathered shoulders. "You'll be fine." He nodded toward Duff. "Just look after him so he'll bring you back." He leveled a funny stink-eye at Duff. "And try to keep the cowboy out of trouble."

Randy tapped his partner on the shoulder. "A'ight, a'ight. My turn and they need to go. They have a long way to travel today."

Bean opened her mouth. Randy waved it closed. "We don't have time for your yapping. Just give me some love."

The large man moved in and enveloped her as Bean sunk into the cook's chest and smelled their breakfast with a hint of last night's dinner. She rested her head flat on his rib cage. The hug was beyond the social niceties. This was what she remembered as family. Or at least her father when he deployed.

Randy quietly eased her apart. "You need to go before I turn into a weeping willow. Don't let him drive crazy. And you keep in touch. Let us know if we can help in any possible way. We're a thousand miles away, but we know people."

They waved until the motorcycle was out of hearing. They hung on each other's shoulders, staring down the road. "We have a new niece." They sighed in unison.

"Did you lift his jacket?"

"It weighs more than a large sack of potatoes." He looked at Niles. "What the...?"

His husband shrugged. "I told you..."

———

THE PRESSURE on his hips hadn't changed in an hour. The small red light was glowing off and on, dimly. He knew to start looking for gas.

"You awake back there?"

"Just thinking."

"What about?"

"About next time visiting my funcles."

Duff thumbed the turn signal as he noticed a few buildings clustered just off the freeway. One had a large sign with fuel prices. It was a dead ringer for a truck stop. "What about next time?"

"The shade of blue."

Duff glanced back. "Shade of blue?"

"What shade of blue I want to paint my Indian."

15

———————

STUCK ON CACTUS

The gleaming cubes of light green glistened in the morning sun, the bottles of vinegar and spices stood sentinel behind the bowl mounded with the cactus, and the long spines from a Ferocactus known as a toothpick cactus, skewered cubes of Nopales as if they were a shish kabob.

The chef and a server stood holding large aluminum trays. Their reflective surfaces lit the table tableau. The infinity pool provided a soft background of water, desert, and sky.

Bean looked at the image in the viewfinder and nodded. Duff took the photo.

He showed it to the chef. The man nodded. "My mentor can only eat his heart out in Paris. There they have nothing but the Eiffel Tower. A piss-poor second for this." He waved his hand progressively at the table, water, desert, and sky. "And they have no Nopales in France. Maybe I should pickle some and send him a care package."

The four stood snickering as the man stood staring down from above. "I heard rumors you added some smashing color to your outfit."

Bean and the rest looked up. "Mr. Kaminski." She held up her red cast. "It's almost Indian red."

Kaminski nodded and descended the stairs. "Chef, you've got the poor girl hooked on cactus."

The chef laughed. "I think you're confused, Mr. Kaminski. The term is stuck, not hooked."

Kaminski smiled as he wiggled his eyebrows. He looked at the photo. "I think you could blow this up and frame it to hang over a certain bed." He winked at Bean.

Duff bent over the teepee of dark leather under the table. He fished into a large pocket and pulled out a thick manilla envelope.

Kaminski bent his head and looked at the jacket as he accepted the package. "I hear you tore up your jacket some."

"Nothing a little shoe polish can't fix. No great harm." He pushed his chin out toward Bean. "Except the most important."

Kaminski smiled sadly. "It'll give her something to talk about in school. I saw the report. I took the liberty of setting you up with an orthopedic surgeon in Vegas. My friend at UCLA highly recommended him. Evidently, he's the go-to guy for some fighters and ballplayers."

"I appreciate that. We can take it out of my pay."

The older man gave him a hard side-eye. "It's covered. Wasn't she on the bike when you were carrying the package? She's on the payroll. I'll just have to find her something safer to do for the company." He nodded at Bean, bent over, directing the chef to take more pictures. "She's got a good eye for marketing."

Duff gave him a return hard side-eye. "Like you do so much advertising."

Kaminski held up his hand, palm up. "Who knows? Maybe

for other people. Like foodie pictures for here."

Duff rolled his eyes to the lower left. "Yeah. We'll talk."

Kaminski slipped the package in his sport coat patch pocket and then jerked and reached into his inside coat pocket. "I almost forgot." He drew out a thin business envelope. "I found a better apartment for you and Bean. There's a school a few blocks away if she wants. You guys can talk about it. In a few days, your housekeeper moves in across the hall, so she'll always be on call. She's exceptionally experienced and knowledgeable and could help Bean if she wanted to home school."

DUFF OPENED the envelope as he sat relaxing after a shower. The plush bathrobe almost wrapped another halfway around him.

"What's the letter?"

Duff rolled his head back and looked over his shoulder at Bean. She stood, swallowed by the white bathrobe as she worked the towel on her hair. Finally, Bean gave up and wound it into a turban.

"It's from Kaminski. It's about our new apartment, how we're to be accommodated, and how they will apply the whip to you about school."

She dropped next to him on the couch. Then, reaching, she took the letter from him. "No, seriously."

Duff blinked twice at her brazen control. "You read it and then tell me it isn't what I said."

"What's a double master?"

"It means you get your own bedroom with its own bathroom. You close your door, and you can run around buck naked from the bed to the bath to bed, and nobody would know. Or look."

She looked up and studied him for a moment. "You're not going to take the door off?"

He nudged her arm with his elbow. "Not unless you take the door off mine first."

She looked at their legs, matching crossed with feet on the coffee table. She raised the letter again. "Deal."

"Is she going to cook every meal?"

"Unless you want to learn how to cook. I just never thought about it. I never had anyone to cook for, but who knows—maybe it'd be fun."

She continued reading. "We'll see."

Halfway down the second page, she pinched her thumbnail into the paper. "Why do I have to go to school?"

Duff pointed to the last paragraph on the page. "You don't. It would probably be better to take him up on the private tutor. Maybe they can help you make up anything you missed or did poorly in. How good was your schooling going from home to home?"

Her left eye grew wide as she turned her head toward him. But the right eyelid was fluttering. "School? There were schools?"

Duff's face stretched up as he looked at her. "That bad, huh?"

She furled her lips tightly as she turned the page. "I know where England is. It's just west of Los Angeles."

Duff let it go.

She finished the fourth and last page. Then, pensively, she rolled the rest of the pages back into sequence. She tapped the edge on her thumbnail, thinking.

"How much do you think all this will cost?" She turned and then scooted around to face him. "I mean, who do you have to kill to have him pay for this kind of living? I don't think a Joe Schmo truck driver could afford even half of this."

Duff thought as his eyes fluttered. Then he licked his lips. "These are the kinds of things I don't ask about. And as for Joe Schmo, I don't think he would get hired by Kaminski to do the job I do." He looked up at her. "And no, I don't have to kill anyone. He has other experts for that kind of stuff."

He watched as her mouth opened and her eyes grew wide. And then, as his smirk became physical, she punched him in the shoulder. "Ass."

His face showed mock horror. "Why, Beanie, you swore."

She stood, massaging the towel into her hair. "I get bitchy and swear when I'm hungry."

Duff looked at his watch and whined. "We just ate, what, ten hours ago."

She snapped the towel off her head and at the air beside him. "Now."

Duff watched her dance into her room and shut the door. He thought about the door. He had always taken a closed door for granted. But it had never meant security or peace of mind to him—that he knew of. He placed the letter on the table and stood.

As he walked into his room and slowly closed the door, he thought about her and a tutor. And how she was a tutor to him.

His stomach growled.

His phone pinged. The screen lit with the photo of the cactus cube salad. Two hearts in purple followed the thumbs up in the reply.

16

GETTING SETTLED

Bean stood at the door, her stomach churning. Old fears are old because they never die.

The knock was soft but persistent.

Bean stared at the door. It was plain, just like the first door long ago. Except this door had a peephole.

The same knock. Three and then one. Like it was a code or something.

Bean's hands curled into fists. She held her breath.

The woman on the other side of the door was blonde with bright blue eyes. She was not in a uniform—unless a tie-dyed T-shirt with a skull on it was some bizarre uniform. The tattered jean shorts hung only a few inches below the oversized shirt.

"Who is it?" Bean demanded through the door. She watched the reaction.

The woman's hand froze, inches away from another knock. "Ingrid. I'm your housekeeper and tutor."

Bean's face was an inch from the peephole. "Where do you come from?"

The woman smiled. She knew she was being watched. She

turned and inserted her key into the door across the hall. The door swung open. "I live here. Well, I moved in last night. I think you two were out for dinner somewhere. I heard the Harley come back around ten. But Duff left at four-fifteen this morning. Have you had breakfast yet? Or shall I talk about your personal details out here where the neighbors can hear?"

Bean opened the door.

The woman smiled but stood in the hall. Her hand was on her own door.

Bean grumped. "Now what?"

The woman tilted her head. "It's up to you. We can talk there or over here. It's up to you, but I have coffee. Do you have coffee?"

"I don't know." Bean opened the door wide, holding it with her cast.

Ingrid gently pulled her door closed. As she walked in, she smiled. *"Hola. Mi nombre es Ingrid. Debes ser frijol."*

Bean shut the door quietly. "What...?"

The woman held out her arms as she spun around in the open space of the living room, kitchen, and dining area. "I love what you've done to the place. It looks exactly like mine. Except I took that picture and hid it deep in the closet. Someone who never left New York City painted that desert." She faced Bean. "I was just kidding about the frijoles."

"The what?"

The woman cocked her head sideways and frowned. "Fri-joles. Beans. It's Spanish...?" She straightened her head as she walked into the kitchen. She started opening cupboards. "Aren't you learning Spanish in school?"

"No."

The woman turned and leaned her hip against the counter.

"*Française? Deutsch? Swahili?*" She waved her hand in the air. "Forget about Swahili. I'm still learning. So I can't teach you."

"Where do you speak Swahili?"

The blonde snorted softly. "It would amaze you at how many taxi drivers understand Swahili. The language is mostly Arabic and close enough to Farsi. I can get almost anywhere in New York speaking Swahili to the cabbies. Or Russian."

Bean sat down at the table. "How many languages do you know?"

The woman pulled the can of coffee out of the cupboard. She grimaced and turned toward Bean, ejecting her tongue in disgust. "Why don't we talk at my place. At least I have real coffee."

Bean shrugged and stuck out her tongue and smacked at her lips. "I need to brush my teeth. I'll be over in a few minutes. I need to get the taste of hangover out of my mouth."

She watched the slight uptick of the blonde's eye before the smile and laugh replaced it. It clinched her credentials of a smartass.

Ingrid opened the door. "If you want to shower also, feel free. I like the T-shirt. But maybe some pants would be good." She softly pulled the door behind her.

Bean looked down. "Dang."

———

"So how did you learn so many languages?" Bean took a deep smell of the coffee and then a sip.

"My dad was an officer in the Navy. Wherever he was stationed, we were with him. The military on foreign bases doesn't have the greatest schools, but shopping off base is the best way to learn a language." Ingrid pulled out a chair and sat. "Are you sure you don't want any breakfast?"

"I'm good. So how many do you know?"

Ingrid smirked. "Breakfasts? Several."

Bean narrowed her eyes. "So it's going to be smartass against smartass? I get a lot of practice with Duff."

Ingrid snorted. "I grew up with the Grand Master and his Dragoness."

Bean sipped a long pull on her mug with her one eye looking over the rim. She was going to wait it out.

"Knowing is not the same as fluent. Fluency comes with reading, writing, and dreaming in a language. But just getting by enough to shop or find a toilet is easy. Kind of like a parrot."

"You said you couldn't teach me Swahili because you were still learning it. How much do you know?"

"Probably a few hundred words. If we went to Tanzania, I could probably get us into some fun or trouble. But enough to get us food, water, a bathroom, and a place to sleep. And maybe it would be with or without lions."

"Where do you take classes?"

Ingrid looked at the short stack of boxes. Then, getting up, she moved three of the boxes and opened the fourth. Pawing through, she found a small book and tossed it onto the table. The paperback was a government information edition for diplomats. It looked old and well used.

She sat back down. "I was clearing out my father's house last year and found this. I wish I had known years ago that he was learning a new language. It was always fun to talk with him in different languages."

"But he passed away. What about your mother?"

Ingrid looked at the book. Bean started to tell her it was okay not to talk about her mother. But the woman looked up. "I guess I was not much older than you when she died. We were in Germany. Dad was attached to the Embassy there. Her heel broke on the cobblestones, and she fell in front of a truck."

Bean drew in a stinging breath through her nose. "That's horrible."

Ingrid slowly bobbed her head. Her eyes were on the book, but her focus was far away. "Years later, my father and I were at a state dinner in Italy. The speaker was a few people over, and it was the president of Italy. Dad started softly chuckling and couldn't stop. Finally, he had to excuse himself. I caught up with him later and asked him what was so funny." Ingrid looked up with a half-smile. "He said he had an image pop into his head. It was Mom hobbling up to St. Peter, swearing. When St. Peter asked her what she was swearing about, she took off the broken shoe and slammed it down on his desk. She leaned in and told him it was her favorite pair of high heels, and they broke."

Bean frowned. "She wasn't mad that she was dead, just that she had broken her shoes?"

Ingrid smiled and slumped down in her chair, hugging the mug of coffee. "After that, I could never think of Mom any other way. For whatever else she was, she was a perfectionist about her clothes. Dad had three pairs of shoes. His boondockers, his dress shoes, and his running shoes. She had the proper pair of shoes for every outfit or event. It was Mom."

"What about you? How many shoes do you have?"

"I'm kind of like dad: sneakers, flip-flops, and a pair of nice sandals for an elegant event. In my line of work, I need nothing more. Navy brat to the core." She pointed at the stack of nine boxes. "There is my estate along with the two boxes in the bedroom. I was too tired to unpack. I notice you two are all moved in. When did you get here?"

"Day before yesterday. But we were busy with some stuff and didn't unpack until this morning."

Ingrid's eyebrows rose. "So you got up with your...?"

"Uncle. And no. I heard him get up and leave. But I was just getting up to take a shower when you knocked."

"But you said you unpacked this morning..."

"When I took a shower. I pulled out the other two shirts, a pair of jeans, and underwear."

"But... what about...?" She pointed at the small stack of boxes.

Bean rolled her lips in a smile and gave the stack of boxes a condescending look. "Kind of hard to stuff that onto a motorcycle, don't you think?"

"A motorcycle? That's it?"

Bean twitched her head, agreeing. "Yup. So if the three of us go out to dinner, it will be either a tight fit, or we get to practice our Swahili with a taxicab."

Ingrid moaned. "Probably more like my gutter Russian. So it's Swahili, eh?"

Bean shrugged. "It's probably just as useful as gutter Russian."

"Where are you at with the rest of your schooling?"

Bean tilted her head as one eye fluttered closed. "I kind of stopped paying attention a few years ago. I can do enough math in my head to know if someone is trying to cheat me. English, well, I can read. I know who George Washington and Abe Lincoln were. What else?"

Ingrid stood and stepped to the coffeepot. "Okay, so first I'll get my hands on some grade assessment tests, and we'll go from there." She turned and leaned against the counter as she sipped on her mug. "Did you get any classes about the constitution and how the government works?"

"I know how a certain part of the government doesn't work."

The blonde cocked her head in a question. "Which part?"

"Child Services."

17

WE NEED A BREAK

The pen scribbled across the yellow pad as the right hand curled around the book's last few pages and the back cover. The hand and cover paused in the upright position as the left finished the thought.

The apartment's front door clicked. Bean looked over the top of her new green reading glasses. Her breath caught in her throat. Ingrid stepped back from the stove. The wooden spoon hovering in midair over her protective left hand cupped below.

The door swung cautiously inward and stopped, opened only a foot. A hand reached around the edge—the fingers gripping the door. The tousled curly head of hair peeked around the edge and locked eyes with Bean. Duff growled in a stage whisper. "Who wants to run away with me?"

Bean shook with laughter as she raised her hand.

Duff looked around the edge of the door and into the kitchen. "Want to run away with a strange man and his sidekick?"

Ingrid put the spoon back in the pot and slowly stirred as

she watched Duff ooze only halfway around the door. "We didn't hear the motorcycle."

Duff chuckled. "You spoke English."

Ingrid's eyes grew large and wild. "Well, what did you expect? You scared us half to death."

Bean leaned back, placing her reading glasses on the closed book. "*Ongea mwenyewe. Mimi tu...*" She looked at Ingrid. "What's Swahili for farted."

Ingrid frowned. "I think it's *nilishindwa*. And I know I spoke for both of us. You sat frozen in fear. You were about to piss your pants instead of just fart." She turned to Duff. "You scared her. You should be ashamed of yourself. And why are you standing in the door?" She glanced at the clock on the stove. "And what are you doing home? It's only four-thirty."

He didn't move. "We only ran up to Carson City. Short day."

Bean narrowed her eyes. "Where's the bike, and what are you hiding behind the door? It better not be a puppy."

Duff pushed the door open more as he looked back into the hall and clapped his hands. "Come on, boy. Come on."

He pushed the door wider as he threw the down sleeping bag at Bean. The red missile hit her hands as she squealed. "Camping!" She pulled the bag down to her chest. "Full moon or dark?"

Duff cocked his head in a smile. "Dark of the moon." He stepped around the door with two more bags. "I got you one too, Ingrid. We never talked about sleeping out under the stars, but I figured I'd offer."

Ingrid raised her eyebrows as she blinked. "I... well, I've never been. I never thought about it, but you would think a Navy brat would have done something out in nature. We just never did."

Bean nodded. "Yeah, and you would think a Marine would have taken his kid out…" She frowned. "I guess, after all the camping and stuff he did for work, he didn't want to do it for fun. I just never thought about it that way."

Bean brightened and leaned back in her chair. She looked at Ingrid with a smirk. "Have you ever seen the Milky Way?"

"Sure. We're in the Milky Way. Just go outside at night and look up."

Bean beamed at Duff. "She has no idea. Where are we going?"

"Tomorrow is Thanksgiving. I have some paperwork to take to Kaminski. We have dinner reservations for seven-thirty for four. I thought we could camp at the crater on Friday night. But if we drive down tonight, we will have some time for a little spa and cactus tomorrow?" He stepped into the kitchen area. "What are you cooking?"

"Soup."

"Will it last in the refrigerator until this weekend?"

She pointed at the containers lined on the counter. "It wasn't for this week. I was going to freeze it for the future. This is just the vegetable base stock. From this, I can make a dozen different soups."

He pulled his head sideways and asked coyly. "So we might leave in a half hour or so?"

"Sure, but it'll be a tight fit on the motorcycle."

He smiled. "But not so tight in the SUV." He stepped closer to the teacher and nodded his head back at Bean. "Any homework she needs to bring?"

Ingrid laughed and shook her head. "She just finished her last textbook for this cycle. Now she's ready to take her tests to challenge her junior year. But I think a little extra credit would be good for her science requirements. Maybe a little astronomy? Yah?"

Duff turned. "And I rented something that might help with that."

Bean furled her forehead. "What?"

Duff smiled. "It's a surprise. Go get packed."

"What about tomorrow's dinner?" She pointed at Ingrid.

Duff's face brightened as he turned. "Fancy restaurant. Have anything to wear? If you don't, we can take care of it tomorrow."

She squinted. "Clean sweatshirt...?"

Duff winked. "Bring your fancy sandals. We'll leave the rest to Kaminski and the staff." He pointed at the soup. "How can I help?"

———

"You're in 104, Mr. Akens. Bean's tutor is next door in 105." The blond valet handed him the two keys as he looked over at the women. "When we heard you were driving down this evening, the manager said just keep the noise down, but the pool is open to you. Suits are in the suites. As usual, enjoy your weekend."

Duff smiled. "Friday night, we'll be staying at the crater. It's a moonless night."

"It should be spectacular viewing. But it will be quite cold. Technically, desert-wise, we are in winter now. The days just don't warm the ground up enough."

"I got us cots, down sleeping bags, and tents. And always the three rows of seats in the SUV."

The blond tapped his head. "Smart. You can park directly across from the bungalows."

Duff leaned in. "Um, attire for Thanksgiving?"

The blond nodded slightly. "The spa will figure out the women's clothes in the morning. You all have appointments at ten o'clock. Breakfast is by the pool at eight. If you need it to be a little later, don't hesitate to call. After all, it is a holiday."

Duff shook his hand with a bill in his palm. "Thanks, James. There's no bike to polish this time, but make sure this gets spread around for you boys who are working the holiday."

The blond nodded. "Very good, Mr. Akens."

———

INGRID TOOK another bite of the light green cubes. "Who would have ever thought the same picture over Bean's bed at home would hang over my bed here. And then, here we are looking at the same view while eating the same melon."

Bean leaned back in her chair, sipping on a mug of café latte. Her raised leg bent with her foot on the seat. "Nopales or Spineless Prickly Pear Cacti or *Cacanapa Ellisiana,* to be more exact. Grown and harvested fifty miles from here. The chef's best friends own the farm. The photography was a group effort."

"Ah, but it was the master's talented eye. Or I should say, the Mistress's talent directing the shot that day." Kaminski leisurely walked down the stairs.

"Mr. Kaminski." Bean stood. "The cactus is almost gone."

The man leaned over and folded his arm around her shoulder in a side-hug. "Forgive me, my child, but an important call detained me. People in London think we are on their schedule." He turned toward Ingrid as he extended his hand. "And you must be the amazing Ingrid I have heard so much about."

She nodded and shook his hand. "I've been looking forward to this meeting, Mr. Kaminski."

"Please. Sit. And where is the elusive—"

Duff jogged up the few steps next to the pool. "Right here. I had just forgotten why we were here." He handed Kaminski the large, thick envelope.

The man smiled. "Ah yes. But this is not the only reason I wanted you here. And having you all here together makes the other easier. Shall we have breakfast?" He waved at the table.

As they took their seats, the waitress in a starched white shirt and black slacks approached with a coffee carafe. She smiled at Ingrid. "Madame, you're the only one who hasn't established a usual. Have you looked over the menu, or do you need a moment?"

Ingrid waved at Bean. "I'll have what she's having. Our tastes run down the same back alley on most days."

"Excellent choice. The chef would be proud." She winked at Bean and silently glided back into the building.

Kaminski rolled his head toward Duff. "Is your passport current?"

DUFF'S FACE FELT FROZEN. His nose ached but in a good way. His mind replayed the night's joy of setting up the powerful telescope. It hadn't revealed spinning nebulas or whirling galaxies, but finding hundreds of tiny stars among the Pleiades or the Seven Sisters was just as impressive. It turned out Ingrid had some background about the stars and constellations. Class had continued for not only Bean but Duff as well.

He took in a breath of cold desert air and cracked his eyes open.

The two mounds of red ripstop nylon greeted him. They almost looked like discarded piles of fluffy red, except for the two hands holding two identical mugs. Two faces with identical black wraparound dark glasses peeked out of the pile of red fluff extending over their heads like tight-pulled hoodies.

The two hands moved in unison, the mugs reaching their destinations in harmony, the length of sips identical. A pause. Another sip. Then they returned to their original position as if they were choreographed.

One mouth cracked. There was no movement. "He's trying to figure out who is who."

"He probably realizes he should have bought different color sleeping bags."

"In his defense, the space blankets only come in reflective silver."

"He could've looked for camouflaged ones."

"So we would blend in with a forest of mirrors?"

There was a soft snicker but no sign from which. "We don't shop in those stores."

"He shops?"

"It used to be only when his clothes were dirty."

The coffee mug dance resumed.

"Should we check for a pulse?"

"Nah. Wait for the smell of rotting."

Duff chuffed. "You know I can hear you."

"You missed a beautiful sunrise."

Duff looked around at the cloudless sky. "What? It got light?"

"That's how it usually happens."

The coffee mugs rose. Paused. Then lowered.

"Any coffee left?"

The two mugs moved to the sides of the chairs and turned upside down—not even a drop.

"Someone forgot to pack enough to last for stragglers. We poured the last a half-hour ago. Next pot is at the Trading Post."

Duff sat up. He thought for a moment and unzipped his sleeping bag. He stood and then stumbled out into the cinder field behind the women. A minute later, he was back and grabbed up his jacket. Slipping it on, he remembered why he needed a softer jacket for warmth in the desert.

As he stumbled to wake his legs up, he remembered how long it took for his body heat to warm up eighty pounds of gold. He leaned the backs of his calves against the large cinder ball. Then, as his steaming morning stream disappeared into the thirsty desert floor, he scanned the solitude of the crater area.

No birds. No rabbits. Nothing. Everything one would ever think would be in a desert wasn't here. Even the tiny remnants of sagebrush were only sample-sized. He didn't know what tumbleweeds looked like when they were growing, but nothing looked like the prairie balls he had watched race with the wind across the interstates.

He turned to find the camp had disappeared. Two shadows were already in the SUV. Either someone was hungry, or they wanted a real bathroom.

18

NEW JOB

Bean pushed the chunk of French toast through the puddle of strawberry syrup. She glanced up through the top of her eyes. "So... new job, eh?"

Duff harrumphed and looked up. "It looks like. Are you two okay with the new schedule and me being gone for maybe a week at a time?" He looked at Ingrid. "You're involved too. Thoughts?"

Ingrid looked to Bean. Duff recognized the checking with the other for the okay to proceed. Duff had noticed the new habit lately. It could be a woman thing, or they talked more than they let on. And it wasn't just schoolwork.

He waited.

"She needs a driver's license."

Duff watched over the brim of his coffee mug. Bean stayed focused on the bite of bread.

"Her eighteenth birthday is coming up."

Duff listened, but he ignored Ingrid. The only important words would be out of the younger mouth. And they would start with the word *I*.

Ingrid continued. "The last home she was in, she ran away. So that makes her a fugitive still."

The small square of bread at the end of the fork paused. Only a fraction of a second, but it was a hesitation. The information was something new to her. She hadn't thought about her standing. The only name she used was Bean. Everything else was secure behind the now quivering lips.

Duff waited.

"What if you're away on one of those trips and something happens? I don't have any authority to take her to a hospital or get any kind of medical treatment." Ingrid hung her head sideways and frowned at Duff. "Are you listening to me?"

Bean stopped pushing the French toast around and looked up at Duff. She turned and looked at Ingrid and back at Duff.

Duff's eyes locked on Bean. He took a long, gradual sip of his coffee.

Bean put down her fork. Dabbing the napkin at her lips, she kept staring at Duff. "Are you going to answer her?"

"No."

Bean put down her napkin as she glanced at Ingrid's open mouth. "Any of it?"

He shook his head a fraction of an inch.

"Why?"

"Because, when we get back to Vegas, she's fired, and we have to leave."

Ingrid's mouth opened wide. Her questioning face turned to incredulous.

Bean drew a deep breath loudly through her nose. "Close your yap, Inkie. In this joint, you can catch flies or worse." She looked back at Duff. "Let's start with her being fired."

"Five months and she only taught you ideas you can read in a book or look up on a computer. But she missed the important things."

Bean narrowed her eyes as she blindly reached out and pushed Ingrid's jaw closed. "Such as?"

Duff gently set his empty mug on the table. "In Colorado."

"What about it?"

"I quietly minded my business, reading the paper and having breakfast." He held up his hand as her mouth opened. "And then you rushed in and kidnapped me."

He pushed his hand forward as she opened her mouth to jump in again.

"Doreen didn't say take her with you. Doreen didn't say she needed a fast motorcycle out of town. Doreen didn't say, this girl is in trouble, and only you can fix it. Nope. The only thing Doreen did was order an extra breakfast and stick it in your face. And then she dressed the deputies up and down and sideways for being the town jokes. Not once did she try to speak for you. She knew by your behavior you could walk and talk for yourself."

"What's that got to do with firing Ingrid?"

Duff blinked. "So I understand you have a birthday coming up. What do you want for your birthday?"

Bean slumped back into the booth. She reached out and grabbed her coffee mug. It had become a universal shorthand between them. She was thinking. Duff looked in his empty mug and caught the waitress's eye by raising the cup. He could tell there was no steam coming from Bean's, either.

"A motorcycle."

"Learn how to ride one first."

"A truck."

"Same applies."

"A driver's license."

Duff reached around to his large wallet. Unsnapping it, he reached in and drew out a short stack of cards. He tossed them onto the table in front of her. "There's seven. Take whichever one you think will work for you. But I don't advise the one saying you can transport a nuclear bomb."

Bean leaned over the spread of licenses. "Which one is that?" She looked up at a grinning Duff. "Ass." She pushed the stack back to him. "I mean one of my own."

Duff side-glanced at the now silent Ingrid. Instead of directing, she watched the relationship and hopefully thought about her job.

"Do you have a certified copy of your birth certificate?"

"No."

"Do you know where we can get it?"

She hesitated. "Maybe... no."

"Where were you born?"

"San Diego."

"Was your dad a marine then?"

"I don't know. I wasn't paying attention then."

Duff gently blew at the steam from his coffee. "It might make a difference, or maybe not. If you were born on a military base, it might make it federal jurisdiction. But I would think they still had to file with the state of California. But Child Services would probably have a copy or at least be able to tell us where we go to get one."

Bean closed in on herself at the mention of Child Services.

Duff furled his lip. "I know. Or at least I understand. But once you start down the path for one, then you need to deal with the other. But after the ordeal, you will have… What do they call it when you hit eighteen?"

"Aged out."

"So you'll end any control they have over you. And you'll have a driver's license."

Bean glanced over at Ingrid. "But why do you have to fire Ingrid, and why do we have to move?"

"She had five months to get you ready to be an independent woman on your own. She failed."

The woman wrinkled up her face in indignation. "How?"

Duff looked at the angry woman. "When did you have the conversation with her about getting her driver's license?"

"It wasn't a single conversation. It was her talking about how she'd like a motorcycle of her own. Something she could drive to the store instead of having to get a ride."

"And when did you have a conversation about her being a fugitive? Because I'll bet that never happened. Just now was the first time you told her of her legal status. That's not what a private teacher is supposed to do. So when did you think the subject would come up? At the DMV? While she's standing in front of the one person who has the authority to give her a license? Even every Mexican working in the kitchens of the casinos knows you must have documents. The difference is, she was born here. The birth certificate she is legally allowed… no, even encouraged to possess is somewhere. But you didn't have those conversations. Hundreds of hours together, and nada. Nothing. Zip. Zilch. Zero."

Duff could she Bean getting worked up. He leaned back and sipped on his fresh coffee. He'd had his say. It was now up to Bean.

"No."

He looked over the brim of his mug.

Bean was calm. But it was the Bean he had seen in Colorado. It was the one with a broken wrist on the highway in California.

"No. She's not fired. Yes, she might have... Okay, should have talked to me about it. But it's not a reason to fire her."

Ingrid rested her hand on Bean's shoulder. "No. He's right. I let you down and overstepped my boundaries. Even if I had your interest at heart, I still went about it the wrong way."

Bean turned on her. "No. It's not right. Yes, it was wrong not to discuss it, but it's as much my fault as yours. We just didn't. But everything else... *Ulifanya kweli.* You did right. I have three more courses, and I can challenge the rest of high school. And that is more education than I've had in the last three years. We've talked about taking an advanced placement test for a community college. Five months ago, I wasn't even thinking of finishing high school. I'd probably just try to get on the shift with Doreen or..." She waved her thumb behind her. "Betty over there. But now, I'm thinking about what I want to do with my life. Not just get a job. And not just be a deadbeat anchor on the big guy here."

It was Duff's turn to object. "Hey! I never said you were an anchor. And I wasn't planning on changing the locks on your birthday."

Bean snapped her head around. "No. But you were planning on firing the only other friend I have in the world. And then what's this bit about moving?"

Duff fluttered his eyes closed as he shrugged. "It's a possibility."

Suspicious, Bean's eye's narrowed. "Where?"

"Probably somewhere in Los Angeles." His eyes glanced toward Ingrid. She was still watching the interaction.

The blonde lowered her mug. Her voice was calm but quiet. "Do you want to drop me off at a bus station, or should I find my own way home?"

Bean's eyes popped wide. "No." She looked at Duff. "No. She comes home with us. And nobody is getting fired. Nobody."

Duff pushed out his palm. "And there you have it. The final word."

Bean narrowly eyed the two of them. "What?"

Duff held up his hands. Ingrid hid behind her mug, but she winked at Duff when Bean wasn't looking. The nod in return was slight then he went into hiding behind his own mug.

Bean jumped. Reaching into her back pocket, she pulled out a phone in a chrome case. She flicked it open. The text was from Kaminski. She read it and looked up at Duff. "He wants to know how the telescope worked. How did he know about the telescope?"

Duff rolled his head to his left shoulder and smiled goofily. "Maybe because it's his telescope?"

Bean scowled. "But you had it in the SUV in Vegas."

"Nope. I had a similar locked case in Vegas. The telescope they swapped out for that case."

"What was in the other case?"

Duff shrugged his face and one shoulder. "No idea."

Bean held up the phone. "And that's another thing. Is this a burner?"

Duff snorted. "No. So don't throw it away or lose it. It's from Kaminski." He pointed at Ingrid. "Same as hers."

Bean turned an accusatory look at Ingrid. "Is this a cartel thing?"

Ingrid shrugged. "It came with the job. It was in the apartment and preloaded with numbers for Kaminski, Duff, and you. It just took a while to get your phone to you."

Duff rumbled. "You didn't seem to need it."

Bean was incredulous as she held it out. "Are you kidding? Have you seen the camera on this thing?"

19

I NEED HELP

The Algebra problem wasn't making sense. Bean had read the chapter three times before she remembered the saying about doing something over and over the same way and expecting different results.

She looked out the window at the sky. The blue never seemed to change. Washed out and still hot. She thought about pictures and movies where Christmas was, about snow-covered trees, snowmen, and hot chocolate. She liked the desert, but only at the resort or the nights at the crater. Vegas, or near it, was about seven hundred of the same-looking homes and some sagebrush. They went to dinner once in one of the big casinos. Walking through the gambling area, Bean started coughing from the smoke. She didn't see the attraction. They never went back.

She thought about the algebra equation as she looked at the chrome-covered phone. Finally, she picked up the phone and called up the voice help. She read the equation into the phone and wrote down the answer. She worked backward on the solution and proved it to be the wrong answer just as the door opened.

Ingrid had been shopping. She put the bag on the other chair and looked over the worksheet. She laughed. "What did you do? Ask the phone to do your math?"

Bean dropped the pencil and leaned back. "It didn't make sense. I read the chapter three times. There's just something I'm not getting."

Ingrid pulled out the end chair and sat. "Let's see what you did here." She looked over the original work page and then looked at how Bean had worked backward from the answer to prove it wrong. "Where did you learn to do this deconstruction?"

"It's just the same, but backward." Bean frowned at Ingrid. "Two plus two equals four. So if two plus an unknown equals four, then the unknown is just four minus two."

"But this is a lot more complicated than simply add or subtract. I can follow what you did here, but I don't think I could do it on my own. We're rapidly reaching the end of my math teaching."

Bean rested her head on her fist. "You didn't get fired, so now you're going to quit?"

Ingrid stood with a raised eyebrow. "*Hakuna bahati kama hiyo, mdogo.*" No such luck, little one.

She pulled some vegetables out of the bag. "I said, this is at the outer limit of my math. But that's not all I teach. *N'est-ce pas?*"

Bean shifted with the choice of language. "*Oui.* But what if I want to learn more math?"

Ingrid pushed her lower lip out. "We find you a math tutor for higher math."

"We can do that?"

Ingrid's voice echoed from the lower refrigerator. "Ask Mr. Kaminski. He holds the purse."

Bean stared at her phone. There was an answer there. It just wasn't obvious. She picked it up and turned in her chair. Looking out the window, she thought about what to say. Being only seventeen had never seemed so unimportant.

She pulled up the texting screen. Suddenly she was just a little girl pulling on her father's pants seam. She could almost smell the wool uniform. Her right hand curled at the memory of the dark blue pants with the red strip down the seam. The red strip she would pull on to get his attention when there were other adults around.

She typed in, *Can we talk?*

She stared at the words. Her thumb hovered over the arrow to send it. It was a little girl asking for permission to speak. It wasn't the message she wanted to send. She hit the backspace twelve times and looked out the window. As she thought about the math, she thought of a larger problem. But the one could lead to the other.

She turned around and typed in the math problem. It looked right.

She thumbed the arrow. The problem now sat in its own bubble.

She turned in the chair. The sky hadn't changed. But what had been washed out before now had depth. There were still no clouds, but she could tell the miles to the distant, hazy mountains.

She jumped. Startled. The phone in her hand vibrated again. Ingrid looked over from the kitchen.

Bean smiled at the name on the caller ID. She thumbed the phone open and pushed the green icon. "Hello?"

The voice on the other end rumbled like happy rocks tumbling in a mountain stream. "I see you have a problem. But I don't think I can help with the answer."

Bean giggled. "Just a moment." She held the phone to her chest as she stood. She looked at Ingrid's inquiring face. Turning toward the sliding glass door, she laid her head back over her shoulder. "Excuse me. I have to take this call." She giggled as she slid the door shut behind her. "I always wanted to say that."

"Great to hear from you, my dear. How are you doing? How is school? And what is that... math problem?"

"Mr. Kaminski. Everything is fine now. Duff worked it out with Ingrid. And we're all on the same page as to my education and stuff. Well... kind of."

"Kind of?" He cleared his throat. "Who is this, and what have you done with my budding superstar photographer?"

Bean giggled again. "Well, I'm kind of in a pickle. That math problem is in the new book. I've read the chapter three times, but it doesn't make sense."

"What about Ingrid? Isn't she there to help?"

"That's the problem. This is the next step in math, and it's beyond her. She says I need a more advanced tutor."

"Then hire one. What's the problem?"

"She said to ask you because it's your purse."

The deep rumbling chuckle rolled from her phone. "You only have one problem, and that is finding the tutor. I might suggest putting up a flyer in the math department at the college. Or you can start with the local high school, but aren't they out for Christmas?"

Bean squirmed her lips. "Probably the college, as well. But do we have money to hire a tutor?"

"My dear, we have money to do anything you want to better yourself."

Bean swallowed and sat down on the small, bleached wood bench. "Good, because I want something else, too."

"What's that?"

"A driver's license… and a new name."

"Let's start with the driver's license."

"Duff says I need to find my birth certificate to get a driver's license."

The word slowly drew out of the phone. "Yes…?"

"I don't know where it is."

"Do you know where you were born?"

"Kind of…"

"What state?"

"I'm pretty sure it was California."

"What city?"

"San Diego… But my father was a marine, and Duff says the Marine base is not in San Diego."

"Well, technically, he's right, but I'm not sure it would matter. Who might know?"

"Child Services. I was nine when my parents died, and there was no other family."

"Okay. So we start with California Child Services. Where was the last foster home you were in?"

INGRID GENTLY CUT the carrots as she watched out the glass door. The conversation was only an inaudible murmur until the air-conditioner kicked on. Then all she could hear was the air from the vents. Animated, the young woman moved from hand waving in the air to sullen dejection. It was like watching a kabuki dance on a shogi screen with no sound. The movements told a story, just not one she recognized or knew.

Slowly, the dance wound down, and the dancer became a sitter, reclined in the wooden chair with the phone to her ear. Whatever the conversation was, it had a more settling effect on Bean than anything since they had returned from Arizona.

Ingrid sliced the zucchini into strips. As she finished each, she peeked at the tableau on the porch.

The threat of termination had been Duff's message for her to back off from fighting the girl's battles. For a man who professed to just drive things, he was smarter than he showed. Once she stepped out of the way, Bean had been showing initiative and direction. From simple things such as shopping for vegetables to even choosing to help with cooking. Ingrid noticed the girl's bathroom had become a neater organized bathroom of a woman. A cloth hamper had appeared where the still five T-shirts used to get tossed in the corner to wait for laundry. There was even a matching one in Duff's suite as well. She had been afraid to ask who the initiator was, but she was betting on Bean.

The door slid open. Bean took one last glance back at the hills and stepped in, closing the door behind her.

She came over and leaned her hip against the counter. Then, picking up a finger of the zucchini, she took a bite. "How are you planning to prepare them?"

Ingrid looked up. "I was planning to batter and fry them tempura style. I got jumbo shrimp, broccoli florets, and mush-rooms. Everything okay?"

Bean nodded as she looked at the chopped vegetables. "It's fine. I'd leave the veggies raw. Batter-fry the shrimp, but leaving the veggies as finger salad would be easier and faster. Duff might be a little late getting out of the airport." She looked up at the woman and smiled. "I'm just saying. I'm going to take a nap before Duff gets home. I want to hear about Amsterdam."

Ingrid watched the young woman walk into her suite and close the door. First, she looked at the deck on the other side of the glass door, and then she looked back at the closed bedroom door.

Walking to the sliding glass door, she looked out at the deck and chairs. Everything looked the same as usual, appearing as if nothing had changed. There was no evidence of sparkling magic powder or fairy dust. Ingrid looked back over her shoulder at the bedroom door.

Something had changed.

20

NEW

Bean slid her thumbs into the tops of her jeans and pushed with her hands against her butt. The air smelled like the back of a bad restaurant. She didn't know what was rotting, but she guessed all the green vegetation along the canal. Looking up and down the canal, the closest thing to a boat was a half-sank board with a large white bird perched on the part sticking out of the water.

"It's a crane. Also, there are black and white ones with a red splotch. Those are sacred Ibises that escaped from a private zoo." The woman turned and rolled her eyes to show her disbelief. "Or so the local legend goes." She turned to include Duff and Ingrid. "The developer named Kinney built the canals in 1905. He envisaged people would paddle or pole their small boats about the development to see friends. But as you can see, he never designed spaces for the boats to dock or tie up."

Duff frowned, thinking about the three blocks they had walked along the canal to get to the house. "What about cars? I mean, in those days, cars weren't exactly common."

The agent held up her finger with an ah-ha expression on her face. "But they expected a lot of deliveries: furniture, milk, food, and anything else you could order through their version of the internet. Come on. Let's look at the back."

She held the clicker and pushed the button. The doors of the garage opened, blocking half the alley. Bean snorted. "Yeah, that works."

The agent had heard it before and waited it out as the doors continued to open until they were flat against the fence. "City code says the doors have to roll up or open not to block traffic."

Duff looked in the small garage. "Well, either her car will fit, or my motorcycle. But not both."

The agent nodded sagely and pushed the second button. "Motorcycles are high crime. You might want to park it in here." The back wall split and opened. The second garage area wasn't as deep but had a workbench to one side. "The owner also rides motorcycles. So he had to hide this addition from the city and homeowners' association until word got out and others on the board wanted the same hidden motorcycle garage."

As they walked through the house, the agent continued. "There aren't any secret rooms or hidden panels. But the plumbing, electrical, Internet, and cable were updated only five years ago when they expanded the upstairs. So you have one suite down here and two full master suites upstairs. The appliances are all under warranty, so just call, and we'll send someone out. The answering service is twenty-four-seven. If the toilet plugs—try the plunger before calling. My husband hates coming out for a three-minute job. He's old-fashioned that way. He wants to get dirty if he has to fix something." She spun on her heel. "Any questions?"

Duff turned to Bean and Ingrid. "They're the ones keeping the home fires burning, so it's up to them." He held his palms up. "Thoughts? It's your choice. The apartments in Century City, the condo in Westwood, or this."

Bean snorted. "A hundred-year-old house on a smelly stream."

The agent hummed. "Hundred and eleven, to be exact. And the smell, you'll stop noticing by tomorrow. I grew up across the canal. After a while, other parts of L.A. stink or smell, but Venice smells like home. It's all the grass and plants. The air hangs in here instead of getting washed out by the sea breeze."

Duff sensed a need for time. "Can we think about it tonight and let you know tomorrow?"

She glanced at her watch. "Sure. It is getting late, and if you need a late lunch or want an early dinner, the boardwalk is four blocks down there. There are lots of great places to shop or eat."

Stepping in, Ingrid nodded curtly and held her hand toward the door. "Okay, we have your card and will call you tomorrow." She guided Bean and Duff out the front door and down the sidewalk along the canal.

A block away, Duff looked at Ingrid hard. "You want to explain the bum's rush?"

Ingrid stopped and faced Duff. "Her accent is only slight, but she grew up in South Boston. She may have had a tough time growing up and getting where she is now. But I don't have time to hear some fantasy tale about how she grew up just down the canal from the house she just *knows* would be perfect for us." She stopped and looked at Bean and then back at Duff. "It may not be your money, but I'm willing to bet it somehow comes out of your paycheck. So tell me, which of the three is the most expensive living arrangement?"

Bean snorted. "The house on the canal that still stinks."

Ingrid pointed at Bean. "Even a teenager can see that. And it was also the one she was pushing hard to rent. She probably gets a bonus for renting the house attached to a twenty-four-hour repair service. That just happens to be her husband. My guess? Her husband is in the house more often than you would be. A little research might even turn them up on the title." She leaned her butt against the end of a bridge railing and crossed her arms. "So condo or apartments? Which is the more economical, and which is the best living situation?"

Duff looked around, lost. "I don't know. She didn't mention anything about rents. I'm guessing this is a trick question, and so I'm going to say the apartments."

Ingrid gently shook her head. "Nope and nope and out of the question." She held up her hands and started counting off on her fingers. "The rent is out of hand because it's near the college. Even on a three-year lease, the price will never be reasonable. Plus, the parking is open, so your bike would disappear before the new year." She bent back her third finger. "I opened all the cabinets. There were bait traps for cockroaches, ants, and mice." She looked at Bean.

Bean shuddered. "And I didn't like the condo. The area is all business. I didn't see a market or restaurant that served breakfast. There were none Doreen would ever step foot in."

Ingrid frowned. "Who's Doreen? But good catch on the market. It was two miles or so down near Westwood and didn't look friendly."

Duff took a long breath in through his nose. "What do you think we should do?"

"What are the criteria for your work?"

He shrugged. "Near the freeways to downtown L.A. and then down to LAX airport. For Bean, it would be good to be near a school to find a tutor. Other than that, secure for the bike and secure to live. I'd feel better if it were a neighborhood where you two could walk around in the evening and still be safe."

"So a house."

Duff nodded.

Ingrid held out her hand. "I'll drive."

"Where are we going?"

"Dinner." She pulled out her phone and typed in a few entries. After a minute, she looked at Bean. "Italian or American?"

Bean looked at Duff. "Italian?"

Duff breathed softly out his nose. "I guess. Unless they have Sikh food."

Ingrid's eyebrow rose. "Oh, good catch." She typed and scrolled. Soon she smiled. "Got it." She stuffed the phone in her back pocket and looked around. "Where's the car?"

———

THE INDIAN RESTAURANT made their mouths water from the street. The glass door swooshing open bathed them in a tsunami of smells, from food to spices. Bean beamed at Duff. Duff licked his lips and showed her his wide eyes.

A young girl showed them a table near the front window. Bean gave her a soulful look and nodded toward the kitchen. "But all the smells are back there."

The girl frowned. "The noise and talking too."

Bean smiled. As she took the menus from the girl and walked toward the back table, she watched the child who stood with a patronizing glare. "You've spent way too long in a happy home. Who is in the kitchen?"

The girl scurried to catch up. "My father and uncles."

Bean stopped short of the back table and turned on the girl, horrified. "Men? Just men? Who is directing them how to cook?" She winked at Duff and Ingrid.

The girl shied. "My grandmother."

Bean moaned theatrically. "Okay, we'll stay." She turned to the table and placed the menus at the three positions.

Ingrid stepped up to the girl. "When, and only when, she has time. We need to speak to your grandmother." As the girl nodded, Ingrid thought. "She speaks English, doesn't she?"

The girl laughed. "No. She speaks British. She was born in south London and moved here after marrying my grandfather. He was an American sailor." The girl bowed and scurried to the kitchen.

As they looked at menus, a woman came out of the kitchen. She looked at the table and turned to gather four glasses of water, placing them on the table in front of Ingrid, Bean, and Duff, with a fourth at the last side of the square table.

Duff looked up. "There are only three of us."

The woman held his gaze as she adjusted the wide shock of white into the large bun of black hair on the top of her head. As her granddaughter had advertised, her words were a mix of clipped Cockney and drawn vowels. "Have you ever worked in a busy kitchen?"

Duff's head ticked in denial.

"It's always as hot and sweaty as a ditch-diggers armpit. And if I must come out and talk to customers, I'm going to get off my feet and drink some cooled water." Her serious face split in a wide smile.

She turned on Ingrid as she swallowed half the glass of water. Then, setting the glass on the table but still holding on, she cocked her head to one side. "What can I do for you, miss?"

Ingrid smiled as she recognized the disarming charm her grandmother used on her. She held out her hand. "My name is Ingrid." As they shook hands, she continued. "This is Duff and Bean. They are my charges."

"Nice to meet you all…" But her narrowing look turned back to Ingrid.

Ingrid pointed at Bean. "This is your favorite granddaughter. She needs a safe neighborhood to live in, so you're comfortable visiting. Where should we live?"

The woman took up the frosted plastic glass and slowly sipped the rest of the water. Then, thinking, she got up and fetched a carafe of water. As she stood and refilled her glass, she watched Bean. Finally, she cocked her chair and gently lowered herself down. "What kind of student are you?"

Bean looked at Ingrid. *"Je! Ninajibuje?"* (How do I answer that?)

Ingrid smirked. "Honestly."

The woman watched the interaction. "Does she speak English?"

Bean looked at the woman. Her voice was soft. "I think I'm a good student. But I'm getting better."

"What language was that?"

"Swahili. We've been learning it together."

The woman looked at Duff with an open face. He held up his hands. *"They…* have been learning Swahili. I'm just trying to catch up." He pointed at Ingrid. "She's the tutor. And Bean's been homeschooling to make up time."

The woman pushed a long white tendril of hair back into the bun. She pursed her lips as she nodded in understanding. She closed her eyes for a moment as she sipped on more water.

Setting the glass down, her face became soulful and sad as

she looked at Bean. "How often do you visit your grandmother?"

Bean frowned. She leaned back in her chair. She tilted her head back, cocked to one side. This was the most important question.

Her voice was flat and even with conviction. "Never enough. Depending on how good your goat..." She looked to Duff."

"Biryani."

Bean waved her finger at Duff. "Yeah. It depends on how good your biryani goat is."

The woman narrowed her eyes and leaned in. "Lamb is better. It soaks up more of the turmeric and cardamom. It gives it more earth." The woman smiled. "But have you tried pulao?" Her eyes rolled around in her wide eyes as she softly licked her lips.

Bean rolled forward and leaned in with a smile. "I need to visit my nana more often."

The woman laughed and gathered up the menus. "You won't need these. What kind of house do you need?" Her finger wagged back and forth at Duff and Ingrid.

Ingrid smiled and shook her head. "I'm the housekeeper and schoolmarm. We need three bedrooms with three baths. He has a big expensive motorcycle we need to lock up—preferably not in the living room. I drive a minivan and would like to garage it too. We also need a better math teacher. She's starting calculus and wants more."

"I'll make some phone calls. Enjoy dinner. I'll be back."

At the door to the kitchen, the woman stopped her granddaughter and pointed back toward the tables.

The girl cleared the larger table and set places for eight people. She laid a large lazy Susan in the middle and gave it a spin, and then placed dishes of condiments on the spinning circle and glasses of water at all places. Next, she set out one-liter glass carafes between each place setting. She turned to the three when the table was right and waved her hands. "Grandma says you will eat with us tonight."

Duff looked toward the three other tables of diners. From the look of the empty plates, they had all but finished eating. He glanced at his watch. It wasn't late, but it wasn't early. His stomach growled.

They got up and moved.

21

———

DINNER

Duff felt left in the dust as the spinning table of dishes slewed left, left, and then back to the right. The etiquette of eating *this* with your hands and *that* with a piece of flatbread naan and the *other* with a fork had his eyes and mind swimming. Bean with the granddaughter kept up a constant low-voiced chatter as they swung the lazy-Susan as skillfully as the three sibling cooks.

The grandmother, Bet, poked Duff in the ribs. "You need to eat something. You're wasting away as you just sit there. You're looking like those kids in the posters."

Duff looked down at her finger, poking at his side and back up to her smiling face. "The starving kids in Africa posters?"

The granddaughter laughed. "She is talking about my music posters. I have old posters of Rolling Stones, Kiss, and The Ramones. She thinks they are all starving."

Duff laughed. "Don't show her a picture of Mick now."

The girl rolled her eyes. "The music died in 1987. All they make now is noise." She looked at Bean. "What's your favorite music?"

Bean chuckled. "One hundred sixteen-inch Indian Chiefs at eighty."

The girl frowned. "Is that a band?"

Ingrid laughed. "No. It's his motorcycle."

The three cooks looked up at the word motorcycle. The one thumb pointed at the one in the middle. "David has a Vespa. Does that count?"

Duff looked at the man. "What size?"

"A1983 one-fifty. But it's bored to twenty over, and I put a carburetor on it from a two-fifty."

His brother laughed. "He races it."

Bean frowned. "Wait. A Vespa? Like a little scooter kind of Vespa? You race it?"

The table laughed. The man held up his hands and shrugged. "Why not? It's cheap, and they race turtles and frogs. Why not scooters?" He pointed at Bean. "And don't count them out. I've seen some old scooters from the fifties hit well over a hundred."

Bean looked incredulously at the granddaughter. "On a scooter?"

The girl, Lena, shied her face toward Bean so her uncle couldn't see her. "He's talking about kilometers-per-hour, not miles. It's like only about sixty miles per hour. Not so fast."

One by one, the cooks picked up the dirty dishes and moved them to the back. Bean started to rise and help, but Lena grabbed her arm low and pulled it lower. Below the table. She carefully shook her head. Her whisper was little more than air. "The men do the clearing. The women sit. We make the nest; the males tend it."

Bean smiled across at Duff. His forehead furled.

They all turned at the sound of the bell above the front door. The tall black woman in tribal dress and a scarf stepped into the restaurant. A slender Asian woman followed close behind. The white stick cane with the red end stood out. She felt out and took hold of the other woman's elbow.

The grandmother rose halfway and waved. "We're back here, Aisha. I'm glad to see you brought Toki." She sat as they watched the two women make their way through the tables of the small restaurant.

Duff watched the practiced teamwork. The tall woman, Aisha, walked close but not touching the backs of the chairs. Toki, the Asian woman, clicked the end of her cane before them, ensuring a clear path. It was an action smooth from years of practice.

Bet patted the table softly next to her. "The boys have eaten and are cleaning up. Sit here."

As they sat, Bet continued with introductions. "This is Aisha and her wife, Toki. Aisha is from Ethiopia, and Toki is from Garden Grove." She turned and started the introductions for Toki's benefit. "To your right are Lena and her new friend Bean. Say hello, Bean."

"Hello."

The table waited. Lena snickered. Bean gave her a stern look, and then her eyes opened wide. "Oh, I'm sorry. It's very nice to meet you." She glanced at Ingrid and then back at Aisha. *"Jambo, Bawana."*

Aisha laughed gently. "Very good. And as much as I appreciate the attempt to greet me in my tongue, French would be more apropos. They speak Swahili in the middle belt of Africa or the Bantu belt. Ethiopia is at the mouth of the Red Sea and has more in common with Arabic and French. The missionaries who took me in only spoke English and French. But we do have a family in our neighborhood who speak Swahili. They have a young boy about your age."

Toki held up her hands, palm out. "And don't look at me. I speak Orange Spanglish and Valley Girl. I'm a southern California banana through and through. I don't even like sushi."

The table laughed at her roller coaster up and down of valley girl talk.

Ingrid cleared her throat. "I'm Ingrid. I speak nine languages from being a Navy brat. And Bean and I are learning Swahili to satisfy her language requirement to graduate high school." She looked at Aisha. "*Oui, je parle français. On peut s'entraîner un jour.*"

"Oh, *oui*. I would love to have coffee and practice sometime."

The heads turned at the deep rumble. "And finally, I'm Duff. But it's good to hear who speaks what."

Bet offered her hand at the two women. "Aisha and Toki live in our neighborhood. So, as you can see, they have reason to want a safe neighborhood, as well.

Aisha nodded. "Bet said you were looking for a house for the three of you?"

Ingrid took the initiative. "Yes. We are three, not a couple with a child. I'm the tutor and housekeeper. Duff is away many days, but he also has a valuable motorcycle we need to lock up securely. Preferably, we need a house with three master suites. But we could make a regular house work where we girls share a bathroom."

Bean looked in horror at the woman. "Speak for yourself." Her eyes grew as everyone laughed.

Ingrid shrugged. "Okay, you get the master, and Duff and I share the tiny bathroom."

"Would a house with an apartment over the garage work?

There is an iron gate leading into the backyard and garages. I even think the Jacuzzi works."

Toki laughed. "She's joking about the Jacuzzi. It's a birdbath with a fountain."

Bet wrinkled her face. "Are you talking about the yellow house? When did the Robertson's move?"

Aisha looked at Bet. "In a couple of days. He got a new posting in Germany." She turned to the rest. "He's with the state department. So the house and apartment are fully furnished. Would that be a problem?"

"Just the opposite. Bean and I own enough to fill the bags on the motorcycle." He looked at Ingrid.

She snorted. "I was a navy brat. Everything fits in a seabag. Well... okay, so I grew up. But the five or six boxes fit in the minivan."

22

—————

WHERE NOW

Bean scrunched down in the chair. She rested her calf on the table and crossed her other over the lower. She looked over at Ingrid. "How do you think the other half lives?"

The blond knew Bean was being flippant, but it was still an insensitive statement. "They either live closer to the ocean or don't have time to sit in the sun. Probably ninety-eight percent of the world would kill to be in your seat right now."

"I was just joking."

"I know you were. But just the clean water to make that tea, most of the world can't see through a glass of water. As for the ice, a major portion of the world has never seen or experienced ice. Outside the United States, most beer is served room temperature instead of ice-cold."

Bean shook her head in confusion. "Is that a problem? Room temperature beer?"

Ingrid realized she had dropped into the wrong department for the lesson. "Forget beer for a few years. Coffee. Oops... no." She sipped her iced tea and looked south across the expanse of the city.

Bean knew coffee. She narrowed one eye as she stared down at her teacher. "What about coffee?"

Ingrid waved it off. "Forget it. It's a bad old joke."

Bean's feet dropped to the deck as she sat up. "What joke?"

"Nothing."

"It's something. And you brought it up. Now give."

"It was an old joke."

"About coffee."

Ingrid's head rolled toward Bean. "And about Americans."

"What's the joke?"

Ingrid took in a slow breath and let it out softly. "Most of the world used to joke that only ten percent of the coffee in the world was good to great."

Bean thought about it. Finally, shaking her head. "I don't get it."

Ingrid smiled toothily. "Americans drink ninety percent of the coffee in the world." She waited. Nothing. Her head rolled back to face the sun.

"Is that true?"

It had been several minutes, and she was almost drifting off to sleep. The words roused her. She looked at Bean. "Is what true?"

"About the coffee. Do we really drink that much coffee?"

Ingrid thought about how to explain it all. "How many mugs of coffee did you have for breakfast?"

Bean thought. "Three, I think. Maybe only two. Why? It wasn't a lot. I think Duff would have had three or four."

Ingrid took her legs off the table. "Go close up the house and meet me at the van."

"Where are we going?"

Ingrid gave her a silly look and shrugged. "Out for coffee."

"But we can make it here…?"

Ingrid stood. "Do you have an espresso machine in your back pocket?"

"No."

"Then I'll meet you at the van." She shooed her with the backs of her hands. "Go."

As Ingrid watched Bean rush down the stairs and across the small lawn to the main house, she dialed one of her new numbers. "Bubba. We need to go to coffee." She listened to the rat-a-tat of the excited woman. "No. Espresso. The real thing. I think Persian coffee… No. Let's take it one step at a time… Okay, it might be better if we pick you up. Okay, we'll see you in ten minutes."

———

BEAN'S EYES reflected the large copper machine. It had levers and dials and more things going on that were missing from the coffeemaker in the house. "So how does it work?"

Bet draped her arm over the young woman's shoulders. She winked back at Ingrid. She pointed at a pipe coming from the wall. "You see that pipe? That is the water supply. But when I was a young girl, and my nana would take me with her shopping, the boys would bring the water up from the river in buckets and pour it in the top where that cap still is today."

Bean looked at her with a frown. "Where is the river?"

"No. When I was a little girl in India, it was a rite of passage for the boys. They must carry the water before they could ever drink the coffee."

Bean pointed at the large body of the machine. "So that's full of water?"

"Not anymore. Now they just have the pipe from the wall."

"So why have the enormous section that takes up so much room?"

Nana patted Bean's shoulder. "Did it impress you? The big copper belly?"

"Well... kind of."

"Well, that's its job now—impressing you. So you will come again. The little red machines down the street do the same job... but not so impressive."

The older woman smiled warmly and pointed. "See how he carefully measures the coffee grounds and then presses them down? He is adjusting how strong the coffee will be."

Bean gave her a side-glance. "The more grounds, the stronger the coffee."

The young man pressing the grounds shook his head. "No, the harder I pack the grounds, the slower it takes for the steam to make it through the grounds and the stronger but more bitter the espresso. So the balance is the talent of the barista. Make a strong but not bitter cup of coffee." He slipped the unit into the machine and pulled the handle to the center. He stuck a small cup under each nipple.

Slowly, frothy tan cream poured out into the two tiny cups. He started a second one next to them. The steam gurgled and screamed as he worked the machine as if he were playing the organ. He played even noisier with the steam that gurgled through the milk he had in the pot in a silver pot. Finally, he topped off the tiny cups with a spoonful of frothy milk and placed it on the bar in front of Bean. "Enjoy."

Bean looked at the tiny cup that was less than full.

Ingrid smiled and pointed at the cup. "This is how the rest of the world drinks coffee."

Bean took a sip as Bet and Ingrid watched, their cups inches from their mouths. Bean blew on the hot liquid and took a sip. The deep flavor filled her mouth, and then she turned toward Ingrid as she swallowed. She looked in her cup at the few drops washing the bottom. "It's good, but…"

Bet laughed and offered Bean the cup she was holding. "This time, a tiny sip. Make a little noise as you suck more air than coffee into your mouth. This is how you eat the smell of the espresso."

Bean frowned. "But that one is yours."

Bet smiled. "I never drink coffee. Only herb tea." She nodded at the bar as the barista put down the larger mug of steaming tea.

Bean watched Ingrid as she softly slurped at the tiny cup. And then she tried. But two sips, and it was empty. "Not much there."

Ingrid laughed. "No, there isn't. Only about ten percent of what you drank at breakfast."

Bean pointed at the tiny cup. "But this tasted better."

Bet laughed with her mug in front of her face. "Americans drink ninety percent of the world's coffee." Her eyes sparkled at Ingrid.

They sat in the front window sharing some small pastries as Bet shared about growing up in India. About how the family wasn't poor, but how pastries such as these were only for special occasions. And how most of the country never experienced this kind of extravagance or even espresso. "Much of the world, even where they grow coffee such as Tanzania and Rwanda, the people don't drink it. Maybe only the farmers."

Bean grimaced. "Ouch. Don't they pay them?"

Bet nodded. "Oh yes. But a good wage there is not what you

would think of as a good wage here. In much of the poorer countries, what a person makes in a year of working long and hard is less than you spend each week for groceries. Even in a country as close as Haiti, the average income is less than two hundred dollars a year. My nephew in Mumbai pays his housekeeper and her husband—his driver—less than a hundred dollars a month for the two of them."

Ingrid leaned in with a knowing smile. "But they live with them, yes?"

"Oh, most certainly. They are like one big happy family behind their gates."

Bean stretched her neck and looked sideways at the woman. "What does he do for a living?"

"He works for a computer company. He could work in the San Francisco area, but he would have to make half a million dollars to live as he lives in Mumbai. But in Mumbai, he lives like a king on a third of what he would be paid here in America." She smiled. "Not all people dream of coming to America. Some live better at home and work through the Internet." She poked softly at Bean's arm. "So you study math superb. And someday, you get a great job like my Rashid."

Ingrid sucked the last drop from her cup. "Or you maybe become a nanny housekeeper." Her smile was large and sincere.

23

MATH

"Bean, Danny is here." Ingrid watched the young boy park his moped in the backyard. Bean had been leaving the gate open for him since he started tutoring her the month before.

He only lived a few blocks away in the neighborhood. So he could easily carry the books and laptop in his bookbag. But he loved the status of riding his version of a motorcycle around the neighborhood. He was the only sixteen-year-old in the community with their own transport.

Bean bounced off the wall as she slid into the kitchen in her stocking feet. "Can we study up on your deck? There's a plug there so we can be at full power and everything." Her face beamed, and Ingrid didn't think it was from the short run from her room.

Ingrid looked out into the backyard at the young, lanky boy. The large, asymmetric mop of black curls made his head look out of balance, but it also encouraged the urge to run fingers through them to straighten the look. She knew the attraction well. And she also knew the boy did not see the effect his hair had on others. But Ingrid also saw how he lit up when he interacted with Bean. There was something mutual there, but they didn't know what.

She turned back toward the frozen Bean, her mouth open, forming excitement and the possibility of even a thank-you.

Ingrid nodded. "I'll bring up some iced tea and finger food after I run the vacuum. Duff will be home tonight, and I don't want him to think we live like slobs when he's gone."

The thank-you cut in half by the sound of the slamming of the sliding screen door.

Later, Ingrid placed the plate of cut-up fruit and vegetables on the small table behind the two. She peeked over their shoulders at the pages of diagrams and equations she didn't recognize beyond it being math. In a short month, the boy had taken Bean past anything she would have learned in high school to the work he had been doing at the junior college. Even at only sixteen, his math professors were encouraging him to make plans to head east to UCLA and stop trekking down to the beach and Santa Monica City College.

Ingrid was sure Bean was also receiving lessons on riding the small moped. Around the neighborhood might not need the helmet, but Ingrid had noticed Bean's helmet kept moving and hanging differently on the peg in the entry hall. She might have to have the talk with Duff later tonight.

As she walked back into the main house, she noticed a FedEx truck parked in front. The gal bounced out of the side door and walked across the lawn to the front door.

Ingrid opened the door.

The FedEx agent looked up from her electronic tablet. "Marika Kuuskoski?"

Ingrid stalled with her mouth open.

The woman looked back at her control pad. "Or... an... Aching Bean?" She looked back up, hopeful for success.

Ingrid reached out her hand for the thick envelope. "She's in the back. Busy."

Back on comfortable ground, the woman handed out the electronic unit. "I need a signature."

Ingrid ran the back of her fingernail across the screen. Little more than a line. The agent took it back and was poised to type in more.

"Last name?"

Ingrid smiled. "Beans."

The woman's thumbs jabbed at the screen, and then she turned back to her truck. The woman drove down to the next block a few seconds later and ran a package across the street.

Ingrid looked down at the large envelope. The return was from Colorado. Child Services. The smile slowly tugged at her one cheek.

She stood at the table, holding the envelope. Then, looking out the window, she watched Bean and Danny on the deck. She felt like a peeping Tom.

Turning, she walked into Bean's bedroom, lifted her pillow, and placed the envelope under the covers. She smoothed the blanket until the low bulge didn't show. Only Bean would know it had arrived. Then it would be up to her when she shared or talked.

24

BREAKFAST

Duff had blown through their lives and house like a tornado on a thirty-one-hour schedule. The coffee mug touched lightly in the sink at four in the morning as Duff ran some water into it. His left hand wadded up the paper towel he had used for a plate. The slice of wheat toast with butter and jam would hold him until he made his way into the executive lounge at LAX. He would indulge in a banana, a cherry Danish, and more coffee there. He looked out into the backyard. In the city, there was never any real dark. It wasn't the desert; it wasn't the open spaces near Las Vegas, but it somehow felt comfortably like home. He was sitting a lot, but he wasn't the driver. Only when he was home did he feel the comforting weight of the leather jacket. As a precaution, he had researched and invested in a light leather sport coat with a Kevlar lining the salesperson guaranteed could stop or mitigate the effects of a nine-millimeter bullet.

He turned at the sound of the light knuckle on the front door.

He stopped at the door, bent, picked up his briefcase with the laptop in it, and opened the door.

The dark man in the suit stood down from the front stoop on the walkway. His voice was the soft wind in the early morning. "Good morning, sir."

Duff pulled the door closed behind him. "Good morning, Leon."

The man turned and led the way to the car. He opened the back door and waited.

Duff stopped at the door and smirked. "You're not letting me drive this morning?"

The man smiled. It had become their game. "No, sir. Never, sir. I need my job. I have a daughter with a very expensive mouth."

Duff shook his head in despair. "Still letting her eat, huh?" Duff ducked into the backseat.

As Leon closed the door, he moaned. "It's getting worse, sir. Not only three times a day, but she wants to snack now as well."

Duff chuckled as he put on his seatbelt. Over the course of two months and the hours of driving, he had heard of the trials and daunting burden the man suffered under the hand of his twenty-six-year-old daughter. She was a third-year medical student at UCLA who wanted to specialize in geriatrics and oncology. *To prepare for the day, she had to take care of Leon.* So her youth and his were being spent practicing.

He had raised her by himself since she was six. Now the tables were slowly turning with some comedy injections.

As the man settled into the front seat, Duff noticed a sparkle at the bottom of the man's right ear. Two days earlier, it had only been the dull glow of a small ball of gold. Then it had looked tiny and discrete on the man who could have played pro football as a defender. Now, the sparkle was markedly larger.

"I see she won the argument. Does she also have a suitable date lined up as well?"

The man's hand touched the sizable diamond as he shook his head. "I only wanted a carat, but she said it would make me look too feminine, and with my size, two carats were the smallest. Do you think it's too large? It feels like it weighs a pound or more."

"Nah. You're good, Leon. I like a little panache in my driver. I mean, I'd get one… but you won't let me drive."

The man glanced in the rearview mirror as he turned up the on-ramp. "This isn't one of the pansy diesel trucks you have those fancy driver's licenses for. This is a one-thousand-horse, positive-traction, limited-slip, hoity-toity, full-blown gentlemen's city-trolling wagon."

Duff continued the usual trolling of the banter between them about vehicles and engines. "Oh, only a thousand today. This must be the four-banger. Because the one you had on Friday was a full two-thousand or more, or I'll eat my jacket."

The light of the man's eye glanced back. "I think we need to talk about girls instead." He reached forward and turned on the local traffic report.

Duff knew that just below where he could see, the man had a computer pad with nothing more than the map of their route. Alternate routing hovered softly in yellow. Duff never tried to lower the windows, but he guessed they armored the vehicle to some extent.

Duff took his laptop out of his briefcase. "How long to downtown, Leon?"

"Twenty-eight minutes, sir. No traffic at this hour."

Duff watched the laptop boot up. "Just don't speed on my account."

"No, sir."

LEON OPENED the back door as Duff walked out of the building.

Duff looked at the tint of pink in the upper air and the few clouds floating over the diamond district. "It looks like it's going to be a beautiful day, Leon." He looked the man in the eyes. "Perfect day to take your daughter to the park and teach her how to fly a kite." He smiled at the man's look of suffering.

"The last fun thing I tried to teach her was how to play hopscotch. She cleaned my clock and told me it was obviously a game for little girls and old men. After that, she never played again."

Duff ducked into the backseat. "Well, Doctor Frankenstein, you've created a monster."

25

BREAKFAST AT HOME

Ingrid enjoyed walking across the small piece of grass. The common yard was the only portion she felt was theirs and theirs alone. She knew it was silly to feel possessive about something they were only renting, but the feel of the semi-green on the bottoms of her bare feet felt like what she thought home would feel like.

The sliding back door was unlocked and slid open. Ingrid stepped into the still of the house, where a tinge of hot metal hung in the air. She glanced at the stove. The small frying pan was still on the stove, but the small red light was off. The red light on the coffeemaker was off, but the pot was half-full. It had run its two-hour cycle.

She stopped at the sink. It was empty.

Hesitantly, she felt the side of the coffeepot. Still warm enough. Glancing out the back window over the sink, she thought about mornings and routines.

"I don't know if the coffee is still warm enough."

Ingrid startled and turned to see the back of Bean's head and shoulders hunched at the table. "Do you want more? I can make another pot."

Bean sat up, looked at the ceiling, and then turned in the chair. "Yeah. That would be good. I think I miscounted the number of spoons. I wouldn't drink that if I were you."

Ingrid took a cautious sip. Her left eye shuttered closed as her right grew large. She poured it down the sink. "Reminds me of the coffee my grandfather used to make."

"Espresso?"

Ingrid shuttered. "Nope. Just bad." She poured the rest out and rinsed the pot. Then, filling it with fresh water, she started making a fresh pot. She glanced in the sink again. "Duff still asleep?"

Bean sounded distracted as she had turned back to the table. "He left a few minutes after four. The car picked him up."

Ingrid frowned as the coffeemaker burbled. "Usually, he leaves his mug in the sink..."

"I put them in the dishwasher."

Ingrid opened the dishwasher and looked in. She knew she had set the dishwasher to run as the last thing before she went back to her apartment last night to write letters. She expected to find the clean dishes and the dirty. There were two plates and a mug. A single knife and fork were in the silverware holder.

Bean glanced back. "I put them away."

Ingrid nodded and turned to stare out at the backyard, hoping for some sign that she would wake up at any moment. She felt the cool of the stainless-steel sink on her fingers. The tiny chip on the edge of the Formica counter was there under her thumb. Everything was the same... and yet... not.

The snap of the coffeemaker brought her back to the kitchen. She began to pull the pot but walked into the dining area and grabbed Bean's mug instead. The coffee really was bad. The cup was almost full.

Thin folders and papers covered the table. Bean was intently reading the thick folder. Ingrid noted the dark and battered edges of the folder. It would be older than the unblemished folders.

She rinsed out the old black water and poured coffee into the mug. Placing it at Bean's elbow, she looked at the obvious work. "You ready for breakfast?"

Bean stopped reading, laid down the folder, and took up the coffee mug. "Thanks. But I already made myself an omelet. I left you some tomato, onion, and ham already chopped. It's in a bowl in the refrigerator. And we're down to only a few slices of bread, so I wrote it on the shopping list."

Ingrid set the coffeepot on the table and lowered herself into a chair. As she stared at Bean, sipping her coffee. She looked for the girl she had met only a few months before. That girl was hardly left. Even how she now tied up her long hair. The ponytail became a bun with chopsticks. And she hadn't noticed.

Bean shifted in her seat, her face still hidden behind the rim of the mug. "What?"

"Who are you, and what have you done with my little girl?"

Bean softly snorted as she put her mug down with a smirk. "One, I was never your little girl. And two, I'm about to be eighteen. By every law in the land, that will make me my own person. An adult."

Thinking of the unusual relationship they all had, Ingrid set down her mug. Then, laying the back of her upper arm out along the table, she leaned her head into her hand. Her face was complacent.

"Well, soon to be a woman. What did you have in mind to do with your life?"

Bean opened her mouth. Blinked. And closed it. She looked at all the paperwork on the table as she thought. "I thought about world peace and curing cancer…" Then, looking up, she smiled. "But I think I'll get my driver's license first."

Ingrid didn't move. She waited.

The bristling slowly melted into a caved slump. "I don't know. I want my driver's license. I like math, and I think I'd like to go to college…" She looked up. The look on her face was more hurt than need. "Did you go to college?"

Ingrid had wondered when the subject would ever come up. Her one shoulder and her face grimaced into a mockery of a shrug. "A little in Germany. A little in Italy. Some credits here in the United States. More in Mexico until they figured out I didn't have a visa and dropped me at the border. But basically, about the same as what I would have gotten here at a city college. But a formal teaching degree? No."

Bean held out her palm. "And for everything Duff has a license for, he didn't get those in college. And as for earning a living…?"

Ingrid pursed her lips and then sucked them back in.

Bean laughed. "Yeah. I know." She waved her hand around at the house. "I don't know what he makes or even what he is doing now. He used to drive in Vegas. But now, the car picks him up and a few days later drops him off late at night. He says what he does is all legal… but how do I get a job like that?"

"What about asking Mr. Kaminski?"

Bean's eyes got big as she leaned away from the conversation. "I would think that would be asking for Duff to get fired. I think it's a don't ask, don't tell kind of thing."

"But it's legal. Or so he says."

Bean nodded. "I've looked at the stamps in his passport. And sometimes, when he gets in, he just pulls the trash and money out of his pockets and cleans it up later. I've never flown before, but I don't think seat 32C is in First Class."

Ingrid snorted. "More like the middle of the screaming baby section."

"How many hours from here to Amsterdam?"

Ingrid closed one eye and shrugged. "Ten, maybe twelve hours. Long flight in the crying baby section. Maybe we should treat him better when he's home."

Bean cocked her eyebrow. "What, a pleasant home-cooked meal?" She rolled her eyes. "I'm just glad he's home. I do everything but fawn all over him. I don't know what could make him happier. But I noticed what you cook for his first night home is not the same as what we eat when he's away."

Ingrid sat up. "You want a change of menu? What would you like?"

Bean's smile pulled back into an evil smirk. "Biryani."

Ingrid licked her lips lasciviously. "Lamb Biryani."

"Tonight. I have something I want to ask Lena about."

Ingrid poured the last of the coffee and then realized it was less than warm. Taking up the two mugs, she started for the kitchen. "What's with all the studying? Is that the stuff that came the other day from Child Services?"

"Yeah. There's a lot here, but not once does anyone mention…"—she looked up, knowing this wasn't a subject she had discussed with anyone but Duff—"um… abuse." She turned back to the large folder.

Ingrid put down fresh mugs of coffee and sat.

Bean's head twitched a half glance. "Thanks." Her hand felt

out for the mug. Her left hand's index finger was marking a line as she read farther.

Ingrid noticed the header on the page. She had seen thousands of documents with the same heading—Department of Defense.

"Is that about your father?"

The mumble sounded distracted and distant. Her right finger held a place while she referred to the line under the left finger. She read and reread the lines. Grabbing her mug, she leaned back and buried her face into the steam and gently sipped as she thought.

"Evidently, on my birthday, I'll be eligible for survivor benefits being held in a bank somewhere since I was nine. I'm also supposed to have been receiving survivor benefits from Social Security, but I can't find where they were ever paid or even filed for." She looked up at Ingrid. "How do you file for these? Heck, how do I find any of this? You asked what I wanted to do." She held her hands at the paperwork. "I want to survive this. Well… and get what I was supposed to be paid all these years."

"What rank was your father?"

Bean frowned.

Ingrid gently put her hand on the girls. "It matters. If he were just a grunt or a sergeant, his pay wouldn't have been that much, and the death benefit would be small. Some, but small."

"He was a captain."

Ingrid's eyebrow raised. "So not a small deal." She pointed at the folder. "How did you get all this?"

"I asked Mr. Kaminski if he could… um… talk to Child Services for me."

"Intercede. It means to mediate or be the go-between, between you and Child Services." She smiled as she bounced her head. "Smart move. I'm sure it was a small thing for a guy who can find me on the Via Roma with a hangover and has me in Vegas three days later."

Bean leaned on her left arm and rested her head in her hand. "What is the Via Roma?"

Ingrid rolled her eyes under her eyelids. "It's a major boulevard leading into Rome, Italy. It makes Wilshire Boulevard look small, and there are lots of people walking up and down, shopping, eating, seeing, being seen, and..."

Bean chortled softly. "And recovering from the night before."

Ingrid hummed. "More like the month or summer before."

"So maybe he would know how to find these benefits?"

Ingrid pointed at her phone on the table. "He's in your phone, just like he's in mine. But why not talk to Duff about this?"

Bean furled her lower lip in under her upper. Ingrid noticed just a tiny line of white teeth marking the top from the lower.

Ingrid stood. "I need to figure out the shopping. You'll work it out. After all, you got all this on your own. Well, with a little help."

26

DINER CONFERENCE

Bet passed quietly through the swinging door. The early dinner reservation had stirred her interest. The men were still in the early evening's "let's make a lot of noise now" stage. She looked at Ingrid sitting by herself at the family table. Bean and Lena sat huddled at the two-top in the window. Not a sound escaped their girl's cone of silence. Bet remembered those years when she was growing up in a small village outside of New Delhi. Girls always had their secrets. It was how they survived.

She braced her hand on the large table and gently lowered herself into the chair. All the while, her eyes never left the two girls. "Any idea what that's all about?"

Ingrid harrumphed softly in her chest. "If this were France or Italy or anywhere else and anyone else, I would say it's boy trouble. But with Bean…?"

She looked over at the older Indian woman in her traditional dress and the red dot on her forehead. She had embraced America, but slipping back into her traditional sarong was as easy for her as slipping on a T-shirt and pants to go shopping. Ingrid envied her for having the two worlds to walk in. One day a modern woman in America, and in the evening, the host from New Delhi, in a traditional Indian restaurant.

Ingrid thought about her roots. A fifth-generation American of mostly upper Midwest farmers from Sweden. The most traditional she got was eating a danish and making terrible impressions of the movie *Fargo*. Even saying "Yeah, you betcha" sounded more like she had just spit out a mouthful of manure than a growing-up accent. Her roots in tradition ran as deep as her jeans and bras from Target. She had gotten used to the bras from the Navy base's Post Exchange and only found Target's cheap stock matched the same feel and fit she was used to.

LENA GLANCED at the back of the restaurant and leaned in toward Bean. "What boy?"

"A boy. Any boy. Have you or not?"

"I haven't even kissed my father goodnight. Much less some boy. I mean... I'm Indian. There are strict rules and customs."

Bean sat back. She chewed on her lower lip. Her only resource, she could think of, turned out to be no help at all. "What if the boy is Indian?"

Lena's head jerked in a shake. "Wait. What? What, boy... I mean... for you to kiss? From the neighborhood? Who's the boy?"

Bean narrowed one eye. "Danny...?"

Lena's eye got impossibly large as her mouth opened to match. She leaned in close. Her voice was all breath. "My betrothed, Danny? Danny with all those yummy curls, Danny? Mister Moped, Danny?"

Bean smelled a stinking fish in there somewhere. Her finger

shook back and forth as she leaned in. Their foreheads almost touched. "Back up there—Danica Patrick. What betrothed?"

Lena leaned in with a soulful look like she would start sobbing at any moment. "Our fathers became best friends when they were young. They promised their firstborn would marry if they were a boy and girl. So you see, they have betrothed me even before our fathers married. It is big bad juju if we don't marry as our fathers swore to. For me to be a girl, and Danny to be a firstborn boy—is kismet. The planets have aligned for this to be."

Bean watched her. Her face was tranquil. Almost too bored. Lena held her stare, but her mouth quivered at the corner. They both started laughing at the same time.

Lena glanced back at her grandmother and Ingrid. The women were paying attention but having their own conversation.

"Okay. He's not my betrothed. If there is one, it will probably be some old troll from India." She smiled and cocked her head. "So... Danny, huh? And what exactly have you two been studying all these weeks?"

Bean narrowed her eyes in warning. "Math. Oh, and there are also our conversations about... math. And computers too. He's a nerd. I swear. If I weren't afraid of scaring him, I'd just jump over and kiss him just to see if he's a boy attracted to girls."

"What else would he be?" Her face twisted for a moment and then popped open. "Oh."

Bean nodded with wide eyes of her own. "Yeah. That."

Lena shuddered, her face in a scowl. "Nah... Not Danny. No." But she paused. "Do you think?"

Bean shrugged. "I don't know. But before I jump him, I

wanted to know if there was some taboo I might step on. I don't want to lose him as a tutor. But also, I'd like to… well, you know… a friend too."

Lena held up her finger and stood. Then, looking at the single late-lunch customer reading, she walked to the back. A moment later, she returned and slipped into her seat. Her smile had canary feathers sticking out. Bean laughed.

"Nana says it was his grandmother who was the last to come from the old country, and she was from a westernized family. Her father came to finish his doctoral work at Berkeley… in math." She leaned back and smirked. "I don't think they adhere to any of the traditions. So you're safe to trip him and beat him to the floor, as my brother says."

Bean snorted. "I think your brother has a dirty mind."

Lena's eyes rolled as her head lolled to one side. "Everything about fourteen-year-old boys is nasty. Especially his socks. They reek worse than the garbage cans behind a fast-food place."

Bean frowned. "But not the garbage cans behind here?"

Lena stood and waved her hand. "We don't throw out food here. Come on. I'll show you. Everything gets eaten."

"Everything?"

The girl stopped at the large family table. "Nana. Tell Bean what happens to leftover food."

The woman frowned. "There's no such thing. Anything left when we close is boxed into dinners and taken to the homeless. It is against our religion to waste food. Too many are starving in the world."

Lena took Bean's hand. "Come on. I want to show you something."

Bet grumped. "Lena, we're going to eat soon."

"I know, Nana. We'll be back in a few minutes."

Lena guided Bean through the wonderful smells of the kitchen. "If there isn't much left at the end of a busy night, we make more. We take about two to three dozen dinners to a different location each night. Many homeless end up sharing a single meal with two or four friends. They are worth watching and learning from."

True to the girl's word. The trash cans were neat and clean. There was no food smell. Mostly cut up and bundled cardboard or washed cans neatly smashed and stacked in boxes for recycling.

"Why so clean? I mean, I like that it is... but why make such an effort?"

Lena pulled Bean down the alley to the street, where they watched for a break in the traffic before running across to the next alley. She held her finger to her pursed lips as she guided Bean toward the approaching large garbage bins of another restaurant.

Bean cringed as they got close. The foul smell stung her eyes —large bins, splattered with multicolored stains, years in the making.

Bean started to say something but gagged instead. The sound startled three rats that bolted out of the top of the bin and slunk rapidly down the alley.

Bean grabbed Lena's arm as both of their eyes bolted wide open. They laughed nervously at having been frightened. Then, they turned around and rushed back to the street and around the corner.

Lena pointed at the garish sign or the popular restaurant. Even Bean had now heard of it. They had never eaten there, and now, never would.

Laughing, they burst through the door of the family restaurant. The stern face on Bet brought them both up short. Chastised in an instant, they scurried toward the back with looks of chagrin.

Bet leaned into Lena's face and rattled off verbal chastisement to match her stern look.

"Yes, Nana."

Bet swept the air with her finger and pointed at the bathrooms. Lena leaped to be out of range. Bet turned her scowl on Bean. "You, too. Wash up. Wherever you were, I know it was dirty. I can smell it."

The two women watched the retreating mischief-makers as the bathroom door closed. The snickering was behind tightly clamped lips. Bet leaned into the service window and told her sons they were finally ready for dinner now.

27

COURT

"**I** can take you."

Bean stood in the doorway and thought about Ingrid's offer. Looking up, her face told Ingrid everything about how she would like to be taken and guided, like a child. But then, there was a strengthening resolve.

Bean's lips unfurled. "Nah, I need to do this alone."

Ingrid nodded somberly. "Okay. But call if you want me to come get you after."

Bean paused. With the door half shut, she looked back. Her smile was small but friendly. "Okay. Thanks, Ingrid. It means a lot, you having my back and all."

Ingrid softly answered a closed door. "Any time, kid. Any time."

———

THE BUS WAS fifteen minutes late, but the driver flashed his lights at the connecting bus, so it waited. As Bean rode, for the second time, the farthest trip she had ever traveled alone, she watched the sky turn from the orange-pink to a dirty blue. Morning crept into the sky as the traffic crawled onto Wilshire Boulevard, heading for downtown Los Angeles.

The last time, she had left earlier and arrived later. The county courthouse was overwhelming. Herds of people caused flows and eddies in the large halls. The marble floors and granite walls echoed the sounds of hundreds of shoes, dozens of conversations, and the general rustle of people moving.

She smiled at one guard. "Good morning, Felix."

The tall black man's face opened in an enormous warm smile. "Well, if it isn't the little Beanie Baby. How are you doing?" His eyes suddenly jumped as he remembered. "Is this the day?"

Bean beamed. "It most certainly is. And I couldn't have done it without you. I owe you."

The man looked around dramatically. His partner rolled her eyes. She had worked long enough with the friendly giant. She turned and leaned, looking down the other corridor. The man's hands were flapping to draw Bean in. Her head was barely above his flat, hard stomach. She could hear his heart beating as they hugged.

As he stepped her back, he held her shoulders. "Now remember—if the judge or anyone tries to give you guff. You come fetch little Felix, and I'll sort them out. Who you supposed to appear before?"

Bean pulled the paperwork out of her back pocket and unfolded it. She scanned the top page.

The man reached over and pulled the top two pages. "Here." His finger pointed about three-quarters of the way down the page.

Bean squinted at the faded print. "Lopez then a y and then Esp... esper...?"

Felix's partner turned back around from ignoring them touching. "Julia Lopez y Esperanza." She smiled at Bean. "Name change, huh. You got the best. When I started, she was Juanita Garcia and working on her first divorce. The guy was an LAPD jerk. Then she met Lopez. I worked as a waiter at their wedding, just to see her dress. They were such a romantic couple. The man had an enormous heart."

Felix nodded but added, "Until it blew up one day. He dropped dead in front of his chemistry class at the city college. It was a small family service, but hundreds of us stood across the street."

Bean frowned with her thumbnail on the name. "But what is the little y and the Esperanza?"

"Oh *majita*. The *y* is Spanish for *and*. Esperanza is the deputy district attorney you no ever want to go up against. He is *muy tiburón*."

Felix leaned over. "He an effen shark. He snacks on new lawyers for breakfast. But he treats little Julia like she be the goddess come to heal his wounds." He glanced at his watch. "You best be getting upstairs. You late."

As she turned, he grabbed her shoulder. "You ain't packing any heat or a knife, is you?"

Bean grimaced and shook her head in repulsion.

"What's in the backpack?"

"My paperwork."

Felix waved at the guard at the metal detectors. "Johnson." He pointed down at Bean's head, then chopped the air to the left, and ended with a thumbs up.

The man nodded and waved his hand at the lane for lawyers, guards, and judges.

Felix smiled at Bean. "You scoot. And stop back after."

"Thanks, Felix. You're the best."

———

BEAN HAD STOOD in the hall waiting with the rest of the people seeking a name change. She listened to the stories. The boisterous woman in the plaid cotton shirt and what would pass for dad pants over the cheap flip-flops. "They spelled my name Tawna, but my mother, in her eternal 'Bama accent, pronounced it *Tanya* like Tanya Tucker."

The woman next to her frowned. "Don't she pronounce it *Tawnya?*"

Flip-flops snorted. "Not if she be ignorant and from 'Bama, she don't."

The young woman in the waitress uniform was talking to the tall, slender person next to her in the nineteen forties-style shoes, floral dress, and long gloves in their hand. They had forgotten to shave close that morning. "My father said when I was born that I was as black as a magpie bird. So the nurse who was hard-of-hearing wrote Maggy."

The young woman or man gushed in little more than breath. "What are you going to do?"

The waitress snorted. "They both passed away last year. I've always loved the name *Lucinda*. So today, I am Lucinda. What about you?"

She held out her long, slender hand. "Candice. Candice Mary Creedy. Glad to meet you, Lucinda."

The waitress beamed and shook her hand. "Likewise, Candice. But what about the nickname?"

They giggled. "Candy is dandy."

Bean smiled. There were so many stories.

The woman in a marshal's uniform waddled down the hall to open the door. "Okay, listen up, people. We will call you in alphabetical order. So it don't matter where you sit. There be plenty of seats for everyone. So just find you a seat and set. The judge is running late this morning, so she will be here any minute but will truck no dawdling. So grab you a seat, and we get started."

Bean filed in with the others and took a seat near the back aisle. She knew they would probably call her near the middle.

"All rise for the Honorable Judge Lopez y Esperanza."

The judge rushed in from the small door behind the raised desk. "I'm sorry I'm running late. Please be seated. Bailiff, please call our first victim." A light snicker rippled through the congregation.

"Alvin Rosenthal."

The man rose and slowly, using his two canes, made his way to the front. The conversation between him and the judge was short. She reached across the bench and shook his hand. She then stamped and signed his paperwork. Handing him one copy, she nodded at the bailiff.

"Barbara Smyth."

Some conversations were a bit longer, and occasionally, Bean could hear snippets. The judge's face barely changed from doing the same to a halfhearted smile. Some hands she shook, most she didn't.

"Charles Creedy."

The tall, slender woman stood and strode to the bench. The

conversation was brief. The judge stood and bent forward, offering out her hand. Candice hesitated. The judge smiled. "Welcome to your life, Candice." The hand moved forward, and the judge took it in both of her hands. The smile was genuine and warm. Her eyes slow blinked as she nodded and sat back down.

Candice turned. Her face was radiant, her life was hers, and her stride self-assured. Bean stuck out her fist, and they fist-bumped as Candice left.

Bean was still floating in thought about the boy who maybe hated himself, who decided whom they wanted to be. So many stories. So close to home.

"Marika Kuusakoski."

Nobody moved. People looked around.

"Marika Kuusakoski? Is there a Marika Kuusakoski here?"

Bean jerked. The name…

"Here. Sorry." She rushed to the front.

The judge looked at the paperwork. "Reason for changing your name?"

Bean opened her backpack and pulled out the files. She placed the larger one on the bench. "This is my father's service record until they killed him when I was nine. I'm sorry, but I don't have the police report from a month later when my mother committed suicide." She laid the other folders next to it on the bench. "These are the places and homes I spent the next eight years in with Child Services. Not what you would call happy years. The report missing is when I ran away from my last home in Colorado. I kidnapped a man on a motorcycle to take me with him. He didn't know me, but he had a spare helmet. He's looked after me like a big brother ever since."

"I'm assuming his name might be Akens?"

Bean nodded. There was something in her throat. "Yes, Duff Akens." The croak sounded more like a toad in the night.

The judge looked up. "And the first name of Bean?"

"He never asked my name. He just called me that from the moment… um… I kidnapped him. I don't know why, but it fits. Fits comfortably."

The judge looked down at the paper. "And the other?"

Bean licked her lips. The lower lip sucked in, and she bit. "The name my father called me."

The judge quietly laid the paperwork down on her desk. She reached for the large folder. "May I?"

Bean nodded.

Used to reading stacks of documents and files, the judge leafed through the folder. She stopped at only a few places. "A captain."

"Yes, ma'am."

The judge reached for the other folders. The bailiff fidgeted. The judge cleared her throat. The courtroom was hers to command and hers alone. She leafed through a few of the folders. "You moved around some."

"Yes, ma'am."

The judge looked up with a wry smile. Her voice lowered. The conversation was only for them. "My father was a marine. You can call me Your Honor, Judge, or Julia. Just don't call me late for dinner."

Bean smiled. "Yes… Julia."

A sad wave passed over the judge's face. She stamped the paperwork and looked up. "So you kidnapped a keeper?"

"I think so. But I don't know what's next beyond Friday."

"What's Friday?"

"I have my emancipation hearing."

The judge frowned. "That should have preceded this."

Bean shrugged. "I guess there was a scheduling problem."

"What name is the hearing under?"

"I guess my old name."

The judge pointed at the benches. "Take a seat. We'll get this settled." She turned to the bailiff. "I need this run down." She pointed out the names and what she wanted.

The bailiff looked at the crowd of people on the benches.

The judge raised an eyebrow. "Do any of them look like they're about to riot?"

"But protocol says…"

The Judge scowled and turned to look at Bean. "Who helped you file your papers?"

"Felix. In the lobby."

"Is he a sheriff or a marshal?"

Bean shrugged and pointed at the bailiff. "Greenish brown uniform."

Julia smirked. "Go get him." She turned to the bailiff. "Next."

Five minutes later, Bean and Felix showed up in the back. A woman was walking away from the bench with a smile on her face. The judge waved them forward.

She laid out what she wanted Felix to do. Then, she turned to the bailiff and nodded as the officer left with Bean in tow.

An hour later, as the judge was wrapping up some paperwork at the bench, Felix and Bean returned. Other than the bailiff, they were alone.

The judge passed the paperwork to the bailiff. "I need this conformed, filed, and ten copies of page three." The bailiff left with a side-eye at the other officer.

The judge rose. "Come on. Let's do this in my chambers.

These new shoes are killing me." She opened the single door behind the bench and waved them in.

Her office wasn't large or plush, but Felix noted the photo on the wall and pointed to it. "I had forgotten you took the bench under Brown."

She snorted with a smile. "Moonbeam and I go way back. He introduced me to the singer we won't mention." She sat. "I've seen you around."

"Yes, ma'am. I even worked security at your last wedding."

"Why aren't you working for me here?"

"They like me up front. I'm a large target."

"Do you think you could handle the tedium here?"

His mouth curled up on one side. "It would be like retirement. But then, if I were in here, I wouldn't have met the Beanie Baby." His thumb wiggled in the air.

The judge smiled at Bean. "I think there's a lot more in your story than just ten pounds of files."

Bean blushed and shrugged.

The judge looked at a small monitor near her desk. "Felix, could you open the door, please? The unlock is silent for a reason."

The bailiff brought in the paperwork. The judge shuffled the papers and then looked at Bean. She stood. "Please stand and raise your right hand."

Bean raised her hand.

"Do you swear that all of this is the truth to the best of your knowledge?"

"I do."

"Do you swear to be an upright citizen? For example, not to run any red lights in my vicinity, not to spit on any sidewalks, eat your vegetables, and brush your teeth regularly?"

Bean snickered. "I do."

She signed her name and stamped the document. "Congratulations. You're now a human being. You may go forth and sin within reason. But no more kidnapping unsuspecting bikers."

28

———————

JUST RIDE

Duff rolled over. He didn't remember a lump in the bed before. He scrunched his eyes and tried to clear the cotton balls from his sight. He rolled over and looked at the door. It was a dark rectangle in the dim gray of the wall.

He closed his eyes and thought—the flight from Singapore to South Korea. The layover was only an hour. He wandered around and kept moving. The flight to San Francisco and then the quick hop back down to LAX. The midnight ride to the diamond district. Then home. He got home just short of three in the morning.

He tried to focus on his watch. Too dark and too blurry.

He picked up his phone. 5:03.

He forgot what he was looking for and drifted back to sleep.

The lump moved.

The warm back found the warm back.

Two soft sighs barely filled the room as sleep resumed.

———————

THE THUMP of laundry flopped on the bed. The two large lumps twitched. The fluffy gray blanket turned back at the two corners. Two blurry eyes squinted at Ingrid with her fists buried in her hips.

"What are you doing home?" She turned and addressed the other face. "And what are you doing in his bed?"

Duff scowled over his shoulder. "What the…"

"I heard him come in. It was three in the morning. I was peeing. And I was cold. His blankets are warmer. His back is hot. And who made you mom?"

Ingrid scowled as she thought. She finally gave up and turned toward the door. "French toast in ten minutes."

Bean crept past her, dressed in sweats and double socks. "Gotta pee." She then disappeared into her bedroom.

Minutes later, the microwave dinged. Ingrid dropped another slice of bread into the egg and cinnamon mix and over to the griddle. The coffeemaker pinged.

The soft sound of stocking feet on the slate floor assured her that Bean was behind her. Her eye was still watching Duff's door. The microwave opened and closed.

Bean gently placed the plate of bacon on the counter next to the griddle. She crunched on a piece of bacon as she leaned closer to Ingrid, cooking. "I'm not saying you have a dirty mind. But you have a dirty mind."

Ingrid stifled a giggle. "I'm not saying you're emancipated. But you're old enough and emancipated enough to make up your own mind about whose bed you jump into; without my okay."

Bean turned and leaned her butt against the edge of the counter. "But it's true. Sleeping with my back against his back is better than an electric blanket." She looked over at the older woman. "Remember how cold it got out there in the desert?"

Ingrid flipped the French toast and looked out of the side of her eye. "Yeah…"

Bean smiled toothily. "I wasn't."

The woman turned her head and frowned. "You were on the other side of me. I was between you two."

Bean bared her teeth and snapped them on the slice of bacon. "Nope. Not all-night." She chewed. "I woke up and went to pee. When I came back, you were moving, so I started making the coffee."

Ingrid thought as she served up the toast. "That good, huh?"

Bean's eyes were enormous as her head rode up and down. The grin was large. "But I claimed it first."

Ingrid growled and turned her head toward Duff's room. "Breakfast is served or thrown in the trash. Your choice Mister Akens."

The door opened. He had gift bags in each hand. He placed them on the table where the girls would sit. Then he sat down.

Bean never turned around. She started chuckling. "Let me guess. The lord and master has arrived and graced us with his presence for us to serve." She looked at Ingrid holding the large platter of French toast.

The soft snort told Bean everything. "I'll get his coffee."

As Bean and Ingrid sat, they both eyed the small bags. Bean narrowed her one eye at Duff. "If something jumps out of there, you're never going to sleep safe again."

Ingrid pushed her bag with her fork. "And she's already proven she can sneak into your bed without you knowing."

Duff sipped on his coffee. "Jeez, a man goes away for four

days and gets nothing but suspicion when he comes bearing Christmas presents."

Bean sat up, frowning, futilely reaching for her phone where there was no pocket. Finally, she shot out of her chair and into her room. A moment later, she walked out, staring at the display on her phone. She placed her phone face up between her and Ingrid. The display was a cartoon of Santa and a reindeer relaxing on the beach. The current temperature was seventy-three, with an expected high of seventy-eight.

Duff snorted as he spread strawberry jam over his French toast. "Satisfied?"

Bean sat back, dazed. "What happened to November?"

Duff shrugged as he took his first bite. "We went to Arizona. Remember?" He looked curiously at Ingrid, who was unusually quiet.

Ingrid watched her hands stack her French toast. She glanced up and then kept her face down. "It's been a busy time."

Duff held his mug near his face. "Aren't the stores filled with Christmas stuff?"

"We have the food delivered."

"What about...?" He looked at her and frowned. "Everything?"

She chewed and nodded.

His scrutiny turned to Bean. She was chewing slowly as her left hand gently turned the bag around and around. The random graphics he knew wouldn't give anything away—especially where he had gotten the present.

Duff leaned over to get in Bean's sight. The unusual move jerked her head up. "What?"

Duff raised an eyebrow as he nodded toward the bag.

Bean thought for a moment. "It's a T-shirt." She forked

another bite into her mouth and chewed. Her face was deadpan. The game was on.

Ingrid frowned and picked up her bag. Then, squishing it, she smiled and put it back down. "But you didn't even feel it...?"

Bean shrugged. "Rule four."

Ingrid frowned. "Rule four? There are rules about gifts?"

Bean pushed out her lower lip. "It's not about gifts. It's about life."

Duff pushed his empty plate forward, took up his mug, and leaned back in the chair. It was days of long flights, but he also knew he had missed something along the way.

The blond set her fork and knife skewed on the plate. Then, pushing the plate forward, she folded her arms along the edge of the table. "What is rule four?"

"Only gather what you're replacing in your pack."

"But how does that mean a T-shirt?"

"I have three T-shirts in my pack. One will go if this is a great T-shirt."

"What if it's not a great T-shirt?"

"Rule five."

Ingrid turned in her chair as she frowned at Duff. Somehow, she knew he was at the root of this. She did their laundry. He had three T-shirts. Three jeans. Three pairs of socks. With flying, he had added three plain light-blue dress shirts and three slacks.

She looked back at Bean. "Rule five?"

"Always be ready to walk away or donate whatever doesn't fit in your bag or on your body."

Ingrid waved her hand at Bean's sweatshirt and pants. "And that would make the sweats...?"

"Rule five."

Ingrid glanced at Duff. The man wasn't moving other than to drink his coffee.

"I'm afraid to ask, but what are rules one through three?"

Bean snorted. "Never stand when you can sit."

Duff cleared his throat. "Never sit when you can lie down."

Bean finished by raising her mug, tapping it to Duff's, then said, "And never pass a bathroom without making use of it."

Ingrid nodded as she looked into the side of her eyes of memories. "The three laws of travel. My father drilled those into me since I was two." Her lips furled with other memories. "My mother always kept half a roll of toilet paper in her purse. I still do." She sipped on her coffee, thinking.

Bean nodded. "The roll is in the left side-bag, toward the front."

Duff scowled and growled. "Well?"

Bean growled back. "I'm thinking."

"What about?"

She looked up at the squashed ego, not getting the reward of her opening her present. "I really like the three I have now."

Duff shrugged his one shoulder. "So… it's a walk-away."

She smirked as she reached for the bag. "Walk-away, my ass." She paused. "Unless it says something stupid like *I got stoned in Amsterdam*, with a picture of a diamond ring."

Duff laughed. "That shirt was in Antwerp."

She pulled the string off the bag and opened it. She reached in and pulled out the shirt wrapped in pink tissue paper. Duff pulled her plate out of the way. She laid it on the table and unfolded the paper. The five cats guarding a mug of coffee stared back at her. The legend said *Het café van vijf katten*. Bean ran her hand down the image painted in the style of the Dutch Masters.

Ingrid opened her shirt. It had a single cat sleeping curled around a coffee mug. The mug was labeled *cafeïnevrij*.

Ingrid snorted. "Decaf. I would never." She hugged the shirt. "So you went to a cat café in Amsterdam?"

Bean held hers over for Ingrid to read. "What does mine say."

"The Café of Five Cats." She turned back toward Duff. "It's in Amsterdam?"

He raised his eyebrows. "It may be. The shop had cat T-shirts from all over the world."

Bean narrowed her eyes. "But where was the shop?"

Duff smiled. "Other side of the world. Singapore."

Ingrid closed her eyes as she thought. "Which means it was Christmas there yesterday."

"Kind of. It was Christmas eve when I landed. The shops were all closed when I left. Well, except the Crazy Cat Lady."

He looked at Bean. "Well?"

She smiled and spread it across her front. "Rule four point one."

He raised one eyebrow.

Bean laughed. "Pack tighter."

———

BEAN LEANED against the sink facing toward the living room. She sipped on the glass of water distractedly. Her mind was years ahead—and blank.

Absently, her eyes watched Duff come out of his bedroom and quietly close the door. He looked his usual—boots, jeans, sweatshirt out of respect for the time of year, and the heavy leather jacket. Then, silently, he strode to the back door.

Bean's brain clicked. "Oh, hell no. Not without me."

He chuckled and looked over with a smile. "I was wondering if you were alive."

She put the acrylic tumbler in the sink. "Warm up, Red. I'll be right out." She bolted for her room. The cat T-shirt was on her bed. Without a thought, she pulled it over her sweatshirt. She stuck her thumbs into her waist to slip off her sweatpants. Instead, she pulled her jeans on over her sweats, socks and then pulled on the tall cowboy boots. Smiling, she picked up the thin wallet and slipped it into her back pocket. Her phone she stuffed into her other pocket. She pulled on her leather jacket with the white fringe as she marched out to the backyard.

Red thumped to a beat that synced with her heart. They hadn't been out for a ride since October. Duff handed her the matching helmet. Except hers had a decal on the back—a cat with a bubble helmet and a laser rifle. The cartoon was Space Kitty. It was the closest to Space Cadet Bean wanted to get.

"Where to?"

Duff shrugged. "I was just thinking of maybe just hop out to the coast and wander down. See how far we get."

"Fuel?"

Duff looked at the meter. "Half."

"Oil?"

It had become their routine. "Changed the oil just before Thanksgiving. No leaks on the garage floor."

She slapped his shoulder. "Stop that. She's not an incontinent Milwaukee dribbler."

Duff thumbed the gate opener as he toed the transmission into first gear. The bike rumbled between the fence and house as they left.

Quietly, Ingrid watched from the sliding glass door of her

apartment. A soft smile tugged on her face. There was a strange bond between those two she knew she would never be part of. The tossed salad feeling of being thrown over her boyfriend's head, bouncing off the windshield of the car, crumpling along the roof of the vehicle, before hitting the ground to roll under the truck that would kill all of them but her—was still fresh in her mind—twenty-two years later. She would never even touch a motorcycle again.

29

COAST

The sun felt good on their dark glasses. The dark wrap-around trapped the warmth. They had stopped earlier on the highway. The extensive structure on the map said it had once been a marine animal park. Bean had laughed and poked Duff. *What, so the dolphins could come swing on the swing set?* Duff had rolled his eyes and said it was probably just for the halibut. They had pulled the wool scarves and heated chaps out of the trunk.

The day was sunny, but not all that warm.

The stoplight changed from yellow to red as they glided up to the line. Three young boys crossed the street in bright colors and black wet suits carrying their surfboards. The one smiled and gave them a thumbs up. Duff nodded back.

"Must be good to have a fan."

Duff looked over at the Sheriff's patrol car. The deputy in short sleeves was tanning his one arm. Duff figured his right arm was tanner than his left from the looks. And his partner was the same inverse.

Duff smiled. "Ya gotta take them where you can get 'em."

The deputy rocked his head at the truth. "Nice day for a ride. No traffic."

Bean snorted. "Great ride, but no place to eat lunch."

The deputy held up his index finger. The light changed, but neither moved. There was nobody behind them. Instead, the driver was plugging something into their onboard computer.

The deputy rolled his head out and smiled. "Got ya covered." He pointed down the beach. "See the pier?"

They nodded.

"There's public parking on the land side. The parking is usually timed, but not today, for Christmas." He looked back in the car at the driver. "Hank says to park in the pickup area for the pier. Nice and public for safety, but if anyone can write a ticket, it's us. So park there and out at the end of the pier is Ruby's. We probably won't be far behind ya." He nodded at something the driver said. "Hank just confirmed it. They're open and desperate for hungry bikers and cops."

The light changed to red.

The cruiser rolled ahead. The deputy waved them forward. "Come on. Ignore the light. We'll show you where to park."

Duff let out the clutch, and the bike chuffed slowly behind the car. The deputy's arm and hand pointed at a small area where two youth bicycles stood locked up at the end of the pier. "Just park next to the bikes. It makes the kids feel like part of a gang." He waved as the car made a U-turn and shot back up the highway with flashing red and blue light. At the next block, it turned inland.

Duff looked up and down the wide sidewalks. The only person was an elderly man walking a small white dog. Bean snickered. "Looks like the coast is clear."

Duff pulled up next to the bicycles and parked. They stowed

the helmets, scarves and set the locks. Looking down the pier, Duff glanced over at Bean. "Let's hurry and have lunch before the deputies get back."

She scowled, sensing a joke. "Why?"

"I don't want to have to leave the state. And you don't have a great relationship with sheriff deputies."

She spun and tried to kick him in the seat of his pants. She was slow. Not by much. But slow.

The young Latino at the rail was fishing with an unusual pole. The heavy-duty rod was short and as thick as his thumb. As they got closer, Duff cataloged what was at the man's feet. Bicycle rim, bait box, bucket, hammer, and a few lumps that defied classification.

Duff smiled as he watched the man cast the large magnet back into the water. "Looks like a good haul today."

The man with the fuzz on his upper lip and a tiny soul patch on his chin pushed his lower lip out as he appraised his catch. "Maybe twenty pounds so far. Not the worst day. It's the quiet that is the real payday. I usually only haul at night. But with Christmas this year, the restaurant closed for the day. I don't know where my regulars will eat, but I'm here in the sunshine."

"Enjoy the sunshine." Duff shot the man the thumb and pinky hang loose sign.

"It's why we live here, *ese*. Why we live here."

As they neared the end of the pier and the restaurant. Bean looked at Duff. "What was he fishing for?"

"Metal. I don't know what scrap is worth. But he gets some time in the sun, some metal to sell, and some time for a little quiet." He looked at her as he opened the door. "Something I used to relate to."

"But not anymore?"

Three waitresses threw up their hands in a touchdown move and cheered. "They're here!"

Duff laughed and side hugged Bean. "Sometimes."

Bean looked around at the empty restaurant. "Jeez. That cop wasn't joking. Is it always this dead?"

The husky brunette with the name tag reading Tiny laughed. Duff figured it was a nickname from childhood. "Nah, most of the time, this place is moving and shakin'. We are a destination at the end of a great walk. Breakfast to dinner, we usually run fifteen minutes to an hour for a booth. But Christmas is always dead. Later it will pick up." She pulled two menus and turned. "Hank didn't say how many. So I put you in the primo booth over here." The window looked north up the coast. "Get you two anything to drink?"

Bean sloughed off her jacket. "Two coffees to start. And where...?"

Tiny pointed back by the front door. "Where you came in."

———

TINY GLIDED up to the table and poured more coffee. "Was I right?"

Bean snorted and smiled with pursed lips. Swallowing, she nodded. "One hundred percent. Disgustingly childish. But sometimes, a girl just needs to indulge in ketchup dipping. And the shrimp are good." She wiped her mouth and looked at Duff.

The napkin slapped across his mouth as a dribble of juice ran out the side of his mouth. Finally, he settled for a thumbs-up comment. How do waitresses know just when you have a mouth full of food...?

Tiny nodded. "When I'm behaving myself, that Albacore

melt is my go-to at the end of shift. It fills in all the nooks and crannies." She zipped the imaginary zipper across her mouth, turned, and left to join the other two waitresses with their noses in their phones.

Bean watched the waves nudging the sand. The most dangerous looked only a foot high. Somewhere she had heard the term flat surf. Most of the ocean appeared to be just that. "Have you ever lived near the beach?"

Duff tracked where she was watching. "My driver's license says I lived only a handful of miles from here."

Bean turned and studied his face. "But you never went there to find out. Why?"

He shrugged. "I don't know. Maybe afraid of what I might find. Maybe what I don't find. I don't know."

"Find. Like what?"

"Maybe a family who has been missing me for three years, and I do not know who they are." He looked hard into her face. "Can you imagine what it would be like to a kid? They think daddy is home, and I have to tell them I have no memory of them?"

Bean looked back out at the surf. She knew… in a way. She looked back. "Okay, so what if there is no house or family?"

"Then, I would need to ask, was I ever really there? Was there a house before they built the gas station? Or did the empty lot once have a house on it? It's a very complicated thing."

"Do you ever have dreams?"

Duff squinted as he looked at the last few fries. "Kind of. But I don't know if what I'm dreaming is a memory or just a bad dinner. None of them are full or clear enough to remember what they were when I wake up. For months, I hoped I would one day wake up and remember everything. But it never did. I'd wake up and remember yesterday, or the last month, or what time I needed to be at work. But nothing from years ago."

Bean pushed her plate to the end of the table. "Does that bother you?"

Duff pushed his plate out and turned to sit sideways, leaning against his jacket. "Not anymore."

"What changed?"

He looked over at her eyes. There was genuine concern. "You."

Her mouth opened, paused, and closed.

"When you kidnapped me, I was just moving from one place to a place I'd been before. When the phone call came, the dump truck into a hole in the ground already bored me."

Duff's finger slowly drew a circle on the table. "The drive from the top of the mine is two point six miles. It takes about forty minutes to make the trip. There's a large boulder with an orange paint mark about the seventeenth minute. It says, *now entering hell*. Every driver laughs the first time they see it. The second time down, you look for it. By the second day, you forget it's even there. In a ten-hour day, you drive six times into hell. By the first paycheck, you think you could drive the seventy-ton dump truck down and back with your eyes closed. Some guy tried. They didn't need to test his remains for drugs. They didn't care."

Duff looked out the window at the surf. "Kaminski called on Wednesday evening. I told them Friday would be my last day. I didn't care. I knew I'd never do that kind of driving again. Maybe you can't do it with your eyes closed, but a monkey could do it. It's just a big truck on a big road, and it never gets out of the first four gears."

Bean snorted softly. "And then you got kidnapped."

Duff snorted with a rocking head jerk. "It was just strange enough to get my attention. But dinner cinched it. If you had turned your nose up at the strange smells or the guys in turbans... I already knew I'd leave you there."

Bean leaned forward with gigantic eyes. "But oh, my gawd, the Biriyani."

Duff smirked. "The lamb or goat?"

Bean leaned back. "Either. And the guys were so..." She stared off into space.

"Open?"

Her head rolled. "More than friendly. It was like you told them I was with you, and they treated me like longtime family..." Her head rolled back as she thought. "I don't think I was even treated like that on the marine base. Only with you."

"What about Kaminski? Or the boys in Bodega? And how about the old couple who helped us on the highway? Which I keep meaning to ask... how is your wrist?"

She waved it in the air. Then changed it to grabbing the clutch on a motorcycle. She laughed as her right hand throttled the gas. "Ready."

They laughed as the two deputies walked in. They approached the table.

Duff laughed. "At the count of three, you run that way, and I'll go this way. Hello, deputies. What was the hurry?"

Hank rolled his eyes. "Every year. Someone gets the little candle lights for their tree. They turn them on, but they look so real. Drunk Uncle Chester grabs the fire extinguisher, and the ABC sets the new alarms off, and... well, you can figure out where it all goes from there. How was lunch?"

Duff thrust his jaw out and rocked his head with a smile. "Radical."

Hank turned slightly. "Tiny, did you feed them those surfer drugs?"

She came out of the back. "Honey, it was the only way we could calm them down. They said the cops had jumped them, and they only escaped with the shirts on their backs."

Duff gave Bean the stink-eye. They both chuckled softly.

Hank held up his hand. "We didn't mean to barge in on your lunch. Enjoy your Christmas and stay as long as you'd like. We need to refuel before the next set of twinkle lights. Or someone's puppy eats a chocolate bar, and we have to explain their expensive candy doesn't have enough real chocolate to hurt the dog, but it can put an extra ten pounds on the hips—which is ugly on a six-pound poodle."

"Thanks. And Merry Christmas to you guys too. And thanks for working the holiday."

Hank chuckled as he walked away, but he looked back. "It pays triple time, and we're both already in overtime at the start of our twelve-hour shift."

Tiny came over to drop off the check and clear the plates. Duff waved to her to stay for a moment. He fished two hundreds out of his wallet. He laid one hundred on the bill. "Will this cover ours and their bills?"

She looked at the large bill. "And with a fat tip left over. Really, you don't have to."

Bean looked up. "Yes, we do. If it weren't for them, we wouldn't know you were out here."

Duff looked at her and then at Tiny. "How many are working in the back?"

"Two. The cook and dishwasher."

Duff counted out five one-hundred-dollar bills and handed them over. "Pass these out and tell them thanks for working. I know what it's like to work all the holidays that everybody else gets off. You guys probably have families. But this is our Christmas dinner. So thanks."

She took the money and wiped at her eyes. There was no sound as her mouth formed the *Thank you.*

Bean pushed out of the booth. "I need to pee before we go."

Duff slipped out behind her and hefted on his jacket. "Rule three."

30

____

WHAT IS GOING ON?

They leaned on the pier railing, looking south. The afternoon was waning. The clear blue sky had become golden with the sunset.

Duff looked at Bean, looking down the coast, more at the sky than the water. Her eye was wet, but no tear.

Duff cleared his throat. She glanced over and then back out at the sunset.

"My father called this kind of sunset a honey sky. They're rare here because if you get too much pollution, you get orange or red. If you get clouds, you get the moisture fracture, and then there is all the gold, orange, and reds or pinks. But if the weather were just right, he would take me down to the beach, and we would watch for honey skies. There were a couple of ratty old beach chairs in this one cove, on a dune. It was our favorite place to sit." She wiped her eyes and pinched the snot from the end of her nose. "He said when he was over in the desert, almost every day, he saw a honey sky—and he thought about us."

Duff thought about that moment in the desert.

As they walked down the pier in the gathering gloom, Duff thought about the desert and then his bed.

"Do you want to explain what was going on this morning in my bed?"

The no was soft.

But a few minutes later and a mile down the beach, she told him to pull over. He pulled into a parking area. Turning off the engine, he leaned to set the kickstand out.

Bean gently grabbed his jacket at the shoulders. "Don't. Just sit."

The silence softly draped down around them. The soft sound of the small waves washed out past the sand.

"Since my dad died, and then my mom…" Her voice cracked. "I trusted no one. Everyone lied to me. They said they would look after me, but they never did. Instead, they moved me from one molester to the next. Some were just creepy. Others were more hands-on. But one thing was consistent—they lied. Until you. You said you would take care of me, and you did. You said you were going to feed me, and you did. You said you would get me my own room with a lock, and you did. Everything you said you were going to do, you did."

She took a deep breath through her nose and let it out slowly. She looked out into the gathering dark, where she knew the ocean was.

"I didn't know what you wanted from me. But that night in the desert, I was cold. My hand was under the blanket sleeping bag. It was near your back, and the heat was just broiling off you. So I snuggled. I didn't know what would happen. But if anything had, I think I would have been okay with it. But it didn't. We slept, and that was it. You rarely ever touch me. It's not like you're afraid of me or something. It's like you're just comfortable. I think if I took your hand when we're walking… I think you would be okay with it and see it for just that—being together and holding hands. So last night was kind of like that. I had missed you this week. And when I heard you come in, I was going to come in and talk to you. But you were already asleep. So I stayed in case you woke up and wanted to talk. And there it is."

Duff gently rocked his body and head as his hip pushed against hers. "So you weren't trying to get in my pants?"

She pushed on his one shoulder as she shook her head. "Dumb ass. I already know where the gold and money are. There's nothing in your pants."

He flinched then turned around. "Hey…"

She slapped his shoulder where she knew there were no protective bars of gold. "Drive."

He started the engine and pulled back out to the street. He could feel Bean moving around but couldn't figure what she was doing.

She tapped his left shoulder. "This next light is Beach Boulevard. Turn left."

"Kind of hard to turn right." He glanced back and could see her face illuminated by her phone. "Where are we going?"

"Just drive where I tell you."

He nosed the bike left through the light.

Twenty minutes later, they were in a mixed residential neighborhood. Most of the signs were in Vietnamese. A few were in English.

"Pull over here, at the liquor store."

They stopped and got off. Bean looked around. "What's here?"

"The address on your driver's license. Come on." She led the way into the small convenience liquor store.

She approached the man behind the counter. "Excuse me. Do you speak English?"

The young Asian man rattled off some diatribe in Vietnamese. He finished with, "Of course, I speak English. This is the United States."

She looked at him. A smartass knows another smartass. She held up her phone. "The street signs out there are not in English. Is this *this* address?"

He squinted at the address on the phone. He reached to un-pinch the display. Bean pulled it back and spread the display until the address filled the screen. "No touching. We hardly know each other."

The guy looked at her and smiled. Then, glancing at the address, he pointed across the street. "It's over there. The church."

She turned and pretended to look through the windows covered with advertising. "It looks new. Do you know when they built it?"

He sat down on his stool, spreading his hands and arms out along the back counter. "Sure. About two years ago. They just had their first anniversary this last summer."

Duff took a half step. "What was there before?"

Bean looked at the area above the counter. The packs of cigarettes in the plexiglass shelving were old. Every small convenience store she was sent to buy beer or cigarettes for her foster parents survived on cheap beer and constant sales of cigarettes. She looked at the man's fingers. There were no yellow stains, and his teeth were bright white and perfect. His right hand slipped back along the edge of the counter until his elbow cocked at an awkward angle. The thumb flexed under the counter. Bean caught movement out of the corner of her eye. The large monitor showed six high-definition panels. One was Duff and her. One was the church across the street. The square with the motorcycle only saw the front, not the license plate.

The Asian man crossed his arms. His T-shirt stretched, revealing more time spent in a gym than behind a counter in a small convenience store. "An old house chopped up into apartments or something. I think the city took it for taxes."

Duff shifted his weight. "Is there anybody who might remember who lived there?"

"Lived there? Nobody. It was sketchy as all hell, man. People came and went all the time. Most of us thought it was a drug house, but even cops came and went over there. And then one day… nada." He slapped his hands in a flat slide. "Next thing we know. They are tearing it down, and the Pres is building a church. But nobody lived there. At least when I started working for my uncle. And that goes back over seven years."

Bean grabbed at Duff's arm and turned him toward the door. "Okay. Thanks, man."

Duff stopped her at the bike. "What was that? The guy has been here seven years. I have questions."

Bean looked down the street. "No, you don't. Get on the bike. We're heading that way." She whipped off her scarf and pulled it across the back fender, hiding the license plate.

Duff nosed the bike out onto the street and headed in the direction she had pointed. He could feel her twist to look behind them. In the distance, there was a car approaching. She pulled the scarf back over her neck and opened her phone. Duff could see her face illuminated by the phone.

"Turn right, and then I need you to break every traffic law."

"What?" But he turned right.

"The dude called friends. Not friends of yours. We need to get out of here fast—as fast as you can go. But turn left at the light. That will take us down to the freeway. Take it west."

Duff turned left, running the red light. He shifted into fifth before he hit the next block. Then, as he slowed to turn onto the freeway on-ramp, he saw the headlights fishtail around the turn five blocks back. The bike roared up the ramp and was moving hard past a hundred as they dropped across the freeway into the fast lane. He reached forward and turned off the tail-lights. He had always wondered why the switch had been installed.

"Get off ahead and go right."

Duff downshifted as they descended the long ramp. He looked left at an empty street. Pausing at only thirty, they leaned into the turn through the red light. He quickly regained two more gears. The speed limit sign blurred by.

"Go past the light and take the second left. It looks small, but it runs west and north."

Duff barked into the wind. "We need gas."

Bean switched apps on her phone. "Take the left. There are several about a mile up the road. Take your pick."

The red bike flashed through the bright major intersection and slowed for the turn. Then, easing over, they sped up smoothly along the wide two-lane. Half of the gas stations in sight were open. Duff chose the fourth open one and nosed up into the bright lights. He parked behind the island closest to the building. A chunky, middle-aged woman strolled out of the office with a red rag in her hand. She methodically rubbed on something in the rag.

"Nice Chief. It looks like a one-eleven or one-sixteen."

Duff looked up as he unscrewed the cap. "You know Indians?"

She smiled at a personal joke. "I've got three. Well... two that run. I'm restoring a twenty-three racer. We had to recast the jugs and pistons. My dad is helping. He's still got eleven. The newest is the one he brought home from Vietnam. It had belonged to the French Foreign Legion's Asian Expeditionary Forces. They left it when they pulled out, and we took over. He was the only one who knew how to make it run. He brought back the machine shop and parts as well. All Uncle Sam wanted was for him to stay and keep the jeeps running. They shipped, and he stayed for three more years."

Duff held out the twenty, and she held out the piece of chrome. It was the metal trim for a front fender. The war bonnet trailed back and tapered out where the trim ended. Duff showed it to Bean.

He stepped over and held it next to the one on his Chief. It was almost half as long again, and his bonnet was short.

She held out his change. "It's custom. A friend of mine casts them. The devil is in the details. That long war bonnet is the sale when he goes to bike shows."

Duff handed the trim piece back with an appreciative look. "What are you going to put it on?"

She harrumphed. "I've got all of mine. I just polish, bag, and box these for him. It fills the night."

Bean peeked through the door into the small convenience store. "You sell cigarettes?"

She glanced back into the building. "Yeah. What do you need, sweetie?"

Bean fanned her right hand. "Just curious. How much do you sell?"

"Price? Five bucks, twenty-five."

Bean's eyes opened. "Whoa... But no. How much of your business is selling cigarettes? I'm doing a paper for school on small neighborhood businesses and what they survive on."

The woman's head rocked in understanding. "We make pennies on a gallon of fuel. So if I sold you a pack of cigarettes, I'd make more on the pack than I just made on your dad's fuel."

Bean furled her lower lip as she thought. "So a small shop in an Asian neighborhood... with no gas...?"

"It would keep them alive. Milk and cookies spoil and break. Or get stolen. The margin on beer and wine is also small. Cigarettes, hard liquor, and drugs are where the margins are. In some neighborhoods, it's all three."

Duff pulled his gloves on. "Thanks."

Bean glanced at her phone and then pointed north at the road. "Does this hit the freeway?"

"Which one. The Long Beach? No. But it turns north, and you can catch the new one out to LAX."

Duff nodded. "That works. Thanks again."

She waved. "Any time for a fellow Indian rider."

Bean smiled. More family connections that come and go.

31

THE LITTLE THINGS

B ean still had her scarf on. But sweats and socks replaced the riding gear. She leaned against the doorjamb of Duff's room.

Duff looked up from his phone. He had gotten as far down as a T-shirt, jeans, and bare feet. "What's up?"

She shrugged. "Still kind of wound up."

He glanced at his phone again—six hours until wake-up. And then a long flight over the north pole. He knew he would sleep on the plane. He laid the phone on his nightstand. "Come on in."

She sat on the corner of the bed and then moved to curl across the foot. He watched her coil and uncoiled like a cat, finding the perfect spot.

"Some night, huh?" He leaned against the padded headboard attached to the wall. He watched her pick at the stitching on the quilt.

He waited.

Finally, he got up and moved into the bathroom. He closed the door most of the way and shucked out of his jeans. He pulled on the lightweight sweatpants. He stood at the sink and mirror, thinking about the evening. He squeezed out a pea of toothpaste and started brushing. His left hand put the cap back on and lined the tube up in front of the small plastic rack holding his two toothbrushes.

"When we were running...?" Bean probed.

Duff elbowed the door open and nodded as he brushed.

"It wasn't the way you usually drive."

Duff spat. "I don't remember ever driving a hundred. Even on a freeway."

Bean squinted loosely and shook her head. "That's not it. The speed wasn't important. It was how you... I don't know. Kind of... attacked the street. Then, once you got going, it was like someone else. Someone who knew how to get away. What it would take." She looked up. Her head cocked to one side. "It wasn't scary. It felt... I don't know... safe somehow."

Duff put the toothbrush in the holder and grabbed the small towel. He patted his mouth and stood, holding the towel to his chest. "I wasn't even thinking. I knew you would tell me where to turn or go next. It was just my job to get there." He put the towel back on the counter and turned off the light.

"It was as second nature as us taking a ride down to a new market you had been to before. I just drove."

He sat down on the bed and leaned against the headboard.

Bean sat up and crossed her legs. Her right hand picked at the left's thumbnail. "That's what I mean. It wasn't something new for you. You just... drove. It's what you do, but I don't think we knew you knew how to drive like that."

Duff worried at a slight bulge in the sweats near his knee. "What I was wondering, most of the way back, was how you knew the guy was... bad?"

Bean stopped picking at her nail. She looked around the spartan room. "It's the little things. Some things are like the bedroom door missing. Other things are a louder warning, like the bathroom door. At first, I noticed the cigarette packs were old. Not like last month, but months old. Dead cockroaches in the slide thing they're in, kind of old. Even the most popular brands were faded. The red should have been hard, bright red, but was more pinkish. And then I saw his hand slide along the back counter. He was feeling for something. If he had worked there for even a year, he would have known where a button or something was. He didn't. And then I looked at the security camera monitor. It wasn't a snowy black and white like most stores. It was like watching regular TV. The six cameras were high definition. They wanted to see exactly who was who. And one camera was covering the church across the street. I got the feeling his job was to watch who showed up at the church. It was just all wrong. Like it was camouflage. Like one of those hunting things."

He frowned. "A duck blind?"

She thought and then shook her head. "No. Those are in the grass on a pond. I was thinking more like those things up in a tree where they're hunting deer."

He squinted one eye. "I think it's still called a blind."

"No matter what it's called, I think that's what the liquor store was. I don't think the neighborhood buys anything there. I know I wouldn't go in there."

Duff rocked in agreement. Absently, he picked up his phone and checked the time.

Bean knew the sign. He would be out the door at four in the morning. She got up and patted his knee once as she padded to her room.

Duff watched her. "Good night, Bean."

Her hand half waved in the air to something mumbled.

———

DUFF LOOKED up from the table. The black car was backing in the driveway. Duff looked at his wristwatch. He was early.

He pulled on his leather bomber jacket. He had put the extra time in Singapore to good use. It was every bit as bulletproof as his motorcycle jacket. And there were also secret pockets he had learned to use as well. He picked up the briefcase and opened the door.

The dark-haired man wasn't who he was expecting. "Where's Leon?"

"Car trouble. And the schedule has changed. My name is Andrew. Shall we go?"

Duff lofted the briefcase into the car first. "We're still going to Encino?"

"Yes, sir." The driver closed the door behind him.

The drive up and over the hills was never long at the early hour. It was the race to the airport where the time could get away from them. Duff tapped on the laptop as they took the off-ramp at the bottom of the hill and turned onto Ventura Boulevard. The Encino diamond center was one of the closest guarded secrets in the jewel business, mainly because the usual diamonds passing through Encino were uncut and of investment size and grade. Encino was a collecting location, filtering in from many places other than Africa. Duff knew he would pick up two or four bags the size of his fists. Even uncut, they could buy almost any large mansion in the greater metropolitan area. His return from Antwerp would be of a much lesser value.

As he put the laptop into its lock-down pocket, Duff looked out the window as they were pulling into the parking structure. He noticed a narrow light gap at the top of the window. He could hear the truck team leader explain that truly bulletproof windows are much thicker and can't be rolled down. This glass wasn't anything other than tinted.

Duff stepped out of the car with his briefcase. "I'll be right back."

As he checked the four bags, he hefted the weight of each. He looked at the man dressed in all black, even down to his yarmulke. "They're heavier than usual, Simon."

The man smiled softly. "There are many orders. These will have to be cut, matched, and set before next high holy days."

Duff raised an eyebrow. "Shopping days are holy now?"

The man shrugged with pursed lips. "Nu. What are we going to do? We're only agents of the market."

Duff chuckled as he placed the four bags in his briefcase. He snapped it shut and made a show of spinning the locks. "The car was early. Can I use your bathroom?"

"Sure." The man pointed. "It's in the same corner it was last time. Why move it?"

Duff jerked his head. "As long as it flushes." He stepped to the door and closed it behind him.

As he sat on the toilet, he grunted and strained as he quietly opened the briefcase. Slipping off his jacket, he placed the four bags in pockets between the two shields at his lumbar. He flushed and stood. Slipping his jacket back on, he placed the briefcase on the counter and made a production of washing his hands.

He opened the door, turned off the light, and then nodded at the man as he came out of the bathroom. "I wouldn't go in there for a while. But thanks." He waved his hand before his nose. The man smiled and shrugged. Bodily functions were a natural thing.

The driver, Andrew, was waiting by the door. Duff slid in, holding the briefcase with its precious cargo.

His fingers drummed as they retraced their path back toward the freeway. Finally, at the turn to pass through the residential neighborhood, the car pulled to the curb.

"Why are we stopping?"

Andrew got out as the rear passenger side door opened. A tall man with long dark hair and a beard leaned in with a silenced gun drawn. The deep, jagged scar on his right cheek pulled the bottom of his eye out of shape and made it look like he was crying. The man smiled and growled. "You should have stayed dead in Pittsburgh." The gun kicked twice in his hand. "And one for good measure." He shot at Duff's head, already down near the floor.

The man leaned in farther and smiled. "I'll take that, my old friend. You won't need it where you're going." He pulled the briefcase from under Duff's arm. He hefted the weight and smiled broader.

The door clicked shut in the early morning neighborhood. The small, dark Porsche started and drove off. Just another dark Porsche in a city awash in a sea of Porsches.

Duff's phone lay on the floor of the car. The screen lit up. The text was from Bean.

"Where are you? Leon is here with the limo."

32

———

HELPLESS

Bean stared at the door. She hated the door. Hate was not a strong enough word for what she felt. The light knock came again.

She jumped at the vibration in her pocket.

Reflexively, she pulled the phone from her pocket and looked at the caller ID. Kaminski.

"Hello?"

The voice never changed. It was always cheerful, upbeat, and happy to talk... except now. Bean could sense the strain.

"Bean? It's Izzy Kaminski. I need you to open the door, please."

"Why?"

Leon had left her alone several hours before when they couldn't find Duff. He had gotten a call and just said he had to leave. She hated being treated like a child as much as she hated being a child. Except now—she wasn't. But the treatment wasn't matching up with the permit in her pocket.

Kaminski drew in a long breath. She couldn't even picture

him by the pool. In fact, it didn't even sound like the man she knew.

"Please."

Bean stared at the small peephole on the door. She didn't even want to look through it. She wanted Duff. She wanted to be on the back of the motorcycle with the wind on her face and tugging at her hair. She wanted everything about today to be a ghastly nightmare. She wanted to wake up and there to be breakfast, and a swimming pool, and two palm trees, and a desert with mountains in the distance...

"Please?"

Bean sighed. "How do I even know you are you?"

"What does it say on your phone."

"Easily faked."

"How about I know your real name?"

"Not good enough."

"How can I prove it then?"

She thought and then smiled. "Name me one thing I dislike and love."

He chuckled. It was a great riddle, but the answer was from their first meeting. "You hate the prick but love the heart. Cactus. And I wish you were here enjoying it now. But that's not what is happening. Please open the door so that I can explain."

She turned the knob and stepped back. A million bad things did not come boiling through the door. Nobody kicked the door open. The door was only a crack open.

She watched the crack. She wanted a magic shield or a hefty leather jacket—anything to protect her against the unknown on the other side of the gap.

Gently, the crack grew.

A woman's face, the color of creamed coffee, tilted as she

tried to see behind the door. The beaded braids flowed along her shoulder and then fell in a waterfall of tiny clicks that could pass for the sound of tiny fairy bells. She pushed more on the door. A young woman stood in the room with a phone to her ear.

Bean could hear the woman's voice on the front porch and in the background of Kaminski's office through the phone. "I see her."

Kaminski's voice resumed its usual tone. "Bean, this is Elizabeth, but she uses her middle name, Tara. She is Leon's daughter. She will take you to the hospital in a while. Duff is alive but in terrible shape. I'm sorry, I keep forgetting you're not a child. He's in critical condition. Someone tried to kill him. So right now, he's in surgery. Is Ingrid there?"

Bean looked around for the van in the backyard. The backyard in front of the garage was empty. "No. I think she might have gone shopping early this morning. We're out of a few things." Stunned, Bean hadn't thought to wake her up when Leon left.

"Can you let Tara in? I want her with you. Meanwhile, I'll try to contact Ingrid and tell her what's going on. Is that okay?"

Bean realized she had done nothing since being woken at four-thirty by Leon. She thumbed off the phone and waved at the woman. "Excuse me. I have to pee."

The woman nodded and stepped in. Her phone was still to her ear. "Yes, sir. Fast appraisal? She's in shock."

She listened as she quietly closed the door.

"Yes, sir. We'll wait here until I hear from Dad." She snorted. "I've been cooking for my father for twenty years. I think I can cook for a young girl. We'll keep you posted." She thumbed off her phone and stuffed it in her back pocket as she wandered into the kitchen.

Bean found her staring at the lack of food in the refrigerator.

Bean moved toward the coffeemaker. "Eggs in the door. Cheese in the cheese drawer."

Tara slowly eased the door closed as she watched the automaton make coffee. "Bread?"

Bean's hand pointed at the tin box on the counter.

Tara placed the eggs and cheese on the island next to the stove. She walked around and looked at the two rounds of fry bread crammed in the breadbox. She frowned and wondered if they ate bread. She thought about her father and wished he had eaten less bread. She pulled out the flat bread and turned them over in the air, looking for mold or worse, from being exposed to air or worse. They disappeared from her hand.

Her head turned, following the two frisbees of bread.

"It's called naan. It's Indian." She drew a long knife from a slot on the island and laid the naan on the wood board. Then, faster than a pizza chef, Bean separated the disks into wedges. She threw the wedges onto a tray and shoved it all back into an appliance on the counter.

She then grabbed two plates out of the overhead cabinet with one hand while pulling forks from a drawer with her other. She turned and set them on the counter. Bending, she took a frying pan out of the oven. Opening a drawer, she pulled out a can and sprayed the pan. Dropping the can back into the drawer, she hip-checked it closed.

Bean looked up. "Are you eating?"

Tara froze.

Bean waved the large French chef's knife in the air in a metronome move. "Yes, no? It's a simple question. The sooner we get this shit done, the faster you take me to the hospital. Personally, I don't give a rat's ass if you eat or not. But I know you have marching orders, and if I don't eat, you don't take. So. Are you eating?" The metronome kept ticking.

Bean grabbed two eggs and held them in her hand. The knife flashed, and the two shells cracked. She emptied the contents into the pan and looked back up.

"Obviously, you're stuck at hello. So I'll back up. Around here, we speak a basic form of language called English. Or, if that's too complicated, *Ninazungumza Kiswahili.* But if Swahili isn't your speed, maybe French."

The deep black eyes were ticking with the movement of the knife. "Yes."

Bean grabbed another two eggs. "Fuck you. I don't speak French. So it's Swahili or English." The knife chopped into her palm, and she turned out the two new eggs into the pan. Grabbing a fork, she stirred the eggs in the pan. She turned down the heat and grabbed the block of cheese. Four chops and four slices of cheese lay on the board. She grabbed the slices and put them on the solidifying eggs.

Turning, she opened the refrigerator. She pulled out a drawer and looked at the limp green cilantro. Shrugging, she threw it on the board and chopped. Scraping the fine pieces up, she spread the green across the melting cheese. She turned off the stove and picked up the pan.

Bean looked at the woman. "What do you do?" She washed the omelet around in the pan and flipped it to close in half. She noted the dark eyes got larger. She flipped the omelet one more time in the air, and it landed on the cutting board. Pan on the stove, the knife flashed in the air, and there were two halves of omelet on the board. Bean served them onto the plates with the large knife.

Bean hip-checked the silverware drawer on her way to the dining table. "Silverware. I only need a fork, so don't get fancy."

She dropped the plates and turned back to the kitchen. "Coffee. Yes or no?"

"Yes."

"See if there is any milk left in the refrigerator. Sweetener is on the table."

Bean grabbed the coffee carafe and two mugs.

After the second bite, Bean leaned back and watched the woman over the edge of her mug. "You didn't say what you do."

Tara dabbed at her lips as she cleared her mouth. "I'm a doctor. Well, almost. I'm a third-year medical student."

Bean put down her mug and hacked another chuck of the omelet. Then, getting up, she rushed to the countertop oven. Grabbing a plate and a mitt, she poured the naan onto the plate, set the plate on the table, and took a piece. She forked the chunk of omelet into the naan and took a bite.

"Perfect." She looked at Tara. "So why is your dad at the hospital and not you?"

The dark eyes narrowed to black lines. "How much do you know about my father?"

Bean took another piece of nan and pushed the plate toward Tara. "He drives. My guess is the limo is bulletproof, and so his skills go far beyond just driving. Does he carry a gun?"

The black eyes opened and looked around the table.

Bean shrugged. "So I guess I know more about the man I've never met than you know about your own father."

The woman who thought she was in control, only to find she wasn't, timidly took a piece of the bread. She took a small bite. Her eyes opened wide. "What is this?"

Bean widened her eyes and rolled them. "I told you. It's naan. It's from India. You are tasting six herbs and spices, giving it depth, heat, and heart. What did you grow up on, Wonder Bread?"

The low hum of the automatic gate opener sounded through the east wall. Bean forked the last two bites into her mouth and picked up her plate. "Ingrid's home. I'll be right back." She dropped the plate in the sink and ran a splash of water.

Opening the sliding glass door, she walked out into the back.

Tara placed her plate in the sink next to Bean's and ran the water while watching the two women talk.

———

BEAN SAT on the plastic chair, toying with her phone. The book had once been engaging. She looked down the hall, distracted. The tall black man in the black suit was talking to a nurse. She disappeared and then came back with a large plastic garbage bag. Even from a distance, Bean could see it wasn't light. He turned toward Bean. The bag hung from his fist. He looked at the elevators. Bean stood and met him at the elevator. They didn't say a word.

The doors closed, and Leon pushed the lower-level button. His voice was a deep rumble of air. "Don't say a word."

The door opened, and they turned down the long hallway. At the end, Leon opened the door. The small parking garage had only three cars in the dozen slots. He opened the back door of the vehicle. Bean's face told him everything. He closed the door and opened the front passenger door, and she climbed in.

He walked around, opened the trunk, and dropped the bag in with a dull thud. Opening the driver's door, he slid in to find Bean trying to figure out the complex seatbelt. He leaned over and arranged the five-point racing restraint. "Hit here, and it all comes apart."

Bean slapped the center, and the straps fell away. She quickly reassembled the system and smiled, tightening the straps to her frame. She turned as Leon started the car. "Who's watching Duff?"

He nosed the heavy car out of the garage. "The doctors, nurses, and my two guys dressed as nurses monitoring machines that monitor the access. He's in excellent hands."

They drove down the large boulevard. Bean's eyes were as active as Leon's. "Do you want to tell me why you wanted his clothes? You know they're all cut to ribbons, don't you? The paramedics just can't leave anything nice."

Bean snorted. "My guess is they might have cut the sleeves of his jacket. But they ended with pulling it off him, anyway. Where did they shoot him?"

He glanced over. "In the head."

Bean rocked her head and shoulders. "Nowhere else?"

"The paramedics said head."

Bean watched the neighborhood as they pulled up. "Back up the drive."

He looked at her.

"Back up to the gate. Ingrid will probably open the gate. Then back up to her van."

He turned the car around and started backing up. The gate opened.

Bean smiled. "Let me ask you something."

"Go ahead."

"How much training do you have for the pistol in your armpit?"

"A lot."

"And the one down the back of your pants?"

He looked at her as he put the car in park. "Even more."

She hit the center and released her belts. "Let's just say you're trained enough to shoot people. How many shots?"

He drew in a loud breath and slowly let it out as he watched down the driveway. His head ground around. "Three. Two to the body mass and one to the head."

Bean nodded as she opened the door. "Come on. I'll show you where the other two are."

She pulled the bloody jacket out of the bag and draped it over the back trunk of the Indian. Leon was partially right. The paramedics had cut as far as they could up the sleeves. Their industrial cut-anything scissors had made it just past the elbow. The body armor was composite to go through TSA screening but resist any sort of weapon. Including paramedic scissors.

Bean pointed to the bullet in the sleeve. And then, lifting the sleeve, she found the other in the torso.

The growl was a low rumble. "Both would have been heart shots. Small hole. It looks like it's only a seven-point six millimeters. Russian Tokarev." Leon felt the jacket. "Protects the whole back, down to the kidneys." He looked at the inside. "Well made."

He folded the jacket and stuffed it back into the trash bag. "What now?"

Bean opened the trunk of the Indian and stuffed the jacket in. Then, closing the lid, she turned. "I'll clean it tonight or tomorrow."

Leon nodded. "But for now... we wait."

33

WAIT HELL

Tara met them at Leon's favorite burger joint. The Pug was a left-over product of the early sixties. The shape of the round building was a squat brown jug. The photos lining the wall showed it being a popular drive-through liquor store called *The Jug*. The owner had started her own collection of photos—pug dogs dressed as famous characters in movies. But, because of her and her wife's allergies, they only loved pugs from afar. So they handed out dog treats in small bags for Halloween as people drove up with their pugs dressed up and behind closed windows. What started as a joke had grown into an Internet *thing*.

The far-flung landscape of the greater Los Angeles and Orange counties still supported bits and pieces of the old architectural style. A hamburger here, a giant doughnut there, railcar diners, and even a brown jug miniature of a famous brown derby.

Tara rolled her eyes as she sat. She had heard the stories all her life. Each edifice that got torn down or burned up was another stake in her father's heart. "Jeez, dad. Give it a rest already."

Leon's eyelids fluttered closed from the grief he suffered at the loving hands of his daughter. Then, finally, his eyes opened to the image he held hidden in his desk. The photo he had taken of her mother the day he proposed, and she told him he was going to be a father. The one was a clone of the other in the photo. Now almost two decades gone by.

His growl was more noise than bite. "Just because it isn't your history doesn't make it any less important."

She opened her mouth to set him straight, and his hand shot up, stopping her.

"Tell us what the hospital said, or I'm going down there dangling a doctor over a ledge."

Tara blinked three times as Bean smiled and gently slugged the big guy in the arm. He looked at her and jerked his hands into a *what* position. Bean snorted and grabbed one of his hands with hers, interlacing the fingers. She turned to Tara.

Tara looked at the younger than hers, slender white fingers, interlaced like boyfriend-girlfriend, with her father's deep walnut sausages. She blinked. "Um...?"

Bean did her best imitation of Leon's growl. "Hospital."

Tara looked up. Blinked. "Mr. Akens. The bullet entered just above the lower cranial crest. It pierced the skull above the medulla and at an oblique angle. It rode the inside of the skull and shattered the left occipital orbit and the temporomandibular joint. He's being kept in a halo state as they watch for swelling. In a few days, they'll go in along the jawline and in front of the ear to repair the orbit and temporomandibular joint. After that, they'll keep him in an induced coma for at least two weeks. If everything goes well, you can probably see him in a few weeks through a window. Then, because of the open-top brain surgery, they will keep him in an isolation bubble for about a month."

Leon's one eye narrowed. "Doctor, your bedside manner hasn't improved."

Bean squeezed his hand as hard as she could. It didn't seem to affect him, but he stopped and looked questioningly at her.

Bean growled at him. "She did fine." She turned back to the medical student while she pointed at her head. "So the bullet went in here, rode around, and came out by the eye and... jaw?"

Tara bobbed her head once. "Yes."

"The rest is because of some kind of damage to the brain and stuff...?"

"Yes." Tara looked at her father. "She's quicker at this than you were." She turned back to Bean. "He helped me study. We had the body parts on cards, with photos on the other side pinned up all over the house. He was still getting the hang of anatomy when I was finishing my second year."

Bean rode her head back and forth with her lips curled. "I had a stack five inches thick. I drilled every other hour unless Duff was home. When he was home, it was playtime. I took the test a couple of months ago along with my foreign language test."

"What language?"

"Swahili with a minor in French."

The woman's head tilted forward, and her eyes grew large. "Why Swahili? I mean, you told me that on the first day. But I thought you were just messing with me."

"Why? Because you're Black?" Bean snorted. "You can ask the same about French. Where can you practice around here? Everyone speaks Spanish... Well, kind of."

Bean rose onto her left hip and pulled out a thin wallet.

Reaching in, she pulled out a card. She laid it in front of Leon. It was her driver's permit.

"We have two or three weeks. I need to pass my driving test for a car, a motorcycle, and a large truck before Duff wakes up."

Leon pointed at the name on the card. "I thought you two weren't related."

Bean narrowed her eyes. "Is that a problem?"

"Maybe..."

Bean reached into her left back pocket and pulled out her phone. She scrolled through the nine names in the directory so he could see. Her thumb hit the fourth. The file filled the screen. She hovered her thumb over the green dial button. The contact name said *Izzy Kaminski*. The name inferred more of a personal relationship. She looked hard at Leon.

He closed his eyes and thought. "You're only seventeen, and you're already worse than her."

Bean put the phone away. "Don't worry. I'll pay you."

He side-eyed her. "The car is no problem. I'll have to make arrangements for the other two."

"I said I would pay you. Whatever it costs, I've got it covered."

Leon looked at his daughter. "I want updates at least twice a day. Even just to tell me he pooped or his blood pressure was up or down. *Capisce?*"

She nodded.

Leon stood and looked at Bean. "Come on. Let's go for a drive. I need the distraction, and I don't want you calling the boss."

34

EATING ASPHALT

The falcon floated upward above the heat of the asphalt. On any game day, the Dodger fans fill the square mile of the parking lot. When they aren't here, the openness never goes to waste. The Los Angeles police officers hold unsanctioned races and practice high-speed chase maneuvers. Fathers in the know bring their children to the one place they can't damage the family car. The aging gray of the asphalt still produces a mass of rising hot air the birds came to play in.

The blackout wrap-around dark glasses only reflected the medium-sized motorcycle turning figure eights, scribing smaller and smaller circles and then weaving down a long series of slalom cones to race back through the marked zigzag of turns and chicanes to the large yellow flag. And start it all over again.

The instructor had given up yelling. It was now all on the rider to run the drill repeatedly until the pass was flawless and under five minutes. The reward sat waiting near the yellow flag. The black and white paint on the squat Harley had been scraped, dented, rubbed, and thrown up on. But those officers who trained on the motorcycle, older than most of them, bought and wore the black T-shirt with a white meatball and the black number sixty-five, with pride—until the shirts crumbled from their bodies in gritty sand. And then they bought more.

The man with the silver flattop haircut snapped the stopwatch.

Leon didn't twitch. "Time?"

"Four forty-one."

Leon understood the man the day they had met decades before. "When are you going to tell her?"

The man watched every lean, toe touch, shoulder drop, and throttle twist. Nothing passed his watch. "Is it true about her and your car?"

Leon's head rolled over as his fence of pearls spread across his face. "Which part? How she parallel parked on the first shot or J-hooked between the cones on the third try?"

The steel mirrored aviators rolled over and mirrored the blackouts. "How fast?"

"About thirty on that third pass. But she said she was hungry. It must have been low blood sugar. This morning, she snapped the turn flawlessly at over forty. She also drift-turned the beast into the parallel slot on the first shot. If I didn't know the truth about their relationship, I seriously would think there was Duff's driver's blood in her."

"How many days of training?"

Leon stood and watched the motorcycle snap off turns on the blocks of zigzags. He could tell she was forcing the bike down. It's called muscling through. And it would wear out a rider. He looked back as he started walking toward the track. "You mean hours? About eight total. I want to put her on a skid plate and see what she can do." He held up his hands as Bean rode up to him.

The older training officer watched the man explain how one pushes the handlebar to make the motorcycle turn sharper. It was counterintuitive to move into the lean, but it was exactly what the dynamics of leaning were all about. He had tried to get Leon to stay with the police department and become an instructor, but then he had a kid, and soon after, his wife died... He needed a solid job without bullets. But he watched how he communicated with the girl. He was a natural. But then, she had only spent a few hours to be where most officers were after weeks.

She hit the start, and he clicked the stem on the watch. Leon didn't even look back. His saunter said it all. He had told her; she would do it. He grabbed the bottle of water and, still ignoring the motorcycle behind him, drank deeply.

Leon sighed heavily. Turning, he straightened the director's chair and sat. He heard the click of the watch. The man stood.

Putting his fists on the small of his back, he bent back, cracking something. He turned and looked at Leon. "Eight hours, huh?" He glanced at his watch. He knew they would finish here in less than six. "You're getting slow, kid."

He waved at the motorcycle, turning the circles. He pointed at his baby. Sixty-five. The nineteen sixty-five panhead had been his personal motor. He bought it when they retired it with seventy-thousand miles on the meter. After a complete rebuild, it got a racing meatball and number painted on the tank. It was his joke about winning bets with street racers in the middle of the night. The racers never thought a cop would rebuild the engine to produce twice the horsepower and then drive it to work. He figured taking a hundred dollars and beating the racer in front of their friends was better than writing a useless ticket.

Leon watched his old friend explain the switch of the left and right foot controls. The lowered center of gravity was something a rider had to feel. She started the motorcycle as the man scribed a large circle with his hand. She slipped the clutch and eased out into the parking lot. Several cops leaned against their cars while they sipped coffee and watched the training. To them, it was just another cop.

Leon rolled up and pulled the phone out of his sweatpants. He looked at the screen. "Leon."

"Sir, I'm trying to deliver a truck and trailer. But the GPS is trying to take me up to Dodger stadium. Is your business near there?"

"Come on up. You're doing fine. Park it behind the blue shade canopy next to the motorcycle training. But, please, just don't hit the motorcyclist. The studio hasn't insured her yet."

"Got it. Which studio?"

Leon rolled his eyes. Los Angeles. "If I tell you, I will have to kill you, your family, and your third-grade teacher. Then my daughter would get your dog and dress it up for her dolly tea parties."

The connection snipped off as the truck appeared at the bottom of the large parking lot.

He slipped the phone into his pocket and then pulled it right back out. The text said no change. It was his daughter. He poked a thumb up and a heart for her. He slipped the phone into his pocket as his friend sat.

The man drained half of the bottle of water. "Now that is scary."

Leon smirked as he looked over. "Did she let you get your whole lesson out?"

"No." He snorted. "I tried to explain how the Harley foot controls differed from the Moto Guzzi, and she looked at me and said they were the same as the Indian. The Guzzi was like a Vespa racer, and the Harley was like an Indian." He shoved his hands out, palm up. "Who's raising this kid? Wolves?"

Leon snorted long and hard as the large prehistoric-looking Marmon truck parked behind them. "The neighborhood nerd races the Vespa, and her uncle rides the Indian Chief."

The two stood and looked at the truck. "What size?"

"Sixteen hundred to start. Three thousand horse with twin boosters now. Bulletproof from the rubber to the lid. Top speed of one-forty dragging sixty ton."

"No. I mean the Indian."

Leon smiled. "Oh. Not quite as big, but just as fast."

The stats of the truck suddenly hit the man. He looked back at the unusual truck. He recognized the palm-sized Department of Energy sticker with a shadow radiation hazard symbol in the center. His middle finger pulled his dark glasses down on his nose as he turned his head toward his friend.

Leon didn't look. He just nodded his head. "Tomorrow, she gets to learn how to drive eighteen wheels and twenty gears."

The driver walked around the truck's nose and looked at the two men. Leon held out his hand for the clipboard. He growled as he signed. "Don't look around, forget anything you saw, and pick this up on Friday."

The man handed him the two sets of keys. "They'll deliver the cab-over tonight."

"They can pick it up next Wednesday." He handed the clipboard back. There would be no paperwork. He had the keys, and they wouldn't be breaking any laws.

The man walked over to get into a white car. The car turned and was a dot in seconds.

Leon turned at the sound of the stopwatch.

He looked over the shoulder of his friend and former trainer. The stopwatch had stopped at four minutes, fourteen seconds. Again, Leon felt the side glance. "And your personal best was…?"

The growl was deep and personal. "Four twenty-six." He turned his head and looked at Leon squarely. "Can I come watch tomorrow?"

Leon snorted. "Hell, cater the training from Maggie May's, and I'll let you strap into the cab all week. Heck, bring the wife."

The man went back to watching Bean throw the quarter-ton of motorcycle around. "She threw a litter last month. But I can bring the babysitter as well. They would love to get out."

Leon scratched his chest through the hole in the middle of the white meatball and the five. "Yeah, the Bean might enjoy meeting a dog as big as her."

35

CHECKING IN

The large truck slowed and nosed into the parking area and back out. Blocking the street, the truck lined up the extended trailer at the ambulance bay. Two ambulances stood in the six bays. The trailer slowly approached the building.

One of the ambulance drivers realized the trailer was too tall for the bay and ran out to stop the truck. As he ran out from under the overhang, the end of the trailer stopped a foot from the building—the air in the brake lines released with a loud percussion and hissing.

The security guard, more waddling than running, approached the truck. The door swung open. The driver in leather pants and a black T-shirt backed out of the cab. The sweat down the spine only darkened the black T-shirt. Her long blondish braid swung out and down her back as she hopped the three steps to the concrete.

"Excuse me. Excuse me... but you can't park there. It's emergency vehicles only." The man was out of breath. "Y'all have to move your truck."

Bean turned around. The blackout wraparound glasses only

reflected the panting guard. In her boots, she stood inches taller than the man. He only had her in weight. She watched as he tried to pull up his belt, holding nothing more dangerous than a radio. The sweat-stained white uniform shirt was half out of his pants. She felt sorry for him, but he had chosen his job.

She leaned in and crooked her finger at him. Then, she turned and pointed at the Department of Energy decal. "Do you know what that means?"

He glanced down at the top and arms of her leather jumpsuit, wound up and tied around her waist. The large white circle with the number sixty-five was a hill-valley-hill as it spread across her unrestrained breasts.

She pulled her phone out of her back pocket and held it threateningly. "Well? Do you?"

The man slowly shook his head as his shoulders lost some of their bluster.

"It means if you don't back off and go back to your doughnuts. You will force me to call my boss. He will then have to call the hospital director to tell them the unit leaking the radiation will continue to spew its deadly contents until we can come back on your day off or after they fire you." She cocked her left hip with the thumb hovering over her phone. "What's it going to be, big guy?"

The man took one glance at the two men walking around the nose of the large, unusual truck. Both were wearing the same sixty-five meatball T-shirt. He didn't know who they were or what the sixty-five meant, but he knew he didn't want to know. Especially the larger one. Nobody was smiling. He waved his open hand at the emergency doors and scurried away as best he could.

The two paramedics stood just under the canopy. Their clapping was silent. There was no need to belittle the guard any more than he had been. The one pointed at the top of the trailer. "You scared the crap out of me. I thought for sure you would hit the building."

Bean smiled and patted him on the shoulder once as she walked past. "I've been driving way too long to have that happen."

Jim smiled at the young man as he walked past. "It's her first day driving a truck."

As the man's jaw dropped open, Leon turned him and pointed at what could be a small light on the top corner. "Proximity sensors. But, yeah, it's her first day driving anything with a stick."

The three walked into the emergency department, smiling and chuckling. Two motorcycle cops stood at the nurses' station. One tapped the other and pointed toward the door and the three.

The second turned and leaned his arm back on the high counter. "Wow. The legend, the myth, and a mystery. Great to see you, Jim, Leon, and whomever you are."

Leon raised his dark glasses and smiled. "Son of a gun. If it ain't Gerald Fitzpatrick and Patrick Fitzgerald. I thought you two were working Hollywood Division."

Bean scanned the two nameplates. Owens and Williams. Obviously, there was an old running joke in there somewhere. She stepped forward and extended her hand. "Flash Frijole. But you can call me Speed."

Williams took the bait and shook tepidly. He wasn't sure if he was being punked or just getting his chain jerked. "Nice shirt. Who's is it?"

Jim snorted. "Hers, asshole. She earned it. What was your fastest time on Sixty-five?"

The officer stood straight. Everyone knew their time. "Five forty-eight." He looked at his partner.

"Six eleven."

Leon pointed at Bean. "Four oh one. Jim won't let her take another run. But her first run on Sixty-five broke his record."

Jim's hand brushed over his silver flat-top. "She's younger than I was." Of course, they weren't about to explain her few hours of riding a motorcycle. Nobody would believe it, anyway.

Leon chuffed and rolled his eyes. "Come on, Speed. Let's leave the girls to trade horseshit stories. We have work to do."

As they approached the elevators, they could hear the whining voice. "You're shitting us. That can't be true." Leon snorted softly with a smirk. He guessed Jim had spilled the beans about it being her first day on a motorcycle. The burn of embarrassment runs deep in men vested in a macho world.

As the metal doors whispered shut, Leon snickered. "Speed. I like that. You know, by this time next week, you'll be a legend. And Jim will back it up—even if it dings his record. But he always shoots straight."

Bean bounced lightly on the balls of her feet. "So what's the part about the myth?"

He looked at her and weighed whether to open the door to a new path for her to spend time down. Very little time. "Weapons. Shooting. Combat range."

She kept looking at the doors. "Handgun or long guns?"

He realized the girl had a lot of access to the Internet. It was how she had studied for her driver's license. She had perfect scores taking the three back-to-back in less than two hours.

"Both. But the myth is about time to run the circuit of Bang Town and the distance to score five in the ten-x."

She looked at him as the doors opened. "How far?"

"A mile."

Out of the side of his eye, he watched the evil smirk grow. *Shit!*

Leon tapped a knuckle on the window. Tara looked over. The only thing he or Bean could recognize were her eyes. The white Tyvek bunny suit covered her from feet to the air helmet. Even inside the helmet, she was wearing two layers of masks. She held up one finger.

If someone told them the person in the bed was a man from another state or country, they couldn't tell if it would be wrong. Nothing resembled the man they knew. The crown of latex guard ringed his head from just above his eyebrows. Hoses and tubes ran out of or into his nose. A large tube attached to a plastic access node at his mouth and taped not to move. Electronic monitors covered his chest. Wires were collected and ran over the side of the bed. Tara was watching the six monitors.

Tara stepped to the window and turned on the communication box on one side. Her voice was muffled but understandable.

"He's doing extremely well. His vitals are much better than we had hoped for. There was only the initial swelling the first three days, but that was expected. They reattached his skull two days ago, and now it's just a wait-and-see game."

Bean looked for a switch or something to press.

Tara's eyes twinkled. She understood. "It's voice-activated. It will clip the first word, but it works from the sound. Just talk."

"How did you get to work in there?

The eyes stared at Bean and then looked at her father. He nodded.

"Technically, I'm supposed to know more about this stuff than a nurse who works in these chambers day-in and day-out. But there is no training for doctors... so it was a matter of pulling strings and making it part of my education."

Bean looked at Leon. "Kaminski."

The voice was more mechanical than Tara's usual musical sound. "Kaminski."

Bean frowned. "But if there's no training... they just turn you loose in there? And when are they going to wake him up?"

Tara rolled her eyes. "And now you take all the mystery of the magic away." She turned. "Selina?"

The nurse stood from behind the machines. Only her eyes were above the field of monitors. She waved. Bean guessed there were even more monitors on the other side.

Tara turned back. "Mostly, Selina is watching all the brain functions. She has more monitors than I do on this side. If I take an extra two years of school, they will let me sit on that side. But only if I promise not to touch anything. As for waking him up... they think in a few days. Probably after they take the staples out of his head, it's usually very painful." She looked at the T-shirts. "Old Sixty-five. I guess the motorcycle training is going well?"

Leon rolled his eyes. "That was yesterday. Remember the truck that ran Schwarzenegger over in that robot movie?"

She rolled her eyes. "The one you made me watch seventeen times because you worked on it? Yeah."

"She just drove us over in it. Your uncle Jim is with us. She broke his speed record on Sixty-five."

They could see her laughing. "Girl, we need dinner some night." She looked at her father. "You need to teach her how to drive a car too, you know."

He barked a laugh and then slapped his hand over his mouth. "That was the first day." He bent each finger backward. "Car, motorcycle, and big trucks. She's almost an expert in each, and we're now on day five. Tomorrow we're taking a cab-over bobtail around downtown. She needs genuine experience with tough traffic. And then, maybe we'll stop by the DMV and see if we can't make some appointments for the car and motorcycle."

Bean rocked her head as she pursed her lips and raised one eyebrow at him. "Or… We could always load the motorcycle and car into the tailer…"

The laugh sounded more like scratchy feedback from a microphone. The blue glove pointed at Bean. "I like this girl more and more. Can we adopt her?"

Bean smiled and nodded at the patient. "That position's been filled."

Bean kept looking at her right hand as they rode the elevator down. Finally, she spread the fingers and turned the hand over and back.

Leon scowled. He knew he was getting sucked into something. His growl wasn't a happy bear. "What?"

Bean turned her hand back over. "What do you think? Nine-millimeter or fifty-caliber?" She leaned back and looked at his backside. "Which do you wear in *your* belt?"

36

WHAT HAVE YOU BEEN UP TO?

The bed was in a private room. Special screens across the windows filtered the light. They reduced the wall of monitors down to only one, an IV drip, and the oxygen canella in his nose. The woman patiently waited for him to finish swallowing. Finally, she placed two fingers in his right hand. His grip was better today but would cause no one to cry uncle.

He watched her eyes above her mask.

"You have deep souls for eyes."

She thought about the wording. It sounded like something her father would say. The speech slurred slightly but was an enormous improvement over six days before. After the coma, he only slipped from naps to deep sleep to naps. He was on day six before he made a sound. Day eight before anyone could figure out a single word.

Day nine, he had asked the doctor, who seemed to always be there, for a bean. She had patted his hand and smiled. "Soon. But right now, you're still in isolation."

Tara knew better than to talk much. The drill for post coma was to let the patient control the talking. Their pace would decide where they were on the path of recovery. Usually, the family was an excellent source to figure out what was normal and where they were in relationship to that. Bean had just shrugged and said he didn't talk much. What talking he did was observational. It was situational—no stories of an ill-gotten youth, no war stories, not even memories of growing up.

Her father had slept on the question and Bean's response overnight. He said he had never given it a thought, but it was true. It was as if the man didn't have a past. Nothing outside Bean and work. Their talk about sports was more about Duff asking Leon about what he thought. No opinions came from the backseat—just questions.

"You're drifting."

She looked at her hand. The spoon of pudding was almost in her lap. She looked up. "I guess I was. Sorry." She brought the spoon up near his mouth.

"Where?"

"Where, what?"

Duff swallowed and closed his eyes. She watched the thin bumps under the lids move back and forth, looking for the correct answer. His eyes opened.

"Where were you"—he swallowed again—"when you drifted off?"

She pushed the spoon up, and he opened his mouth. "I was thinking about my father."

Duff swallowed the pudding and then a couple of more times. "Nice man."

Duff's tone was flat. She wasn't sure if he was making a statement or asking a question. She wasn't sure if Duff knew who she was or not. Time would tell.

"Yes. Yes, he is." She held up another half spoonful of

pudding.

Duff looked at it and finally shook his head. "Sleep."

She put the small cup down on the low table. He had eaten almost half. It wasn't about food. It was about extra calories and interaction. The glucose mixture would sustain him, but the pudding was about remembering how to eat and why.

She watched him drift as his eyes closed.

She stood and gathered the napkin and pudding cup, then made her way to the trashcan that stood against the far wall. She toed the lid and dropped the trash in. Then, turning back, she saw him crooking his finger for her to come.

As she stepped to the side of the bed, his lips moved, but there was no sound. She bent over closer.

His whisper was soft but clear. There was no slurring. "They bugged the room. Tell your dad I need to see Bean."

She thought for a moment, then stood. Patting his hand, she nodded. "Yes, the chocolate is not the best tasting. But it is what the hospital gets."

———

THE SIXTH AND ninth holes were just outside the last ring. The third and first were close to the red.

"Well, at least you winged the guy." Leon jammed another clip in his pistol.

"It jumps." Bean pulled on the slide and drew the pistol up to level.

"You're the one who wanted to try the big-ass gun." The pistol barely twitched in his hand as fourteen rounds punched out the red dot on his target. Finally, he shifted and sent the last round through the tiny X in the center of Bean's target.

"Hey. No cheating." Her pace was more about trying to resight after each shot.

"If you're going to show Duff a target, show him one that shows you've been working on it."

Bean shot the last round and laid the pistol down. She peeled the thin leather glove off and flexed and closed her fist. The comment was quiet, and she hoped private. "Maybe next time, I'll take the smaller gun."

Leon leaned around the barrier. Placing a small pistol and cartridge on her bench, he hit the target recall button. "Start over."

She looked at the small gun. "What is this? The little girl's gun?"

Leon stared at her through the yellow wraparound glasses. "No, smartass. It's a Walther PPK. It's chambered to use a thirty-two-caliber round. Same as James Bond. It's light but accurate. The rounds are as common around the world as nine-millimeter. Unlike that fifty caliber you've been dancing around with."

Bean picked up her glove.

Leon held his hand over hers. "No. Try it without the glove. I gave you the glove for the cannon because it will beat you up and tear out the web. This is a martini, shaken not stirred, with two olives and will respect you in the morning."

Bean grouped all six rounds in the black, and one was half-and-half in the red. She hit the recall button.

Leon leaned against the bench. "You can study for knowledge tests on the Internet. Your driving is a gift I can't explain. But this...?" He tapped the target. "This is a good start."

She examined his face for bullshit.

"Okay. This is a lot better than most of the rookie cops after they get out of school. Have you ever had your eyes tested?"

"No."

"I'm going to bet on your eyesight being closer to fifteen-twenty. But where did you learn not to close your offside eye?"

Bean snorted. "There are a lot of videos on shooting on the Internet. They just don't warn you how much the big guns hurt."

Two other shooters down the range packed up and walked past. They nodded at Leon. One shook his hand. They held the door for two women coming into the range with their guns and ammo boxes. Leon had explained how busy the range under the San Diego Freeway was. Bean looked down the line. All nine of the lanes were full.

She looked over at Leon. The man was packing up the half-empty boxes. She frowned.

"Time to move."

Bean swept her bench into her small gun bag. Then, zipping it closed, she started for the door.

Leon followed. It tempted him to lecture her on the lack of care about the gun and bullets, but he was more assured by her response to the need to move.

The gun bags went into the trunk. The five-point seat belts clicked, and the car started—the dark vehicle nosed out of the parking lot. Leon watched the rearview mirror as he handed her the note the man had passed.

Bean silently read the note. They had found seven bugs at the house, three in Ingrid's apartment, and three in the hospital room. She tore the small scrap of paper into smaller pieces and thought about how the bulletproof windows didn't roll down. She stuffed the small wad into her mouth and took a long drink from her water bottle.

Leon looked over and smiled. He pulled off his yellow shooter's glasses and replaced them with his blackouts. The instructor was back to working as the driver.

At the hospital, she stopped him at the trunk. She pulled the last target out of her bag. "They knew where we were. Might as well let Duff know too."

Leon bounced his fist on her shoulder as he smiled. Then, draping his arm over her shoulders, they walked into the building. "If Duffus doesn't adopt you, I'm always up for a kick-ass daughter."

"You have a kick-ass daughter. And she's going to make a brilliant doctor as well."

His face glowed as they stopped in front of the elevator. "Okay. Then maybe a second daughter."

She hip-checked his thigh. "Don't get greedy. Settle for uncle."

They turned to watch the doors close. A hand stopped the doors, and a harried nurse slid in.

Leon bounced on the balls of his feet. "Uncle Leon. I like that."

Bean rolled her eyes as the nurse questioned the white girl and black man. "Nah, I like Uncle Myth better."

The doors opened on the fourth floor. The nurse continued to the next floor. Bean had already found out the fifth was oncology only. She didn't envy the nurse her job.

Tara eyed the target. She had a few of her own from growing up being babysat by other officers. "You can't take it in there like that." She held up her finger. "I'll be right back."

Bean watched her rush off and then looked at Leon. "I feel like one of those jokes they draw about kids being layered with winter clothes until they can't move. Then, the kid goes outside, and a single snowflake falls from the sky. Then the sun comes out and cremates the kid standing there on the sidewalk."

Leon could see her point. They had covered her from the booties to the gloves, the mask, and a hair covering. The only thing left of Bean was her eyes.

Tara came back with a large plastic bag for biohazardous garments or any other waste they needed to seal. There was a double fold-over tape seal. She folded over the outer edges of the target and inserted it into the bag. Folding the seal and pulling the tape shut, she handed it back to Bean. "Now you're good to go. Just remember, the nurse is in command. She'll tell you where to sit and when you must leave. She's going to hold you to the five minutes unless he fades sooner. When she says go, you get up and leave. No last sentiments, just leave."

Bean nodded. "Got it."

She stood in front of the outside door. When it opened, she stepped into the airlock. The outer door closed, and the air in the chamber refreshed. The inside door moved back. The nurse waved her hand at her and pointed to the chair beside the low bed.

Duff watched the new person enter. It wasn't until she was standing by the bed could he see her eyes. His smile was wonky. His voice sounded like he had dragged it down a long dirt road. "Frankenbean. Or is it the mummy?"

"Hey Duff. You look like shit."

"Don't let the pretty..." He closed his eyes and mouth and sucked oxygen through his nose cannula. "... face fool ya. I feel worse."

Bean felt a flutter in her chest and stomach. "I heard you've been grabbing the nurses in places you're not supposed to."

His face was blank. The joke had passed over his head or just fell flat. She didn't know what to do.

His finger rose from the blanket. "My clothes..."

She watched his eyes. The clarity was back. She kept up the lighter conversation tone. "Yeah. I got them. I'm going to have to try to sew the sleeves of your jacket back together. The medics tried to cut it off you, but I guess the leather was too much for them. But I got it all cleaned up and safe. There was lots of blood. I had to work hard cleaning the inside. But I couldn't do anything with the shirt—*that* they did cut off you. And I think the pants are history as well."

He waved his hand that it was no big deal. But she noticed his thumb was up. She got her confirmation. Leon must have been right. But how would Duff know if they bugged the room? And who were *they*?

Duff sucked more oxygen. "What have you been up to?"

She forgot he couldn't see her smile. She held up the target. "Punching paper and some other stuff. I've been hanging out with Leon."

Duff half pointed at the target. His thumb was up and then laid over. He crossed his one eye. "Who?"

They uncrossed, and the other crossed. She had never seen him do the trick, but she understood. "Just a friend."

The nurse frowned at the monitor in front of her. "Um... miss?"

Bean stepped a half step back. She looked at the nurse. "I know." Looking back at Duff, she waved her fingers. "Gotta go. But I'll come back as soon as they let me."

She backed out to the doorway. She needed to rub her eyes with her sleeve but didn't want Duff to see it. Then, turning, she stepped into the open door and wiped her face with her sleeve.

37

MARKING TIME

The group of fifteen holes bled past the red circle. There was no more room, as there was no more red. The buzzer sounded, and the target swept backward as the trolley rushed toward the shooter.

Bean found the new range on an obscure website. The range part had been an old bowling alley. The city had made the owners load more concrete around the building to guarantee no high-powered bullets left the building. The range had the usual distance and a small section of five alleys for rifles at fifty and hundred yards. The ads said they were for dialing in hunting rifles. Bean watched weapons that would make a deer drop more from fright than what the exploding bullets could do.

"How many rounds have you mashed through that Glock?"

She didn't even flinch. She figured he would find her soon enough. "I have thirty clips for the PPK, thirty for the Glock, and twenty for the Desert Eagle. I like the Walther, but it leaves a red ring. The Eagle still wanders. But most are inside the eight. I'm getting comfortable with the larger guns, but they make the

Walther feel like a toy." She looked back at the man in the dress shirt and slacks.

Leon furled his lips and looked at his watch. "It's time for lunch."

Without a word, she turned back to the bench and packed her bag. She saw the shadow of the man leaving the range. She dropped the earmuffs in, zipped the bag, and slung the strap over her shoulder.

She stepped out into the sunshine. Leon was standing in front of the rust and chipped paint of a twenty-year-old Ducati. The orange paint had almost aged to be more of the rust covering than what originally passed for shiny chrome. The custom-painted full-face helmet matched the bike.

"Yours?"

She stopped next to him. "Am I following you?"

He squinted down the street both ways. "Yeah. But in a few miles... keep up."

She coughed in her hand as she pulled up the jacket part of her leather riding suit. "The duke is good to one-thirty. Probably more."

He looked back up the street as he slipped his blackouts on. He bent over to tie his slip-on shoe. "Good. How is your canyon driving?"

She looked down into her bag, searching for something she didn't find. "I've been trolling for races. I'm up a few grand."

He looked back at the door to the gun club. "If we get split up, I'll meet you at two for chowder."

She smiled. He had introduced her to the clam chowder a month before. The county line restaurant had a large parking lot with no cover. But they also made a great chowder.

She was slow getting started, and he was a block away before she nosed to the driveway. The dark gray car with the two men rushed past and never saw her. She snorted. The beater motorcycle wasn't from their world, and they never saw it. She may as well be nothing but a wisp of smog. She pushed the switch forward, and the twin canyon racing headlights went out. She would be just more moving gray noise in their mirrors. She rolled out into the street a half-block back. She let the black jacked-up jeep be her foil with the big tires.

At the stoplight, Bean pulled up alongside the jeep. She snorted at the license plate on the car, following Leon. *This guy is a joker all year long.* She thumbed the phone connection button. "Call Leon."

The answering voice rumbled in her helmet. "Go."

"The two guys following you. The license plate is Juliet King Romeo three six five."

"Got it." The connection clicked closed as the light changed.

The wave surged forward, and Bean let the kid with the zits jockey his jeep back in front of her. The Sunday beach traffic was building. Soon they would break north and south for the freeway. Only the hearty souls would crawl their way through Topanga Canyon. The soccer moms in bloated SUVs could turn the curves through the mountain into a metal game of dodgeball with no winners.

She wasn't sure where Leon would go, but she knew all she had to do was follow the joker. Or get lost and meet up with Leon later.

She smiled. But first, she wanted to get a look at who they were.

As the light ahead turned yellow, Leon played the scofflaw and shot through on red, leaving the two cars between him and the followers waiting at the light. Bean pulled up next to the two men in the car. She clicked the Ducati into neutral and leaned against the car door as if she was a bicyclist resting. Both men looked over. They could feel the grin behind the mirrored face shield. They weren't happy. But their attention was on her, not on Leon.

Bean noted the little things. The tall, slender driver was wearing gloves. She had seen the padding before. It was the same lead powder in Duff's gloves. The passenger was highly distinctive, with the ragged scar down his cheek pulling the bottom of his eye open. The scruffy beard was more of a European look than a lazy Californian's *I don't care what I look like,* look. The long greasy dark hair had gone out of style when she was in diapers. The green tattoo on his neck she had seen on some shady sites deep in the dark side. Russian Mafia.

The passenger yelled at her but didn't roll down his window. It was a little too thick.

The light changed. She held up her middle finger and then stalled her take-off. She smiled as she knew they were now laughing at the doofus on the motorcycle. But she also knew what they looked like. And the driver, she had seen around the shooting range in the last few weeks. He had been shooting some serious targets with even more serious pistols—the kind she couldn't find on the internet.

As she saw them take the on-ramp heading north, she spotted Leon. The charcoal-colored car was all but invisible under the long underpass. She flashed her high beams twice before she also turned and headed up the on-ramp. He tapped the brakes twice. She would see him at two.

The dark gray car was being anything but discrete. She could tell where the men were by the traffic's reaction. The aggressive driving pissed off even the trucks. One blew his horn. She turned on some throttle and closed the gap.

She had taken and raced every canyon from the famous Topanga to Camarillo and back over Point Mugu and the naval missile base. Now it was time for some nasty fun, as only a vindictive teen could produce.

She rode the fast lane, passing cars on their left and keeping in the driver's largest blind spot. She watched to make sure a highway patrol hadn't gotten wind of an aggressive driver. She didn't want their day to end with a simple ticket. She wanted their Sunday to end.

The off-ramp she wanted was less than a mile. The car was in the middle lane. Her escape was clear of trucks or anybody who would impede the assholes. She wound on the throttle and dropped across the two lanes. She would suddenly be at their door.

The steel-toed boot didn't damage the bulletproof door, but it made a loud noise to startle the driver. His reaction took his foot off the gas, allowing her to cross in front and dive for the off-ramp. The professional driver was right behind her. A truck blew his horn along with the work van they cut off. Even on the weekend, the Ventura freeway was busy and fuses short for people who don't respect the rules of the road.

Bean blew the red light as he turned back under the freeway and headed toward the ocean fourteen miles away. But her destination was closer. As she reached her turn, she ensured the car saw where she was turning. Once they committed, there was only one destination. And to make it work, she needed to be there with several minutes to set it up.

To any highway patrol, she would look like just another road racer. But today was a race for her life. And the hundreds of bikers in the canyon would be her salvation.

She slid to a stop in front of the host of bikes parked around the liquor store turned snack bar and motorcycle hangout. The rocks making the building's foundation and expansive patios were laid over a hundred years before. The bikers who came to race or just hang out with others on a lazy weekend had been doing so since the nineteen-fifties. Bean and her prowess with the big Ducati had made friends and allies.

She kicked out the stand and parked the duke where nobody could miss it. The tip of the front tire hovered over the white line, marking the traffic area.

"Hey Barney, you can't park there."

She held up one finger in reply. The catcaller got laughed at by his buddies. Bean kept walking toward the group she hoped would help in the way she needed. The tall, skinny redhead rolled forward off the table he was sitting on. She had made friends with the crew after she beat their fastest rider. She took the hundred and bought them all drinks. It didn't hurt that she liked the women, teased the guys, and could outride them all, but never held it as a patch. She just fit in.

"Bean?" His strained voice was flat. Everything sounded like a statement hiding as a question. She figured the large burn mark along his throat and eating his right ear had something to do with it.

Bean pushed her shield up. "Carrot. I need some serious help. The guys coming after me are coming to seriously fuck me up. Most likely to kill me."

He smirked. "Did you shoot their dog? Because you never want to kill a badass's puppy."

"No. I think it's about my uncle. They shot him in the head a couple of months ago. He's still in the hospital. But now they're after me."

"Who are they?"

Her shoulder slumped. "I don't know. But I'm pretty sure they aren't churchgoing cops."

The man looked back at the group. The leathers they wore weren't for racing. The jean vests were jackets with their sleeves cut off. It was easier to sew patches onto jean jackets than leather. The nods were small but carried the weight of the group.

"What kind of help."

She pulled her helmet off. She wanted to meet this man face-to-face. What she was asking was beyond lending her a twenty or a few gallons of gas to get home. She stepped close and looked up. "The kind nobody wants to see. The kind nobody wants to hear about. If they don't make it back to their car, nobody is going to cry for them. But fair warning. The driver is wearing weighted gloves, and they both probably have weapons."

"Do we want to keep the weapons?"

She thought as she shook her head. "Sell them to an idiot. Cheap."

He chuckled. "We know those kinds of guys. What are they riding?"

"Suits and a gray car. The passenger has a large scar on his right cheek." She hooked a finger at the bottom of her eye and drew it down her cheek for a visual."

"Got it. Where are you going to be?"

She held the helmet over her head. "The bike will get them to stop. When you engage, I'm gone. Oh..." She stuck the helmet on the top of her head and reached for her wallet. She opened it and made a show of taking all the money out. She held it out to the man. "Here. If I owe you more, I'll be up next Sunday."

He thumbed through the thin stack of hundreds and fifties and smiled evilly. "I'll owe you a soda next week. What about the car?"

She paused with the helmet half down. She raised it so he could see her smile. "It's bulletproof. Seriously bulletproofed. You can't even roll down the windows. Do what you want." She pulled the helmet down and looked down the highway as a large dark car came around the curve. She pointed.

Carrot smiled and gave her a thumbs-up. She scurried up the steps and around the back of the store. She would wait and watch through the battered wood fence on the other side. As she looked back, the group was moving as one. It was like pointing a pack of sharks at a wounded surfer from Iowa.

What happened at the store... became a biker legend by the following weekend.

———

THEY SAT along the rock wall separating the highway from the rocky beach. Few people came to the county line between Ventura and Los Angeles for the beach. The sand was sparse among the rocks, and the wind wasn't comfortable. The surf was like a waltz performed to a polka beat. Interesting, but you couldn't find a rhythm to dance to. It was a perfect place to talk without worrying about being overheard. After their lunch on the deck, they had bought ice cream and crossed the highway. Bean relayed what had happened as they walked.

"That's it?"

Bean bit the tip from the orange and vanilla ice cream bar. "Um-hm."

"You kicked their door and then led them up into the hills. And there just happened to be a bunch of bikers who were bored and deadly? And you just happened to be friends with them? That easy?"

She squinted at the surf crashing on the distant point. The violence exploded dozens of feet into the air, only to become a rain of foam. And then do it all again. She bobbed her head. "As easy as sending them down a river in canoes where banjos are playing."

Leon snorted and pushed his tiny wood spoon into the cup of chocolate syrup and vanilla ice cream. "You're not old enough to know about that movie."

She bit off another small bite. "Old enough to know about watching old movies on the Internet." She turned toward him and frowned. "I'm still trying to figure out why they were after you. Or was it me all along?"

"I'm thinking the same."

She sucked the last of the ice cream off the stick. "While we're thinking, why were you late that morning?"

His eyes narrowed. "In all my years of driving. I've never gotten pulled over. But, that day, the officer was a jerk from the get-go. Said my license plate didn't fit the description of the car. Then there was a problem with the registration. He kept going back and forth to his car and radioing in. He even addressed me by my name. But it wasn't until just the other day that I remembered a couple of things that were important."

She looked at him. "What?"

"As I said, he kept walking back and forth to the car. That's the way it used to be before they got radios on their hips. He had the mic clipped to his shoulder, but his radio was off. He wasn't talking to his dispatch. He was talking to someone else. Like maybe on his phone instead."

Her left eye narrowed as she watched the traffic on the highway. "What else?"

"The officer never asked for my driver's license. Only the registration and insurance card. He already knew who I was."

"Did he write you a ticket?"

"Nope. Jus' suddenly, he had somewhere else to be. Gave me my papers back and let me go."

They both turned at the rumble and watched the foam cloud rain back to the rocks.

Bean probed her tongue at her teeth as she watched the dance at the point.

Leon frowned and looked out at the point. "What?"

"I was just wondering if any real cops have died in the last couple of months?"

38

WHO?

Ingrid poured the coffee into the insulated carafe. The day would be warm, so an early morning breakfast on the deck had sounded good. Bean pushed the second omelet onto the plate. Picking up the two plates, she headed for the sliding glass door. "So they let him have the walker with the wheels, and now they can't keep him out of the hall."

The toast popped up. Perfect. Ingrid would have preferred some bagels, but the small shop had run out early yesterday, so they were settling for sourdough with Kalamata olives. She smirked at how life could be rough sometimes. Just having food was good enough for her. The three months on the Silk Route still haunted her. What little food they had, they shared—until it ran out. Then they sacrificed the goats and camels for survival. She had been Bean's age. And it had burned a scar on her soul for life.

She stepped out on the deck and laid the plate of toast on the small table. She filled the two mugs with the coffee and sat. "How many miles a day do they think Duff is walking?"

Bean's fork animated the air as she finished chewing her

food. She took a sip of the coffee and paused. Frowning at the mug. "This isn't French roast."

Ingrid raised one eyebrow. "It is French roasted, but it's not Columbian. It's Tanzanian."

Bean sipped again. "Is there honey in here?"

"Nope. But they grow the beans at a lower altitude, and the earth isn't volcanic. Those two features give it a creamier or butter flavor. So even though the roaster cooks the beans a little hotter and faster, the flavor is mellower. What do you think?"

Bean took a deeper swallow. "I'm in. How did you find out about it?"

Ingrid smiled. "My father took us to Tanzania once when he had R&R. We stayed on a coffee plantation up out of Dar es Salaam. The capital of the country. I never forgot the difference between their coffee and the smell of the plantation. The wild animals wandering through the plants was entertaining as well."

She looked over at Bean. The young woman lounged back in her seat, watching her. "What?"

Bean softly waved her hand away from her mug. "Nothing. I was just... you sounded... I don't know. Like you missed it. Like it was a better time."

Ingrid furled her upper lip and looked down at her hands, softly picking at each other in her lap. "It was. Or at least while we were there, it was." She looked up at the morning. "People weren't trying to kill us."

She shook slightly and tossed her head. Looking back to Bean. "Well... how much is he walking?"

It took a moment, and then Bean found her place. "It's not so much how many miles, but that he goes and talks to all the other residents. There's one guy who has the checkerboard always set up. And the lady who plays scrabble with herself if he's not around. It's driving the nurses nuts. They never can figure out where he is. So when it's lunchtime, they go down the east wing to let him know and find him pushing someone in a wheelchair from the west wing. And then sits with them for company."

Ingrid's open face frowned as she blinked. "Duff? Our Duff? Talking? Did they check his ID at the door?"

Bean's eyes rolled large. "I know, right? But when I was there Friday, I had to track him down. It was lunch, and he had gathered five elderly women at his table. And I'm telling you, it was a full-on six-way hen party."

Ingrid forked the last bite of her omelet into her mouth and leaned back with the last half of the toast. "Who could have guessed. The way to get the man to talk was to shoot him in the head."

Bean crossed her feet on the railing as she leaned back. "I just hope he works it all out before he comes home. The quiet is nice."

The two women watched the empty blue sky—lost in their thoughts.

Ingrid stretched her legs out and crossed her feet. Her toes flexed over the edge of the railing. "Yeah. I miss him too."

————

THE GRUMBLING GROWL BURBLED in the tunnel. Bean pulled on the throttle, and the louder voice thundered off the stone walls. She loved coming this way just for the tunnel. It was the one accurate time she could hear and feel the brute strength of the bike.

They originally built the bike to race the giant road race on the Isle of Mann. The size of the engine placed it in the open class, so the owner had done everything to make it competitive. He just hadn't counted on a heart attack taking all his dreams away. The widow just wanted the racer gone.

Bean had found a mechanic to reassemble the bike, but the gray primer was another matter. Also, the three years waiting in storage had destroyed the chrome. Bean had sat with the partially assembled gathering for an hour. Then, figuring some fresh air would help, she went for a walk. The graffiti had given her the idea for the paint. A friend of Lena's was looking for a project for his art class.

The last blast of the racing pipes at the end of the tunnel sounded more like a gunshot. A very large gunshot. The rock and dirt wall lining the one side of the road gave way to what some would call forest. But what Bean thought was more like large bushes. But the large bushes and trees soaked up the sound of the motorcycle as Bean leaned into the curves.

Bean was almost dozing off as she let the flow of the motor-cycles coming and goings wash over her. The smell of grease and gas was its own kind of perfume. She understood why old racers still hang out around tracks long after they have stopped racing. She imagined it might be the same for horse racing as well. But she would rather take the smell of oil over the stench of horse poop any day.

The small packet dropped into her lap. Her crossed legs on the table didn't flinch. Carrot's boots were distinctive, with the steel slugs screwed into the sides of his heels.

Her hand felt the envelope before she opened her eyes.

She straightened, dropped her legs off the table, and sat up as her hand drew out several documents. She flipped through the passport from Romania. Sergey Milkvetch. The driver's license matched.

"Probably a bogus passport or name. My sister says milk vetch is a flower used in Chinese medicine. But if you're going to give a bad guy attachment to your government, give him a stupid name as a cover. They had tattoos from the Russian Mafia."

Bean nodded and pushed her blackouts up onto her head. "Are they still alive?"

The man shrugged, and his face stretched. Four of the others chuckled. "Maybe…? I heard there was a fire out that way last Sunday night."

She flipped through the driver's ID. No passport, just a commercial driver's license. Nikolai Petrovitch. She opened the folded lottery ticket.

"He didn't win." The group laughed.

Bean tapped the thin stack into order and stuffed them back into the envelope. She held it in the air.

Carrot shook his hand. "Keep it. You might need it down the road to figure out who wanted you so bad—and had a lot of money to spend. The car was interesting. The trunk was full of weapons." He looked down and then back up with a coy smile. "Hard to get weapons."

"Care to define hard to get?"

He licked his lips as he weighed who he thought she was, and now with new information…

"Hard to get, like, shoulder-launched stuff."

Her mind ticked through many movies and even more videos. "Flying targets or big heavy stuff on the ground?"

His eye narrowed. "Yes."

Bean waved him off. "I don't want any of it."

The man relaxed.

Bean held her hand back near her wallet. "So… are we good?"

Carrot leaned in, growling. "No." He held her stare. "Ginger, get her a soda."

Bean smiled and looked up at the bleached blonde. "Um… coffee. Two creams and one sugar."

The woman's face cringed. "One sugar?"

Bean laughed. The woman made two of her, with Carrot as a bonus. She knew they were a couple. "Just one. I'm watching my girlish figure. It keeps the creepers away until I'm legal."

They all laughed. But she felt Carrot's eyes. It gave them all something more to think about.

She reached out, her hand and thumb cocked up. He took it, and they gripped in a pact grip. He would keep her secrets and she theirs.

39

REMEMBER?

The halls were vast but lined with elderly in wheelchairs. Some were asleep. Others only thought they were. Only a few were wandering. The Asian man, without a left hand, was still pushing the pole with the bag of clear liquid and a tube running down to nowhere. A care aide had confided in Bean. The man had been pushing the same pole and bag of water for almost a year. But it was okay because he had pension insurance that would cover anything until he died.

Bean dipped her head into twelve west. No Duff. She walked back to the nurse's station. The heavier woman with the bad dye job and a beehive hairdo that almost covered the pure white roots chuckled when she saw Bean. "Sweetie, it's a good thing you be wearing them racing leathers. That boy be hell-bent this morning. He already done took six laps, and I think he is chatting up Julie in twenty-eight south." She pointed down another hall.

Bean stuck her head in the room. A woman in one bed was propped up and watched a soap opera in Spanish. "Are you Julie?"

The woman turned and looked at her. "No. No *sé*. Julia go garden with *Guapo* Duff."

Bean frowned. "Garden?"

The woman, fixated on the television and whatever was going on in the storyline, kept pointing her finger behind her. Or at the end of the hall. Bean looked down the aisle. There was a door with a window in the top half. Beyond were green plants.

Duff sat in a wheelchair with a woman with a bald head. He was holding her hand as they spoke softly. Even from a distance, Bean could tell the woman was crying. Duff's other hand drooped off the armrest. He pointed behind them. There was a table and bench in a flower-covered gazebo. Bean headed that way.

"Her husband passed away from cancer a week ago. She probably won't last the month."

Bean opened her eyes and sat up. Duff had rolled up to the concrete table.

He smiled. The hair around the scar was almost blending. "Have a good nap?"

Bean nodded. "What's a... whopper? Did I say that right?"

He laughed lightly. "Are you asking about a lie, a fib, or something Esmeralda said?"

"I guess Julie's roommate?"

He pushed his lower lip out as he nodded. "The Hispanic lady. The word is *Guapo*. It sounds like a W but starts with a G. It means good looking or stylish." He ran his hand up and down in the air at Bean's leather jumpsuit. "So around a racetrack, you would be *muy Guapa*. Very stylish."

She rocked her head and shoulders. "Want to take a walk?"

He reached into his pajama pocket and pulled a small plastic box out. Bean recognized the unit she had for checking the bugs in the house. "We're good. That's why I'm in this. I fell and broke the bug on my walker. Leon stopped by and had some information for me."

Bean unzipped the jumpsuit and reached in. She laid the ID papers in his hands. He squinted, and she jutted her chin at the documents.

He looked at the passport. "Shit. This is a fake passport. His real name is Arkady Andropovitch. He's a Russian mafia hitman who works for the shiniest dollar. He's the one who shot me. He works both sides and usually even more. How did you get this?"

Bean nodded her chin to keep looking.

He looked at the other driver's license. His hand dropped, and he leaned in. "Now we're in some serious territory here. Where did you get these?"

"I'd seen the driver around the shooting range the last couple of weeks. But last week, Leon met me at the range, and when he left, they followed him. So I followed them, and let's just say, I had them taken care of."

"Define taken care of." His forehead became a field of plowed rows. Deeply plowed rows. "Shooting range?"

She waved the air. "Just punching paper with Leon." She taped the two driver's licenses. "They won't be a problem anymore." She pointed at the papers. "Which is how I got those. Their weapons and bulletproof car... probably went south."

He stared at her. "I see now a lot has changed while I was on vacation."

"Does that mean you got your memory back?"

He nodded. "How much do you know about computers? Or maybe I should ask, how much has Danny taught you?"

She blushed.

He waved his hand and laughed. "Not about that. Computers."

"Some... well, probably a lot. Why?"

"Do you know what a microSD card is?"

"Sure. Danny carries most of his classes on them. Solid State Disk drives. They look like a Bruce Banner thumb drive. But plug it in, and you get the big guy."

"Okay, but we took a bunch..." Duff wiped his hand across in the air. "Forget it. You'll just have to search until you find it. Take all the metal plates out of my jacket. Hold each one with the casting stamp facing up. Put your thumb on the stamp and press down and try to slide it open. Only two will open. You'll need to copy them. Don't worry about cracking the code to read them. They can just be mirror copied. Make copies and hide some. Maybe give a set to Leon. He'll know what to do."

"What are they?"

"They're the reason these guys tried to kill me the first time. This time they just wanted the diamonds." He tapped his finger on the paperwork. Then, picking it up, he handed it all back. "Keep these safe too."

She studied him and thought about the walker. "How close are you to being able to get out of here?"

"According to the doctors, a few months. But if I got up and walked out now, I'm probably good for a slow walk to the end of the block. Why?"

She shrugged her right shoulder and looked back toward the building. "Nothing really. Kaminski hasn't called in a couple of weeks. So I was thinking of giving him a—"

His hand dropped on hers—cutting her off. He shook his head. He bit on his rolled lower lip as he looked at the flower bed and then out at the street. "Hold off on Kaminski. He's right in the middle of all this somehow." His eyes cleared. "On second thought." An evil grin swept across his face. "These months have been gruelingly hard on you and Ingrid. You two need to take a little relaxing trip. Let him know you're coming. Or at least, call the resort. It's hot, so they'll have room. Talk it over with Ingrid in the house. Don't lay it on thick, but how the waiting and all is grinding on you, and you need to get away. Have her come up with the idea about going to the resort for some spa time. And when you see him, explain how I was doing so good, until I fell. Now I'm back in a wheelchair, and the doctors are talking months. If he asks about my memory, nothing has changed. I don't even remember what happened when I got shot."

She shot her one eyebrow up once. "So a dose of mushroom to go with the cactus."

He laughed and aimed his finger at her.

She sighed. "So then what?"

He leaned in, and his voice quieted. "I get a lot of walking during the middle of the night. They leave the backdoor of the kitchen open to cool the work area. Nobody pays attention to the insomniac who wants to go out and sneak a smoke. I can get some core work and more walking out here. Let's see how things progress over the next few weeks. But find the drives and copy them. Go get some sun and rest, and we'll take it from there."

Bean stood as two caregivers came out of the door and looked around. "I think your escape is over. I'll come by before we go." She leaned down close. "Should I push you back to your room, Grandpa?"

His voice dropped into the slurred speech he had been using. His right hand slipped down and half set the brake. "That's

Hector's job." He waved at the approaching man. "Hector. The wheel don't work."

The man gave Bean a plastic smile to go with the stern look. "It's probably just the brake again, Mr. Akens. But it's time for your meds and nap. I'll get you back to your room."

Bean waved bye-bye as if he was a shatter-pated old grandfather. Duff's eyes rolled, and the tip of his tongue hung in the corner of his mouth.

As she ambled to her bike, she keyed the checker in her side pocket. It vibrated twice. Someone had placed a tracker. It was time to pressure wash the weekend's dirt off. She smiled only after she had pulled the helmet over her head. She checked the tiny green LED just right of her eye. They hadn't figured out how to hide a tracker or bug in her helmet yet. Whoever it was, didn't know how deadly her new helmet could be.

She started the system. "Mac, start bike and bring up map. Search for high-pressure wand car wash."

The map and route ghosted across the inside of her face shield. She smiled widely. Maybe she would let Danny get to second base after all.

She eased out onto the idyllic residential street. "Mac. Text to Leon. Need face time. Temple? End text and send." The green LED blinked once.

At the corner, she followed the map on her face shield. She smiled. Who needs a two-billion-dollar fighter jet when a grand, some kissing, and a high schooler does just fine?

———

THE MEDITATION GARDEN was a quiet three acres in the center of a busy city. What started as a Buddhist retreat became a multidenominational to nondenominational park or garden, open for anyone to come and meditate or just find peace and spiritual quiet in their life. Lena and Bet had brought Bean here the week they shot Duff. Now, her bike in the parking lot was a common sight.

Leon's shoes were off. With his legs crossed, he sat quietly, waiting as Bean approached.

Without opening his eyes, he addressed her more like a mechanic mystic than the big papa bear he was usually. "You just washed the bike. You should run it out on the freeway afterward. The static in the connections affects the timing and spark. It coughed as you made the turn from the south."

Bean sat on the other end of the bench. "Oh, Master Full of Shit. I came in from the west, and the pig needed a bath."

His eye opened, and he looked at her, smirking. And then he looked down at what she was holding in her hand. He carefully took it. Peeling the two gum wrappers off the insignificant item, he turned it over a few times.

"It's a Track Master 742. The feds used to use them a lot. If Radio Shack was still around, you could probably buy their overflow."

He looked at her with a question.

"I went to see Duff. They planted it while I was inside. I found it at the carwash."

He dropped it on the concrete bench. Bending over, he grabbed one of his hard-soled shoes. It was tough as it took three smacks of the size seventeen heel to crack it before the fourth hit ended in smaller parts. He separated the pieces and wrapped two packages in the gum wrappers. He dropped the tiny packets in his shirt pocket. He looked at the young woman he loved like a niece.

"Do you need more gum?"

She grunted softly. "Just the wrappers. Those were my last two."

"How's your uncle?"

"Getting restless. We might have to bust him out of the place before they figure him out."

The man bobbed his head. "It happens." He slid his blackouts down off the top of his head and looked down the garden.

"Something?"

"Probably not."

"I'm going down to Arizona."

"The bike?"

"Nah. We'll take the van. It's just two girls getting away."

"It's bugged and tracked."

She smirked. "I'll find them."

He glanced at her to read her level of sarcasm. "Kaminski?"

She took a deep breath. "How long have you worked for him?"

He watched the couple kneel at a small shrine. He knew the one. They placed a flower and something small on the dais. Leon remembered his day. The flower was called a double delight. A beautiful rose with two colors. And a deep, multilayered smell. The buds don't smell like the full bloom. The flower was his wife's favorite. The coin was a silver dollar he had kept in his pocket since his grandfather had given it to him.

"What are they doing?"

He dropped his head. Embarrassed, he had intruded into their private moment. "They lost someone close. It's the shrine for the dead."

She cleared her throat. "Kaminski?"

"We contract with his company. I don't work for him directly. But about twelve years."

"Ever meet him?"

His head shook as he looked at his hands between his knees. "No. But I've heard bits and pieces."

He looked over at her silence. She was waiting.

"Just watch your back."

Bean nodded. "Duff thinks he's in the middle of all this."

He patted his shirt pocket. "It's possible. But I don't think he had Duff shot or the diamonds stolen."

Bean raised her eyebrow above her blackouts. "Diamonds?"

He looked at her. "What did you think he was doing? Smuggling drugs? On a commercial airline? You can't carry enough to even buy the ticket."

"Was that what he was supposed to do that day?"

Leon ballooned his lower lip as he looked down the garden. The young Asian couple was strolling by now. She was crying into his shoulder—*a child.*

"What are you seeing Kaminski about?"

Bean leaned forward with her elbows planted on her knees as she softly rubbed her hands together. "I'm distraught Duff's not getting better. He fell the other day and is back in a wheelchair. They're talking months more before he'll be ready for a halfway house. I just don't know what to do with myself. So Ingrid will suggest a road trip and some spa time."

Leon didn't say a word., waiting for the genuine answer.

She smirked and shrugged. "We'll see."

40

TREASURE HUNTING

Bean whistled and hummed as she worked. A small sign hung taped to the sliding glass backdoor. *Go away. We'll talk at dinner.*

She cut the aluminum foil into large squares. In the center, she placed rolls of tape she had rolled backward around her two fingers.

With the squares lined out on the table, she turned on the Bluetooth speakers Danny had lent her. She placed them near the bugs in each room. She found the heavy metal thrash band from Russia she had sampled before. Full volume, she hit play. Only the tissue in her ears was saving her. As she picked up the first square of aluminum foil, she watched Ingrid come down the stairs from her apartment.

Standing at the door, she pointed at the note. Ingrid nodded and gave her a thumbs-up, and then rolled her eyes.

Bean found the first bug on the backside of the table lamp next to the couch. She mashed the sticky tape onto the bug and then crumpled the foil, encasing the bug and lamp base.

Each bug became a wad of aluminum foil—breaking or fouling the connection.

She turned on the bug sniffer and strolled through the house. One bug had escaped her early hunt. She considered it to be the most despicable of surveillance. At least the foster parents had been upfront when they took the doors off the bathroom and bedrooms. This was in her bedroom air vent. At the top of the wall, the yellow light lit up next to the glowing red light on her sniffer. It was a video.

Using a dinner knife, she unscrewed the vent cover. The unit was small. Small enough to travel to the sewer.

Bean sat on the toilet, thinking. The noise was distracting. She changed the phone to her original programming of soft rock ballads.

Now in Duff's room, she opened his closet and dragged out his jacket. She hefted it onto his bed. Then, curious, she lifted the jacket that was more than half her weight and put it on. Surprised, she walked around the house. It was only somewhat large on her but fit. She realized for the first time; she had grown in many ways this year, but one thing hadn't changed. Duff was not a big, hulking guy. He was as much the jacket as she was.

Spreading the eighty-plus pounds of jacket over her body made the weight become part of her. It was only the picking up and taking it off that was the strain.

She spread the jacket out on the table and removed all the gold ingots. Each one-pound bar was about the size and shape of a stack of eight credit cards. She made piles ten-high. Finally, there were eight stacks and four extra ingots.

She started pressing and pushing. Push out, pull back, and put on a new stack. Before long, she had eight new stacks and four extras. None were hollow. None opened. None were the treasure she sought. She stared at the stacks. Something was wrong. All eighty-four of the ingots were the same. Solid gold. No electronics. She wondered about Duff's memory.

Turning the negligible weight over and over in her hands, she remembered watching Ingrid weighing out even smaller weights for cooking.

She retrieved the electronic scale. Turning it on, she laid the first ingot on the scale. The scale read one pound with a bit of human goo.

Bean smiled and looked at her hands. "Hmm... dirty hands strike again."

She replaced the ingot with the next. Smiling, she added nine more bars. The scale read just over ten pounds. She placed the next stack. Same. All the ingots were one pound. Something wasn't adding up.

She thought back to the night in the desert. Duff had been specific. His jacket wasn't ninety pounds. It wasn't eighty-four. He had said eighty-eight pounds. She was four pounds light.

She folded the jacket into a condensed square and set it on the food scale. The scale read thirteen pounds and a couple of ounces.

She retrieved her leather jacket from her closet. Nine pounds and four ounces.

She laid the two jackets on the table, hers on top of his. The difference was minor. Both had extensions of the back to prevent a draft on the motorcycle. Her fringe would make up for his jacket's slightly larger arms and girth.

But there was still the unaccounted six-pound and change difference. She had missed something.

She pushed her jacket off and onto the floor and started on

his coat again. She checked the pockets—again. The weighted gloves lay on the floor next to her.

She unzipped the inside pocket. The small, folded map lay with the gloves.

The two top breast pockets were empty except for a tiny inspection slip. Good to know inspector number ten had inspected the custom jacket.

Running her hands flat over the lining, she checked to see if she had missed anything. Stumped, she slipped on the now light leather jacket. Even her used leather racing jumpsuit was heavier. The metal guards on the legs, arms, and back weren't for bulletproofing. They were there to protect the rider in a crash.

She went to the kitchen to make coffee. There was a conundrum, and it wasn't showing itself. Standing at the sink, her hands backward on the edge of the counter, she pushed down. As she rose onto the balls and toes of her feet, her elbows dug into her sides.

Her eyes roved over the small patch of grass. There were two lone iron chairs on the grass. The gardener moved them onto the driveway when he mowed. He commented once how they were missing a small table to put their beer on.

The table was missing. But she felt there was too much of something else.

As the coffee burbled the last of the magical water as it changed into coffee, she pulled the jacket off.

There had been three pockets capping the shoulder leading down into the sleeves. She hadn't felt or thought to feel the inside of the sleeve—in the armpit.

She drew out three more ingots from each side. Then, with the jacket thrown over her shoulder, she carried the gold and coffee back to the table.

She weighed each one—pound, light, pound, pound, pound, light. The two were less than two ounces light but in the scale of this treasure hunt. They were the winners.

With her thumb on the minting mark, she pushed. Nothing. She pulled. Nothing. She looked carefully again. There were extremely fine lines at two corners. She placed her thumb on the mark and pressed. She felt a small chirp or click. She pressed sideways. The top slid open like the lid of a Chinese puzzle box. Inside rested a small fat chip. The difference between this and those on Danny's key ring was that everything was removed from the outside of this chip.

She opened the second ingot. The chips looked identical.

She sat back and sipped on her coffee, thinking about how to have Danny do his magic. Finally, she looked at the leather jacket and smiled.

She replaced all the ingots into their pockets. Only the two chips remained on the table.

Wrapping the chips in an envelope of aluminum foil, she slipped them into one of the zipper pockets of her jumpsuit. She carried Duff's jacket back to his closet and tossed it back in the corner that was its home.

She raised her arm and sniffed at the pit—shower time.

———

"A PIECE OF CAKE." Danny stuck the stripped SSD into the reader. Then he pulled another from a box of drives.

Looking at the monitor, he put his drive back and pulled out a smaller box. There was only a handful left of the larger drives. "It's a bigger SSD and file than I thought."

Bean frowned. "But it will work. Right?"

He stuck the fresh drive into the socket. "Sure. We can copy any file or drive as a mirror. Think of it like algebra. AxC+B=E. The mirror doesn't even need to know its math. It just copies AxC+B=E. You need to crack the encryption to see the numbers. The mirror doesn't know what it is because it's still encrypted. But it will copy it." He looked at the file on the monitor. "It just might take a stronger brute to crack the encryption algorithm. But for a thousand bucks, I can rent time on the monster at UCLA and go full Beast Mode."

Bean watched as he pulled the one drive and stuck another in. He turned as the computer copied the drive. "How many do you need?"

"Let's do three of each to start." She reached into her back pocket and took out her wallet. Pulling out a thin sheaf of bills, she counted eight hundred dollars. "Can this get you started, or do I need to go back to the house?"

He gawped at the money and then closed his mouth. Taking the money, he fanned the bills and examined them. "This will go far." He looked up. "Can we take your bike?"

She smiled. "That's all you want?"

He blushed as she leaned in and kissed him on the lips.

"Motorcycle it is. But I need to go by the house for a few minutes. I'll need some gas money."

He looked at her coyly. "I have a twenty."

She patted him on the cheek and pointed at the computer. "Copy."

He handed her the originals, and she re-wrapped them in the aluminum foil. "Keep a set here, and we'll take the other set. Do we need to buy some more drives if we bust them?"

He reached into his desk and pulled out a much larger external drive still wrapped in shrink-wrap. He held it up and smiled. "One full terabyte. Of course, the new ones are four and eights, but for twenty bucks, what's to lose?" He reached back in, grabbed two more, and pitched the three in his small messenger bag. "Good to have backup."

She smiled as she stood. "That's what I was thinking."

As they rode down the street, Bean smiled. The young boy's hands were riding a little higher than needed and trying to feel through the leather. Bean hoped he'd get better at it when they took the freeway to the college.

She pulled up in the driveway.

"I'll be right back." She smiled at his radiant face. Today was his perfect day—computers, a motorcycle, and getting to second base—even if it was through leather and on the bike.

She stashed the wad of drives and foil in the bottom of the aluminum foil box. Then, refilling her wallet just in case, she stopped in the bathroom for a fast swish of mouthwash—just in case.

As she locked the back door, she turned to find Ingrid standing there with her arms folded.

"Is that Danny out there on the bike?"

"Yes. I'll be back by seven for dinner."

Ingrid narrowed her eyes and cocked her head. "Does he have anything to do with this morning's note?"

"No." Bean blushed. "Man, you have a dirty mind." She leaned in close. "We've got to run, but I promise I'll fill you in over dinner. By the way, we're taking the bike."

———

THE YOUNG MAN was more like thirty. Bean had seen worse slobs, but the flip-flops, Ramones T-shirt, wild head of light brown curls, and thick glasses didn't match the plaid shorts. And none of it was a good look, on a man pushing enough excess groceries to overflow the complaining desk chair.

"I've explained this to you before, Danny. You need to fill out the forms and book a reservation for time on the supermax. You can't just drop in and expect—"

His mouth froze as five hundred dollars dropped into his lap. He looked up at Bean.

Bean shifted her weight to her left hip and unzipped her leathers for a few inches. The black T-shirt wasn't sexy, but it was at least suggestive to a man whose day was staring at a monitor. Of course, he didn't need to learn about the number sixty-five just out of his sight. "How much will computer time cost me?"

He mentally stumbled. "It depends. What are we working on?"

"Nothing you can or want to see. Let's just say it may or may not be of national security interests." She shifted her weight to the other hip. Then, placing her hand at the edge of the open zipper, she raised one eyebrow. "Do I need to show you my NSA identification? Because if I do, we'll need to shut everything down and scrub the computer when we finish?"

The man's face blanched. "You can't scrub Super Max. There are years of information and calculations in there. There is people's life's work tied up in there..."

She withdrew her hand. "Good, then we have an understanding."

He took a deep breath. He knew he was now in a corner he would never get out of. "The government rate is five hundred an hour. But we don't accept cash. I mean, the department usually bills it against a credit card or an account."

She looked at the cash still in his lap. "This one is off the books. What government accounts can you bill it to?"

His eyes grew as he slowly swiveled the chair. He pulled up a list of billable accounts and their time usage.

Danny pointed at one. "They log a lot of time. Even some today."

A few more bills landed on the keyboard as Bean leaned in next to his ear. "Make it happen, stud."

The man's fingers were moving before his mind engaged. "Terminal three."

Danny sat down and plugged in the two drives. He typed in what he wanted and set it in motion. He leaned back in the chair. "Now we wait."

Bean ran her hand along his shoulder. "I saw a coffee stand down in the quad. Can I get you anything?"

He looked up. "Chai? Maybe a Thai chai?"

She winked and smiled. Turning, she took in the computer master. The man had a thirty-two-ounce soft drink laced with caffeine and sugar. "Wally. I'm making a drink run. Anything?"

He pointed to the general area of the quad. "If you're going to the corner coffee, they have a killer blueberry coffee cake…"

She smiled and walked. She brought him a double order. As she sat behind a smiling Danny, she noted the second screen was showing documents he was flipping through. She leaned in next to his ear. "You might not want to know what's on there."

His eyes didn't waver. "Too late. Should I tell you or just a generalized synopsis?" He turned his chair around. "You weren't shitting Wally when you said national security. But it's mildly out-of-date."

She sucked on her iced coffee. "Yeah, it's three years old, but the information is still critical."

He sucked on his straw. "But where would you get something like this?"

She cocked her head. "That is what you truly don't want to know." She looked at the screen. The schematic looked like a missile. "Certainly, don't want to know."

His eyes were enormous, but he wasn't looking away. Instead, he glanced at the other monitor. "I'm sticking both micros onto this drive as unzipped files. There's plenty of room, and it keeps it all in one place."

Bean rubbed his shoulder and neck. "Good thinking. Can we copy it onto the others while we're here?"

"Sure, as long as we're resident, it's in our ram, and I can just... Wait." He unwrapped and plugged in the others. "I'll just octopus them."

Bean frowned. "If the broken files are in the mainframe..."

Danny jerked his head and smiled. "Way ahead of you. Even Wally can't see into our bucket. And when I'm done, the bucket becomes a lump of coal." The farthest monitor cleared. Danny pointed. "That is where we were, and this is what's on our new drives." As he unplugged all the drives, the second monitor also cleared.

He dropped everything into his bag and stood.

As they climbed on the bike, Bean was still worried. "You're sure the system has no memory of what we did or saw?"

"Sure. It says we logged forty-seven minutes on terminal three. We billed it to the Air Safety Board of the Air Force out of some base, and that was all it knows. We could have been playing the latest multiplayer action game for all it knows. Or we were just checking our email like Wally was."

"He has friends?"

Danny shuddered. "*That*, I *positively* don't want to know."

41

SETTING UP

The argument in the backyard was brief. Bean promised to drive slowly. Ingrid said she'd eat cold cereal. Bean leaned in and reminded her the van had bugs and a tracker.

The little Italian restaurant was only blocks from the beach. Bean had found it a couple of weeks before. There were only a few other patrons. And none could eavesdrop on their conversation.

Bean pulled back each finger as she counted off. "Duff missed my birthday. I'm scared his condition isn't improving. He fell and broke his walker. Now he's back in a wheelchair. I don't know if his income stops, and what about the expensive rent?" She shrugged her face and one shoulder. "Easy peasy gently squeezy."

Ingrid stalled with a forkful of lasagna halfway to her mouth. Her milk blue eyes twitched from one of Bean's to the other. She nibbled at the fork of hot pasta.

Bean moved her mouthful of food to her cheek. "Whaff?" A small piece of pasta dribbled onto her chin. She wiped it with the back of her hand.

Ingrid smiled and put the rest of the lasagna into her mouth. She contentedly chewed behind a smile. Then she leaned back in her chair as she pointed her finger at Bean. "There. There's the girl I know and love."

Bean cocked her head and frowned, confused. Finally, she put her fork down and patted at her lips.

Ingrid leaned in. "Where the hell did this full-blown take-charge woman come from? Just a few months ago, you were skipping rope with Lena and tittering about how cute Danny was. Now…"

Bean wiped her mouth on her arm and then looked at it. Her face wrinkled in disgust. And then she leaned in. "Second base. I let him cop a feel through my leathers at eighty miles per hour. What was he going to do? He had to hold on, and I owed him."

Ingrid's one eye slowly narrowed. "Owed him for what?"

"Some serious computer work. Shit that I couldn't do in a million years. The kid has mad skills…" She dug another forkful of lasagna and raised it to her mouth. "Skills I needed, and the people he knows, and access to a monster computer." The chunk of lasagna filled her mouth.

Ingrid held her hand out and grabbed her small finger with her other hand. "I'm just trying to play catch-up here. You got emancipated." She pulled the finger back and grabbed the next. "You got your driver's license and somehow got a motorcycle."

Bean reached over and pushed the next finger down. "Don't forget the name change."

Ingrid's hands faltered and gently lowered as her face crinkled and puckered around her eyes. "You're not Bean anymore?"

"No… I wasn't Bean before. Now I am."

Ingrid's face puckered, and she watched. Somehow, the world wasn't what she thought it was.

Bean cocked her head and reached out. Then, Curling Ingrid's finger over her other index finger, she smiled. "Bean Honey Aikens. Licensed to drive motorcycles, bulletproof cars, and big trucks with large trailers but not doubles or chemicals. So I guess I could maybe haul furniture or hay. But no livestock."

Ingrid dragged down her finger as her eyes narrowed.

"Oh, and I can shoot the eye out of a target at thirty yards with a nine-millimeter, but I'm still a little wild with the fifty caliber."

Ingrid leaned back and let her hands fall limp into her lap. "Have I been asleep or something?"

Bean pushed her empty plate forward and leaned back. "Nah. That's been Duff's job. You're okay. This whole thing with Duff has us both at different angles. You went into full mom mode. The house is so clean it's sterile. And I don't recognize half the stuff in the refrigerator. But me, I needed to do distracting stuff. I've been meaning to get it all done, but maybe over the next year. But the name and emancipation... that came about all at once. And now I have a judge on my side willing to help me if I need it."

Ingrid blinked at the firehose of information. "What career did you choose?"

Bean stalled and then closed her mouth. "I don't understand the question."

Ingrid leaned back as the young waitress took their plates.

"Well, in my timeline, a week ago, you were a high school student. Now, you have everything to be... I have no idea what."

Bean made a happy, wide-eyed face as she shied to one side. "Honestly, I can't think that far ahead. I have too many things right here, right now, that need to happen."

"Like what?"

Bean spotted the waitress coming back and waved her off. She leaned closer to Ingrid. "Duff isn't safe where he is. Right now, everyone must think he's still shattered—mentally and physically. But I need to get him out of there and hidden. Next, I'm not sure how much longer we can stay where we are. For that, I need Kaminski to commit to it on his own." She circled her finger in the air between them. "To be the good uncle or grandfather looking after the favorite, whatever. But that must come voluntarily from him."

"So you need to fly down to see him." Ingrid nodded, seeing the logic.

"No..." Bean circled the finger in the air again. "We. Need to drive down."

"But...?"

Bean jerked her head. "I'm distraught. I need time away from all this. So you'll suggest—when we are in the house with the bugs, going down to Arizona. If it's Kaminski listening, he's got a heads-up when you call. If it's not, they just know we're going down to Arizona. Either way, we're out of the way up here."

Ingrid crinkled her eyes, and her head rolled back. "Out of the way of what?"

Bean smiled and looked toward the waitress. She made the sign for the bill. "They might need to change the batteries in the bugs. Or at least, take the aluminum foil off the one or two I missed and probably put a camera back in my bedroom air vent."

Ingrid's face exploded.

Bean rolled up on her hip to get her wallet. "Yeah. I know. Perverts."

BEAN SLIPPED into the quiet office. It amazed her how many offices in the administration building at a major university were empty—but with working computers and phones. Making a long-distance call wasn't what it used to be, but it was still a long-distance call.

"Good evening. Thank you for calling—"

Bean cut him off. "Is that my favorite fun uncle? Don't answer. Just say yes or no. In case you know who is eavesdropping."

The man quietly squealed. "Yes."

"Okay. Here's your next yes or no question. Can you hide someone for a month or more while they recover from some serious surgery? Of course, they will need good food and gentle care. But they can also pay."

There was a humming on the other end of the line. "No. They've got me on hold. You know how these small-town bureaucracies can be. Just go back to making dinner. I won't be a minute."

Bean could hear the phone being muffled. The sound had the distinct texture of being in a woolen cave. "Of course, we can. Oh... how deliciously clandestine. When?"

"I have to set it up. But soon. I'll call and tell you your shipment is en route. But we don't know when it will get delivered until he's on your doorstep. And the big red monster will need to be locked up as well."

"That's fine. This isn't our busy season, so the distraction will be good. What about you?"

"Working on it. I've got to go." She hung up and spun in the chair.

The disheveled man with wild eyebrows and unkept hair opened the door. He stood blinking. He stepped back and looked at the office number. His face pinched. "This is three-nineteen. Who are you? They told me the office... I have to work alone..."

Bean stood and held her hand out to slide past him. "I was just waiting for my mom. Sorry."

She snickered about the poor guy all the way to her motorcycle. She wondered if he would ever settle down enough to get any work done in the next week. Always wondering who he might find in his office.

————

THE ROOT BEER TASTED BITTERSWEET. The unusual light rain in the early morning had washed away most of the usual haze. By the time hot motorcycle tires started cautiously up the asphalt snakes, cut in the coastal hills, and into the depths of old burns and this year's threat, the roads were dry.

Bean had slept late and took the long way in. The food shack on the coast was little more than a hot truck that had traded its wheels for concrete blocks as its appeal had gained legitimacy. The anthill of young surfers with their uniforms of long scraggly hair and wet skins pulled to their waists and tied, as they scarfed down the burritos, was the confirmation. Good taste at a fair price.

Bean agreed.

From behind her blackouts, she watched the comings and goings of all things motorcycle at the Rock house. The singles usually came, looked around, and then left to try their hand at one of the death-defying serpentine roads in the area.

The groups usually gathered before they left to watch each

other on The Snake before the Highway Patrol arrived. Or had already been. They had watched and filmed the run or crash and were now just hanging out.

She scratched at the center of her chest between the six and the five.

The group she had been waiting for arrived. The rumble had been thundering in the canyon for at least several seconds as they rode the last mile. The nine choppers lined up across the street. A few of the young kids on Kamikaze bikes saw the group coming and made hurried escapes to leave room for the group.

Bean stretched and gradually stood as Carrot approached. They stopped with their two right shoulders touching. "I need your help."

The wild head of red hair shook out as he jerked his head at his wife for them to continue. "I forgot something on the bike." His head waved for her to follow as he turned back.

They sat on the sizeable silvered log covered by tattoos carved by knives or bottle openers. Decades of youthful testosterone and the narcissistic need to leave one's mark, leaving marks to cross over marks, and then get wiped clean by another.

"So we'll need a large van."

Bean nodded. "With a ramp. I can rent one…"

He glanced over. "Naw, we have a couple. They're clean. One even for the bike shop. So we're good." He looked across the street, considering the options. "Stick and I can come to get it this evening. But the other…"

"We're leaving tomorrow morning. So Tuesday or Wednesday would be best."

The man leaned back, rubbing his palms along his leather pants. "Does he know?"

"I'll tell him this afternoon."

"But it's a full-on mask and disguises…?"

"I'm sure they have cameras that work. As well as bugged. So until he gives you the thumbs-up, no talking. Or at least not recognizable."

"Weapons?"

Bean smiled. "They always look great on cameras. Might even make the six o'clock news. But I doubt it. Just don't shoot anyone."

He stuck his hand out to shake. She slapped a fat envelope in his hand and wrapped her hand around it. They both smiled.

"You didn't have to. The car was more than enough."

Bean's eyes narrowed, and her face slumped to stone. "This is more important."

42

GOING SOUTH

The knuckle was dull on the door. Bean reached and unlocked the door to slide it open. Stepping back to the island, she stuffed the second insulated coffee carafe into the second bag. She pointed at the green bag and Ingrid. Then pointing to the red, she patted the sixty-five on her T-shirt.

They picked up the bags and stepped into the backyard. Locking the door, she pulled out the fob and triggered the new over-watch system a friend of Leon installed. Cameras, motion-activated, watched every section of the house. The recordings were stored on a hard drive at Leon's friend's house and Danny's house. Bean could access Danny's storage remotely from her phone.

Bean put the two bags in the back of the van and climbed in. Ingrid backed out as the gate opened. The sky wasn't quite at the pink stage yet as they pulled into the gas station.

Opening the back, Bean took the bags out and quietly closed the door. Leon stood by a large gray car with its doors open. He smiled at Bean's shirt as she put both bags in the backseat. She hugged the big man.

Climbing in, she noticed the extra seat belt straps. She'd teach Ingrid later.

Leon closed the door silently as Bean pressed the start button. She pushed the fob into her jean pocket and smiled up at Leon. The gas gauge read full. It would take them to just outside Las Vegas. The next gas station was already on the GPS mapping.

The large gray car nosed out of the gas station and onto the street. Three blocks later, they were heading north on the San Diego Freeway. They would be crossing the desert in sixty-seven miles. The next hundred miles would be about detecting anyone who may follow them.

"Now can we talk?"

Bean laughed and looked over at Ingrid. "Talk, sure. Sing? Absolutely not. I heard you at that karaoke bar. It was not your pretty side."

Ingrid leaned her seat back and grabbed at the two bags. Pulling the two carafes out, she poured the coffees. She put the one in the cup holder beside Bean. "It's so strange sitting here and having you drive. I've driven in seventeen countries and on both sides for almost twenty years. You take a five-hour crash course…"

Bean's face and mouth flew open in mock indignation. "I. Did. Not. Crash."

They both laughed until a motorcycle shot out from the Ventura Freeway interchange. The bike was low, black, and fast. It crossed all lanes and disappeared down the fast lane. Bean could feel her right calf clench, not to follow. Thinking, she set the cruise control at seventy-four—nine over the speed limit and almost as fast as the few other cars. Most of the early morning traffic was going the other way and into the city.

Ingrid held her mug with both hands, watching the distance where she couldn't see the motorcycle anymore. "That's the way you ride?"

"Sometimes."

"Why?"

Her lips furled as she cleared all three mirrors and the gauges. "Sometimes, it's faster and cheaper than therapy. And I like the therapist better."

"Therapist?"

"The Duke." She glanced over as she grabbed the mug from the holder. "The Ducati. My bike."

"Did you tell Duff about the bike?"

Bean sipped on the coffee. She side-eyed Ingrid.

Ingrid knew the look. She sipped on her coffee. "Yeah. To tell him about the bike, you'd have to tell him about the driver's license, which would lead to the emancipation, and then the whole name change and then the bloody part."

Bean's face pinched. "Bloody part?" The woman had no idea.

"Spending the week with Leon, getting a new shirt that you have worn for weeks solid—buying a motorcycle that shouldn't be anywhere but on a racetrack. Yeah. All that bloody stuff."

"I wash this shirt."

"That explains the coat hanger in your shower."

"Wash it at night when I shower. Hang it. It's ready in the morning."

"And the meaning of the sixty-five in the big white dot?"

Bean smirked as she glanced over. "Took you long enough. The bike I learned how to ride on was a 1965 Harley Davidson. It was the first Electra Glide." She looked over. "That meant they had an electric starter. But it was the last year they made the Panhead engine. So it was unique."

She sipped her coffee and put the mug back in the holder as the freeway merged with another. "My instructor bought it when they retired it. He rebuilt the engine to be bigger and faster than anything else and trained police officers to ride fast but safely. He's rebuilt the bike three times. But it's a legend. And those officers and a few others who learned on it—get the shirt. The first one is free. After that, they cost a hundred bucks."

Ingrid choked on her coffee. "For a T-shirt?"

Bean peeked over. "The money goes to the rebuild fund. I'll probably buy two more."

Ingrid knew the quasi-code she and Duff lived by. "Then you'd have to give up the cat shirt."

Bean snorted. "Nah. I'm expanding to six shirts now. I might even start wearing underwear."

———

THE MORNING WAS BEARABLE. But Bean could feel the heat building behind them. Soon the long shadows would burn off, and the sun would be overhead.

She smiled as Ingrid forked another cube of cactus into her mouth. "This sunrise makes the long drive worthwhile."

Ingrid swallowed. "I think I missed the part between the yucca trees and the sagebrush."

Bean snorted. "You missed most of the drive. Remind me never to get you up before oh-coffee-thirty to go anywhere. You punked out about the fourth turn in the desert."

The third chair pulled out. *"Jambo buwanas.* I hope I didn't miss anything. How is the cactus, my dears?" The man gracefully seated himself.

Bean spread her arms in the air. "Now. Now, my desert is complete." She reached over and covered the man's hand with hers. "*Nimekukosa sana.* I have missed you so much."

He dipped his head in acknowledgment. "That, my child, is called adulthood. And I understand you are now in that age group. So *mazel tov.* What would you like for your birthday?"

Bean spread her hand around. "This. This is the most I could wish for."

"Well then, your time in the spa will not be in vain." He turned to Ingrid. "And you, my dear? I understand your charge passed her challenges with flying colors."

Ingrid pushed the cube of cactus into the side of her mouth. "She has a tough choice to make now. The forty-seven bus runs right to UCLA, but the twenty-four drops her off three blocks from Santa Monica City College."

He raised his index finger. "Ah. But which has the better math program?" He looked at Bean. "I am led to believe you have a fondness and knack for the archaic figures of the Arabic world."

"Actually, Pythagoras was Greek."

Kaminski nodded. "As was Archimedes, respected as the true father of mathematics. But it was Euclid who studied at the knee of Plato in Athens but moved to Alexandria in Egypt to study and perfected the forms and theorems of geometry we use today. But all is with Arabic numerals instead of Roman numerals. So even though mathematics is the product of Greece, it is the numerals of the Arabic world the entire world uses today. It is the universal language."

The two waitresses brought out the breakfasts, freshened the coffee, and silently retreated to the cooler air.

————

THE TWO DAYS they had were precisely what Bean and Ingrid needed. Floating from food someone else cooked, spa, pool, and the glorious luxury of naps. Bean checked into the class Danny had found her and worked through worksheets and lessons as she honed her math skills. Another endeavor wasn't a class or one taught in any school. They moved money around the world. Untraced. Unrestricted. And perfectly legal. Countries did it. Corporations did it. Diamond and commercial gold sellers do it. But the common people are accountable if they deposit ten thousand dollars. Or try to take the same out of the country. But in movies, bad guys transferred millions in the blink of an eye to an offshore account. And she wanted to know where the boundaries of truth were. Unfortunately, there wasn't an app for that.

The massage had finally worked out the knot in Bean's lower right shoulder. She knew she was carrying a lot of her stress there but hadn't realized how much until the masseuse pushed on the spot. The session ran long.

Bean stepped out of the shower, and she bent over to wrap her hair in a towel. The luxury of three large towels was amazing.

The attendant adjusting the stack of towels turned. Her voice was as soft as the small water fountain in the relaxation room. "Mr. Kaminski is waiting for you in the lobby. I think it's urgent."

Bean's eyebrow rose. "I'll be right out."

"I'll let him know."

Bean pulled on the oversized robe and wrapped it around her. Sliding her feet into the slippers, she padded her way out to the lobby.

"What's up?"

The man rose. Concern clouded his face. "There has been an incident concerning Duff. We're still gathering information, but if you could please come up to my office when you're done. I can bring you up to speed."

"What happened? Is he all right? Did he fall again?"

His voice lowered even quieter. "Not here. Please, come to my office."

"I can go now."

He looked at her robe and turban of towel. "I think it can wait until you finish. Evidently, this all happened some hours ago, so a few minutes more won't make a difference. Please. Take your time and do your hair and whatever else you need. I'll be in my office."

She turned and pulled the towel from her hair as she opened the door to the back. "Give me half an hour."

The man pursed his lips as he turned. "Take your time."

BEAN WATCHED the news clip again. The whole incident lasted less than two minutes. The national news would probably pick up the Los Angeles local, and it would be worldwide by the end of the day. Guns, terrorism, and kidnapping took top billing.

The news anchor sounded breathy as she narrated over the grainy video. *"In a brazen early morning kidnapping, four armed and masked men, believed to be members of a Russian mob, broke into a Brentwood care facility this morning. Brandishing weapons and speaking Russian, they pulled one patient out of his bed and fled in a gray van. One man dropped his pistol and fingerprints identifying him as a known international mobster wanted by Interpol for many killings around the world.*" The Interpol photo took up half of the screen for a couple of seconds.

"*A weighted glove, dropped by one of the other men, has yielded DNA, and the authorities expect to match the partial prints taken from the gloves. The van, found an hour later, was burned beyond the ability to gather more evidence.*"

Four people dressed in all black with hoods and guns silently entered and moved down a hall. One pointed a handgun at someone off-camera. The other three entered a door. The next square showed the room with two people in beds. The three grabbed one man out of his bed, moved him into a wheelchair, and pushed him out into the hall, leaving a black pistol on the bed. The five moved back down the corridor they had approached in. The next clip was of them pushing the man in the wheelchair to a waiting van. The four picked up the chair and man and pushed him into the van. Climbing in, they closed the door, and the van drove off.

Bean moved the slide to the man in the bed. She had been in the room enough to know the blurry person with the mop of hair and a short beard was Duff. She sat staring at the screen. One person pointed something at his head. One person helped him get his legs over the edge and stand to turn into the chair. The third person quietly gathered the few personal items into a black bag, taking anything that was Duff. In seconds, they erased the man. Quick, neat, and professional. Almost military. Except for leaving the evidence in the bed and driveway.

Bean licked her lips and realized her mouth had been hanging open the entire time. She stood and headed for the hall. "I need…"

She knelt in the stall. She gagged into the toilet. Making a grand production of the churning in her gut. She didn't know what to expect but watching grainy black and white footage, she knew to be real...

She walked out into the lobby to get a tall glass of the cucumber water they kept there in a twenty-gallon cylinder. She downed two glasses before one of the staff brought her a water bottle filled.

The woman smiled. "We're all extremely conscious about dehydration in this heat, especially if you're doing any of the spa treatments. Keep the bottle and fill it whenever you want. If you use the steam or sauna, take it in full and bring it out empty. You can't feel how much you're sweating—it dries too fast. But you're losing about a gallon a day."

"Thanks. That's probably it."

Ingrid was watching the video with horror on her face. She turned as she pointed at the screen. "Is that Duff?"

All Bean could do was nod.

———

THE MORNING WAS UNUSUALLY cool and muggy. The clouds hung low in a medium gray. Not threatening, but still there. The sky was on vacation.

Mr. Kaminski pushed an envelope toward Ingrid and handed one to Bean. "Our agreement with Duff was his pay was cash and delivered by the driver who drove him around. It was always the same driver and one we vetted vigorously. His payments were more of a salary than by work done. Those payments will continue. I will cover the rents and bills as they have been. There is to be no change. The important thing now is to get Mr.

Akens back and find out why he was kidnapped. We have taken the liberty of tapping your phones in case they call. Any incoming calls other than ones already in your phone books will trigger the tap and start a trace. You won't have to make any overt actions." He looked at each of the women. "Questions?"

43

———

GOING HOME

Ingrid leaned into the trunk with Bean. She mouthed her question. *Are we bugged?*

Bean softly snorted as she stood up straight. "Nope. Found it this morning in the dark. It's on a Ford truck from Montana. That should confuse the hell out of them." They both knew they hadn't figured out who *they* were... yet.

It wasn't as if they did much talking. Bean figured Ingrid's silence was fright from the turn of events. After all, how many people have had a friend or family kidnapped?

Bean pulled into the Lucky Motel near the border of Nevada and California. The sign from the last century, of a hand holding four aces and a queen, had only a few sections of neon left. The recent sign hanging below the hand was the clincher. It advertised Wi-Fi.

Bridget frowned as Bean grabbed her bag and jumped out. She held her hand out like you would when telling a dog to stay.

The woman had bleached hair. The weight could hold off the wrinkles only for so long. And the flower print muumuu Bean understood in the desert.

Bean pulled her laptop out of her bag as she stepped to the counter. "Hi. We've been streaming GOT, and I don't want to miss the next update. So I want to check your Wi-Fi speed."

She booted the laptop as she watched the woman blink in confusion and blew a pink bubble the size of her fist. The bubble snapped as the main screen came up.

The woman's face cleared and beamed. "Let me know when you want the passcode."

"Go."

"Have a lucky day. All caps like you're screaming. All one word."

Bean typed. "It doesn't work."

The woman leaned on the counter. Six inches of cleavage showed at her neckline. Seven more than Bean needed. "Now add four As and a Q for the queen."

Bean spoke as she typed. "A A A A, and a Q." She hit enter, and the screen wiped to a large advertisement for the motel. Bean ran the speed test. The download and upload were off the charts. She looked up at the woman.

The woman smiled and pushed a registration card across the counter. "My son supports us as a professional gamer. He came back from the Stan in a chair. As for GOT, it ended a year ago."

Bean held up both hands. "No spoilers. We're only on season six." She pulled a hundred-dollar bill out of her wallet and pushed it and the blank card back across the counter.

The woman stuffed the bill into her muumuu. Bean assumed a bra. "You were never here. But no funny business."

"It's just my sister and me. She just lost her husband in the sandbox a couple of months ago. I'm bringing her home. But... well, you understand. The Throne has us hooked. Any place decent to eat?"

She pointed. "Doris is the only place not to get poisoned. Just don't play the slots. They don't pay out."

Bean smiled with a thumb in the air as she closed the laptop. "Doris, no slots."

The woman laughed as she leaned her head and shook her finger. "And no funny stuff."

As Bean pushed on the door, the woman added. "And sorry about your sister. I know where she's at. I lost my Homer in the first sandbox."

Bean paused and looked back. "Sorry."

The woman waved. "Say hi to Doris."

———

THE QUALITY of the video wasn't the best TV. But it was in color. When the idiots looked directly at the cameras, Bean snapped a screenshot good enough for a social media algorithm. Two of the three had family accounts. The third was on four dating sites, still looking for love in all the creepy places.

Ingrid pulled another spoonful of ice cream out of the Rocky Road container. She pointed the spoon at the laptop. "The creepiest part is they have the key to the front door."

Bean sucked on the spoonful of Double Fudge Bananas. "I would wire it for electrocution, but Leon uses that door. Maybe it is seriously time to change the locks."

"But who are they?"

Bean pointed her spoon at the screen. "Their uniforms say *exterminator*. But all I see is them installing bugs."

"So they're infestation guys."

The two laughed at the three serious guys, but what looked like a Keystone Cops video.

Ingrid screamed as she rolled over in laughter. "NOOOooo… He stuck his camera right next to yours and didn't even see the other camera? How did he get the job?"

Bean pointed at the lamp as the men looked around to ensure they forgot nothing. "A massive wad of aluminum foil, and they forgot they placed a bug there before? Who hires these kinds of guys?" She turned with a shocked face toward Ingrid. "If these guys turn out to be government… United States government… I want a new country."

Ingrid rolled over on her stomach and growled. "Don't you dare leave me behind."

Bean rested her hand on the top of the laptop. "Again?"

"Nah. You need some sleep." She rolled over, looked at the half-empty container, and grimaced. She put the ice cream on the nightstand and pushed herself up into a sitting position. "What's the game plan for tomorrow?"

Bean looked off into the distance through the walls. "If it's okay with you, I'd like to go through San Diego. There's a beach I'd like to see again." She cranked her head around and looked over her shoulder at Ingrid.

Ingrid guessed it would be near the Marine base. She understood. "I'd kind of like to drive through the Navy base on North Island…"

"Will they let us?"

Ingrid snorted a soft, sad breath. "No… I don't think so. But it would be nice."

"How long were you there?"

"About eleven months. Then dad transferred to the Mediterranean, and we were in Italy. And France. And Germany. And, and, and…"

Bean smiled. She had heard the litany. Marines and noncommissioned Navy left most of the wives and kids stateside. Other kids grew up moving from suitcase to suitcase. Much like foster kids. Except for the parents and countries.

———

BEAN GOT out of the car. As she got close to the Marine, she stopped and pushed her blackouts up onto the top of her head.

"Miss, you can't park there. You're blocking traffic, and I can't let you in because you don't have a pass."

She recognized the stripes of the lowest sergeant. Her hands raised deliberately to her hips, and her forefingers and thumbs spread along her belt. "Sergeant, I'm not going to insult you by calling you *sir*. We both know you work for a living. My father, on the other hand, was a captain. He died nine years ago. My mother couldn't handle raising me alone. She drove off the cliff at Tory Pines. I have paid that price every day—for nine years." She turned and pointed at Ingrid. "See that woman?"

The man's voice was softer and the official bluster gone. "Yes, miss?"

"Her father served here aboard the Kitty Hawk. Their eleven months here were her best memories. He gave his all in the First Desert Storm. She lost her husband last year in the sandbox. She has stage four pancreatic cancer and Alzheimer's. She may be from a different mother and father, but she's my sister and the only person we each have because the glue that held us together was kidnapped three days ago. You may have seen it on the news. They came and stole him out of his bed in the nursing home. What wasn't in the news was that those bad people had shot him in the head two months ago. We didn't know if he would survive or not. But now, we know he won't."

The man shifted uncomfortably. "Miss...?"

Bean put up her finger. "All we want is for someone to bring a jeep. And just drive us around while she lays her father to rest in whatever she has left of her mind. The base can't be that large. What? A ten-minute drive?"

He broke her stare. "Let me see what I can do. But can you park along the fence and let these cars through... please?"

Five minutes later, a lieutenant rolled up in a jeep. The woman talked to the sergeant and then got out of the jeep and walked over. She stuck out her hand. "Hi. I'm Lieutenant Margaret Hanson. Sorry about your fathers. Err, I guess families."

"Hi. Bean Akens, and this is my sister, Ingrid Foster. Can you drive us around the base a bit? Her father served on the Kitty Hawk... and I saw you have a carrier here now..."

"Yes, miss. The Theodore Roosevelt. And it would be my honor to drive you around the base."

Ingrid leaned her head on Bean's shoulder as they rode in the back of the jeep. "I don't know what you said to that Marine, but thank you for this."

The lieutenant never said a word, never pointed out a thing, but drove slowly by the most important points on the base.

When they returned to the front gate, Bean thanked the lieutenant for her kindness and understanding.

Bean bit her furled upper lip. "There's only one more stop."

"Where's that?"

"Out on the beach at Camp Pendleton, there were two ratty, old beach chairs. I doubt if they're even there anymore. But my father used to take me there for sunset." She pointed at the sky out over the ocean. "When the air is clear but hazy like this, the sky would turn a honey gold color. So he told me that when he was in the desert and saw the same sunset, he would think of me and those beach chairs. He called them Honey skies because he had named me for them. My middle name is Honey."

The lieutenant licked the lip she had drawn in. "I'll call the main gate and talk to the Officer of the Day."

Bean shook her hand again. "Thank you. If I had a challenge coin, I'd give it to you."

The woman's eyes turned wet, and she blinked several times. "No need. The memory is more than enough. You take care of your sister."

———

THE SERGEANT POINTED to the two chairs on the low dune. "Take all the time you need. Sunset is in seventeen minutes. I'll be right here when you're ready to go back."

44

THE FUNCLES

The ride was long but fun. Bean kept to the old Highway One as much as she could. She loved the curves as she mastered more and more of the skill of pushing a large bike through its paces. Eventually, she knew she would convert to a lower seat and center of gravity like the Indian or sixty-five. But for now, the English upright seating suited her style.

She learned to ignore the stares she got every time she took off her helmet and pulled her long ponytail out of her leather jacket. She knew she wasn't responsible for the misogynistic attitudes of people toward powerful motorcycles and the people they expected to be riding them. But the urge to give a few the one-finger salute was overwhelming.

Mostly, she only stopped for gas and food. The large B&B in Pacific Grove recommendation had come from a woman who was shocked when Bean ordered from the outside window of a chowder house a block from the beach and the Cayucas pier. "Why honey, that is exactly what I get every time we come through here. Are you going to walk on the pier and eat? Because that's what I do."

Bean had leaned in the window and asked them to double the order.

They had named Ester Williams Thompkins after her mother's favorite swimmer and movie star. "Mama tried to teach me how to swim, but I sunk like a brick. It wasn't until I was in high school, I started getting these boobies and some float in my boat. Then, they couldn't get me out of the water. I've lived near water ever since."

They stopped about halfway out along the pier. A fisherman wasn't using the bench, allowing them to put their iced teas on it. "Where do you live now?"

"A little place in the central valley. People know Wasco for oil and sheep. It don't have nothin'. But it's home now. Well, for now, at least. My Thomas passed this last winter. I'm just trying to figure things. I keep thinking maybe a trailer here on the coast. But we've been in Wasco for forty-one years."

"Is there a river or lake there?"

The woman laughed. "Nope. My Tommy, God love him, built me a cement pond." She looked at Bean's frowning face. "A million years ago, there was a television show about some hill-billies from back east moving to Beverly Hills. They called their swimming pool a cement pond. Well, Tommy didn't know a swimming pool from a cesspool, but he had a tractor. A friend had a cement shooting gun. So the next thing I knew, he had dug out a quarter acre, and his friend shot it all down like it were a stucco house."

"So it's an enormous swimming pool?"

The woman almost choked on her clam chowder. "Nope. That there stucco cracked sixteen ways to north, and by spring, we had frogs and three ducks. So we threw in some fish and let nature have her way. I'm too old to be swimming, anyway."

When they finished eating, they walked the rest of the pier and half the town. If Bean wanted a grandmother, she knew where to find her. They had never had children. And they figured there were plenty in the small town to spoil, anyway. Her husband had always worn the Santa suit she sewed for him. And eventually, he grew his own gray beard.

The B&B in Pacific Grove was known for a different teddy bear in each room. If you wanted, you could have the bear to take with you. Bean knew exactly where the bear in the white chef's hat and coat would fit in.

Duff wobbled out the front door with a cane as she pulled up the driveway.

She turned off the bike and leaned back into the pack strapped behind the seat. They watched each other through the black visor of the full-faced helmet.

Duff waved the cane. "There's no more room. You might as well clear off."

She cracked the shield from the mask. "Well then, I guess we'll just have to bury you in the backyard so I can have the bed."

He held the cane up to his hip like a shotgun. "This here is loaded, you know."

The two men came out the door and braced Duff. Niles scoffed loudly and stepped down the three steps with his arms outstretched. As Bean pulled off her helmet, his arms were around her neck, and his mouth was at her ear. "Save us." They both leaned on the motorcycle to keep from falling over.

The three men stood admiring the bike.

"It looks like you never washed it."

"You missed a spot of chrome on your rust."

Duff finally broke with the poking fun. "Is it as fast as it looks?"

"Faster. The guy designed and built it up to go race at a place called the Island of Man."

Randy choked and cleared his throat. "It's an Isle, not an island, and the man has two N's, not one. They have goats there with six and eight horns. The Manx cat always has six toes and usually weighs over twenty pounds. But the race you're talking about is the oldest road race in the world. It's the original Tourist Trophy. It's about thirty-five miles long, and the racers on bikes like this circle the track in less than twenty minutes. The tight turns are faster if you can pick up your bike and turn it around, and with the small bike, they do. But these monsters, you have to walk. The backstretch down the hind-end of Snaefell mountain, the bikes can hit three hundred and fifty kilometers or—"

"Two hundred and twenty miles-per-hour."

Niles leaned in with a raised eyebrow. "Oh. We're all grown up and interrupting the man cooking your dinner now?"

Bean blushed only behind her ears. "I do math. And my speedometer reads in both miles and kilometers."

Randy looked at the speedometer and turned with enlarged eyes. "How much of that have you used up?"

"Most of it. My best was coming up here."

He pointed at the speedometer. "Where are you going to burn most of three hundred and ten?"

Bean flopped her finger out and then pointed at the speedometer. "*Kilometers.* That's only one-eighty in the miles column. I looked at the map and backtracked to King City. The highway patrol isn't out along there until after they've had breakfast at seven." She looked at Duff. "Remember that long straight coming into Arizona?"

He nodded.

"It's kind of like that. But with the GPS, you can see the curve coming at the end. It's only a big sweeping double S, but I wouldn't want to hit it at over a hundred."

Duff frowned as he scanned the single speedometer and the single tachometer. "Where's the GPS?"

Bean snorted and picked up her helmet. Then, reaching in, she turned it on. "Here, put it on."

She pulled her cell phone out of her pocket and tabbed to the map. She looked at the black face shield. She knew what he was looking at.

The voice was muffled. "A fighter pilot has less information."

She smiled and cracked open the shield. Putting her mouth close to the crack, she smiled. "Call the Funcles."

The voice in the helmet responded. "I have two Funcles. Randy and Niles. Which do you want to call?"

Duff laughed. "Call Randy."

They all laughed as Randy's hip pocket rang an old-school wolf whistle. The man blushed as he answered the phone. "Yes?"

Duff chuckled. "Are the oysters ready yet?"

Randy hung up. "Pushy customers." He looked at Bean. "So you never stopped when you called an hour ago."

She patted the tank. "Nope. And what looks like stock is almost seven gallons of fuel. So with over a three-hundred range, I can go until I need to stop to go."

Duff looked up from looking in the helmet. "We need to talk."

Bean smiled. "Danny says he can rig up a half-drop face shield for your shorty."

Duff set the helmet on the front of the gas tank as Bean unstrapped her bag. He turned and draped his arm around her shoulders as they followed the two men into the house.

"Imagine my disbelief on the drive up here. Carrot is talking about some superstar motorcyclist racing a monster through the scary canyons of the coast range... and I'm just wondering if he's talking about someone else or it's the drugs. And then you pull up here on the monster. And you have Wonder Woman's helmet."

"She doesn't wear a helmet."

"You know what I mean. When did you get a driver's license for a motorcycle?"

"The same day I got the rest of it."

He frowned. "The rest of what?"

She fished the license out of her wallet and watched his face.

He held it up as his elbow held the screen door open. "Where was *I*?"

She smirked. "I think you were still asleep that day."

"Day?"

"Well, in the week, I learned to drive all three. Well, it took most of the week because there wasn't a hurry. But I didn't want to waste any time at the DMV, so we loaded Leon's Beast and the sixty-five in a fifty-five-foot box trailer, and I pulled it with a freightliner cab-over. We opened the back and asked the test bunny where she wanted to start. I think I made her day or week or something. She never stopped giggling until I put the Beast into a side drift through an intersection and ended up parallel parked heading the other way. Some old guy on the one corner gave me two thumbs-up."

"Where was Leon?"

"In the back, giggling."

"What about the bike?"

"If there had been a second seat, and she could have found a brain bucket, we would have gone for a spin in traffic."

45

ANYTHING

They had been running and rerunning the video of the break-in and bug planters for over an hour. Duff was getting good at stopping the video and enlarging the still to make out the faces. Unfortunately, he didn't recognize any of them.

"Do you think they're connected with the Arkady guy?"

Duff puffed out his lower lip and pulsed it as he thought. "Probably not." He pointed at the guy sticking the camera in the vent next to Bean's camera. "I think he would shoot someone this stupid."

He looked over at Bean. "Do you think Danny's supercomputer can do facial recognition?" His finger tapped on the man's face on the screen.

"Let's see..." She pulled out a flip phone and dialed one of the few numbers.

Duff frowned at the old phone. "Whose phone?"

Bean smirked. "Burner. Sixty bucks, and it comes loaded with two hours' worth of time. You can load more time, but hooking onto a Wi-Fi is free. I got some for Danny, Ingrid, and

Leon just in case." She reached into her pack and found the small box. "Here's yours and an old-school charger." She reached in and pulled out the teddy bear in the chef's outfit. "I got something for Randy."

She held up her finger as she looked down. "Archimedes, it's Lot's wife."

She waited and then saw Duff's questioning face. "He's going into his bedroom."

She jerked as there was a sound on the phone. "Yeah. Camping on the beach is different. But it gets me thinking. You know the three guys in the video? I wondered if the Big Max can do facial recognition and figure out who they are beyond social media? We need to know who they are and who they work for."

She nodded at Duff. "Nah, I don't want it to be traced back to you or even close. Go ask my big sister for two fists of paper. I'll call her and tell her you're coming. And any ideas about the other stuff?"

Her face rolled through several gyrations as she listened. "Okay. Great. I'll be back in a couple of days, and we'll get some biryani or something. Thanks. Yeah, I miss you too. Bye."

She slipped the flip phone into her pocket. "He'll run the faces and let me know."

"Lot's Wife? Archimedes?"

"He's a math geek, and I haven't looked back yet. If I ever do, I'm toast."

"I think it was salt."

"Either way, if you look back, you've stopped moving forward."

Duff ran his finger along the edge of the table. "Sometimes, being able to look back can shed light on your path forward."

"Your memories."

He nodded. "My memories."

"At least you remembered where the smart drives were hiding… kind of."

Duff frowned in confusion and then frowned harder and made a clown's frowny face when he looked at the three drops of coffee left in his mug. He looked at hers.

Bean snorted. "Hah. Long gone."

Duff grumped. "Randy thinks too much coffee isn't good for my brain healing." He closed one eye and fluttered the other until Bean laughed. "Anyway. But you found the two ingots…"

"Yeah. But only after I put your jacket on."

"I don't understand."

She cocked her head and made her eyes large. "The armpits?"

"What about them?"

"Where's your jacket?"

He went to his room and retrieved it. She had forgotten how heavy it was. She was glad for the lighter alternatives she chose for her jumpsuit and jacket.

Bean spread the jacket on its back. "Show me where you thought they were."

"I don't know. I just knew they were there. The guy showed them to me, then how to open them and put them back."

She frowned. "Guy? What guy?"

"The Russian spy. In Canada."

She held her hand on his chest to stop him. "Okay, we'll get to that in a minute." She poked his chest and then squeezed his arm like it was fruit. "You've been working out?"

He growled. She laughed and then pointed back at the jacket. "If the ingots are worth more as data than a gold ingot, where are they safe?"

He shrugged. "The armpits?"

"Did you ever take them out?"

"No."

Bean reached in and drew out the two in the right armpit. She weighed them up and down with one in each hand and then handed them to Duff. He weighed them up and down, then shrugged.

Bean took them back. "Right. They are so close you need a scale—a very accurate scale."

She led him into the kitchen where Randy was working. He looked up. "Need something?"

She handed him the two ingots. "Which one is lighter?"

He weighed them in his hands. He held up one. "It's very slight. Maybe only a few grams or so, but lighter."

She slid the ingot apart slightly. "Do you have a scale that accurate?"

"Of course. I grow my own herbs, don't I?" He turned and drew a thin scale out of the small stand of cookbooks. Laying it down, the screen lit and cleared to zero.

Bean gave him the gold ingot. The scale froze. Randy gave a low whistle. "So that's what a pound of gold looks like." He looked up. "Good meat is prettier."

Bean laughed and handed him the ingot with a secret. It was two ounces lighter. She handed him the chip.

Duff blinked. "Twelve grams. That makes the ingot two ounces lighter." He turned to Bean. "How did you find them?"

She put the chip back in the ingot and pushed it closed. She pointed at the scale. "Ours isn't so fancy, but we have a scale as well. You just never cook."

As they turned to go back into the dining room, Bean looked at the coffeepot. It was half-full, but the red light was dark.

Randy's shoulders slumped. "He drinks too much coffee. It's not good for him. I've read articles."

She pointed at the pot. "No, he doesn't. And right now, I need him awake and thinking. So you can cut him off at lunch." She stopped in the door and leaned back. "And as someone much younger and wiser than you… don't believe the Internet. It's just people drinking coffee and making shit up."

She found Duff examining the armpits of the jacket. "The four on the outside, and your arm, would protect the two in each pit." She shrugged. "It's a theory. Now explain the guy in Canada."

He sat down, and his eyes glazed. "I had a job—more courier than driver. In fact, I flew into Canada. Toronto. Just north of there is a lake. Lake Simcoe. There's a bunch of small villages around the lake. Innisfil is tiny. Maybe only a few hundred people in the area. The guy was out on what was probably a family farm at one time. I only knew I was to take a cab and get dropped off. The transport out was part of the deal."

Bean cleared her throat and nodded thanks to Randy as he set down two new mugs already prepped. "And you would take a job knowing only that?"

Duff shrugged, his face behind the mug and steam. "Sometimes less. Kaminski called, and I was at the general aviation in thirty minutes. Two hours later, I'm standing in the guy's driveway." He shuddered. "He looked like death hit by the defrost setting in a microwave. He took me into the dining room. The leather jacket, gloves, and riding chaps were on the table. He told me to put the jacket on. He helped me at first. And once I had it on, it wasn't so bad. He said I'd get used to it. The money and other papers were all stacked on the table. He opened the jacket and showed me the first pocket. Then he explained the bulletproof nature of a million in gold. As he stuck the money into the large pockets, he explained how Russia had poisoned him with plutonium. He was dying, and it was painful."

Duff took another sip of coffee as he looked at the jacket. "The guy was a double agent. The schematics were the most advanced stuff Russia was working on. He knew they were going to get rid of him, just not when. All the gold and money were his running stash. In case he needed to run. But with the plutonium killing him, running wasn't a choice—but getting the stuff to America was. I could drive anything, so he knew the Indian would work. But what we didn't count on was the Russians would be at the meeting and know his motorcycle. But what they didn't count on was I wasn't him. Once I figured it was a trap, I ran. Arkady shot me in the back, and I went down. Hitting my head. The scalp bled a lot, and they figured I was a goner no matter who I was."

"So everything in the jacket was yours. What about the spy?"

He nodded. "The bike too. He signed over the pink slip. As I got to the end of the lane, the house blew up." He looked around as his eyes dampened. He cleared his throat, but his voice was still gravel. "A couple of months later, I was in Los Angeles and got it put in my name."

Bean closed her eyes and grimaced as she held up her index finger.

"What's wrong?"

She farted and slumped with a smile. "The oysters. Obviously." She made a wonky face. "But no. The church down in Orange County."

His face lit up. "Ah. Yes. That's where Kaminski comes in. Legally, the CIA is forbidden to operate on American soil."

"Supposedly."

He bobbed his head. "So they have private contractors doing stuff for them domestically."

Bean pushed her lower lip out. "Like, Kaminski…"

"Like, Kaminski."

"And because the guy didn't know you or me…"

"We were a threat."

Bean picked up and dropped the two ingots on their edges in a drumbeat. "So how do you want to play Kaminski, and what do we do with these? Especially now that we know what they are."

His hand gently laid down on hers. Stopping the double-tap of the ingots. "Let's talk about something else for a minute."

Randy stuck his head in. "A minute is all you have. Lunch is almost ready. And no grubby hands at the table today."

Duff, with gigantic eyes, pulled his head away from Bean. *They* had been told.

AFTER LUNCH, they sat on the front porch. Even though the road was a through street, Duff couldn't remember ever seeing a car drive by.

Bean stuffed her hands in the pockets of her leather jacket and slumped down to almost laid out. "What's on your mind?"

"Lot's wife." He looked over at her.

Bean nodded. "Okay. What about her?"

"I've been looking back these last few weeks. There's a big difference between forty-two and eighteen. But not really."

She rolled her head toward him. "Is this going to be the talk?"

He snorted. "Not like you think, smartass." He frowned at her. "Unless there's something you want to share…"

She harrumphed. "Not hardly, Grandpa. I've got my sights set on something with a lot more curls than that mop of yours. Don't the funcles know any hairdressers?"

He ran his fingers through his shaggy hair. "Leave my hair out of this. But it's a lifetime before I would even think of retirement, and you have an even longer lifetime before you."

He looked down the road and then back up it. "A year ago, I had big plans. I was leaving Colorado. I think your plans were almost as long-term. Get to the border and then figure out what was next. Since then, we just… floated along."

He looked down at his hands in his lap. "With all this time, and my memories back, all I've done is think."

Bean murmured: "What about?"

"Down the road."

Bean looked one way and then the next.

"Ass." They both chuckled. "You've got the driver's license and motorcycle thing done. Although, I noticed it's more rust than blue. Still want blue, or have you changed your mind?"

"It blends in better."

Duff shoved his lower lip out. "Point taken. Make a note to repaint the Indian. But you also have some interest in math. So there is the question. What do you want to be doing in, say… five years? Studying math for like engineering or something? Or something else?"

"I don't know. I've been thinking a bunch about something Bet said when we first met them."

Duff frowned. "Go easy on me. I'm new to all this remembering stuff again."

Bean held up her coffee. "How's your coffee taste?"

He took a sip. "Fine."

"Now imagine what it would taste like if we had to make it from the mud puddle out there in the middle of the street."

He looked out at the street. He stood and looked down the street and then up the street. "What puddle?"

Bean stood and stretched. "Yeah. Exactly. Now imagine if you had to walk a couple of miles with two empty five-gallon containers to get the mud puddle water. But when you got there, it was gone, and you had to hike another mile to get it from the stream where people bathed, cows drank, pissed, and worse."

He narrowed his eyes at the serious woman beside him. "You've changed. Why can't I just get the water from the tap in the kitchen?"

She turned. She sucked loudly on the last drop in her mug. "That's the point. *You* can. But half the world can't." She opened the screen door and walked in.

Duff looked at the street as he listened to the voice in the house.

"Randy? Your fun niece needs some delicious yum-yum to remind her why she needs to come back."

Duff kept staring at the road and thinking of water he couldn't see through. His thought was barely his outside voice. "Fun niece?"

46

CLOSING THE DEAL

The crater was colder than she remembered. But alone, it was the perfect space for the way she felt. She watched the distant lights that she knew were blazing stars. Some were smaller than our sun, but most in the visible light were larger or multiple stars circling one another.

She had watched a short bit of a movie about an astronaut adrift in space. She had lost interest and clicked on the next video and next and next. Here, there were no alternatives. This was the Internet. This was the only channel on the giant screen. This, for her and billions before her, was it.

Another girl in rural Iceland had maybe gotten up early to do some chores before school, and she was looking at the same sky, but from a different angle. Bean thought about a girl in maybe Mongolia, or Russia, or China, going about her day working, but thinking about the night sky. She didn't need to talk to the other girls. There were no words: only the endless black and the stars.

Bean sipped on the still-warm cocoa. It wasn't as good as Ingrid made, but okay cocoa, the sky, and the crater were enough. She looked toward the hazy lightening of the edge of sky to the east. That would be the 10:23 moonrise. She drained the last of the warm chocolate and stowed the collapsing mug.

Adjusting the space blanket over her sleeping bag, she snuggled down into her nest. The conversation with Duff kept replaying. He wasn't sure, but it made sense to insure diamonds. The man Leon introduced her to at the diamond mart. The man with the curls hanging from in front of his ears. The man who wore a black suit and a black hat on a hot day. Even he said they would always insure the diamonds against loss in transport. And as Leon said: That man should know. They had been his diamonds.

Even more important to her was the last thing the man told her in confidence. He had stopped her at the door. "Just so you know. We insure raw diamonds against the loss of their potential. But if you bring in some raw diamonds, there is no way I can tell if they are mine or Joseph Smolensky's down the street. Five million dollars of raw diamonds are five million dollars of diamonds. What sets the price is weight, color, and inclusions." He nodded his head in a shrug. "And how it can be cut."

He raised his two hands out at his sides. "So if by some chance you were perhaps to find a small bag of some pretty stones... Maybe we should do some talk. I recently got a bit of a somethink from an insurance company. *Nu*, I might be interested in some pretty little rocks."

———

THE WOMAN SET the bowl of water on the table and left.

Bean had unwrapped the layers of foil while she sipped coffee. She waited for her omelet with bacon chips, onions, Ortega chilies, and two slices of American cheese smothered in salsa from a large can. The bread came from a bakery at least a few days away... It could prove to be a long day.

Her conversation with Kaminski's secretary was short.

"Do you know who this is?"

"Yes."

Bean watched the other people in the Trading Post. "Do you know where I am?"

There was a long pause. Bean guessed the man was calling up a program on his computer. "Yes..."

"Good. You can do the math—after I eat. I will be down. No hanging out at the pool, no spa time, no extra stuff. Just Mr. Kaminski."

"He's not here." The man's voice wavered. Bean figured he was stalling.

"Every other bug you had on me is dead. This phone will be dead in a minute. It is in his best interest that he is there when I arrive. Otherwise, we'll go talk to the Russians. Am I making myself clear?"

"Yes."

Bean dropped the phone into the bowl of water she had asked for. She watched the lines of tiny bubbles.

Raking her upper front teeth over her lower lip, she looked across the restaurant and store. Nothing had changed. The woman with no name tag or introduction when she took an order wore the same plaid flannel shirt: mostly reds, some greens, and worn thin at the elbows and neck. The sleeves turned up two folds to expose the large silver and turquoise armbands covering most of her lower arms. The jeans were more elastic waist dad-pants, worn here and there, polished dark in other spots. The length wasn't quite long enough to hide the limp or the brace sneaking into her right leather orthopedic boot.

She hadn't noticed so much a year ago. Then, she had only watched the things she considered a threat to her. Now she saw and cataloged everything. So much wasn't the same anymore. She looked at the phone at the bottom of the bowl of water—so much change.

———

KAMINSKI READ each file under the photos. Each rap sheet boiled down to the salient points. Each criminal's header carried the most relevant charges or talents they brought to the team or dragged with them in baggage.

The one photo stopped him. In the background was a bed with a teddy bear leaning up against the pillows. Above the bed were a large poster of a sunrise across the desert and a bowl of green cubes. The bed and room were stark, except the two items making it the girl's room, not the man's. In the foreground, a man's face and his hand placing a camera into the air vent, the header read: *Child porn: possession to distribute, pedophilia, stalking, aggravated assault, and rape of a minor while a minor.*

At the bottom of all three sheets was the name of the company they worked for.

Bean shifted in her chair. "As you have noticed, these are not the kindhearted people who would stay here."

He looked over his reading glasses at her. "Don't be so sure. Character has nothing to do with money."

She dipped her head. "The exterminator company hasn't bought a single chemical for eradicating insects since it started in two thousand and four. It has bought a bottle of drain cleaner a few years ago, as well as a snake and plunger. My money is on the second guy. He just looks like the sort who enjoys a beer or two with his double burrito lunches. Not the sort you would hire directly…" She pulled a small electronic pad from her jacket and turned it on. "But the bug company is owned by a shell company in Louisiana. It's owned by a shell investment firm in New Jersey, which is owned by a holding company in Houston, Texas, with only three people on the board. Two are… um… legal types with sketchy references, and the third name is—"

Kaminski held up his hand to stop her.

Bean lowered the electronic pad. "Really? You guys were so confident of not getting caught that you didn't even run a shell in the Caymans or Switzerland? How dumb do you have to be to do business with the State Department? I'm a silly little eighteen-year-old girl, and I had you in under thirty minutes. The sleaze-balls you have doing your dirty work were even easier."

He gently tossed the papers onto his desk. "How much do you know, and where is Duff?"

"Duff missing is why I started digging."

"Have you heard from him?" He eyed the large manilla folder still on her lap.

Her eyes narrowed. "What is it you really want to know?"

Kaminski pointed at the envelope. "Maybe that's a start?"

Bean flipped the envelope onto the desk. As the man opened it, she cocked her head. Studying his eyes, scanning what she knew was the top page. The math was beyond her, but she was getting there.

"Three years ago, you sent Duff to Canada to interface with a Russian double agent. Someone in the State Department or Homeland wanted what the guy was offering for sale. The price was five million. High then, but it was to be his retirement going away package. The top pages are the eleven he sent to verify what he had. The rest prove that I have the complete file and cracked the encryption. But thirty minutes after they received the original eleven pages, you had Duff in the air. I think it's worth more now."

Kaminski looked at a few more sheets and laid them on the desk. His thumb and knuckles rubbed along his chin. He put his reading glasses down and looked at her. He had estimated she was smart, but he was out of his league here.

He raised his finger and picked up his cell phone. He dialed a number, not in his contacts. "It's me. You need to come right now. And come ready to wire at least ten million to an offshore account." He listened for a moment. "No. But the same information you looked at three years ago just surfaced. The courier has what you still want, and they have... And they have cracked the encryption. So it is ready for the open market." He looked expectantly at Bean. She nodded. "But the clock is ticking. And don't try to be smart. They're nine steps ahead of you already." He snipped the phone off. "He's twenty minutes away. But you know Phoenix traffic." He wavered his hand in the air.

Bean glanced at the old chunky dive watch she had picked up at a pawnshop. The time on her phone was always accurate, but glancing at a wristwatch sent a message beyond just checking time. "I'll take some coffee."

Kaminski stepped to the door. "Stephen, can we get a carafe of coffee and some cactus...?" He looked back at Bean, who shook her head. He looked back at his secretary. "That'll be enough."

He sat back down. Putting on his glasses, he looked at a few of the printed pages. "I know you've been learning much-advanced math, but do you understand this stuff?"

Bean sensed he was trying to get back to their old relationship. He wasn't the enemy she thought he might be, but probably the ally he had always been. "I've been studying computer science too, but not at the level to crack a sixteen-digit encryption in forty-one minutes, but as for the math, I understand enough to understand it's about fuel burns, drag, and other stuff involving missiles. Some is about surface-launched, some air and others have depth and range designations."

Kaminski frowned. "Sixteen-digit…?"

"It takes a very large supercomputer that has shared resources to draw on. A gaming laptop could do it in about a hundred years. If you don't unplug it."

Kaminski sighed as he took off his glasses. With the glasses entwined around his middle finger, he pinched the bridge of his nose. He rocked back in his chair as the secretary brought in the tray. The man started to serve, but Kaminski waved him off.

Kaminski served a spoonful of cactus cubes into one bowl and then the next. He portioned them out randomly into each bowl. Bean watched the actions meant to show that neither bowl nor cactus was tainted.

She reached forward and poured the coffee from the carafe. She sweetened and creamed them equally. She watched his face. She remembered he didn't use cream.

He took the mug she handed him. He sipped. "I have never used cream. But then, you knew that. It was only something my grandmother did. The men poo-poohed it as a woman thing. But it tempers the bite of the roast. I might start."

Bean stuck a chunk of cactus in her mouth. "Duff."

Kaminski mirrored her. "What do you want to know?"

"How long has he worked for you?"

The man sighed and leaned back with his coffee mug. "Oh

goodness. I think close to fourteen or fifteen years. I recruited him from the State Department. They were underutilizing his talents. He had worked for a few years with the Department of Energy. They transport anything having to do with energy—even explosive warheads or rods for nuclear plants. So one day, he's driving a van. Next, he's in a bulletproof truck with four other guys, and the next, he's flying an airplane with a recovered bomb. But nothing required his mind. Which is quirky but brilliant."

"Is he worth the pay you pay him?"

"Some days, yes. Most jobs of just the driving? No. But then, he introduced you to the game. You have potential." He pointed at the stack of information. "Let's just say I saw the potential and invested in that future."

"But I won't be working for you."

He took another bite and smiled. "I didn't invest in my future, my dear. I invested in your potential. Your future. Call it a scholarship." He glanced at his thin gold watch and then smiled. "Traffic."

Bean sipped on her coffee. "If you knew, why didn't you tell him?"

The man shifted in his chair. "Memory is a funny thing. But if you push to remember, often, it just hides deeper. Better to just keep him close and hope he recovers." His head leaned forward. "And I'm assuming with all this, he has."

Bean nodded as she put the empty bowl on the corner of the desk. "And if we finish, and he still hasn't shown?"

Kaminski pushed his lower lip out and shrugged. "Then I'll buy the information and do a stick-up job on him later—if that works for you." He stuck the last cube of cactus in his mouth and smiled. "So when we're done, what happens?"

"I have copies of everything. Who, what, where, and when. They are in safe places that will release the information to the right places and people if anything was to go wrong. Then we disappear. Nobody comes looking for us. And we live quietly on a ranch in Montana."

He smiled and snorted softly. "Somehow, I don't see you or Duff as ranch people."

"Don't forget Ingrid."

He shrugged his face in agreement as if to say, *There is that.*

The phone on his desk hummed softly. Kaminski pushed a yellow button in the corner. "Yes, Stephen?"

"Sir, the valet says a man has arrived for you. He gave his name as Hiram Abiff."

"Tell them to let him pass." Kaminski turned off the intercom.

He leaned forward with his elbows on the desk. "Before he gets here, let me show you my credentials and that I'm on your side—always. No matter who hired the idiots in Los Angeles. And yes, if you give me the information, I will turn them over to the proper authorities."

Bean nodded.

"The man coming. His real name is Khalid Adorn, but he uses David to make him sound less... Arab. He was born in Palestine but is an American and works for the State Department. He suffers from an addiction to Thai food, has high blood pressure, and has bad indigestion. Use that as you can. His cap on paying for the information is probably ten million, but he's going to squeal and moan at anything over the original five."

Bean rocked as she pressed her lips into rolls. Finally, the rolls became a smile. She wondered how these guys would fare in the shade of the old oak tree with Carrot and gang.

The knock was soft.

"Come." Kaminski stood as the man entered.

Bean slumped a little more casually in the chair. Kaminski was right about the man. He was not only overweight, but the red at his ears and neck meant his high blood pressure was out of control.

"David, this is… um… Libby. Libby, this is David."

The man half stuck his hand out, but Bean only nodded. Then, uncomfortable, the man sat.

Kaminski looked at the three sheets of paper with photos and documentation. She smiled.

"There's no need for duplicity here, David. Or I should say, Khalid." He picked up the reports and held them up randomly before setting them face down on the desk. "She already knows everything. And probably knows what you ate last Thursday."

Bean's head rolled over until she looked directly at the man. "I won't tell your wife, but you need to switch to Indian food instead of that Thai. It will lower your out-of-control blood pressure and high cholesterol. And about the sweet young thing…"

The man blushed around the neck. Bean rolled her head back to look at Kaminski. She winked with the eye the other man couldn't see.

Kaminski handed Khalid the stack of math and schematics. Bean interceded and removed the last two pages. Each had a photo and rundown of who they were and worked for. She added a small package from her pocket and passed it all back to Kaminski. "We already removed these two from play."

As Khalid looked at the top secrets from Russia, Kaminski studied the assassins.

Kaminski's eyebrows rose above his reading glasses. He took the glasses off and quietly tapped them on the papers. He eyed the two thin wallets held together with a rubber band. "How removed are we talking?"

Bean thought for a moment. The night they moved her to Colorado, she had sat on the front porch of the house. She had thought about running. What she thought was just a neighborhood dog came trotting up the street. As it passed under the streetlight, she could tell it was a coyote. He wasn't skulking through someone else's territory. She was in his. The people built the neighborhood in his neighborhood, and he would continue to trot down the road any time he felt like it. The coyote ruled the desert.

Bean shifted and shrugged. "Only the coyotes know where they buried the bones."

The State Department glanced up and squirmed at the image held out so casually. He looked at the leather pants and the cryptic black T-shirt. The large sixty-five could mean anything—or something he didn't want to know. He guessed the person and clothes rode the sketchy-looking motorcycle parked at the valet station. The closest he wanted to be to that world was watching the Mad Max movies on his big-screen television.

He tapped the edge of the papers against his thigh. "You have the rest of the information?"

She smiled softly. *First comes the test.* "The file was zipped and encrypted to a little over a megabyte. The encryption was a sixteen-digit cipher within a twenty-four-digit rotating reverse drop-out code." She held up a thin micro thumb drive. "To crack it in your lifetime, you will need a supercomputer much larger than the one at the DOD—which they won't let you near... since that last incident."

She smiled at Kaminski. "There are only seven computers capable of doing the job. One is in Russia. It did the original encryption. Three are currently reserved until the middle of the century as they try to figure out if there even was a big bang or was it just a whimper. They buried two in research work for a couple of large companies, and then, there is mine."

She looked at the small piece of technology. "Three years ago, the price for this was five million. The original holder was poisoned and then burned to death. I'm not pointing fingers, but the only people who knew about him and where he was at was your organization. Inflation, death, and scarcity have driven the price up."

Khalid growled. "How much?" He had blinked—and lost the negotiation.

Bean held out her open, splayed hand. "Ten. But wait, there's more." She pulled a silver chain out of her T-shirt. On the end was another fatter thumb drive. "On here is the entire file cracked and stabilized." Her eyes opened wide as the man's forehead frowned in confusion. "Oh, you didn't know about the program in a program, did you?"

"Program within a program? What does that even mean?"

"It means the first time you ran the encrypted file without the password, it would run fine. But the second time, bits of information will become wiped. So by the time the file gets to your analysts, any pieces of critical data would be meta-gibberish."

The man's ears and neck were now a deep red. "Meta-gibberish. How much meta-gibberish are we talking about?"

Bean looked at Kaminski and winked. "Enough for your superiors to question what it was you wasted fifteen million dollars on." Her head ground around to face the man as she held up the drive. "This information on the state-of-the-art Russian missiles is worth billions, but for the next twenty seconds, I will sell you this and the safe word for fifteen million. In one minute, either we are transferring funds, or I'm going to"—she glanced at her large dive watch. "My other appointment. *My zdes' chisty*? Are we clear, comrade?" She held up her watch and pushed the timer.

"I don't have authority to pay that kind of money."

Bean looked up through the top of her eyes and over at Kaminski. The man held up his hands and rolled his eyes. Bean tapped her watch. The man's neck was getting close to purple.

"Five…"

"I would have to get authorization…"

"Four…"

"It would take time…"

She stood. "Three…"

The man started blustering.

"Two." She wiggled bye-bye to Kaminski and turned for the door.

The man exploded. "Okay. Fifteen." He slumped back into the chair.

Bean pulled a card out of her back pocket. "Into this account. Now."

The man tried to save face. "I need a computer."

Kaminski stood and held out his hands at the keyboard and monitor. "I already got you into your account. Libby here was so kind to give me your codes."

The man rose and glowered at the young woman who beat him.

Bean smiled sweetly. "Just remember, you're doing this for the safety of the free world. *And* it's not your money."

She looked down at her small pad. The script for the series of transfers waited—already set. She had run several test routings using most of the money from the bottom of the Indian. The diamond payments had routed through Antwerp, through Sweden, and to their ultimate destinations.

She confirmed the balance of ten thousand was now fifteen million fatter. She felt sorry for the poor banker in the Grand Caymans, but as she hit enter, the balance was once again ten thousand.

She pulled the chain off her neck. "As agreed and paid for." She handed the man the thumb drive and chain.

The man growled as he draped it over his head and tucked it into his shirt. "And the code word?"

She smiled and held her palms out from her sides. "We're in Arizona. It's all around us." She rubbed her abdomen. "Or in some of us. The word is cactus. All lowercase."

47

―――――――

CHANGES

The lion has a reputation for being the king of the jungle. But the lioness is the one who hunts and is the more deadly.

The tawny fur of her back dappled from the bushes shading her. The dappling camouflaged her from prey who may distract her or warn her prey. She was in striking distance. Her hindquarters swayed in place as she prepared her hind feet in the soft soil. The strike on the young woman bent at her work, oblivious to the danger, would be instantaneous. The lioness's tail twitched uncontrollably.

The muscles bunched, the hind feet set, and the cat exploded across the short distance. Two galloping strides and the front paws spread in their prey-felling reach.

Just as the golden puppy bit down on the cat's tail.

The lioness flipped over in midair. The fifty pounds of cat and forty-five pounds of dog bowled Bean over. The three tumbled in the soft earth between the rows of coffee bushes.

"Help. Help me. Someone help this poor defenseless woman

from these wild beasts. *Mtu aniokoe kutoka kwa simba na mbwa!* Save me from the vicious lion and dog."

She grabbed the lioness by the cheeks and kissed her on the lips. "Are Daddy and Danny home, Simba?" The dog nuzzled up under her arm, licking anything it found. A human face, lioness face, hands, paws. Everything was fair game. The large flat tongue of the lioness reached out and washed the dirt from Bean's face and the dog's nose."

The voice was as much laughing as commanding. "Honey, Simba, let your mama up. No killing the boss lady before dinner."

The tall black man wrapped in the tribal orange skirt laughed. "Oh, most decidedly. Not before we eat."

Bean lay on her back, clutching her children to the sides of her chest. "Gaspari! It is your job to warn me of any wild animals preparing to attack me."

"Yes, bwana. I was protecting you from this dangerous coffee bush. The children be *mjomba* job."

She looked at Duff. "He's right, you know. The tribe gave Simba to you."

One of the tribe's goat tenders had found a dead lioness and her two small cubs. So when Duff and Bean started the project to drill a well, build a natural filtration system, and have it run all by the sun, the boy had found the third cub, Simba. When they had a meeting with the tribal leaders, the cub had climbed into Bean's lap and fell asleep. Propriety dictated that the chief could only give such a special gift to another man. So Duff was the recipient. But as he explained, he had to give it to his niece because only she knew how to be a mother. The tribe agreed. And Bean became *Mama wa Simba,* mother of lions.

Duff kneeled as Honey raced over to find a new face to lick.

"Gaah. She spends all day with us just lying around while we work. But come home, and it's all play and licking time." He put his face into the face of the golden lab mastiff mix. "Huh. Honey. Just licking time with mommy?"

Bean sat up as the lioness filled her lap with her body and the air with her purr. "What did the chief say about Simba?"

Danny ran his fingers through his hair. "They couldn't believe she had grown so much. A month of steady food makes a difference. It affirmed the choice of his gift." They both rolled their eyes.

Bean curled into the cat and scratched her belly. "Did you scare all the children? Huh, my little princess? Did you?"

Danny dropped onto the ground beside Bean and helped with the scratching. "Babysitter is more like it. She still remembered everyone and was just another of the wild children running around the village. After lunch, when everyone took a nap in the heat, she hunted out Push, the boy who found her in the bush, and snuggled into him as if she was a tiny kitten again."

Bean smiled. "They have amazing memories. And they are a pack or pride animal, so anyone who is or was in their pride is until they die."

"But what do you do when she grows up? When she's four hundred pounds?"

Bean frowned. She had only been a lioness's mommy for a couple of months. "Hey, Guaspari?"

The older man stood from tending the bush. "Yes, bwana."

"What do we do when Simba becomes a woman?"

He laughed. "You have listened to the stories too much. Simba is a lion. She will only be a lion when she is five times your size. She will not be a woman like you."

Bean snorted and shook her head at the logic. "Yes, but when she is five times my size. What do we do with her?"

The man rubbed his chin under his lower lip. "How big Honey get?"

"About twice my size."

"Do you throw her out then?"

Bean twisted around and scowled at her foreman. "Why would you even think that?"

The man gently twisted his head to crack his neck. "Why were you thinking the same about Simba?"

"But she's going to be huge. What do I do?"

The man laughed. "I think you need a bigger bed."

She bent back into the face of her cat with a reward of a large rough tongue. "Hear that? *Mjomba* Guaspari is going to build us a giant bed."

The man snorted. "I think first you need a bigger room for such a bed."

"Ooo, we get a bigger bedroom too."

Bean looked up at Danny. "How did it go with the solar panels?"

The metal bar banging around in the iron triangle on the back porch had a universal reaction. All work stopped. It was the ten-minute warning—time to wash and do anything else you need to do. But the meal would start hitting the table in ten minutes, non-negotiable. If one eats, the farm eats. What had started as a collective of only five field hands and a single cook had grown into a small village. The Masai had little use for money other than what it could buy. Bean had sat down with the chief and some elders and worked out a strange barter system. The workers came and went as the farm needed work or not. Bean and Duff supplied food and goods the village needed or wanted. They tilled a large area of the farm to raise produce to feed everyone. By the second year, they were even taking produce to the market. The coffee wouldn't produce a crop until at least the third or fourth year.

Bean stood at the head of the massive table. This never changed. All thirty chairs would fill during harvest, and Duff would be at the other end. But tonight, it was only an intimate group of twelve. The covered space could eventually hold two tables when they needed to build the second. Right now, they focused on building a kitchen building next to the dining lanai.

When the cooks and Ingrid showed up with the last bowls of food, Bean nodded, and they all sat together.

As they ate, Danny talked about teaching the village youth how to install the solar panels and how the system worked so they could repair and maintain it. The idea was not to just give a village water but to teach people how to do the same over and over for other villages. The panels, controllers, and batteries had to be imported, but once the equipment was here, installing and maintaining was the endgame for the locals, along with the clean water. Eventually, Bean had her own agenda. Electric lights for students to study under in the evening, and maybe a medical clinic or two.

Danny pulled out his phone. He shifted through the photos and found what he wanted. He pulled the little stand out of the back of the case and stood it in front of Bean. He touched the screen.

As the day ended around them, the sky changed from blue to a honey hue for just a few seconds, and the little screen came to life. The sound was tinny, but the images were the only important part. The children gathered at the end of the pipe.

Suddenly, water came splashing out of the pipe as the children cheered and danced, throwing water at each other.

As the short video ended, the small whisper came from behind Bean.

"*Tena, shangazi.*" Again, auntie.

She turned. Everyone, even Duff and Ingrid, clustered behind her. She nodded her head. "Tena."

The fire in the pit was down to embers. They rarely burned a frivolous fire, but tonight seemed the right time. Ingrid had made cocoa and then gone to bed. Bean looked over at Duff but spoke to Danny.

"When will the filtration system be working?"

"We're trying a new system with sands and a local version of duckweed. The entire system is about forty feet long but can process"—leaning over with one eye and brow raised— "in theory, about two hundred gallons a day."

She frowned. "That doesn't sound like much."

Danny smiled as Duff rumbled from the other side of the fire pit. "That's huge. Remember, this is only the water for drinking and cooking. The water for bathing doesn't need to be filtered. For that, we just need to pump. In a week, when it's full, the cistern will hold almost sixteen thousand gallons. They will have enough water to last them through a month or more if they have to."

Danny added. "If the filtration system works as well as we think, they can build a much larger one and expand to supply drinking water for the Moobi tribe. They have been walking through the draw to the river, and there are some intermarriages, so it's a good fit."

Bean put her hand out and took his. "When do you have to go back?"

"Three days. I'll catch a hop over to Kigali in Rwanda. From there, I pick up a Sabina flight up to Belgium and then a polar flight straight to Los Angeles. That gives me five days to recover and write up the report on this, and then school starts."

"How many hours?"

He squinted as he did the math. "I'll be on the move for forty-three hours once Duff drops me at Arusha airport."

"But in June, you'll bring Lena as a graduation present?"

He rolled his eyes. "I sent pictures of the work and the farm. Especially Simba and Honey. I think even Nana wants to come too."

Bean pushed her lower lip out. "See my Nana? Yeah, I think we can cover that. But you know. She is getting old. She'll have to stay at least a month."

He laughed. Duff snorted as his head leaned back—asleep. They both snickered.

Danny leaned in and kissed Bean. "I'm getting old too…"

She patted his hand. "You can always stay."

The lioness rolled over in her sleep between them and groaned.

He shook his head. "Lena is going to lose it. Hugging a real lion."

Bean looked down at the cat the size of a medium dog. "You know, you won't be back for six months. She's going to be bigger than you by then."

He hummed. "I think I can live with that." He looked up. "So, have you thought of the name?"

"Which? The farm or the organization bringing clean water?"

He snorted softly. "Both."

"I think so. The single coffee berry has two beans inside. It's kind of like my day. I run the farm, and then I run the NGO for the water. So I wear two hats."

He squinted one eye as he slowly turned his head to one side. "So... you're two Beans?"

She smiled in a smirk. "Two Beans are better than a hill of beans."

ALSO BY BAER CHARLTON

The Very Littlest Dragon: NEW Editions
(All-new full-color ebook, a paperback with
coloring pages, and a full-color Collector's Edition hardback)

Stoneheart — Pulitzer Nominee 2015
Angel Flights
What About Marsha?
Pirate's Patch
Flat Surf
Secrets of the Gold

JOLIE "ROCKET" ROBERTS SERIES
Dry Bridge of Vengeance – Book One
Dry Ridge of Redemption – Book Two

THORNY WALLACE SERIES
Death in the Valley – Book One
Light to Light – Book Two

SOUTHSIDE HOOKER SERIES
Death on a Dime – Book One
Night Vision – Book Two
Unbidden Garden – Book Three
Boomtown – Book Four
One Day Under the Grass – Book Five
Southside Hooker Series: Books 1–5 Box Set

(Collector's Edition hardback & ebook available)

I Drink Coffee and Make Shit Up
One Writer's Journey Without Signposts

BAER CHARLTON

ABOUT THE AUTHOR

Bestselling author Baer Charlton graduated from UC Irvine with a degree in Social Anthropology, monkeyed around for a while, and then proceeded onward with a life of global travel, multi-disciplinary adventure, and meeting the memorable array of characters he would come to describe in his writing. He has ridden things with gears, engines, and sails, and made things with wood, leather, and metal. He has been stitched back together more times than the average hockey team; his long-suffering wife and an assortment of cats and dogs have nursed him back to health after each surgery.

Baer knows a lot about many things in this world. History flows through his veins and pours out of him at the slightest provocation. Do not ask him what you may think is a simple question unless you have the time to hear a fascinating story.

You can find more at
www.mordantmedia.com

9 781949 316209